Seasons in Purdah

Keeper of Secrets ... Translations of an Incident

The House

Seasons in Purdah

Anjuelle Floyd

NOJ Publications

Berkeley, California

ISBN 978-0-9787967-4-7

Published by NOJ Publications
P.O. Box 9405
Berkeley, CA 94709
www.anjuellefloyd.com

Cover and Interior by:
Iryna Spica of SpicaBookDesign
www.spicabookdesign.com
and
Six Penny Graphics
www.sixpennygraphics.com/

Edited by:
Lori Zue
Karlyn Thayer < www.constructivecritiques.com/>
Shonelle Bacon <www.clg-entertainment.com/#/services>
Jennifer Magnani <www.expertsubjects.com/Editing/>
Naomi Long <www.expertsubjects.com/Editing/>

Printed in the United States of America

"We see only that, which we feel we can confront."
—Anonymous

"Everything we see is a shadow cast by that which we do not see."
—Dr. Martin Luther King, Jr.

"In your light I learn how to love. In your beauty, how to make poems. You dance inside my chest where no one sees you, but sometimes I do, and that sight becomes this art."
"I died as a mineral, and became a plant. I died as plant and rose as animal. I died as animal and I was Man. Why should I fear? When was I less by dying?"
"Don't grieve. Anything you lose comes round in another form."
—Jalal ad-Din Rumi

Indian Summer

•.•.•.•.•.•.•.•.•.•

Chapter 1

Sahel breathed in the September night air of Indian summer as Titus helped her out of the car. Again she coached herself, *hang in there*. Within minutes they would be inside the ballroom and seated at their table.

Titus closed her car door. The beep from the car signaled he had engaged the anti-theft system. He lifted her hand and placed her fingers around his upper arm. "The temple's just up this way."

"Okay." She nodded. They started forward.

With stomach churning, Sahel carefully followed Titus's lead into the flow of footsteps made by others moving towards the Masonic Ballroom at the corner of Porter and Fourth.

"Are you all right?" Titus asked as they walked.

Honestly? Sahel thought. This was no time for truths. "I'm fine."

"No you're not."

A voice arose within Sahel, one that only she could hear against the sound of shoes worn by men in tuxedoes and ladies' heels muffled by their gowns. Sahel tried to smile. The voice inside her spoke again. "You don't want to be here." And then, "You'll be okay," the voice reassured. *You seem so certain.* Sahel conversed with the voice through her thoughts as she walked alongside Titus.

Nothing is for certain, except for death, rebirth, and love, the voice said.

Sahel tightened her grip on Titus's upper arm.

Myriad sounds swirled around Sahel inside the ballroom, people discussing their lives, those of their children, husbands, mothers and sons. Endless bits of conversations, none of which included Sahel, left her feeling isolated and imprisoned within the burden she felt she had become.

As on so many occasions in the last year, Sahel cringed at the thought of her weaknesses and vulnerabilities. Unable to live, unable to die, her life was a dark pit; Sahel frozen at a moment in time that had occurred nearly twelve months earlier. Like her mother who had rarely left the house, except to see her doctor, Sahel now remained home, eschewing contact with anyone except Titus, her father, and her physician. A malfunctioning heart had high-jacked the life of Sahel's mother. Blindness now served as Sahel's warden.

Sahel willed herself to remain present amid the sounds of joyful greetings and what she imagined to be spirited hugs and kisses of people greeting each other. She gripped her arms and tried to envision Titus receiving his award, Surgeon of the Year.

He deserved it, needed it. If only she could fix his heart. But Sahel could barely get through the day. The river of anxieties that rarely strayed from the banks of her awareness washed onto the shore of her thoughts. She felt so broken. How would she manage when their guests arrived at their table? And then there was the matter of food. What if she dropped a knife or fork? Sahel would not be sitting beside Titus. All eyes would be on Titus, who was being honored.

Sahel had not attended any such event since the accident a year earlier. When obligation demanded his presence, Titus always went alone, paid his respects, and immediately returned home.

Tonight was different. He was being feted and wanted Sahel to be present. *I've got to get through this evening. I owe him that much. If only I could have brought my cane.*

A hand lightly touched her shoulder.

"Sahel. It's Clarissa Murdoch. I don't know if you remember me, but ..."

The pendulum of Sahel's heart swung back and forth. The dialogue in her head edged toward silence. Carefully, she turned towards the voice, extended her hand into the darkness, and again formed a smile.

Chapter 2

M

oments later another hand landed on Sahel's shoulder. "It's me, Carl." She turned. Carl lifted her palm. "How are you doing?"

She squeezed his hand, felt glad to have Carl present. "I know how you hate these things," Carl said.

"Not as much as you." Sahel smirked.

Like Titus, he had grown up with Sahel, the three of them living on the same street. Positioned between the flatlands and hills of Oakland, they had grown up in solid middle-class country, the children of hardworking parents who knew the value of a dollar and that perseverance with tasteful frugality yielded solid earnings. "Too bad we can't leave and make some of your mud cakes."

Sahel chuckled at the memories. As children, Titus and Carl had gathered in her parents' backyard where Sahel directed the mixing of mud and water, which they poured in pie pans discarded from her mother's kitchen and dried in the sun.

Presently she considered the dark soil Carl had provided from his mother's flower garden behind their house down the street. "It was always soft and moist, the dirt you brought," Sahel said.

"My mother was always watering her flowers."

"I wish I could see them, your mother's hydrangeas. They were so beautiful, blue like a sun-filled sky." She reached for Carl's other hand. He placed her palm to his face.

"They're long gone." Carl's mother had died five years earlier, his father passing in the year that followed. Sahel had remained by his side, ever present during the planning of both funerals and then afterwards.

Carl said, "You'll never see my mother's flowers again. Neither will I. They're long gone. But there are other flowers you can see, that I want you to see. If only you'll let me—" Again Sahel squeezed his hand, but this time with a firmness that said No to Carl's wish. "It's too risky," Sahel said. "I can't put Titus through that, not again."

Sahel was blind and Carl, a neurosurgeon, wanted to perform a procedure to return her sight. "What about what he's put you through?" he said.

"We've been through this." Pangs of old frustration rose in Sahel.

"There was no way he could have known I was down there looking for the ring." Sahel shuddered at how stupid she had been. She had lost all reason when seeing the ring gone from her finger. Her heart had pounded, her chest expanding to near explosion.

"It's not the accident," Carl said, his anger subsiding, but only in the wake of a new demand. "He keeps you in the house, won't let you use your cane."

Sahel grew angry in her defense of Titus. She hated feeling torn, being pulled in two directions. Carl had given her the cane. It had been like that, Sahel loving them both, Titus and Carl, her best friends, loyal until the end and she vowing to never choose, during childhood. And now ...

"He discourages you from taking classes or any training to adjust to your loss of sight. And then forbids you to have the

14

surgery," Carl said.

"Titus isn't holding me hostage." Sahel withdrew her palm from his grasp. So much had happened in the last twelve months, much of it filled with Titus and Carl arguing about the loss of her sight and the best way, if possible, to get it back.

Known as the Three Musketeers throughout their lives, Sahel, Titus, and Carl had grown up attending the same parish for Mass each Sunday and the parish school during the week. All three had attended and graduated Cal the same day. While Sahel had pursued and earned her doctorate in psychology, Titus and Carl had studied medicine, then trained at the University of California, San Francisco, Titus becoming a heart surgeon, Carl a neurosurgeon.

The shared experiences of their lives had bound them forever.

Carl leaned in, nearly touching her ear, and whispered, "I will never abandon you." Sahel felt herself weakening. On hearing Titus's voice, she leaned back from Carl. He lifted her hand and brought the back of her palm to his lips.

What must people think? Her cheeks grew warm with embarrassment. Again she drew back her hand. Titus's voice softened amid those of what Sahel assumed were a group of elderly physicians, most of them on the board that chose who the medical society would fete each year. "I've congratulated Titus," Carl said, his voice near once more. He pulled away.

"Where are you going?" Sahel asked.

"A patient in the hospital. With all the doctors here, I can do the surgery with the operating room assistants I prefer." A neurosurgeon whose specialty was brain injury, Carl was judicious and controlling to the point of freakishness about the nurses he chose to assist him in surgery.

Yet unlike Titus, his desire for excellence never reflected anger or frustration, rather a calm and clarity that dipped to the point of inaudibility when most annoyed, action that left Sahel feeling safe as compared to Titus's more overt stance of voicing his irritations. And yet she loved Titus. His pain was truly hers. She would never let him go despite the many ways he reminded, if not evoked, her deceased mother's spirit.

15

"I wish you wouldn't go," Sahel said, but on speaking the words Sahel chastised her selfishness. A patient lay in the hospital waiting for Carl.

She regretted having pulled her hand from Carl. He was a friend and her doctor. Yet even Sahel knew that much of the timing of the surgery lay in Carl's avoidance of witnessing Titus receive the award. Though friends, Titus and Carl were competitive, a quality that bound and tore at the knot that stitched their souls.

Like Sahel before the accident, Carl found balm for his wound in healing others. "Tomorrow at Mass. Will you come?" Sahel asked. A futile question at best. Carl had not attended Mass since serving as best man for Titus when he married Sahel.

Three weeks after the accident, he had moved to San Francisco. A busy practice served as his excuse for missing Sunday Mass. "It depends on how tonight's surgery goes. I'll see what I can do." He patted her hand. "In any event, you're due in my office Thursday morning."

"Nine a.m. sharp." Sahel said the words knowing and underscoring Carl's penchant for punctuality and her difficulty in getting up and dressing for going out. Were her neurosurgeon anyone else but Carl, she would have long stopped keeping her appointments. "I'll be there," she said. Again Carl lifted her hand and this time planted a kiss upon her head. He then left.

With Carl gone Sahel touched the crown of her head and fingered the sensation left by the imprint of his lips. An uncanny sensation of being watched washed over Sahel. She turned her head to the right. No one spoke to her. Blindness was such a bitch.

A vision spread before her.

Two people.

A man and a woman.

They were arguing.

They were in an office. Darkness painted the windows. Lights throughout the city below streamed across the nighttime sky.

"What's come over you?" The man stood back.

16

"Daddy never includes me in the decision-making around here."

The woman set her hand upon her hip. "I'm just as educated as all of you men. I bring in the same amount of money. Why doesn't he give me more responsibility?"

"Your father respects the work you do."

"Then why does he have you here working late and inspecting charts? I've been coming here since I was ten years old and watching him work. I used to do my homework over there in that corner."

She turned and pointed to a small desk and chair. "Why can't we work at this, you and me, together?" She whipped around and stared at the papers filling the desk.

"I'll speak to your father," he said. He walked back behind the desk.

"And that's just the problem," the young woman retorted. "He's my father, and your boss, but I have to go to him for any kind of promotion."

"Surely you don't envy my becoming partner?" He opened his arms in fear and frustration. The woman said, "I just want to be acknowledged and rewarded for the work I do here, too. I don't plan to stop work when I get married."

"And neither would I want you to."

"Then why is my father always talking about when you take over running this brokerage?"

He inhaled deeply. After a momentary silence he said, "Your father wants to protect you." He strode around the desk to Sunetra. On his approach she stepped back. "Have you been talking to my father behind my back? You promised that we would both go to him and announce our plans to marry. None of this ancient stuff of you asking him for my hand."

The man glanced away.

"Have you spoken with my father?" The woman drew near.

The man clenched his jaw.

"Answer me," she demanded of him.

"I spoke to him." He faced her. "I was afraid. And I didn't want you hurt by the possibility that he might say, 'No.' I thought if I honored your traditions—"

Sunetra slapped him and then said, "As if him telling me not to marry you would stop me from doing so?" She knitted her carefully sculpted brows, kohl outlining her eyes.

"I wanted his respect, and blessings." The man massaged his cheek. "That's important in your culture. And to me." His hand slid from his cheek.

"You're not marrying my father or the Hindu culture. It's me that will be your wife." The young woman touched her chest. "But not if you insist on carrying out all this foolishness."

"Why is it so hard for you to see that I love both you and your parents?" James said.

"I love them too. But I need to know you're on my side."

"Where's the war?" he demanded.

"Where the hell have you been the last thousand years? Women have held no power or independence over our lives. Slaves to our parents and husbands is all we're worth."

"I don't want to make you a slave."

"Then why would you go behind my back and speak to my father about us marrying, particularly when you promised we'd do it together?"

"I'm sorry. Truly. I didn't mean to hurt you."

"That's what you all say."

"Sunetra, I love you." The man grasped her arms and pulled her close. He then kissed her lips.

"Let me go." She pushed back and escaped his arms. "I don't want to be just a wife. I want to be a woman in the world and moving under my own power. I won't be dependent like a child upon you or anyone."

"And I will give that to you."

"I don't want you to give me anything. I'm a person in my own right. I don't need you or anyone to—"

"But I need you. Can't you see that?" The man then whispered, "Without you I am nothing. Nothing."

The inferno of fury in Sunetra's eyes dissipated. Her passion for freedom turned into compassion. Reaching up, she took the man's head into her arms. He nudged his face in her breasts, breathed in the scent of amber mixed with the faint aroma of curry that Sunetra's mother seemed to use in all she cooked.

18

"Don't leave me," the young man said. "Don't ever leave me."

Footsteps sounded from out in the corridor of the brokerage. The man and Sunetra exchanged glances, her pale brown eyes darkening to dusk.

"Somebody's here," Sunetra said. "They're breaking into the …"

Venturing into the dimly lit hallway, he saw no one. Only the empty metal scrub bucket, most probably left by the janitor eager to get home.

He returned to the office, and there he found Sunetra removing the lock from the black semi-automatic glock.

"What the hell is that?" The fear in the man's tone scratched his throat. "Put that away. There's no one out there." He approached her, reached out his hand, and grasped her palm with her fingers clenching the gun's trigger.

Footsteps resounded once more, this time growing louder. "I told you someone was here," Sunetra said. She pulled away and went out, he following her into the other room.

Sahel's vision ended as quickly as it had arisen. Darkness settled once more. Sahel had never experienced anything like this even before losing her sight.

A hand softly lifted her palm. "Carl? You've returned," she said, emerging from the break with her usual reality.

"No. James Bolton," said the man holding her hand. Geraldine, a friend, then spoke. "Sahel. There's someone I want you to meet," she said in her familiar tone, a mixture of excitement and determination.

Chapter 3

J

ames Bolton was an interesting person. Unlike Titus or Carl he seemed to hold no agenda. After Geraldine completed the introductions, he sat next to Sahel. Engrossed in conversation with the physician to Sahel's right, Titus sounded excited and peaceful for once. Pleased and happy for him, Sahel attempted to tamp down her anxiety concerning how she would handle the food and eating by leaning left and going deeper into conversation with James. "So tell me about yourself."

"What do you want to know?"

"Whatever you want to tell me."

Sahel searched the canyon of silence that emerged between them, encapsulated within the din of muffled voices floating about them. Titus's voice then pierced the cascade of conversations. "I was just saying to Harry Miller that we've got to add this new procedure to our roster. I'm losing ten patients a month to the group in the city."

Sahel imagined everyone looking to him. Tall and lean with a thin mustache he kept neatly groomed, Titus was a handsome man. Sahel tried in vain to conjure images of him from her memory.

Abandoning the task, she again leaned towards James.

"Am I that difficult to talk to?" Sahel straightened the lap of her gown. The clanking of plates and silverware grew louder. "I suppose dinner's coming," she said. She grew anxious in James's silence.

A waitress then said, "Fish or steak?"

Sahel splayed her palms upon the lap of her dress in an effort to remain calm.

"Fish," James said.

"And what would she like?" The waitress's words descended upon Sahel.

"I think the lady can answer for herself," James said. "Ask her."

"Excuse me, miss." The waitress leaned down and spoke to Sahel. "What would you like?"

Sahel turned slightly towards the waitress and said, "I'll take the filet mignon."

"They only told us it was steak. I'm not sure if it's—" the waitress began.

"Filet mignon," Sahel reiterated, and then, "My husband was on the menu committee, Dr. Titus Denning."

"Yes, ma'am. I'm sorry." The waitress's words ascended from the depths once more, but with what seemed less fervor. "And what kind of salad dressing would you like, ma'am?"

"Ranch." Sahel then reminded the waitress, "You didn't ask Mr. Bolton what type of dressing he wanted."

"Oh, yes sir, and what would you—"

"Same as Mrs. Denning," James said. "Ranch."

The waitress left.

"I hope I didn't offend you," James said.

"Well, at least you're talking. And quite the opposite." Sahel felt strengthened. "Are you always so abrupt?"

"I don't like it when people are overlooked, mistreated."

Again Sahel ran her hands across the lap of her gown, but this time with passion and less out of anxiety. The darkness felt less foreign; Sahel became less alien to those around her against the calm of James's words. A warhorse for the weary. "People aren't comfortable around me." She spoke her truth.

"Are you comfortable around you?" James said.

"Your salad, madam," a man spoke. The waiter's arm whisked by her face leaving a light draft that, from its path, caressed her cheek. The aroma of sautéed onions, mushrooms and white wine filled her nose.

Titus's voice to her right continued leading the discussion on surgery. She placed her hands upon the edge of the table and inched her fingers in search of the plate.

"Would you like me to hand you your fork?" James said.

"No. I'll be fine." Her fingers began to shake. In an effort to find her knife, Sahel's finger tipped over her water glass. Oh, my god. She pushed her chair from the table. Her stomach began to churn as she imagined all eyes upon her. "Get me a napkin," Titus demanded. She felt him grip her hand. "It's all right. They're bringing napkins," he said.

"I'm sorry," she said in a fearful whisper. The world began to spin. Her hands trembled. "I need to get out of here."

"Let me wipe your dress," Titus spoke softly.

Sahel felt herself crumbling within in the silence of what she sensed were those around the table staring at her. "Please, I need to get out of here."

"Okay. I'll take you home." Titus sounded worried. Sahel felt crushed. "Can't I just go outside, catch my breath? Isn't there a door on the other side of the room?"

"Okay," Titus said. Geraldine spoke. "Titus, you stay here. Let me help her."

"Take my hand." James grasped her palm. Sahel pulled away from Titus and reached over and took hold of James's other hand.

He lifted her to stand.

Seconds later they were out on the veranda.

Sahel clenched the stone balcony and took a deep breath. The heat writhing in her cheeks subsided.

"You don't like these sort of things, do you?" James said as she leaned over and breathed in once more.

"It's the food," she said weakly. Sahel felt herself about to throw up.

"Would you like me to bring you a plate out here?"

"No! I said it was the food." Calming, she went on. "This is my first time out since ... losing ... my sight. I'm sorry."

Again silence descended.

"Please don't do that," Sahel snapped. "Talk to me when I say something."

"I'm sorry, but you remi—"

Sahel tried imagining what caused James to go silent with her and yet defend her to the waitress taking their orders. "I mean you no harm. It's just that—" James attempted once more.

"Is my hair not right? My gown not fitting?"

"No. You look very lovely. If anyone didn't already know ... it's not apparent that you're ... blind," James said.

"Well, the waitress certainly knew."

"Perhaps that was because your husband had spoken to her prior to taking our orders."

"You overheard them?" Sahel exhaled heavily. She felt incredulous.

"I'm sure he meant no harm. I saw them speaking. And then she came to us."

Sahel gave a sigh of disgust that flowed into despair. "I'm sure he was worried, trying to protect you," James said.

"He's always worried," Sahel retorted.

"He loves you," James said. Sahel turned towards him.

"He feels guilty," Sahel said.

"For what?"

Sahel wanted to talk, but she had met James fewer than forty-five minutes earlier. She grew suspicious of his easy manner, and her growing comfort in his presence. "Where are you from?"

"I grew up in Richmond."

"Do you still live there? Geraldine said you were her

godchild. But she's never mentioned you."

"I've been living in Marin. Just over the Richmond Bridge for the last two years."

"Where? Sausalito?" Sahel grew intensely curious.

The voices of Titus and her father, Essien, drawing near silenced her thoughts.

"There you are," her father said. He placed his hand upon her shoulder. "Titus said you had a little mishap at the table."

"I spilled a glass of water," Sahel said with a bitter smile. "But I'm all right now."

"Good, good." Her father caressed the back of her hair, drew her close, and kissed her forehead.

"Would you like to come back inside?" Titus intervened.

"No. I'm catching my breath," Sahel said. "At some point I've got to take some classes," she retorted in a whisper.

"Now is not the time to discuss that," Titus said in restrained frustration.

They could not continue living in denial of her lack of sight. "I'm blind, Titus."

"There'll be time for all that." Titus lifted her hand and she felt her father step away.

"The time is now. I can't keep coming out and embarrassing myself, and you, like this. I'm a wreck."

"It was just a glass of water," Titus said.

"It could have been a disaster."

Essien intervened. "I don't know about that."

"What if I'd had coffee?" Sahel said, turning towards his voice.

"We don't need to rush into anything," Titus said.

Sahel then considered James, whom she imagined observing the sordid inner workings of her family. "Have you met James?" she said. "Or has he left?"

"I'm still here."

She felt Titus turn, his grip on her hand tightening. "Essien Ohin," her father said. "I'm Sahel's father."

"James Bolton," James said, to which Titus added, "Titus Denning."

"Titus is my husband." Sahel then turned her head in the

direction of James's voice. "James is Geraldine's godson."

"Oh, really." Essien's voice held an aura of excitement. Having dated Geraldine for over a year.

"James lives in Marin," Sahel said.

"Where in Marin?" Titus questioned tersely. Always the inquisitive and distrusting one.

"South Marin. Just over the Richmond Bridge," James said.

"There's the federal prison, San Quentin, immediately over the bridge," Titus snapped. Sahel hated his tone. Yet she too was curious.

Footsteps drew near and then Geraldine's voice. "Titus, they're about to call for you."

Titus caressed her arm. "Are you sure you won't come back inside?"

"You go and receive your award." She patted his hand on her arm.

"You don't need another distraction. I'll stay out here."

A moment passed. Titus then said, "I'll be ready to leave in the next half hour." Disappointment echoed in his words. He lightly kissed her cheek.

"I'll be fine," Sahel assured once more. "James is with me." She searched the space between them and touched his cheek.

Essien and Geraldine accompanied Titus back inside the ballroom, leaving Sahel with James out on the verandah.

"There's no way you can be a distraction." James's words stroked Sahel's ears. She felt him closer than Titus or her father had stood.

"I make Titus nervous. This is his night. He shouldn't be thinking of me," Sahel said. "He worries when he can't see me."

"That's what happens when you love someone. And when they're as beautiful as you."

Sahel's face grew increasingly warm. "I fear the only thing that distracts Titus's anxiety is when he's performing surgery."

"I'm not trying to come on to you. Just stating the facts."

The heat in her cheeks intensified. "You speak as if you know me."

"Only what I've seen." James's words now emanated from a distance. "I know what it means, feels like, to love someone.

26

And then not to have them around, to be unable to see and help them."

Fearful of what she could not identify, Sahel took in breath.

"What happened?"

"She died."

Sahel exhaled. She wished for the inner voice to rise up and tell her what to say. Again she took in breath, and in a moment of deep and confounding fear, wished for the woman in red to appear in her mind.

"Do you believe in reincarnation?" James was again close.

"I don't know much about ..."

"Do you believe?" he repeated, this time in a firm whisper. His words, and the warmth of his voice, again brushed her cheeks and strummed the desires of her heart, awakening and opening against her fears. Sahel parted her lips and was about to speak when James said, "You remind me so much of her. Sunetra." She sensed James about to kiss her and then on angling her head, she reached out. But nothing was there.

"James ..." she called. No answer came.

Chapter 4

Moments before James left, Sahel had felt him about to kiss her. Now at home and sitting before the bureau in her bedroom, she pondered James's question. *Do you believe in reincarnation, that the dead can speak through the living?* The darkness surrounding her grew cold. Sahel gripped her arms. She was wearing a nightgown, her shoulders bare.

Titus's hands descended upon them, providing welcomed warmth. "Thank you for coming tonight," he said, then proceeded to unclasp the pearls about her neck.

Sahel reached back and cupped her palm to Titus's cheek now brushing hers. Titus's lips then nudged their way into her neck beside her shoulders. She wished she had seen him accept the plaque, Surgeon of the Year, from Calvin Bennett, President of the Oakland Medical Society, and senior partner of the cardiac group with whom Titus practiced.

Sahel tried to imagine their cheeks, hers and Titus's, beside each other, one dark and one light, in the mirror's reflection. Unlike other nights, Sahel grew wet and warm. She envisioned herself as the woman in the vision that had unfolded before her, Titus the man. But they, she and Titus were not arguing.

"I need you," Titus whispered in the lowest of tones. "Forgive me." A tear slipped onto Sahel's shoulders from Titus.

Despite silent urges to enroll in classes for the blind, Sahel had yet to accept her blindness as permanent. She batted away Carl's words from earlier. "I need to see you looking back at me." The surgery brought too much risk, demanded more hope and faith than she possessed.

The string of pearls slid from her neck, down between her breasts and onto the carpet, a sound ever so faint, but registered by Sahel with heightened senses.

Sahel leaned back into Titus's arms with greater ease than she had ever known. Gently he lifted her into his arms, kissed her head, face and cheeks, then took her to the bed.

After the wedding, Essien had invited Sahel and Titus to join him in the house that Sahel had grown up in. "I'm here all alone and Sahel knows where everything is. Please." His voice had been despairing. That her father had not wanted to be rid of Sahel in her brokenness further shattered her heart, casting her into a dwelling place of thankfulness and anger, antipathy that always led to despair.

After their acceptance, Essien bequeathed them his and Lillian's bed. "Make it happier than what your mother and I were able to do," he had whispered to Sahel as she and Titus, on their honeymoon night, stood facing a door she had been able to see but six weeks earlier.

Titus drew the covers upon them. The bare skin of his chest against hers stirred memories of James's words out on the veranda. *Do you believe ... in life after the death? Do you believe?* James's words settled upon her spirit.

Titus's whispers grew sweet. "I have always ... always ...

loved you." His passion entered Sahel's body, and for the first time since they had married, pierced her heart and soul. "I ... need ... you," Titus moaned.

"I love you," Sahel whispered words that until this moment had evaded her voice.

Titus's lips touched to her neck. James's question to Sahel out on the verandah perused her mind, and penetrated her thoughts.

"Yes, I believe ... in life ... life ... after ... death ..." Sahel uttered within. Slowly she surrendered to Titus's love. Redness filled her world.

A sliver of her vision rose and died. Sunetra said, "If we were to marry, I can't make you my entire life."

"I wouldn't want you to," said the man, his face a teddy-bear brown face, bore a soft genuineness and sadness.

Chapter 5

T

he next morning Sahel entered the sanctuary with her hand on Titus's arm and followed him to a pew. Moments after sitting, she felt a presence that again she was being watched. "Good morning, my dear," greeted her father. He kissed the top of her head. Geraldine then patted her shoulder.

Those not aware might think Sahel and Titus did not share a residence with Essien. Last night, as on many recent occasions, Essien had spent the night at Geraldine's home.

On hearing Titus address James, Sahel turned back.

"Good morning," James said. He lifted her hand. "It's good to see you, too."

"I wish I could say the same of you," Sahel said with a chuckle.

Titus said nothing in response to her humor. A brief twist of pain, barely noticeable upon Titus's face, said that he had yet to make sense of what life had dealt his wife.

"Your father's invited James to brunch," Geraldine said to Sahel.

"Oh, wonderful," Sahel said. Her confusion about his question from last evening dissipated. But now she found something familiar about his voice, as if she had heard it before even meeting him. She grew warm with a familiarity that extended deep inside her.

"It'll be nice to have you join us," Sahel said.

The organ sounded. Titus tapped Sahel on her shoulder and she turned around.

"Good morning, Sahel," said Father Richard. She extended her hand into the darkness, whereupon the priest received her palm and pressed it between his. "Titus," the priest said, and Sahel imagined him shaking Titus's hand.

Throughout the service she thought of James, the feel of his hands, warm and trembling last evening. What runs through his mind when seeing me? She longed to see his face. Were that to happen by anything not short of a miracle, she would be lost for words. In a strange way, blindness had its positives, such as not having to face herself in the eyes of another. And yet that was exactly what Carl desired and wanted. "I want you to regain your sight. I need to see my reflection in your eyes, you looking back at me," he had said. But to do that meant accepting the guilt of what Sahel felt had been her betrayal. Sahel was Titus's wife. She loved and needed him, and he her. Another part of her held affections for Carl. She could not imagine life without him. And yet ...

Sahel's thoughts lunged back to Titus making love to her last night. It had felt good, his passion pulsating throughout her body, enlivening her soul and drenching her parched spirit. This had occurred only hours after meeting James. His abrupt abandonment of her on the verandah seemed strange. Essien had rushed to her seconds later.

"James said he needed to leave, that he was not feeling well," her father had said. "He asked me to convey his apologies."

"Oh," Sahel had said.

Hours later and enveloped in Titus's arms, she had reconsidered James's question. *Do you believe in reincarnation, eternal life?* The question had haunted her each time Titus had gone deeper into her body and unleashed the energy of his love and desire. "I love you, need you," Titus had whispered with each thrust. And then on coming, "Please forgive me."

"Yes ... I do," Sahel had whispered back.

Titus's hands, firm and soft, had kneaded her body and soul into surrender. The door of her heart lay open when he had finished.

Sahel wished to have her sight back, if only to thank him for being so patient after her stupidity. The accident had been her fault. But Titus viciously blamed himself. So did Carl, but without the venom of self-recrimination with which Titus's fangs of guilt continuously bit himself, something that Sahel had come to realize but most others did not recognize or know existed.

A handsome and successful surgeon, Titus was revered by his patients and respected by nurses. Surgical residents appreciated his patience and willingness to teach. His excellence at wielding a scalpel or directing a laser continually impressed colleagues. Operating room technicians, along with the residents who assisted, relished any opportunity to observe him repair a heart, and learn from his expertise.

Few could imagine let alone realize, in the wake of Sahel's accident, the depths to which Titus fell, the result of qualities rooted in the less altruistic side of his humanness, aspects common to all who have ever lived and loved beyond themselves. That the frustration he had displayed the night of the incident reflected an aspect of personality all individuals possess did not matter. Titus held himself to a higher standard.

Last evening, lying within the darkness of their bedroom, Sahel had received his passion. The experience, the first of its kind since they had taken their vows, provided a flicker of hope amid the loss of Sahel's sight, if only to nurture the flame of desire in Sahel that one day she would look into Titus's eyes, see herself, and not feel repelled. Then and only then would his love cease to repulse her and frighten her, and liberate not only her but also Titus.

The priest completed the homily. Titus assisted Sahel to stand, the touch of his palm taking her back to the previous night. Warmth traveled through her. She smiled. And then searching the space between them, she lifted his left hand to her lips and kissed it.

Sahel held fast to Titus's arm as they approached Father Richard in the line to receive Eucharist. Titus guided her forward as he had done during their wedding Mass. On reaching the priest, Sahel silently counted to five, her way of waiting, as Father Richard placed a wafer upon Titus's tongue.

She spoke the number five in her mind and then turned to Titus to receive her wafer, the second one that Father Richard would bless and give to Titus, as he had done at their wedding, and which Titus would place upon Sahel's tongue. With the bread melting in her mouth, Sahel signed the cross upon her chest as she knew Titus also was doing.

Again she took hold of his arm and followed him to the Eucharistic minister holding the chalice of wine. As always since the accident, after he had sipped, Titus brought the cup to Sahel. She gripped it, her fingers touching his, steadied it, and drank. Titus placed Sahel's hand on his arm and she followed him back to their pew.

Carefully he assisted her to kneel. There, beside him with palms together, she prayed and asked God to help her survive her blindness. In the darkness Sahel had surrendered to, she found her way to accept and receive Titus's love.

Chapter 6

S

ahel greeted James and Geraldine on their arrival at the house. "Please come in." She extended her hand and he took it. "Zelda is just putting out brunch."

"I'll go help her," Geraldine said. Her voice trailed off into the sound of footsteps. "I imagine Geraldine is wearing those wonderful black stilettos," Sahel said, wrapping her arm about James's.

Sahel envisioned him smiling as he spoke. "We'll be eating out on the patio," she said.

"That should be nice. The sun is really pretty today."

Indicating with her cane the direction he should guide her, Sahel said, "Through the kitchen." The two had nearly cleared the foyer when voices bounded from the study.

"I don't care what you say, she's not having the surgery," Titus shouted.

"She's your wife, not your child," blasted Carl.

"I hope you like Spanish chorizo," Sahel said as they entered the kitchen, her effort to distract James from a new version of the escalation that had been brewing during the last few months.

Following James's lead, Sahel stepped onto the patio. On hearing Zelda speaking with Geraldine, Sahel said, "Zelda, this is James. James, this is Zelda. And she makes the best chorizo with scrambled eggs."

"James Bolton," said James. "Just call me James." From the sound and ease of his voice, Sahel concluded James worked in a profession that required comfort with introductions.

She said, "Zelda's husband runs a highly sought-after landscaping business."

"The table is prepared," Geraldine announced.

"She's on the other side of the table, by the tree," Sahel said.

"She is," said James.

Sahel smiled.

"How long had you been without sight?"

"A year."

"A year too long," said Geraldine. "Carl's been trying to get her to undergo this procedure—"

"I thought we agreed not to discuss this," Sahel said.

"Okay. Okay," conceded Geraldine. "Then again, maybe James can —"

Sahel felt James move. "I'm going. I'm going," said Geraldine.

"She's gone into the house," James whispered as Sahel turned her head.

"To get the cantaloupe," Geraldine called out. "I heard that."

"Please sit, Mrs. Denning. And you too, James," said Zelda. "I'll bring out the eggs and chorizo."

"Let's sit." He led her to a chair, and pulled it out. Sahel found her way to sit. "A warhorse for the weary," Sahel said as she had last evening.

"I don't like to be poked and prodded."

"But it's not you that's being herded," Sahel said. On folding her cane, placing it on her lap, Sahel realized she had only met James last evening, less than twenty-four hours ago.

"Would you like some water?" James asked.

Sahel slid her hand onto the table, located her glass and handed it to him. "Where's your father?" James asked. "And Titus?"

"Daddy's probably on the phone with a colleague or one of his many students."

"He teaches economics at USF."

"I see Geraldine has filled you in on Daddy." Sahel ignored the question about Titus's whereabouts.

James took her hand and placed her fingers around the glass of water. She sipped and then, finding the table, carefully set it on the surface. "No spills or messes this time."

"Why were you so worried last night," James said, "about the food, and eating? You're fine at finding the food on your plate. It's quite amazing."

"A year is a long time to go without eating. I have my own method. Or rather Zelda devised one for me. She places meat at the three o'clock position, vegetable or fruit at the nine o'clock. It's been a year since the accident. Eggs always go at the six o'clock.

"And without her present and preparing your plate, you were ..."

"I need to get a better system. A week's notice was not long enough."

"But last evening you said that Titus was on the committee that planned the menu. Surely you knew about the event in plenty of ti—"

"He didn't learn that he had been chosen as the surgeon of the year until last weekend," Sahel explained.

"Have you ever considered taking classes for the blind?" James's question came seconds later.

"It's crossed my mind. Then there's the research, getting the phone numbers and making the calls," Sahel said. "Like I said earlier, I'm not who you think I am."

"I would agree with that. I guess what bugs me is why you're stuck here letting them do it. But then again, maybe this is your way of taking care of them, letting them show you how much they love you, giving back what you've given to them."

"I think it's a little more sinister than that," Sahel said. She fingered her cane.

"Then you like having them dote on you, their minds forever worried if you've fallen and can't get up. If that's the case I would think that you'd—"

"I took a bottle of pills eight months ago. My father's medication for back pain. It relaxes the muscles in correct doses. Too much, which is what I took, and you stop breathing," Sahel said. "I wanted to die."

"I would imagine that you were also hurting."

"Terribly. But to take it out on them ..." Sahel shook her head.

"It wasn't right. Had I not come back ..." Again she shook her head.

"Which was it—you coming back or Titus saving you—that hurt the most?"

"A little bit of both, I suppose," Sahel said. "Titus happened to come home early the afternoon I took the pills. He normally doesn't arrive home until after six. That day, he came home at two. Geraldine had found me upstairs and unconscious. She had just told Zelda. Titus discovered the bottle by the bed, called the ER and drove me to the hospital. He ran the code. My heart had stopped beating, but he got it pumping again. I owe him my life."

"What do you mean?" James asked. He leaned towards Sahel.

"When we opt out, take our own lives, we don't escape. Instead we commit ourselves to having to do it all over again. We're stuck. The life we abandoned still has unfinished work that waits for us."

"But can't you just pick up in the next life from where you stopped?"

"That's what we'd like to think. Or at least I did."

"What changed your mind?" James asked.

"Dying and seeing the anguish and hurt on the faces of those I had left, Daddy, Carl, Geraldine. And then there was Titus."

"But if you were dead, how could you see—"

"Trust me, I saw them. And don't ask me how." Sahel

40

unfolded her cane, stood, turned and, with the cane before her, plodded the way towards the house.

James came to her and touched her hand. "What I asked you last night, about life after death, reincarnation, I meant it. It wasn't some game," James said. He gripped her wrist.

Sahel turned towards his voice. "I know." With that she removed his hand from her wrist and went inside.

Chapter 7

S

ahel entered Carl's office.

"It's good to see you using that," Carl said.

"We're coming along." Sahel smiled, still feeling the joy of the previous evening with Titus. Carl grasped her hand, placed it on his arm, and took her cane.

Sahel she interwove her arm around his. Carl led her from the foyer to the study.

She asked, "How did your surgery go last night?"

"Swift, smooth and quietly," Carl said. He helped her sit. "The perfect time to do it."

"I missed you at Mass this morning. In fact we all did," said Sahel.

"I doubt that. Besides I had to—"

"Let me guess—the patient from last night. You had to look in on him or her. Or was it Sunday rounds?" Sahel queried.

"I do live in the city." Two weeks prior to Sahel marrying Titus, Carl moved across the bridge to San Francisco. "It's not so easy getting over here now."

"You make time to walk me around the lake each week."

"Wednesdays are my half day off. I'm already over here. And I enjoy your company."

"Your disguise for getting me out of the house."

"Well, Titus certainly isn't going to do it. Left to him, he'd keep you cooped up here—"

"Will performing Saturday night surgeries become a staple in your life like Sunday rounds?" Sahel interrupted once more. They entered the study. "Or is it just one more way to justify missing Mass?" Carl had not entered St. Maria's since serving as best man for Titus wedding Sahel.

On reaching the sofa, Sahel moved to sit. Joining her, Carl folded the aid and laid it upon the table beside him. Carl, too, was given to hiding "*the thing*," as Titus called it. But Carl's dislike of Sahel's cane lay rooted in other hopes.

"Don't you have residents to see your patients?" Sahel pursued.

"I do, but the buck stops with me."

"You're a horrible liar, Carl Pierson," Sahel said.

"So perhaps I am."

Sahel heard the click of Carl's penlight. Immediately she prepared for his fingers to stretch open her eyes. "Just lie back and relax." The traces of the light she had seen in the initial weeks after the accident had faded, a symptom that when further examined showed the need for surgery to restore her sight. Carl's pain was now becoming hers.

She neither squinted nor squirmed, indicating what Carl feared. He clicked off the penlight and then lifted her hand. "I need to get inside your head and fix this," Carl said.

"We talked about this last night." Sahel shook her head. "I won't put Titus or Daddy through this. Or you."

"I don't have to perform the surgery." Carl protested. "But as your doctor—"

44

"You're my friend. What if I die? Then you'll be like Titus, forever feeling responsible."

"On the matter of your blindness, he is."

"I say he's not," Sahel retorted.

"If he hadn't been so angry and impatient. Hotheaded."

"What's done is done. I don't want to discuss this. I was pig headed. It's in the past," Sahel said.

"You weren't ready to get married."

"I was stalling. I see that now," Sahel said. "We've always loved each other, Titus and I. And just because my mother liked him it didn't mean he was wrong for me."

"Your mother was wedded to the idea of your marrying Titus and not me, the dark boy who looked like your father."

"And what of me?" Sahel said. Her skin was darker than Carl's.

Silence ensued. The subject of skin color was painful. And yet it was their bond. Carl started once more. "I'm not trying to come between you and Titus. I just question this hole he's got you stuck in. You don't use your cane except at home. No classes for the blind. And no surgery, god forbid."

"He's afraid."

"I'm afraid," Carl said. "That you'll never regain your sight."

Carl's words from last evening returned. "I need you to see me, Sahel. I need you looking back at me and me knowing that you see my face. That's all I want. Trust me."

Sahel said, "We'll get through this. And we'll be closer than ever."

"And if not, I suppose you'll just take the pills again." Carl's words were cold and incisive. Sahel momentarily grew still. When she moved to stand, he grasped her arm. "I'm sorry. That was a low blow." His voice was a whisper.

Sahel eased back onto the sofa. "You mean well. But I won't take this from you or anyone." Sahel would not let go of the joy she had experienced in Titus's arms last evening. It was the first time they had truly made love, Sahel allowing all of him in and receiving the gift of his love and commitment unfettered.

"What's gotten into you?" Carl chuckled. "The old fight is back."

"Don't change the subject." Carl's words had hurt. "I'm not giving up."

"Not if I can help it," Carl said.

"And that's the point. You're not helping."

In Carl's silence Sahel realized she had struck his vulnerable place. Again his plea from last evening returned. *I need you to see me.* She said, "Titus and I are married."

"More reason for him to support you in having the surgery." Gone was the joviality in Carl's tone, bitterness having stepped in.

"Forgive me, but he's not as narcissistic as you are. Titus doesn't need to see himself in my eyes. He wants me alive. This is my decision," she added.

"I'll never accept that."

"Perhaps if you found your way back to Mass, you'd—"

"You didn't feel that way six months ago." Carl referred to the incident with the pills.

Sahel withdrew her hand from Carl's.

"I'm sorry. It's just that—"

"Things have changed, Carl." Sahel had told no one about her out-of-body experience. She had seen Titus and Carl fighting to save her. The voice of her father pleading for explanation of her attempted suicide, blaming himself for having left his bottle of pills lying around, all remained with her. She could not rid her memory of the torture on Titus's face. Despair and hopelessness fleeing his body as if stabbed in the chest, and yet blood refusing to drain, had changed Sahel.

Sahel's heart had ceased beating. Moments passed wherein she hung between life and death. She had found herself in the ocean. There, beneath the water's surface, she had met the woman in red whose face she could not recall.

Sahel said to Carl, "I refused to let Titus operate on my mother. Had I chosen differently, she might be alive."

"Your mother's heart was worn out." Carl defended his counsel to both Sahel and Essien against Titus performing open-heart surgery on Lillian. "The operation would have killed her."

"Then you should understand Titus's position despite how much you hated Mama," Sahel countered. "Even you regret

46

having prevented Titus from doing the surgery."

"I hated what her death did to you," Carl said.

Sahel shook her head. "Don't you find it a little strange that we're back in the same place as with Mama, only this time it's me and my surgery we're discussing? I couldn't have lived with her dying in the operating room. That was my greatest fear. I won't put Titus or you in the same position."

"Your mother was not your friend. She loved Titus because he was just like her," Carl said.

"On that you're wrong. He may be fair like her, but that's where the similarities end. I don't want to talk about it anymore—"

"Talk about what?" Titus said. The door to the study going shut resounded. Titus's footsteps drew near. The sofa cushion beside her gave way; Titus sat next to her.

Sahel collected herself. "We were just discussing Carl's having become a lapsed Catholic." Titus lifted her hand. She plastered a smile. "It seems he's growing comfortable doing surgery late on Saturday nights when other doctors aren't around."

"As far as I'm concerned, it's the worst time to perform anything but emergency surgery. That is, unless you want the person to die," Titus said.

"No sane physician wants his patient to die," Carl snapped. Titus lifted Sahel's hand.

"The key word is sane," Titus retorted.

"Then again, when the doctor can only think of his needs and not that of his patients, one has to question—"

"That's enough," Sahel said. Well aware of the point to which Titus was driving, she moved to stand. Titus helped and joined her. Carl's palm landed upon her back. How she longed for the war between her two best friends, not unlike brothers, to end. *How do you marry the brother who lives in your soul and remain faithful to the one that holds your heart?*

Sahel's decision to wed Titus had spewed, what amounted to kerosene, upon a slow burn. Her decision to forego the surgery had sent flames devouring the forest of bonds knitting the three.

"Where's Daddy and Geraldine?" Sahel said, then thought of

47

James. She turned back, motioned for Carl to retrieve her cane.

"We don't need the thing." Titus placed her hand to his arm.

"Try to behave yourself," Sahel said to Titus. "We have a guest in the house." Only too glad to defy Titus, Carl opened Sahel's hand and placed the cane in it.

"Who?" said Carl.

"James Bolton, Geraldine's godson."

"Oh, you mean that character from last night out on the verandah?" Titus snapped.

"Watch your tone," Sahel said. "If you took the time to speak to him, you'd see that he isn't some character, but really a nice person."

"Well, forgive me for having questions about some person I just met via Geraldine, my all-time favorite non-member of this family who asserts she knows what's best for everyone. The man who left you out on the verandah alone last evening," Titus said.

"James wasn't feeling well. He told Daddy to come to me."

"Anything could have happened in those three minutes," said Titus.

"It was barely a minute."

"You were out there alone."

"Who is this man?" Carl said.

"Geraldine's godson," Sahel repeated. "I told you about him."

"And just what do you know about him?" Carl said. "I like Geraldine, but leaving you on the verandah alone was not a smart thing to do. Then again, if Titus had allowed you to take your cane ..."

"Would you just shut up about that blasted cane?" Titus said.

On the heel of his words, Geraldine rushed into the study. "Please! Come quick! It's James."

"What's wrong?" Carl said.

"He's collapsed on the patio," Geraldine said, her voice fading.

"You two see to him." Sahel pushed them off, urging Carl and Titus to go.

Chapter 8

S

ahel pushed open the door leading from the kitchen and placed her cane onto the patio.

"Is he allergic to anything?" Titus barked.

"Not that I know of." Geraldine's voice was feeble.

"The paramedics are on the way," Essien said from behind Sahel. He helped Sahel onto the patio. The warmth of the Northern California sun landed on her face.

"What's happened?" Sahel angled her head towards her father.

"We were sitting at the table, Geraldine and I, eating and talking with James," Essien spoke low. "One minute he was fine. I noticed he was silent, so I looked across the table and saw him slump over."

"Is he awake now?" Sahel gripped her father's hand.

"Titus and Carl are checking his arms." Essien whispered. He placed his palm upon her back and drew her close. Geraldine squeezed Sahel's hand.

"What's wrong with him?" Sahel forced strength into her voice and whipped back memories of having found her mother, Lillian, in the throes of her first heart attack. Sahel had been thirteen and home. Essien had been lecturing to one of his classes at University of San Francisco over in the city.

"He's going to be all right," Essien said. He patted Sahel's hand. And then added, "James is a good person."

"He seems to have lost a lot of weight," Carl commented.

Sahel let go of her father's hand and, with her cane before her, moved towards Carl's voice. Drawing near, she accidentally poked Titus.

"Ouch." Titus gruffed. "Sahel, we're trying to—"

"What's wrong with him?" she again demanded.

"That's what we're trying to find out," Titus said. "James. Can you hear me?" Titus spoke loudly. Sahel's cheeks grew warm in recalling how, when she had taken the pills, Titus had called her name. Then came the sensation of his hands to her face, turning her head side-to-side, and then pinching her cheeks in an effort to revive her.

Sahel's sensate, kinesthetic memory was a crazy and unwieldy thing. Until last evening it had remained bereft, and empty of images. The vision she experienced had displayed no attachment to memory, at least not to Sahel's.

Sunetra. The name of the woman in the vision now penetrated Sahel's thoughts.

She recalled how the vision had evaporated when James lifted her hand. She had thought him to be Carl having returned. Or had it been the other way around—Sahel wishing for Carl only to have Geraldine introduce James into her life?

Carl said of James, "His pupils are fixed and dilated."

"What does that mean?" Sahel knelt and found James's shoulder.

"Geraldine. Please, help her." Titus called to Geraldine, wanting her to take Sahel away.

Geraldine helped Sahel to her feet. Sahel stepped back. The

memory of lying upon the gurney in the emergency room returned.

The pain of the breathing tube guided by Carl's hand scraping its way down her throat, soared to the surface of her consciousness and disoriented her.

The voice from last evening as she and Titus made their way to the ballroom rose within Sahel. *Nothing is real except life, death, and rebirth*—the voice now said. *Titus is scared. Don't let him push you around. It's not the time. James needs you.*

"I want to know what's wrong with James," Sahel said. A truth was being withheld. "Somebody, speak to me."

Sirens, fast approaching in the distance, grew louder.

"I'm at a loss." Carl sighed. "Once he's at the ER, I'm sure—"

"And who says he's your patient?" Titus said.

Carl came to Sahel. "And I'm late for my surgery. The emergency room physician will take care of him," Carl said, ignoring Titus.

"I want you to look in on him." Sahel turned left, to Carl.

"I have a surgery case for which I'm already late."

"Please, he's my friend," Sahel said.

"You hardly even know the man. You only just met him," Carl said.

"Please, he's sick and needs our help," Sahel said. Carl sighed.

Titus came to them. "The paramedics are outside."

"Okay," Carl succumbed. He drew Sahel into his chest and kissed her head. "My case should take about three hours. The ER doc should be Ana Desai. I'll tell her to page me if anything arises."

"No, have them call Titus," Sahel said.

"Who do you want to take care of him, Sahel?" Carl asked.

"All right," she acquiesced. "You don't need to be disturbed." Sahel regretted her ambivalence, the dilemma of her life, the inability to choose and decide.

"I'll have Ana call Titus if she needs to speak to someone while I'm in surgery." Carl was terse. "I'll check on James as soon as I've finished my case. Will that please you?"

51

"Yes, now you need to go," Sahel said on succumbing to her confusion wrought by her faults. "Thanks," she added with a half smile.

The paramedics entered the house and took James to Berkeley General, Geraldine going with them.

Chapter 9

T

he afternoon stretched into the evening. No one from the hospital called about James. Sahel became hopeful. "Probably a bad case of the stomach flu," Essien advised. At Geraldine's request, he had remained home.

After seeing James off with the paramedics, Titus set about to dictate notes from patient charts. "I'm way behind on charting my surgeries. Wait any longer and I'll be on suspension," he said.

"But what about James?" asked Sahel.

"Ana will know what to do," Titus said. Ana Desai, the head physician of the emergency room at Berkeley General, had been present the afternoon that Titus had brought Sahel in unconscious from having overdosed on Essien's muscle relaxants.

"I just think one of us should be there when he wakes up."

"*If* he wakes up," Titus retorted. He and Sahel were now in the study, Sahel having followed him there from the patio.

"Don't speak about him like that."

"Okay, I'm not certain if he'll wake up. I hope he does, but with someone like that, you never know."

"And who is someone like that?"

Titus sighed. The door to the study went closed. Titus returned to Sahel, gently grasped her shoulders, and in a low voice said, "If I'm correct, Geraldine told you that James was her godson."

"That's right."

"Doesn't it strike you as just a little bit funny that she's never mentioned him before?"

"Well, perhaps—"

"Think about it, Sahel. She says he's like a son to her and yet we've never heard of him, never met him until now. She's been dating your father for at least two years. And yet she asked him to stay here while she goes to the hospital to be with James," said Titus.

"You don't know that," Sahel said. Titus's last words had stung.

Sahel's mother had died but fifteen months earlier.

"Come on, Sahel. Everyone knows your father was seeing Geraldine long before your mother died."

"And was that such a bad thing? Mama was dying. He had to find a way to cope."

"Then why chastise me for speaking the truth?"

Tight silence ensued. Ambivalence and the inability to choose, was Sahel's life, her challenge, a trait that marked her personality, and that so frustrated Titus, a surgeon, and a person of decision. This propensity for seeking out the gray areas of life, and dwelling there in refuge, had stoked the flames of their argument the night of the accident.

Titus said, "Your father struggled a lot that last year of her life. But it wasn't just with your mother's bad heart."

Sahel ignored Titus's statement. "My father's relationship

with Geraldine has nothing to do with my concern for James, and your lack of it. This is what I don't like about you. Always judging people before you get to know them, just like Mama."

"I'm nothing like your mother!"

"Yes, but at times you can be everything like her," said Sahel. The swinging back and forth of the two sides of Titus's personality tore at her. At times he was loving and kind to the point of extracting tears from Sahel. At others he bordered on the edge of crass indifference. Yet never did he exhibit this behavior with patients.

"Okay, Sahel," Titus said. Again, he sighed. "What would you like me to do? Go to the hospital and query Ana for every 't' and 'i', nook and cranny about James's condition? Never forget he's a full-fledged adult. Have you ever considered he might not want us prying into his life?" Titus had a point. Again he caressed Sahel's shoulders. The feelings from last evening and the intimacy she had experienced with him during Mass that morning returned. "Even if I asked her," Titus said, "Ana would feel torn about giving me the details of James's condition. I don't want to put her in that position. Let Carl finish his surgery. He'll call as promised." Titus drew Sahel into his chest. Despite her annoyance, she felt warm and safe. If only it could be this way with them all the time.

Sahel calmed. Titus then settled his lips upon hers. Again Sahel found herself in the throes of desire. Once more, she surrendered to Titus's passion and her need to have it fill her. It was a strange affair, their having made love last evening. The dry spell they had weathered since marrying after the accident had ended.

In recent months Sahel had neither desired him nor felt repulsed by him. Instead, she felt dispassionate, not unlike how she had felt the afternoon she had taken the pills. Sahel's psychiatrist, Dr. Leonard, had attributed it to Sahel's depression due to the loss of her sight.

Now, having met James only less than twenty-four hours earlier, she had come back to life in surviving her blindness and her attempt to take her own life. Sahel felt at home in the arms of Titus, whose hands had revived her heart.

Titus drew her closer, his body hardening against hers. She lifted her head. Titus kissed her. She lay back in his arms. He carried her up the stairs. "But what about your charts?" Sahel said.

"They can wait. You can't. And neither can I." He proceeded up to the landing.

Sahel rested her head on his chest and closed her eyes. Her cane lay on the desk in the study below.

Chapter 10

T
hey all gathered at the hospital that evening.

"How is he?" Sahel asked Carl when he touched her shoulder on approach.

"Let's go into the nurse's office," Carl said. Somberness coated his words.

Inside the private space Sahel sat and placed her hands upon her lap. Against rising anxiety she remained quiet. Geraldine was the closest James had to family, as far as Sahel knew, the acknowledgment of which further drove home the truth of Titus's earlier comment. We know little or nothing about James. Sahel felt a bond with James, one that had tightened in the four hours following his collapse.

"It's not good," Carl spoke. His words sounded ever more weighted.

"What's wrong?" asked Sahel. A moment had passed with nothing emanating from Geraldine.

"After running some tests, Jeremy Caynard, head of infectious disease, spoke with Harold Lattimer at UCSF." Carl dispensed the information at no one directly.

"Harold Lattimer?" Titus questioned. "He's the head of the HIV Lab at UCSF."

"Does James have HIV?" Sahel turned, searching for Geraldine.

"Yes, my dear," Essien spoke, "I'm afraid he does."

"He has more than that," Carl said. "He's in the throes of an AIDS crisis."

"Did you know this?" Titus said. He was speaking to Geraldine, who had yet to say anything.

"She did," Essien defended. "But—"

"Well, why the hell didn't you tell us?" Titus said.

"I don't know what that has to do with him right now. How is he?" Sahel launched her question into the torrent of allegations and interrogations fired by Titus.

"It has everything to do with his condition," Titus said. "This man is highly contagious. We could have been infected."

"I doubt that," Sahel said.

"This is no time for sympathies. The man is carrying a virus that leads to terminal illness if someone gets infected with it."

"Well, unless you're afraid that Sahel is about to sleep or have sex with him, I doubt she'll be affected." Geraldine finally spoke.

"Then again, with the way you're behaving—"

"That's it." Titus lifted Sahel's hand. "I've had enough of your—"

"What are you doing?" Sahel snatched her hand from Titus's grasp.

"This woman has no respect for us," Titus said. "Never has, never will. I will not allow her to speak to me, nor to you, this way."

"Well, it's true," Geraldine said.

"What's true?" Titus shouted.

"You're jealous, forever worried that Sahel is going to leave you. And the reason for that is you don't have what it takes to make her happy. You know it. We all know it."

"Geraldine, I wish you wouldn't say things like that," Sahel said.

"Well somebody has to. You won't," Geraldine retorted.

"But Geraldine—" Essien tried intervening, but she continued.

"Your blindness has you bound to Titus. It's the only reason you marri—"

"That's enough!" Carl shouted. "I'm using this office as a favor from the head nurse. We can't stay here forever. What I need to know from you, Geraldine, is have you known about James's illness? And if so, for how long?"

"Yes, I've known about it." Geraldine spoke softly, almost penitently. Another silence ensued.

"And for how long?" Titus demanded.

"Since he was infected." Again she lowered and softened her voice, as if embarrassed and fearful.

"And how long has that been?"

"Titus, please," Sahel reprimanded.

"Eight months."

"So you knew of Dr. Lattimer."

"I've met him."

"Met him. Know him. What do you know of James's condition?" Titus demanded.

"Enough to know that you would reject him had I told you what he had."

"And so, despite your so-called love for Sahel, the child and daughter you never had, you introduced her to this apparent godson of yours without telling her or any of us of his condition."

"None of this matters," Sahel said. She reached for Titus's hand. "It's James we're concerned about."

"Clearly, Titus disagrees," Geraldine said.

"Geraldine, you may have your feelings about Titus, but this doesn't explain why you didn't tell us what's going on with James after his collapse. Had he been cut or bleeding, we could have been exposed," Carl said.

"And I for one have patients to care for," Titus said.

"Exposure to end-stage AIDS is not something I care to transfer to them, never mind contracting it myself."

"I feel the same," said Carl. His words landed hard. While Titus had always held a firm distance from Geraldine, Carl had sought to welcome and make her comfortable as part of the family.

A third long silence ensued, broken later when Carl sighed. "We don't mean to point fingers. I couldn't care less how he got the virus. I just like knowing what I'm working with. After seeing to him back at the house, I went straight to the OR. Of course I washed my hands as I prepped for surgery, but—"

"I think what Carl is trying to say, what we're all trying to say," Sahel started. She searched for and gripped Titus's hand. The strain in Carl's voice moved Sahel. "We're concerned and want to help," she said. "But to do that we need to know everything. We have no judgment."

"Maybe you don't," Titus blurted, "but—"

"This is not helping James," Essien said. Geraldine let out a muted moan. It was like the stunted bleat of a goat.

"Let us help you," Sahel said. "You and James."

"And how can you do that? By giving him a death sentence?"

"No one's saying he's dying," Sahel said.

"At least not for now," Carl said. "But we do need to be prepared for the possibility," he explained. "Apparently, Dr. Lattimer had difficulty keeping his T-cell count up." He paused as if waiting for Geraldine to contribute. "He's had James on several combinations of drugs, all to no avail." Again Carl waited. "In any case, it now seems his T-cell count has taken a nosedive from its already low level."

"When did that happen?" Geraldine cried out. "We were just over in the city on Friday."

"So you knew all along how seriously ill he is?" Titus said.

"Titus, please." Sahel tugged at him and then said, "What are you doing for him right now?"

"This is not my specialty, but Jeremy is coordinating a regimen of treatment with Lattimer, a mix of medicines that can hopefully stimulate James's immune system to kick out some T-cells. They're on the phone as we speak. It's touch and go until that happens."

"When can we see him?" Sahel said.

"Oh, no. That's not happening," Titus shot back.

"He can't be left alone," Sahel said.

"I, for one, am going to see him right now," Geraldine said.

"Perhaps he is resting," Essien proffered.

"Resting or not, no one's going to see James this evening or even tomorrow. He's not allowed visitors until his T-cell count rises."

"But he needs me," Geraldine pleaded.

"He's sleeping right now," Carl said. "What I suggest is we all go home now, so hopefully, when things get better, we'll have our wits about us to support him."

"That sounds like a very good plan. Thank you, Carl," Essien said, and then made arrangements with Geraldine to drive her back to the house.

On their way out of the nurse's office, and while Carl was offering thanks for the use of it, Sahel asked Titus, "Are Daddy and Geraldine still here?"

"They're almost to the elevator."

"Would you catch them? I want to speak with Geraldine."

Titus groaned. Seconds later Sahel held Geraldine's arm, the two of them walking towards the exit of Berkeley General. Titus and Essien had gone to the parking garage to retrieve their cars. Carl had gone to check the status of the patient on whom he had performed surgery that afternoon. "I'll look in on James after seeing my patient," he promised Sahel.

With her hand to Geraldine's arm, Sahel exited the elevator and entered the lobby of Berkeley General. "I'm available to help James in any way I can," Sahel said. Geraldine led her to the front entrance of the hospital.

"I know you are. And truly I'm sorry." Geraldine stopped. "I should have told you that James was sick."

"How did it happen?" Sahel softly asked.

"He's not gay."

"And what if he were? Should that matter?"

"I know it doesn't to you. But it does to me," Geraldine said.

"I'm sorry about that." Sahel felt Geraldine's arm tremble.

"We love you, and James."

"How can you say that? You hardly even know him." Geraldine's voice cracked, emitting a pain that enveloped and fueled her words.

"He's been kind to me."

"But you don't know his life." Geraldine was now crying.

"Would you like to tell me about that? Maybe it's too difficult for him."

"No, no." Geraldine moaned. "I can't. It's too much." She pulled away from Sahel.

"I'll hold what you say in strictest confidence." Sahel would not ordinarily be so intrusive. But she felt Geraldine's ache intensifying.

"I know you would," Geraldine agreed.

The need to unburden herself pressed upon Sahel's senses. "You love James very much and that tells me he's a good person."

"If only that Sunetra could have seen it—his goodness. She was so selfish." Vehemence stitched Geraldine's words.

Sunetra. The name shocked Sahel. The woman in Sahel's vision last evening. "I love you, Sunetra," the man had said. "I need you to be honest with me, James," Sunetra had said.

James.

Sunetra.

They had been the couple Sahel witnessed arguing in her vision.

To Geraldine she now spoke, "Tell me about her."

"No. No. I can't. I won't. I refuse to invoke her presence. She's at the root of all James's problems. It's Sunetra that's causing all of this right now," Geraldine sobbed. Sahel had never heard or seen Geraldine in this way. "I'm sorry, but I have to go. Titus will be along. Tell your father I'm taking a cab."

Chapter 11

S

ahel explained to her father that Geraldine had taken a cab. "Most probably back to the house for her car."

"I suppose she needs some time alone. Waiting at the hospital this afternoon took its toll," Essien said. Then, on kissing Sahel's forehead, added, "You and Titus don't wait up for me." He was headed to Geraldine's house to provide comfort, as Sahel was certain Geraldine had done for him during those days immediately following Sahel's suicide attempt.

The ride home with Titus was quiet, with Sahel contemplating the events that had led up to her mother's first heart attack.

A heated argument ensued earlier that afternoon between Sahel and Lillian.

Lillian scolded Sahel for arriving home late from school. "I was at the library studying," Sahel pleaded.

"Where were you?" Lillian's pink lips against her white skin had been terse and sharp like her words. "And don't tell me you were alone. You were with that Carl Pierson," Lillian said. "You spend too much time with that boy. He's dark like you," Lillian reprimanded. "He's no good. I won't have him smearing your name."

"We were just studying," Sahel said. "He's my friend."

"There's studying. And then there's studying. Only so much involves books."

Lillian's pinched face took on a quizzical demeanor, as if her own words had befuddled her. Sahel could not understand how her mother was so aware of her feelings for Carl.

Sahel's grades were excellent. She kept her room tidy, helped out wherever she could around the house, worked diligently to make herself invisible.

"You think I don't know what it feels like to want someone," Lillian said. "To need her so much that even when she's gone, you dream of her, hoping to bring her back. But you can't." She was speaking of Titus's mother, Cecile Denning, who had been dead for two years. Remaining in New Jersey with Cecile's sister, Titus had yet to return home to Oakland.

"You can't forget Titus," Lillian implored with eyes that were wide, red, and filled with tears.

"I haven't forgotten him," Sahel said. "But I do have to study."

"Shut up!" Lillian slapped Sahel. "Don't talk to me about studying. I know what you're doing—you and that Carl." Sahel had been studying for the entrance exam to gain entrance into Oakland Catholic Prep High School. She and Carl were in eighth grade, the remaining two of their Three Musketeers.

"He's dark like you," Lillian snapped. Have you thought of what your children would look like?"

Like me—and him, Sahel thought.

"This country doesn't like dark, hates what's black. Can't you get that through your head?

64

Lillian's words sliced through Sahel like a scalpel, leaving a deadening pain in its wake and drawing Sahel from her reverie of longing for Titus.

Carl was an easy substitute, one who drew Lillian's ire in the face of Sahel's subtle rebellion, a person Sahel could have easily loved, had Titus not returned. Sahel started out the door.

"Don't turn away from me, you little slut." Lillian grasped Sahel's arm. They were in Lillian and Essien's bedroom, Lillian standing with her back to the mirror. Her brush that Sahel shared, and now used, lay upon the mirrored vanity. "Titus will open doors for you."

But he's gone.

Yet, more than his absence, what affected Sahel was Lillian's obsession to make Titus her son-in-law, or perhaps the son she never had, and mold him into the symbol of her disdain and anger towards Sahel. Fair skinned, Titus resembled Sahel's mother, Lillian, even more than Sahel.

Even then Sahel loved Titus. She also feared who he might become should he return to Oakland with Lillian aching from the death of his mother, Cecile, Lillian's best friend. Titus was Lillian's only link to Cecile.

An early adolescent unsure of herself and life, Sahel doubted her mother's love. Lillian seemed like a demon from the deepest caverns of Hell, sent by God to torture Sahel for coming to Lillian as a child dark as night and bearing no resemblance to her mother except for the length of her hair.

The anger and frustration of loss brimming in Lillian's eyes energized Sahel's every nerve and fueled her self-disgust. Her love for Titus and all he represented outshone the affection she refused Sahel.

Again Sahel tore away from Lillian's piercing stare. Again Lillian went after her. Reaching the doorway to Sahel's bedroom she cried out, "Oh, no." Sahel turned back to see Lillian gripping her chest. "Oh, my god," she dropped to her knees, and thudded upon the floor.

"Mama. What's wrong?" Sahel knelt down and brushed her mother's face. "Talk to me!" Unable to speak, Lillian responded only with her eyes. Realizing the fear lying in them, Sahel grew terrified. At thirteen Sahel perceived doubt and regret that only she, Sahel, had been present to save her mother.

Now some twenty years later, and riding in the car beside Titus, Sahel tugged at her fingers, as she had when nervous or frightened as a child. She nearly pulled them from their sockets outside the emergency room.

Undergoing her first heart attack, Lillian nearly died at thirty-eight years old. She needed a heart transplant. Sahel blamed herself—despite the extensive explanation given by the cardiologist. The wait for her father's arrival felt interminable; Sahel's fingers had grown sore and stiff. They experienced shock when only hours later the physician described the weakened and poor condition of Lillian's heart.

The vortex of memories ended with Titus lifting her hand and helping her from the car. She had not even felt the car slow and then come to a halt in the driveway. She gave Titus her hand. She had no choice but to allow him to guide her towards and into the house.

Sahel had left her cane at home.

Chapter 12

Sahel did not want to shower. Her mind was on James. "No, you go first," she said to Titus.

On entering the bedroom upstairs, Titus had asked, "Would you like to shower first?"

"Okay," he now acquiesced, "but before I go, would you like something to eat? Something to drink? Are you hungry?"

The meeting at the hospital with Carl explaining James's condition had been intense. "No, thanks, I just want to lie here, maybe call Carl, and see how James is doing." Sahel found the way to her side of the bed, and stretched out.

Titus touched her hand. "I know you care for James, but I don't want you getting too involved with him."

"What do you mean? He's dying." Sahel pulled back her

hand and sat up. She felt Titus sit upon the bed.

"This is not going to be easy. If you really care for Geraldine, you won't get drawn into this. You'll stay strong for her. She's going to need you and your father's help." Titus sounded somber and sympathetic.

Sahel felt herself withdrawing. "It doesn't help to give him a death knell. You sound so negative."

"It's the truth, Sahel. I spoke to Carl afterwards while you were with Geraldine. Dr. Lattimer told James last week that he had probably less than six months to live."

"Okay, well last time I checked, seven days is a far cry from six months, 180 days."

"There's no need for you to rush in and try to save him. The man was probably long gone before now. Whatever he's been through is linked to however he got the virus."

"And just what do you mean by that?" Sahel flashed her palm. "Then again, don't answer that. You're always so judgmental. Just like Mama."

"This has nothing to do with your mother. I am nothing like your mother. Even your father has concerns abou—"

"Don't bring Daddy into this." Sahel swung her feet onto the floor. "You're always putting people down, tearing them apart, talking about how they're not good for me."

"Well, if you're talking about Carl and how he's never really loved you, then yes, I would agree."

"How can you say that?" Sahel stood. "He's your best friend. Mine too."

"Carl Pierson stopped being my friend when he made it clear that he was willing to have you undergo risky surgery just to make him look good."

"He only wants my sight back," Sahel said.

"Like I don't? And why do you always defend him? Last time I checked, I was your husband. You're not Carl's eyes. He can see just fine without you." Titus grew silent. "Then again, maybe you believe Geraldine, that I want you to stay blind so that I can keep you by my side, locked up here in the house?"

Sahel began to tremble. All discussions of any consequence between her and Titus seemed to circle inward to this point.

68

They had experienced no laughter, no joy, until having met James two nights ago. Sahel needed James. She did not want him to die. Speaking with him had awakened something within her, opened her heart to Titus, a door that she now feared would close. "I love you," she said to Titus.

"I love you. I don't want to lose you. James, for whatever has happened to him fairly or unfairly, has a terminable disease that is contagious."

"It's not like I'm going to sleep with the man," Sahel said.

"Do you want to?"

"Why would you say that?" Sahel was shocked. "Of course not."

Despite their argument Sahel and Titus fell asleep in each other's arms. Hours later the phone rang. "It's Carl," Titus said. "James is not doing well."

Titus hung up the phone. He and Sahel dressed and left for the hospital.

Sahel stepped from the elevator and heard Geraldine's voice. "I need to see him. He's my godson. Why can't you understand that?"

"It's not that simple." That was Carl. And then another voice.

"We're doing all we can, Mrs. Paynter, to save James."

"And what is that? One minute he seems fine, the next you're telling me he's dying, there's no hope. Why aren't you trying to save him?" Geraldine demanded. "Surely there's something you can do. You can't just let him die without trying."

Sahel tightened her grip on Titus's upper arm as they moved forward. On drawing near the voices, Titus placed his arms to her shoulders. "What's going on?" Sahel said. "How is James?"

Carl introduced Sahel to Jeremy Caynard. Carl then said to Caynard, "And of course you know Titus."

"I want to see James, Dr. Caynard," Geraldine said.

Sahel turned to Carl's voice. "Why can't she see him?"

69

"It's not that we don't want her to see him, it's just that—"

A voice entered the corridor. "Dr. Caynard, he's crashing."

Titus left with Caynard. "You and Sahel stay here," Carl said. He walked Sahel to a wall. Geraldine was with her.

"What's happening?" Sahel reached out for Geraldine.

"They're all across the hall in James's room." Geraldine's voice was feeble and low. A piercing resonance of a heart monitor filtered into the corridor, one continuous shrill, and no longer beeping.

The somber shrill enveloped Sahel. She recalled the afternoon she had died.

Chapter 13

S

he had swallowed the pills while in the bedroom where she and Titus now resided, what had been her parents' bedroom for nearly forty years. She had then found her way down the hall to her childhood bedroom. Sahel had lain down, drawn the covers to her neck, and prepared to never awaken, had closed her eyes.

All twenty-five of the pills that were her father's muscle relaxants dissolved in her stomach. Darkness descended. Floating past sleep she entered the death, or so it seemed.

Moments later, and to her amazement, she had come alive. Instead of lying on the bed, Sahel hovered above as if hooked to the ceiling. Her body lay stretched on the bed below.

By the doorway stood Geraldine, frightened and trying as best she could to answer questions Titus was firing at her. "How long has she been this way? When did you find her?"

"I don't know. I got here just after lunch." Geraldine turned to Zelda standing beside her and Zelda added, "An hour ago, Mrs. Denning said she was going to take a nap."

"Christ!" Titus shouted. Sahel's soul, her consciousness, whatever survives death, watched from above as Titus tapped the wrist of her body limp and lifeless. "Sahel," Titus called her name again.

"Sahel. Wake up." Fear clouded his eyes.

Sahel's spirit grew cold and anxious. She had not planned on this. Taking the pills, releasing everyone from the prison of her blindness, was to be her final act.

In seeking death, the heaviness of the last six months had lifted.

Sahel's soul had taken flight from her body. She had regained sight. And yet her spirit ached for the pain those she had left were experiencing.

Titus hit Sahel's wrist once more. "Sahel!" He was sitting on the bed. "Can you hear me?" He turned Sahel's head side-to-side upon the pillow. He pinched her cheeks. "Sahel! Wake up! Sahel!" Again he pinched her cheeks, and slapped them. Titus then pulled open her eyelids. His eyes, black like Lillian's, ran murkier than a backwoods swamp.

Zelda signed the cross and continued praying with her rosary.

Titus glanced at his watch while checking Sahel's pulse and then said to Zelda, "Gather all the medicines and put them in a bag."

Zelda ran out of the room, Geraldine remaining. About to lift her body from the bed, Titus bent over and lifted a brown pill container from the floor. Again his eyes grew wide, but this time darker. An ache flooded Sahel's spirit, nearly extinguishing it.

Titus lifted Sahel's body from the bed, her head lolling as if her neck were broken. "Tell the paramedics I'm a doctor and I've taken her to the hospital. Then call Essien," he instructed Geraldine. Titus rushed out of the bedroom, down the stairs, and out to the convertible. He placed Sahel in the passenger's seat.

"I'll be along as soon as I speak with Essien," Geraldine said. Titus strapped Sahel in and closed the passenger door.

"These are all the medicines that were in the cabinet," Zelda said.

She held out the zip-lock bag of medications.

"I don't think I need them, but just in case," Titus said on grabbing them and rushing around to the other side of the car.

Now crying, Zelda again signed the cross. Geraldine grasped Zelda's hand, clenching a rosary.

Now in the driver's seat, Titus started the car and sped off.

Up Highway 13, the Warren Freeway, and fast approaching Tunnel Road, Titus called the ER while moving into Berkeley. "It's Titus Denning. Get me Ana Desai." Seconds passed, his breath deepening.

"Hi, Titus. Got a heart coming in?" Ana said.

"It's Sahel. She took some pills."

"What and how many?"

"Soma, a muscle relaxant. I don't know the count. She's not breathing."

"What's your ETA?"

"I'm almost to the Claremont. Four minutes," Titus said. Traffic was light to nil.

"We'll be ready," Ana said and then added, "Bring her around to the back."

With one hand on the steering wheel, and fear filling his eyes, Titus tore the fingers of his other hand through his thick, dark hair as if to grasp his head and scream. A chill landed upon Sahel's spirit in observing the torture biting at his. The rage boiling within him enwrapped her soul. This was not what she had sought.

Titus sped around to the back of the emergency room at Berkeley General, and brought the convertible to a stop. He hopped out, rushed around the passenger side, and pulled open the door.

Carl and two orderlies guiding a gurney ran to him as he lifted Sahel from the car. "Ana called and said you were on your way in," Carl explained.

"She's aspirated and isn't breathing." Titus placed Sahel's body on the gurney.

"We've got to clear her airway." Carl joined Titus as the two pressed onward through the doors of the emergency room.

Titus loves you. Lillian's voice extolled again like the bells of a church sounding out that a funeral mass was about to take place.

Get away from me, Sahel retorted.

On entering the emergency suite, Ana Desai, chief of the emergency room, greeted Titus and Carl. Quickly she examined Sahel's wrist, the back of her hand and then wrapped a cuff around Sahel's arm.

"She's aspirated a lot," said Carl. He stood inspecting Sahel's throat. "I'll get a line in."

"Her pressure's dropping," Ana announced.

Titus looked up at the monitor above the bed. His face darkened. The wave popped up and down, making successively smaller peaks.

"She's crashing," Ana yelled. The line went flat, its beep becoming one continuous shrill sound.

"Where're the paddles?" Carl jumped up.

Ana rushed to the crash cart and brought it to Titus, who had already begun chest compressions. One-one thousand, two-one thousand, three-one thousand. Beads of sweat poured from his forehead. One hand crossed upon the other and pressed her chest with all his might.

Sahel had never witnessed him this way. She observed more of what she had not planned nor anticipated. By Sahel's estimation she would have been cold and stiff, too late for any possibilities, had Titus arrived home as usual, at five p.m. or later. She had counted on watching her death play itself out. Sahel's spirit grew anxious and cold. Fear, like that filling Titus's eyes on discovering the bottle, now shrouded Sahel's spirit, which began to fade. Her soul swirled in an ether of shame and regret. The ambivalence and indecision that had ruled her thoughts and actions underneath a veneer of equanimity now ruled her reality.

She had made a choice, though terrible, and acted upon her

feelings. And while some part of her consciousness floated in a space between life and death, Sahel felt finality drawing near.

Cool waters filled the space around her and subsumed her. All grew dark and murky. Again, and to her surprise, she did not lose consciousness. Sahel instead became more aware and alert to her surroundings.

She was beneath the ocean's surface. In the distance stood a figure, what seemed a woman. The woman was wearing a red robe flowing amid the ocean's water. Her face was a soft shade of chestnut, what others might describe as butterscotch. The woman approached Sahel and said, "Death is never what we think."

"I didn't want to see this," Sahel declared in her thoughts.

"You've regained your sight," the woman said.

"I didn't want it back, not this way."

Again the woman read Sahel's thoughts and then said, "What do you want?"

"I don't want to be a burden."

"And whose burden are you?" The woman's face settled into sharp focus. She was beautiful, like an angel. And yet there was a strength and purpose about her. Her melancholy eyes shone bright and clear against the red robe. The woman appeared determined to complete her task. She said, "What is the true weight holding you down, preventing you from giving, and accepting love?"

"I've never blamed Titus," Sahel rushed to answer. "I love him."

"By accusing yourself, you convict and prosecute him," the woman said.

"He committed no crime." Sahel grew angry.

"Oh, but you have served as both judge and jury."

As much as the woman angered her, Sahel felt gifted in that the woman presented the other side of Sahel, a part of herself that Sahel kept hidden and that she avoided in an effort not to become like her mother, Lillian.

The woman stepped back. Her face slipped out of focus. Sahel grew frustrated and fearful that her ambivalence had returned, was now ruling the situation in a way she could not control or halt.

"You cannot come here." The woman's voice was then firm against the brightness of her robe—red, effervescent, and streaming with life. Bubbles rose from Sahel's nose and mouth while the waters around the woman remained calm and still.

"Go back." The woman held up her palm. Sahel reached out to grasp it. The woman wafted farther back and beyond Sahel's reach.

The woman's face blurred once more.

Sahel tried moving forth but felt weighed down. She looked down and saw that her chest and arms had returned. Naked, she stood in the waters now edging toward freezing. Sahel lifted and inspected her ebony arms. Sadness mixed with anger and dismay encompassed her spirit. The coldness, reaching a point of what felt near freezing, pierced her soul. Her engagement ring from Titus, bearing a pear-shaped diamond, floated past. Sahel tried but failed to grasp it.

The waters drained away.

Again she found herself hovering just below the ceiling of the emergency room suite. Below, Titus and Carl fought to bring Sahel's body back to life. The heart monitor behind them beeped at a continuous pace.

A tingling sensation started down her arms and then, reaching her wrists, continued into the empty space where her fingers should be. Slowly her fingers appeared. The same sensation spread from her abdomen, going on to her thighs and knees and then reaching her ankles. Sahel saw her toes manifested as if in thin air. The lightness of soul and spirit diminished. The heaviness of regret and shame of her actions settled into the space that was her chest. Her spirit lost energy. Sahel grew weak. She felt unable to remain hovering above. Sahel grew conscious of the weighted burden of life, and then life without sight.

Titus ripped open Sahel's blouse and laid bare her chest. Ana handed him the pair of paddles and then backed away.

"Clear!" He placed the white instruments over Sahel's heart and fired a current of electricity into her chest. Her body lifted off the table. The line on the monitor remained flat. The chill that had overtaken Sahel's spirit intensified the ache in her soul. "Clear!" Titus fired once more, rattling Sahel's body. The line remained flat. "Clear!" Titus shouted and fired a third time and with increased voltage. The shrill sound continued as if entering the dark tunnel of no return. Carl continued squeezing the bag, extending from the mask over Sahel's face, as Ana fell still and somber.

"It's not supposed to be this way," Sahel whispered within her spirit.

The line continued across the screen, never rising.

"I want to see my daughter," a voice spoke from outside the emergency suite against the continuous beep of the flatline. Though weighted and burdened, Sahel's consciousness drifted beyond the emergency room suite. Ana Desai now stood with Essien and Geraldine outside the emergency room. "They're working on her right now, Mr. Ohin," Ana said.

"I need to see her," Essien Ohin demanded, his words filling that part of Sahel hovering between life as she knew it, and what she had hoped, but failed, to achieve. The woman in red had sent her back, barring Sahel from death.

"Titus and Carl are doing all they can," Ana sought to assure.

Sahel's spirit returned to the emergency room suite. The deathly shrill of the heart monitor encompassed the suite below. Titus, holding the paddles, gazed up at the monitor displaying a flatline. The dismay upon his face nearly severed the last flames of Sahel's spirit.

Ana Desai re-entered the suite. Titus threw down the paddles and resumed chest compressions.

The aching tiredness of his hands on her chest seeped into Sahel's soul.

77

"One-one thousand, two-one thousand, three-one thousand." Sahel's chest edged towards warmth.

"Don't leave me. Please," Titus whispered. Carl, sitting near Sahel's head, continued squeezing and releasing the bag attached to a tube in her mouth.

"Four-one thousand, five-one thousand, six-one thousand," Titus counted off another round of compressions.

The lamentations of his soul pierced Sahel's heart and soul. Her consciousness entered Titus's mind.

Sahel saw Titus as a boy, eleven years old. His grandfather spoke the words, "There's been an accident, son. Your parents are dead."

With hands covering his face, Titus, the boy, slumped to the floor, wishing to have been with his parents.

I'll be a better man, he whispered in prayer, *a better husband, a better person.* "Seven-one thousand, eight-one thousand, nine-one thousand." *Just give me another chance.*

The consciousness of Sahel's spirit traveled even farther. She found herself within the car carrying Howard and Cecile Denning, and a huge eighteen-wheeler heading towards them, Howard unable to speak, Cecile simply staring ahead. Sahel saw this from within the back seat of the sedan, where Titus would have been, had he traveled with them.

Titus's parents succumbed on impact, words his paternal grandfather would never speak to Titus or anyone.

Sahel's spirit and consciousness now dwelling in Titus's mind grew tired of resisting life. The fatigue of his hands upon her chest jolted her sadness and regret. It seemed such a cruel and long distance to travel.

No. Titus cried within his spirit as his hands pressed upon Sahel's chest, his soul willing her body back to life. *Not again.* "Ten-one thousand, eleven-one thousand, twelve-one thousand."

The shrill from the monitor remained continuous and firm. Geraldine's words to Essien sifted from outside the emergency room. "Whatever happens, Titus is with her."

"Thirteen-one thousand, fourteen-one thousand, fifteen-one thousand." *Please, dear god, not again…*

A soft rumbling filled her chest.

78

Sahel felt her body having completely returned. She extended her hand, beheld her engagement ring bearing the pear-shaped diamond. It lay beside the wedding band on her left hand.

Sixteen-one thousand, seventeen-one thousand, eighteen-one thou—" With each compression, the energy of Titus's spirit beckoning and willing Sahel to come back seeped from his fingers into her chest. Sahel felt Titus's hands threatening to cramp.

The full weight of life encased in a body bore down upon her.

Beep ... beep ... beep.

Sahel coughed. The shrill was no more.

Beep ... beep ... beep.

All went dark.

Chapter 14

T

he sonorous shrill against the din of voices blew from James's hospital room and pulled Sahel out of her memory. "Stand back." That was Titus against the shrill growing louder. A surge of energy sped through Sahel on hearing him fire the paddles. She jumped as if her chest were again receiving the jolt of electricity. The words grew clearer, last vestiges of Sahel's visions fading.

"Again," Carl said.

Once more Titus commanded, "Stand back."

The paddles snapped, firing a second round of electricity through James's chest. The piercing shrill of the heart monitor echoed around the room. James's heart was not beating.

"Oh, my god." Geraldine released a heavy sob. "Dear Lord,

please don't let him die. I can't lose him. Please—"

"Once more," Carl said.

"Stand back," Titus ordered, and fired the paddles once more. The piercing sound of the heart monitor continued.

Geraldine's moan became a heavy sob. Sahel extended her arms, and searching the way, maneuvered across the hall, and then locating the doorway, entered the hospital room. "Please," she spoke softly on touching someone. "Take me to James." She did not know to whom she was speaking. The person took her hand.

"Try, one more time," Carl said. The shrill of the heart monitor remained firm.

"Stand back," Titus called a third time.

"You shouldn't be in here," said the doctor who had taken Sahel's hand.

"My husband is Titus, Dr. Denning. Please take me to him."

"He's operating the paddles," the doctor said. He grasped Sahel's arms and kept her from moving forward. The paddles fired a fourth time.

"This man, James, is dying. I know him," said Sahel. "Please take me to—"

"Sahel, what are you doing here?" Carl took her hand.

"Take me to James," she said.

"Titus is with him. He's doing all he can to save him."

"And it's not working."

"Let's try one more time," said Dr. Caynard.

"No!" Sahel said. "It's not working." She turned to Carl, "Take me to him. Now!"

"Sahel, what are you doing here?" Titus's words hit her. "Carl, get her out of here. This is ridiculous." Sahel pulled her hand from Carl's grip.

"Sahel, you need to leave right now." Titus grasped her right arm.

"I'm not going anywhere." She snatched back her arm and against the piercing sound of the heart monitor attempted to find her way around Titus. "Where is James?"

"It's me." Carl guided her forward.

"What does it matter now anyway?" Titus murmured from

behind. "It's been six minutes. No heartbeat. "

Carl placed Sahel's hand to the bed. "Give me James's hand," Sahel said.

"But Sahel, he's dea—"

"Give me his hand!" Sahel shouted.

Sahel grasped James's fingers. They felt like ice. "Give me his other hand," Sahel said to Carl. She massaged James's fingers. Slowly Sahel descended into herself as if entering the portals of meditation. "We need you, James. Answer me if you can hear me. Geraldine needs you." Sahel's heart began to race.

James's fingers warmed to lukewarm. "Don't go. Not yet," Sahel said. She grew anxious against the stillness of James's hand.

Oh, my god, what have I done? She began to fear her actions, what they indicated. I've lost it. I've totally lost it. I'm crazy. How will Titus ever forgive me? She began to cry.

And then an image took shape in her mind. Red. A woman, her face ebbing between hues of chestnut and butterscotch. She was wearing a long, red caftan. Her forehead held a small red dot. What seemed a gold necklace draped her head, its small pendant hanging just over the red dot.

The woman spoke. "Titus has already forgiven you. You have nothing to fear."

I've made a fool of myself. Sahel transmitted the words through her thoughts.

"No. You have saved James."

Sahel grew dizzy. Hands settled upon her shoulders. She felt herself pulled back.

The crowd of voices rose around her and then merged into one.

"We've got a pulse." The piercing sound of the heart monitor faded in a series of well-paced beats. "Oh, my god. We've got him back," someone said.

Again Sahel's heart began to race. Her head began to ache against what felt like the room spinning. "Sahel," Carl called. "Help me lay her down," he said. "Sahel," he repeated, and then said it again, and again. Try as she might, Sahel could not speak.

83

Chapter 15

S

ahel insisted on keeping her appointment with Dr. Leonard that
afternoon, something she normally resisted, despite Titus's
concerns that she needed to go home and rest.

After losing her sight, Sahel had relinquished her license as a
psychologist. On learning of her actions, Carl had contacted a
colleague with whom he and Sahel both consulted. A
psychiatrist, the colleague had referred patients to Sahel and she
had done the same. The two respected each other.

Carl and the psychiatrist, unbeknownst to Sahel, contacted
the State Licensing Board of Behavioral Heath in Sacramento,
and explained Sahel's accident. The board refused to accept
Sahel's license without her undergoing a year of psychotherapy.
Initially Sahel ignored the requirement. She began seeing the
psychiatrist after taking the pills.

The failed suicide attempt forced her into psychotherapy,
about which she felt torn and conflicted.

"Titus tells me you gave them quite a scare this morning," Leonard said.

"He worries too much." Sahel gripped her cane lying folded on her lap.

"Perhaps, but a blood pressure of 200/180 is nothing to play with. You fainted."

Sahel lowered her head. "I'm going to see Carl as soon as I finish here," she decided.

Leonard's silence seemed to indicate his satisfaction that she was not ignoring the physical toll of what took place hours earlier. "Something strange is happening with me," she said.

"Oh?"

"I've not said anything, but over the last few days I've been hearing this voice. It sounds like mine, my thoughts. It's not mine. Then again it feels like another part of me. A side of me that I'm just now hearing, able to access."

"Or perhaps no longer able to avoid," Leonard added.

Sahel felt disappointed in that Leonard didn't question the nature of this voice, or suggest that perhaps she was hallucinating.

"What does the voice say?" he asked.

"The truth. What I can't or won't say," Sahel said. "This morning when the heart monitor stopped beeping, when I heard that piercing sound as the beeping line on the heart monitor went flat, it told me to go to him. I did. But then I grew scared. This woman appeared in my mind."

Sahel told Dr. Leonard of the visions she had experienced on Saturday evening, and then moments later how Geraldine introduced her to James, and then of his collapse Sunday afternoon on the patio at her house. "Paramedics came and took him to the hospital. He was resting fairly well until early this morning. Carl called Titus. And we came to the hospital."

Sahel continued, "The woman I saw this morning looked like the woman I saw in my vision Saturday evening. She was arguing with James. She called his name," Sahel continued. "This morning she was wearing a red cape with a hood. In my vision on Saturday night, she was wearing black pants and a matching turtleneck. She was arguing. With James. She called

86

his name. When I went to him this morning after his heart had stopped beating, I realized his voice was the same as that of the man in my vision on Saturday evening." Again Sahel gripped her cane.

"The woman in my vision on Saturday night, and who spoke to me this morning, told me to come to James. I also saw her when I died. The heart monitor had stopped. For both of us. When both James and I died. There were no beeps. Just that horrible sound of death. He was dead. I was dead when I took the pills eight months ago."

Sahel then explained. "Like with me, Titus had shocked him with the paddles two or three times. Nothing had happened. And then I touched him. I held James's hands. And he woke up."

"He came back to life," Leonard said.

His words frightened Sahel. "I don't know about that."

"Titus seems pretty certain that something took place."

"Titus?"

"He's concerned. About you and James." Dr. Leonard also met with Titus each week.

"I weary him, Titus, that is."

"Why do you say that?"

"He seems so much like Mama." Sahel leaned back into the cushion sofa and let go of her cane.

"In what way?"

Discussions of Titus and how he resembled Sahel's mother, Lillian, formed a mainstay of her sessions with Dr. Leonard. Sahel often wondered around what major theme Titus's sessions with Leonard centered. She said, "He asked me why I married him. If I'd done it to absolve him of his guilt about the accident."

"Did you?"

"No!"

"And yet you have difficulty being intimate with him."

"That changed this weekend," Sahel said. She explained making love with Titus on arriving home after the medical dinner. "Something inside me shifted after I met James."

"How so?"

"That's just it. I hadn't even recognized it until last evening

87

when I felt him slipping away from us, dying, like me. It was like everything was happening all over again, my dying, Titus with Carl, the two of them working so hard to save me. And then Titus ripping my shirt off and doing chest compressions. On Saturday evening at the medical dinner, while Titus was accepting his award, James and I were out on the verandah. He asked if I believed in reincarnation. I felt he was about to kiss me. And then he left."

Leonard said, "Have you told Titus about your out-of-body experience?"

"I'm not sure it was that. It was my imagination." That Leonard gave validation to what she had wanted to forget annoyed Sahel. She didn't believe in out-of-body experiences; saw them as the wranglings of the mind of people who had undergone enormous traumas and their way of coping. The psychiatrist said, "I know what you think of the descriptions of what you saw."

"I died that afternoon. I can't explain it. But Titus revived me," Sahel said. "Titus and Carl."

"I did some checking," the psychiatrist continued. "I spoke with Ana Desai."

"You went behind my back and spoke with her?" Sahel was incredulous.

"I asked her to tell me what happened when Titus brought you into the emergency room."

Sahel grew still and cold, like James's fingers that morning and last evening.

"I said nothing of your story, or what you have shared with me over these last eight months."

Sahel gripped her cane as Leonard spoke slowly. "Everything you described matches with what Ana not only told me, but noted in the chart of your treatment that day. Titus tried reviving you with the paddles. Ana said she stepped out of the room, but heard Carl through the door acknowledge that Titus had given you five shocks. And he then started chest compressions. She even told me of speaking to your father outside the emergency."

Sahel's lips began to tremble.

"I checked the chart, your chart. It's all noted. As Ana

88

described. And in accordance with what you've shared with me over these past eight months. Everything you've said matches what Ana noted in the chart and described to me."

"How do you explain what happened? That I remember. That I saw Titus and Carl working on my body, trying to save me. How did I hear my father? He wasn't even in the room." Sahel spoke hoarsely.

"I think you already have."

"You can't expect me to believe or accept that while I can't see what's in front of me—you in the chair on the other side of this coffee table, I saw my own death, observed what happened, minute by minute of what took place after my spirit ... my soul left my body." Sahel's words slowed. Her voice faded. "You can't—" she whispered and then clasped her hands in an effort to stop them from trembling.

"I don't; nor will I pretend to understand what went on the day you died. Neither do I comprehend how you could know all of this. But one thing seems clear."

"I saw it," Sahel blurted. "I know what I saw. And I saw everything I described." Against everything inside her and all her doubts, she claimed she actually had the experience. Sahel countermanded her statements from seconds earlier. "It happened."

Sahel opened her cane and moved to stand.

"Others have experienced what you underwent, many others. Several of my clients have described undergoing experiences similar in many respects to what you've shared."

"So you have a practice of schizophrenics who can't be helped?" Sahel shouted.

"Do you really think you are crazy?" Leonard's voice was close. "Or is this your way of trying to deny who you are, and what you survived?"

Sahel surmised he was standing. She turned her head away from his voice. "I tried killing myself, taking my own life, what I've coaxed many of my clients, at one time or another, away from doing. How hypocritical." It was this nature of thinking that had caused Sahel to surrender her license to practice psychotherapy.

Sessions with Leonard had been rough—him pushing Sahel to depths of introspection she had long avoided. That he was also working with Titus intensified Sahel's challenge of looking at herself.

The psychiatrist said, "It's not uncommon, Sahel, for people such as yourself who have been abused by their parents, particularly the same sex parent, to undergo what we call these out-of-body experiences."

As always when Leonard spoke the words "abuse" and "parent," "same sex," Sahel's skin warmed to a slow burn.

"All of my clients who have stated having had these experiences were mistreated in some way by their parents."

"My mother didn't molest me."

"No, but she was emotionally abusive. She also beat you and then told you it was out of love, that you needed it, that you had earned it." Sahel's soul had remained alive and fighting—despite everything.

Intent on Sahel retaining her license to practice psychotherapy, Carl had researched and interviewed several psychiatrists and found Albert Leonard to be the best for Sahel. On meeting him Titus had instantly bonded with the man. Learning the nature of Sahel's accident, Leonard felt it best for Sahel that he also work with Titus.

"There's something wrong with me."

"Why do you say that?" Leonard's voice was kind.

"Last week when Titus asked why I married him, whether I had done so because of the accident, it hit me that ... that ..." Sahel felt herself crumbling inside. Arching her back, she drew on her reserves.

"I don't think I would ... No, I couldn't have married him without having lost my sight."

"And why is that?"

"It's too hard. Love is too hard."

"Loving Titus?" Leonard queried.

Sahel said nothing of having seen Titus at eleven years old and receiving news of his parents' deaths. "No. Letting him love me."

Chapter 16

T

he journey back home in Geraldine's car started out quiet with
Sahel in the front passenger's seat, her mind caught in the throes
of her session with Dr. Leonard and what Sahel imagined was
Geraldine's private anguish at almost losing James. Despite the
miracle of James having survived, Jeremy Caynard, the
infectious disease specialist, warned that James remained
gravely ill. The disease was progressing.

The car slowed at what Sahel suspected was an intersection.

Geraldine said, "Thank you for saving James last night."

"I only went to him and held his hand."

"You did more than that. I saw the monitor. I was outside the
room, but I saw the monitor. The line was flat, had been so for

at least a minute. I know the scent of death." Sahel had smelled it too. "You brought him back," Geraldine said. An aroma of life had filled the room when Sahel spoke to James.

"That's not what happened," Sahel rebutted.

"Why do you always deny your strength?" Geraldine questioned angrily.

"I'm not denying my strength. I'm just saying that it's not rationally possible for me or anyone to bring someone back to life." Sahel shook her head.

"Titus brought you back," Geraldine said. "He threw down those paddles, put his hand to your chest, and started pressing. When Ana Desai went back into the emergency suite, I held the door open. Your father turned away. Carl kept squeezing the bag over your mouth and nose. He was praying and crying."

Sahel lowered her head.

The images of Titus working to revive her sailed once more through Sahel's mind.

"At one point Carl lifted the St. Joseph from his chest and kissed it." Sahel visualized Titus, his hands upon her chest and making the compressions, forcing, willing her heart to beat, she to breathe.

"He loves me." The words slipped from Sahel's lips. "Needs me."

Chapter 17

T

itus came home that afternoon minutes before Geraldine had
prepared to leave. Neither said much to the other. "I suppose
you know James has yet to regain consciousness," Titus said to
Geraldine. "I'm going back to the hospital," she said. "Sit with
him for a while." With a somber voice she added, "I appreciate
all you and Carl did this morning."

"It's what we're here for," Titus said. The sincerity in his
tone amazed Sahel.

"Still, I thank you." Geraldine said. She kissed Sahel's cheek,
said, "I'll call you tomorrow," then to Titus, "I'll see myself
out," and left.

"I'll go set out dinner," Titus said at the sound of the front
door closing. Zelda always prepared dinner that either Titus or

Essien warmed and brought to the table. "Do you know when your father might arrive home?" Titus asked.

"Not really," said Sahel. Part of Sahel remained in the throes of what Geraldine had shared about James, and also the warmth in Titus's voice when speaking to Geraldine. "He's got a meeting with some of the faculty and then ..." Sahel finally said.

"Are you all right?" Titus asked after some moments of silence.

His words were closer.

"I was about to say that he's probably going to join Geraldine at the hospital and have dinner with her later."

"I'll prepare him a plate just in case he doesn't," Titus said, against his footsteps ebbing into the distance and then returning. "I want you to stay away from the hospital. Don't see James again," Titus said. Tension bound in fear filled his voice.

Sahel turned towards his voice and frowned.

"What you did today ..." Titus spoke firmly. "It was dangerous."

"His heart wasn't beating," Sahel said.

"That's not the point. You're not a doctor. Things can happen. I don't want you blamed for anything."

"Things like what? James was fighting for his life."

"And aren't we all."

Sahel unfolded her cane, stood, and headed for the doorway leading from the kitchen into the foyer. She had struck her cane to the floor and entered the foyer, was headed upstairs to their bedroom, when Titus grasped her arm. "Please." He turned her around.

"Let me go," Sahel demanded.

"I'm your husband."

"It doesn't mean you own me."

"I don't get it." Titus let go of her arm. "Why is it you have time for everyone but me?"

"I'm here with you now," Sahel said.

"But do you want to be here?"

"Yes. But not with you like this. Demanding to have everything your way."

"The pot calling the kettle black. I find that amusing," said

Titus.

Sahel gave a bitter smile. "That I'm black? Or the hypocrisy in your statement?"

"You may hate your skin color. But I love you." Titus spoke with seriousness. "And caring about your safety doesn't make me like your mother."

"How would you know what she was like? You were gone for two years."

"I was eleven, Sahel. My parents were killed. My god. What do you want from me?"

"I was talking about when you left UCSF and went to Columbia." Sahel tightened her grip upon the cane.

"I married Alice because you wouldn't have me."

"You went away."

"Is it really that? That I went away?" The pain in Titus's words pained Sahel. "Not that I got married. But that my wife was white?"

"You got married."

"And you slept with Carl Pierson."

All within Sahel stilled, her tongue numbed by a truth she had hoped Titus would not discover. "How did you know?"

"I didn't. I only surmised."

Sahel lowered her head. The inability to see Titus's face tore at her. That he had perhaps been fishing for evidence to his suspicions angered Sahel.

Lillian's warning came flooding back. *There's studying. And there's studying ... I don't trust that Carl Pierson. He's no good. All he wants to do is soil you. Make you dirty so that Titus won't want you.*

Sahel turned around, extended her cane and found her way to the stairs. She wanted to close her eyes, sleep, and forget about waking up.

Sahel started up. Titus again caught her arm. He grabbed the cane from her hand. The sound of it hitting the front door and falling to the floor resonated throughout the foyer as he placed his lips upon Sahel's. "I love you. I need you," he pleaded. Again he set his lips to hers where they lingered long and hard.

Titus dropped to the floor, caressed Sahel's legs and kissed her knees. Then his hands eased from Sahel's knees, never to stop until, moving past her thighs, he had entered the forest of her passion and pushed open the temple door encasing her heart.

Chapter 18

S ahel lay in bed later that night feeling that she had been tricked, at the least deceived. She quite strangely experienced relief that Titus now knew of her intimacies with Carl. Perhaps for this reason, Sahel did not blame Titus for having hit her with the car. In addition to not having known she was upon her knees on the pavement of the driveway, she now realized he had been driven by the painful rage of abandonment. Sahel felt that same explosive sense of disappointment and loneliness, betrayal and desertion by her mother, Lillian.

Due to James's weak immune system and so as not to put him at risk of an infection, Sahel refrained from visiting him at the hospital. Concern for him propelled her into the boundless caves of her thoughts. On dwelling there, Sahel concluded she had entered a new phase in her life completely defined by her relationship with her two best friends that had over the years so mirrored her interactions and dynamics with her parents.

Thursday afternoon Carl came to visit.

"I suppose Titus told you that James awoke yesterday," he said as Sahel walked with him towards the sofa.

"Geraldine will be happy. She's been terribly worried. I'll go to see James tomorrow." Sahel didn't want to burst in on James and overtire him.

She also shuddered to think how she might tell James of what she had learned of him, and how he might react. The culmination of these events against what had transpired since she had last spoken with James during brunch and before his collapse stood large and teeming with possibilities. Though excited, Sahel felt ungrounded, less secure.

"How's he doing?" She lowered herself onto the sofa and felt Carl sit next to her.

"Fine, all things considered," Carl said. "I'll call Geraldine later this evening."

Sahel sensed a sheath of anxiety, a characteristic Carl rarely displayed, churning underneath his desire to assure. "Is everything all right?" she asked.

"James isn't ready to see Geraldine," said Carl. "In fact, he doesn't want to see her."

"But she's his godmother." Geraldine was probably at the hospital as they spoke.

"The nurses will inform her."

"The nurses?" Sahel was incredulous. "Carl, what's going on?"

Sahel grew anxious. "Is James okay? What are you not telling me?"

"He wants to see you," Carl said.

"Me? Of course I'll visit him, but—"

"I know you care for James—" Carl released another gust of anxiety. "—but Titus and I don't think—"

"Since when did you and Titus start agreeing on anything concerning me?" Sahel released a dry, angry chuckle. "What can the man do to me?"

98

"You fainted this morning. We had a really hard time waking you, never mind your blood pressure was pushing through the roof."

"I don't understand you two. James hasn't done anything to anyone. Why are you so worri—"

"He killed a man, Sahel. His fiancée's father. And then his fiancée committed suicide due to the strain of the trial."

"That's not true. Geraldine has explained everything," Sahel retorted. "James was wrongfully convicted. After reading Sunetra's suicide note, the D.A. had no choice but to find him innocent. The judge dismissed James's sentence. I don't know where you're getting your information from, but—"

"James contracted AIDS while he was in prison," Carl said, "San Quentin, no doubt."

Sahel drew in breath. Geraldine had not explained how James contracted HIV. "I want to see him," Sahel said.

"We need to talk about this," Carl said.

"Take it up with Titus. For once the two of you are on the same page," said Sahel. She stood and struggled to unfold her cane. "As for me, I want to see James."

"I don't know about Titus, but as your physician—" Carl said. She started away.

Carl grasped her hand. "It's not a good idea emotionally, and with your physical condition, to become so attached to someone who's going to be dead in a few ..."

"My emotions? My condition?" Sahel whipped around. "Last I checked, I met James after I lost my sight."

"It took a half hour to get you conscious this morning," Carl said. "I thought you had undergone a stroke."

"You think James caused my blood pressure to spike?"

"It's an emotional toll," said Carl.

"More than I've already been through?" Sahel said. "For god's sake, I'm not having an affair with him, nor do I care to." She exhaled.

"That's not the point. He won't be with us very long."

"And last time I attended Mass, the pictures of neither you nor any of the doctors at Berkeley General, nor Dr. Lattimer, were hanging above the cross," Sahel said. Carl sighed into what became a deep and heavy silence. Sahel shook her head and said, "How does one man who may be dying frighten so many people?"

"You held James's hand. His heart started beating. Then you collapsed," Carl said.

"Surely you don't think I brought James back to life, that he in some way took something from me, something that made his heart start beating again."

Sahel could not resist echoes of Geraldine's earlier assertion. *You saved James's life. You brought him back.* "I only spoke to him," she said.

"I don't know what happened. But if his physical state remains the same, James Bolden will not be with us for long," Carl said. "I don't intend to let him take you with him. I've lost patients, watched them die on the table, not all mine." Carl's voice cracked. "I thought we'd lost you that afternoon in the ER. When your heart stopped beating ... "

The piercing sound of the heart monitor flatlining entered Sahel's ears. Solemnly she said, "You kissed your St. Joseph, and prayed three Hail Mary's?"

"How do you know that?" Carl said.

"Geraldine told me."

"But I said the Hail Mary's silently," Carl rebutted.

"Well, she must have seen your lips moving." Sahel tried worming her way out of the results of her slip. "Someone must have told me. How could I have known? My heart had stopped. I was dead."

A moment passed, taking with it several bricks from the wall of confusion and frustration separating Sahel and Carl. "Only twice have I seen patients revived after their hearts stopped beating for over five minutes. This morning with James," Carl said, "and the afternoon yours stopped."

"Miracles happen every day." Sahel grasped for any explanation she could make worthy of Carl's acceptance.

"The greatest miracle for me would be to see you looking back at me with the image of my face in your eyes," Carl said. Sahel was about to speak, tell Carl she could not tolerate him continuing to address the matter of her blindness in that way.

"But a blood pressure of 200/180 is not going to get you there," Carl said. "I want you in my office tomorrow morning."

"Then you either come and get me or I'll have Geraldine or Zelda take me," Sahel said.

"I'll call Geraldine and tell her to bring you."

"I'm speaking of visiting James, not my appointment with you."

"This is serious, Sahel."

Now Sahel sighed. "And I'll be at your office, tomorrow morning at 9. I will also visit James."

"Thirty minutes. That's all I'm allowing," Carl said.

"And is that to protect me or him?"

"Both of you."

Chapter 19

W

ith her hand on Geraldine's arm, Sahel exited the elevator onto the fourth floor at Berkeley General. A nagging feeling spread across Sahel's stomach as she followed Geraldine, who had remained quiet during the elevator ride up from the lobby and down the corridor. "Here's Carl," Geraldine said as they neared James's hospital room.

Carl took Sahel's hand. "No more than thirty minutes," he said regarding Sahel's visit with James.

"But what about you?" Sahel turned towards Geraldine. "Surely he—"

"Another time," Geraldine acquiesced.

"But you're his godmother."

Geraldine's worry tore at Sahel and pained her. "He needs to speak with you," Geraldine said. "Besides, you saved his life."

She patted the back of Sahel's hand and left.

Sahel grasped Carl's arm and followed him to James's room. "Like I said, a half hour, not a minute more," Carl reminded in a whisper.

He helped her sit, and left.

She would have preferred a few moments of quiet before easing into their conversation. It frustrated her that she could not see James's face. "They tell me you saved my life," he said as she pondered how to address him.

"I don't know about that to be true," Sahel said. "How are you doing?" She turned towards James's voice and smiled.

"Weak, but alive. They tell me that's to be expected."

"You gave us all a scare," Sahel said, "keeping us on our toes." Moments passed, Sahel surmised James had dropped off to sleep.

"I miss her. My fiancée," James said. "It hurts. Her not being here."

Sahel lowered her head. "You mean Sunetra," she said after some seconds.

"I suppose Geraldine told you," James's voice gained energy.

Sahel imagined him moving to sit up or perhaps trying. "Yes, she did."

"Did she tell you that she died?" James asked.

"Geraldine said she jumped from the Golden Gate." Sahel spoke in a low voice, recalled the additional element of mystery Geraldine's words had conveyed. "*It all happened on the same afternoon, James's sentencing. Sunetra's suicide and your taking the pills.*" Sahel said nothing of the barbed vehemence Geraldine had expressed towards Sunetra.

"When Geraldine told me what Sunetra had done, like you, I wanted to die," James said.

An image of Titus flashed upon the darkness encasing Sahel, the torture upon his face when lifting from the bedroom floor the bottle empty of the pills she had taken. "It's painful," she murmured.

"Why did *you* do it?" James asked. "Take the pills."

His words tugged at Sahel. She had forgotten having told him of her suicide attempt. "You're in pain," she said. "You want

104

the ache to go away. But you feel there's no way out. In your mind you're a burden to those who love you and whom you love."

"The only burden you've given Titus is not letting him love you. Not letting him in."

Again Sahel inhaled deeply.

"I've watched him with you. You're all that matters to Titus. Just like Sunetra was all that mattered to me."

"Geraldine said you were wrongly accused of shooting Sunetra's father, Ravesh Desai," said Sahel. "Sunetra shot her father. She wrote that in her suicide letter. When he saw the letter, the D.A. had you released."

James sniffled against the quietness. Sahel sensed him crying.

"You were trying to protect Sunetra," said Sahel.

"I obviously failed."

Sahel's heart sank.

"I guess this is where you ask questions, psychoanalyze me, and figure out why I would fall in love with a woman hell bent on running her father's brokerage, so much so that when she found out that her father wanted me—as her husband—to manage it, what was to be hers, she broke off our engagement." James said. Sahel heard what sounded like another whimper.

"I'm not a psychoanalyst. And as far as trying to configure why you chose to love Sunetra despite what she did, I have no desire to ... I can only say—"

"Do you love Titus?"

"He's my husband."

"Do you love your husband?"

"Oh, since I'm not going to analyze you, you're going to deconstruct me?"

"Do you think Sunetra meant to shoot her father?" James asked.

James's questions stumped Sahel. "I ... I don't know." A voice, the one she suspected was Sunetra's, rose in Sahel's thoughts. *No. I didn't. I was angry. The walls were closing in. I never meant to kill my father, or blame James. I was scared.*

Sahel said, "Sometimes we do things we don't mean,

105

particularly when we've been hurt and feel betrayed."

"Is that why you won't open up to Titus?"

A well of anger opened within Sahel. She unfolded her cane, stood and made to find her way to the door.

"You can run away from me and my questions. And I'll surely die. But the fact that you can't answer me says that—"

Sahel turned back. "I came here to help, not to sit here and listen to you raking through my life."

"Why did you marry him?" James pressed. Sahel stifled a whimper threading for tears.

More moments passed. "I'm facing death," James said. *Death*. The word echoed within Sahel. James continued. "The only conversations I know how to have right now are honest ones."

Sahel tightened the grip on her cane. She had remained standing. Sahel thought of the woman in red, how she had flashed her palm and told Sahel, *Go back. It's not your time.*

"When I'm with you ..." James started once more. "The first time I saw you in the ballroom last Saturday evening ..." A crack pierced his voice. "When I'm near you, I feel Sunetra's presence."

A wind of dizziness passed through her. "I saw her, Sunetra, when you came to me on Monday, the night my heart had stopped beating." James sounded relieved, almost joyful. "Sunetra lifted my hand. She was standing over me. I was so tired, ready to go. But she told me, 'No. Not yet. Go back.'"

Sahel took in breath.

"I reached out for her," James said. "Almost touched her. I wanted so much to kiss her."

Sahel grew cold.

"But Sunetra told me to go back," James explained.

James's words exhumed memories for Sahel, her spirit separated from her body. She had been underwater, swimming, and also ready to die. The woman in red had appeared. Sahel had drawn near her.

The woman had lifted her hand, and opened her palm. Again the words, *Go back*, enveloped Sahel.

Sahel brought her left hand to the cane. "What was Sunetra

wearing when she came to you?" Sahel asked.

"A red cape. It had a hood."

Sahel's chest filled with angst and the fear of a mystery she could not explain, would perhaps never understand. Slowly she made her way back to the chair and sat. She folded her cane and placed it on her lap. "I love Titus. I love him very much," Sahel said.

"Why is it so hard to say it?"

"Two weeks after I lost my sight, I took a knife and locked myself in my bedroom," Sahel said. "My plan was to slit my wrists, stab myself and bleed to death. But then Daddy started calling my name, begging me to let him in. I refused to open the door. Told him to go away. He called Titus. When I refused to let the two of them in, Daddy called Carl." Sahel took in breath.

"Carl came, convinced me to open the door. Titus slipped in. Came up behind me. While I was listening, Titus came from behind and grabbed me. Carl took my hands. The knife dropped to the floor." Tears filled Sahel's eyes.

"I was so tired," Sahel explained. "Titus took me into his arms, patted my head, brushed my face. I was soooo tired." Tears broke into her throat like glass cutting through layers of ice. "He begged me to marry him. I was too weak to say, 'No.' I couldn't fight him any more. His love was the only thing that was going to get me through." Sahel sighed.

"We married six weeks later." She wiped her face, gathered part of her emotions that had spilled forth. "All I could think of when swallowing the pills was how much I would be setting him free, never of the pain he would feel on seeing me dead. Those first months into the marriage were hard, painful. Titus was doing the best he could. It wasn't his fault. I felt so worthless."

"Losing your sight is hard," James said.

"I never felt that Mama loved me. I was a burden to her."

"Titus is not your mother."

Sahel sighed. "I didn't hold Titus responsible. I had played my role. Shouldn't have been back there, on the pavement behind the car. But still somehow, my anger had its way. All the pent-up frustration, the things I could never say or think to say

107

to Mama, came barreling out in little slights and snips at Titus, criticisms for the way he tried to help me. I wanted to step into my dress. He wanted to pull it over my head. I didn't like the way he brushed my hair. When he tried to comb it, I said the comb pulled my hair. He wanted to go right, I said, 'left.'"

Again Sahel sighed, this time long and heavy. Pain rattled in her throat and heart.

"The accident," James started moments later. "Was it how you lost your sight?"

"Yes." Sahel's lips trembled. Again she lowered her head and whispered, "Oh, my god. It was my fault. All ... my ... fault. If only I had given him a date. Just a date. He would have taken care of the rest."

Sahel told James of the accident.

Titus had shouted, "Why can't you marry me? Is it because of Alice, that I was married before?"

"I'm not saying I don't want to marry you."

"Then what are you saying?"

"A major change like this will affect my clients. It's like having a baby."

"Oh, come on, Sahel." Titus had twisted his face.

"I have to prepare them. We'll need some time away. My clients'll want to know where I'm going. That I haven't abandoned them."

"Then tell them!"

"I can't do that."

"Why do you always box us in like this?" Titus had thrown up his hands.

Sahel now flinched in recalling the incident. "We were arguing." An image of Titus, the anguish of rejection twisting his face, flashed onto her memory. She squeezed her fingers around the cane. "I was stalling as always, as always."

"The night of the accident I was so afraid. Mama had died two months earlier in November. Titus was eager to get married, and bitter that I was again holding back, stalling. I felt as though this noose was around my neck, everything he said, his words, pulling it tight."

"His anger frightened you?" James asked.

"He was hurting, truly aching. For the first time I saw that he truly loved me, and how much."

Sahel slid back into the memory, recalled Titus's protestations. "We had been arguing about setting a wedding date. As usual, I wanted to wait. *'What's the rush?'* Titus wanted to make plans. Move forward."

She described to James what transpired.

"Titus said, '*I have always loved you, from the time we took our first communion and played in your back yard, me and Carl helping you make mud cakes—*'

"He always brought the water," Sahel explained. "Carl the dirt. He reminded me of all the times I had watched him and Carl fence. Titus frowned even more." Sahel recalled his sienna face a few shades darker than her mother's.

"I felt the pain gripping his face. It hurt my heart," said Sahel. "But I just couldn't ... I was too scared."

Sahel repeated Titus's words. "'*When my parents died, all I could think of was you. How much my mother loved you; she told me to protect you, and keep you safe.*'"

"His parents were killed in an auto accident. Titus was eleven," she said to James. "I'm all he has left."

Again she shared what Titus had said during their argument. "'*Your mother loved my mother, but your mother was incredibly mean to you. My mother knew it. I knew it.*' I began to cry." Sahel gripped her hands, pulled at her fingers. "I was so ashamed. Titus drew near and grasped my shoulders."

Sahel lifted her head and spoke into the darkness separating her from James lying on the bed. "I hurt Titus that night. I hurt him so much."

She recalled Titus's words, recited them to James. "'*After you there's no one. No. One.*'"

"Everything Titus said that night was true. But his love ... It's so overwhelming. I never knew he had seen so much, that his mother had told him to protect me. How could a child, a boy my same age, protect me?" Sahel spoke in search of an answer.

"He's an adult now." James said. "Maybe Titus's mother was speaking to him of the future, telling him to take you from your mother, marry you and give you a better life."

"I've made his life a living nightmare." Sahel sobbed.

"Your mother loved Titus," James said. "But it sounds like Titus has passion, strong feelings, like your mother."

"How did you know? Who told you?" Sahel asked.

"That your mother loved Titus, or that he is passionate about all he does, including loving you?"

"Both?" quipped Sahel.

"It's in your voice. You're as ambivalent about him as you are about your mother."

"Why do you keep referring to her as if she's alive? She's dead," Sahel said.

"Perhaps in body. But not in spirit. And definitely not in your mind."

Sahel described the escalation of her argument with Titus. "He was holding my hand. I pulled away. The ring must have come off. I didn't notice it until I was upstairs in my bedroom. After Mama died I had moved back home. My excuse was that I didn't want Daddy to be alone." Sahel chuckled, knowing that Essien had been seeing Geraldine at the time. A hard and cold heaviness settled into her stomach.

"When I saw that the ring was gone, it was as though the whole world came apart. Here I was, hesitant one minute to set a date for our wedding then freaking out the next because I had lost the engagement ring Titus had given me. Makes no sense."

Sahel shook her head.

"Your fear of your mother returned when after her death Titus became determined to marry you."

"Mama had kissed the ring just before Titus slid it on my finger. I was standing on one side of her bed, Titus the other. Carl and Daddy were by the window." Sahel sighed.

"Mama had a bad heart—had been confined for the last five years to a hospital bed we'd set up in the living room. Her first heart attack had struck when I was thirteen." Sahel shuddered at recalling how scared she had been, how death had welled in her mother's eyes, the fear that had penetrated Lillian's voice, she barely able to talk and grip her breast.

Oh, Mama, don't die! Sahel had cried when kneeling to her.

"My world was coming together. I was doing what Mama

wanted. And getting the man I'd always secretly wanted. And then ..." Sahel wiped her face, straightened her posture and tried collecting her emotions. "Titus had no idea I was down there on the cement of the driveway looking for the ring. It was dark. I was down on my knees. He was in the car. There was no way he could get out except in reverse. It was not his fault. He would never hurt me. I knew it then as I do now. I knew it then. It's just that ..." More tears pierced her throat growing raw with rage and regret.

"Do you love him?" James whispered.

"Very much. But, oh god, it hurts so much when he loves me back."

"The monsters that are our insanity die only when we embrace all of who we are. Love ourselves. And forgive those who have hated and despised our presence," said James. "You fear Titus's love is rooted in the same craziness as your mother's."

"And who is your monster? Have you slain him? Or her?"

"We're both haunted," James said.

With that Sahel grew dizzy. As on the night of the accident, red consumed her.

Chapter 20

S

ahel lay in the hospital bed. She had collapsed. So vigorously had she relived the moment of the accident, the taillights of Titus's car blaring red, that she awoke with a momentary lapse of having experienced the memory. Neither did she remember having been with James in his hospital room, and nothing of their discussion. She turned her head upon the pillow. Essien lifted her hand.

"How are you feeling?" he said.

"Oh, my head," Sahel said of the throbbing and frowned. She touched her temple. "What happened? I feel as if someone took a sledgehammer to my head." She fought to sit up and orient herself.

"Don't try to get up," Essien said. Sahel journeyed back in time, her thoughts snagging memories. The night of the accident. The argument that ensued. Titus wanting an answer.

Slowly she recalled James. We were talking. I was in his hospital room.

She had told James of the accident, and how it happened. Images and memories of that night beckoned. Part of her remained stuck.

"I should get Carl," Essien said. The sound of his footsteps dissipated into the din of her thoughts. The door to Sahel's hospital room opened. Titus and Carl's voices drifted in.

"What the hell were you doing taking her to see him?" Titus said. "I thought the man was in quarantine."

"He wanted to see her," Carl said. "It was James's risk."

"I don't give a damn whose risk is greater. Every time she's near that man something happens. She loses consciousness. I don't want Sahel with him again," Titus said. "Do you understand me?"

"Like the surgery she needs that you don't want her to have?" Carl said.

"One has nothing to do with the other. Sahel is my wife. And you'd better get used to it. I want you the fuck out of our lives!"

The door to Sahel's hospital room closed. Essien was back. "Carl will be here in a minute," Essien said in a soft tone as if to quell the argument from the corridor.

Again she touched her forehead, Titus and Carl's words rattling her thoughts. The pounding headache made it impossible to speak. Sahel sought escape from the angry exchange between Titus and Carl. She drifted back to her recent conversation with James. *Titus is nothing like my mother.* Sahel had said. *I love him. It was hard to love her. I don't know if I did. Whether I could, really.*

"But you love Titus," James had said, echoing Sahel's truth.

Again Essien lifted her hand. "I'm here with you," he said.

Once more she turned her head upon the pillow, but this time away from her father. She sank into another memory.

"What the hell were you thinking of?" Carl had questioned Titus. The accident had taken place the previous night. Then, as

114

now, Sahel had been lying upon the bed in a hospital room. This time Carl had been on the offensive, Titus defending his actions from which he could neither seek nor offer any recompense.

"I don't know what happened. She was behind the car," Titus had said. "I thought she'd gone inside the house." Sahel absorbed Titus's words from the past. "She wasn't supposed to be there," he had said. "Not behind my car. It's crazy."

The nurse had removed the thermometer from Sahel's mouth, and then lifted her arm and wrapped a blood pressure cuff around it.

Sahel had grown anxious against the sound of Carl reprimanding Titus out in the hospital corridor.

"This is not going to go away," Carl had said. "She can't see a damn thing. Nothing."

"Isn't there something you can do?" Titus pleaded.

"I'm doing all I can. If you hadn't lost control last night, none of this would have occurred. We wouldn't be standing here."

"I would never do anything to hurt Sahel. You can't think I did this on purpose?"

"Everyone knows you have a temper. They only tolerate you because of your surgical abilities."

Silence.

"I would never hurt her," Titus repeated.

Sahel left her eyes closed to avoid speaking with the nurse. Lifting them would reveal a wall of darkness. The nurse had removed the blood pressure cuff from around Sahel's arm and gently lowered it back onto the pillow. Seconds later Sahel had heard a voice reprimanding Carl and Titus. "You both care for Dr. Ohin. But just because she can't see doesn't mean she's lost her hearing."

Tears slipped from underneath Sahel's eyelids. Her life was ebbing away. No more independence. Minutes later and feeling an urgent need to urinate, she got out of bed and tried finding her way to the bathroom.

Failing at the task, she wet her hospital gown. When the

nurse returned she sat crouched by the wall beside the bathroom door.

"Don't let them see me like this," Sahel had cried, stunned and shocked at what she perceived as her incompetence. She needed help, could not live alone. That hurt. The shame of her physical state, what it meant and entailed, ate away at her soul. If only the beast of her hatred and self-loathing would devour her and end it all.

Three weeks later she arrived home with Titus and Essien on either side. "I want to go up to my room." Obediently Titus and Essien guided her upstairs to what had been her bedroom throughout childhood. There she remained, leaving only when Essien coaxed her to eat, until three days later when Carl arrived for the fourth time, demanding that Sahel let him see her.

Sahel had been lying in bed when she was awakened to the voices outside her room. Still unaccustomed to the darkness, she had realized only after seconds of repeatedly blinking that opening her eyes would not eradicate her blindness.

Slowly she pushed herself to sit up. A knock sounded at the door. A second and third followed, and then, "It's me, Carl," he announced his presence. "I'm coming in."

The door creaked open. Sahel lamented the inability to detect any light shining through. She lay back down, turned from Carl, the sound of his footsteps growing louder.

He sat upon the bed, touched her hand, and said, "Are you awake?" Unintentionally, Sahel pulled back her palm.

"You can't hide out in here forever."

"I've been thinking about my clients. What to do with them?" she uttered. Her voice was flat and bereft of emotion.

"I've spoken with Renard Williams. He's made some calls, and lined up therapists willing to take on your clients. Don't worry about that."

Sahel's back remained to Carl. "I can't ignore them," Sahel said of her clients. "Neither do I want to."

"I think they'll understand," Carl said.

"What has he told them?" She whipped over, tried to sit up.

"What have you told them?"

"Nothing." Carl grasped her shoulders. "I've said nothing. Nor has Renard."

"But he called them. What did he say?"

"Only that you were injured, had been in the hospital, and were now recuperating at home." Carl's voice was calm. Sahel lost steam.

"I don't know what to say to them." She lowered her head.

Still in shock, her emotions wobbled back and forth between concern about being away from her clients, unable to maintain her sessions with them, and shame and fear of informing them of what had actually taken place, that she had lost her sight. Carl took her into his arms.

"It's been four days now since you've been home. Your father says you only leave the room when he coaxes you to eat."

"I need time." She pulled away from Carl's embrace.

"You're not alone in this," Carl said.

"I don't know what to do with my life," Sahel moaned.

"First we need to get your sight back."

"It's not coming back."

"Not on its own." Carl then said. "There's a surgical procedure that can restore your sight."

"You're certain about this?" Sahel turned her head.

"I've spoken to a friend of mine in Chicago. We were residents together at UCSF. He's performed the operation several times. His success rate has been consistently above average."

"And where are his patients now?" Sahel said.

"Back living their lives, doing what they did before losing their vision."

Sahel shook her head. It all seemed too good to be true. Titus had also expressed concerns about the types of surgeries available to her. *They all come with a risk.* Titus had said. *I want your sight restored. God, I do. But not at the cost of your life.*

Sahel was afraid. "You need to explain all of this to Daddy," she said.

"I have."

Sahel lifted her head.

"Your father wants what you want."

Again Sahel lost energy, initiative. "I don't know."

Carl lifted her chin with his forefinger. "I love you."

"You can't. Look at me. It's sick."

"My Little Red Corvette," Carl spoke soft and slowly. "If only you'd slow down from taking care of others and let me help you." He sighed.

Carl's words had taken Sahel farther back into their history. With a half smile she recalled a Prince concert she and Carl had attended. An attending physician whose wife, two days prior to the event, had gone into early labor, and given his tickets to Carl.

Carl took Sahel in an all-out effort to cheer her from Titus's abrupt absence. Without forewarning, Titus had left the surgical training program at UCSF in the city and transferred to Columbia in New York.

"I've always loved you," Carl had repeated that moment, sitting upon Sahel's bed, she having lost her sight. Sahel left the memory of the concert, Prince singing "Little Red Corvette" and Carl staring into her eyes.

"Let me help you," Carl had pleaded in a whisper to Sahel who was unable to see him looking at her, or to greet his gaze.

"And what if the surgery fails?" said Sahel.

"Believe me. It won't."

"What are the percentages, the success rates?"

"They're good," Carl said softly.

Titus then spoke. "For the ones who survive." Sahel turned.

Footsteps entered the room, and drew close, and stopped on the other side of the bed across from Carl. "Ask Carl to tell you how many people die from the procedure he's talking about," Titus said.

Sahel turned to Carl.

"It's a good procedure for people who are healthy, and if done in a timely manner," Carl said, then with a solemnity bordering on coldness added, "The longer you wait, the more difficult it is to drain the fistula now forming behind your eyes."

118

"Is that what's causing my blindness?"

"The CT scan shows a small out-pouching having formed. I'm certain it's from the trauma of hitting your head on the pavement of the driveway."

Once more Sahel lowered her head, her thoughts retreating to a place of defeat. "This is not hopeless," said Carl. He grasped her upper arms, and gently shook her.

"Let her go." Titus had touched her arm.

The two of them holding her arms and arguing with each other had driven Sahel into a childhood memory of the three of them making mud cakes.

Sahel had lowered her hands into the bucket of water. Titus to the right had followed, with Carl on her left doing the same. The sun, bright overhead, had cast a sheen upon the water's surface. Their six hands had shone clearly from the bottom. Peace descended in the stillness of the moment.

The beating of their three childhood hearts fell in rhythm, each with the other. The fragrance of eternity touched upon their souls, transcendent of time. Heaven floated upon the deserts of their souls.

The dwelling place reserved for so few became their abode.

Slowly Carl inched his finger towards Sahel's pinky finger and touched it. "Leave her alone," Titus yelled.

"You can't tell me what to do," Carl shot back. "You're not the boss."

The swishing of Carl and Titus's hands stirred the black sand at the bottom of the bucket. A storm arose in what had been calm and silent. Sahel rushed to her feet and ran back towards the house.

"See what you did," said Carl.

"It wasn't me. You messed up everything," Titus said, his words fading as the back door closed behind Sahel having entered the house.

Unable, as in her childhood memory, to run away, Sahel had snatched her arm and hand from their grips.

"You need to tell her the truth," Titus said to Carl. "The

surgery is dangerous."

"Is that so?" Sahel turned towards him. Carl sucked in air. "I want to know," Sahel had demanded. And then filled with frustration, "Tell me," she shouted.

"There's a thirty percent chance you could die," Carl said.

The words entered Sahel's ears, sank into her soul. She lifted a pillow, pulled it to her chest, and lay down, wishing to return to childhood if only to see their hands, one nearly white, another brown, and Sahel's dark as night between them.

In vain she had tried envisioning their three pairs of hands beneath the surface of the water, tranquility stilling them but for a moment. But no such vision came, only a hollowed-out memory in which Sahel lay captive to her blindness, the darkness surrounding her then as now, the latter holding one exception. A year had passed since the accident.

Now with James Bolton in her life, she could, for the first time since losing her sight, see images. The first had burst upon Sahel's thoughts in the Masonic Ballroom, moments prior to Geraldine introducing James and his lifting Sahel's hand.

Now again lying in a hospital bed, with Essien holding her hand, Sahel contemplated that moment of James entering her life. That evening with James differed in so many ways from the routine that had become her life.

James had questioned her out on the verandah and with a passion matching Titus's love and commitment.

"Do you believe... ," James had asked. His interrogation had echoed the certainty Carl held in the surgical procedure he wanted Sahel to undergo and his determination to return her sight.

Do you believe?
Immortality.
Resurrection.
Reincarnation.
We can come back.
Yes, Sahel now whispered within. Yes, we can.

Chapter 21

T

he click of Carl's penlight signaled Sahel to prepare for him to pull her eyes open. "That was a nasty fall you took," he said. "Care to tell me how you were feeling before it happened?" Carl let go of the skin around her left eye and placed his fingers to her right eye.

"I was sitting on the chair," Sahel said.

The argument minutes earlier between Titus and Carl had ended. Essien had left.

"I don't remember." She lied.

"Can you recall the last thing that happened, or what you said?"

Sahel shook her head.

"You do remember any of your conversation with James?"

Carl let go of the skin around her eye and clicked his penlight.

Again she shook her head.

Carl sighed. "I'd like to keep you here overnight, run some tests and—"

"I need to go home. Titus is worried and upset," Sahel said.

"I'm concerned about you. This is the second time in four days that you've collapsed. Both times you were with James. And with this recent occurrence you're unable to remember what was happening before you blanked out."

Sahel could neither ignore nor refute Carl's points of concerns.

"Your blood pressure is 275/200," Carl said. "Higher than on Monday when you fainted."

The thickness of Sahel's headache had dissipated, yet remnants of the intense dizziness she had felt before losing consciousness remained. Again she touched her head. "Your father said you talked of having a horrible headache when you awoke," said Carl.

Sahel moved to sit up. Now as then she felt as if her hospital room would begin another round of spinning. Quickly she leaned over to quell the rising nausea. "Lie back," Carl said as he caught her. "Breathe deeply."

Sahel did as Carl instructed, let her head sink into the pillow, and inhaled deeply. The threat of spinning subsided, as did the nausea. "I cannot stay in this hospital."

"It would only be for a night or so," said Carl.

Memories of the accident were flooding back at will. "You can run the tests. But find a way for me not to have to stay here."

"The techs can run the tests quicker with you here."

"I'm not an invalid. I won't stay here. You can't force me." Her head upon the pillow, Sahel turned away from Carl.

Carl touched her hand. "Sahel, this is serious."

"And so am I. I don't want to be here by myself. Don't you understand? I want to be home. I can't see. I don't know these people, nice as they are. Please," she said.

"You wouldn't have to be here alone," Carl's voice was low. He lifted her hand. "I'll be with you," he whispered. "I'll be with you through every test."

122

Sahel shook her head. Carl squeezed her hand. "He knows about us," said Sahel. "Titus knows we slept together. That's why he left the residency at UCSF and went to Columbia."

"You weren't married."

"I am now. And you're making it very hard for me."

"Because I love you. Or you love me."

"No. Yes. I love you ... as a friend. A very close friend. You're like a brother," Sahel said.

"Then as your brother, who is also your physician, I need you to have these tests. And remaining in the hospital is the quickest and easiest way to get them done."

"You're not hearing me, Carl."

"I love you. And will never stop fighting to get your sight back."

"I don't have to stay in the hospital," said Sahel. "I won't."

"Aren't you listening?" Titus's voice resounded. "She doesn't want to stay."

Sahel made a start to sit up once more. She tried collecting her wits and emotions now tattered and torn by Carl's words.

"How are you feeling?" asked Titus. He touched her head.

"A little dizzy. Carl wants to do some tests," Sahel said. "I want to do them. But as an outpatient." She turned to Carl, still holding her hand. "I need to go home."

Carl signed the forms discharging Sahel from the hospital and Titus drove her home. During their meal, Sahel assured Essien that she would undergo the tests Carl wanted performed, even if it took a week, since she refused to remain in the hospital. At Titus's urging, he escorted her upstairs.

"You shower first," he said on reaching their bedroom and closing the door. "I have to call the hospital, speak with the Jared Nixon and see how our Mr. Madison is doing." A cardiac surgery resident, Jared Nixon, often assisted Titus in surgery. Forty minutes later and still slightly damp, Sahel lay upon their bed as Titus emerged from the bathroom, having also showered.

He sat upon the bed. She reached her hand into the darkness and touched Titus's back. Water droplets, like smaller ones still upon her shoulder and neck, moistened Sahel's palm.

She moved her hand up his back and felt the towel around his neck.

"I want you to have a second opinion," Titus said. "Carl's an excellent surgeon, but he's not the best person to be treating you."

"He's our friend," Sahel said.

"More the reason he shouldn't be treating you. I've let this go on too long."

Sahel withdrew her hand from Titus. A stream of anxiety flooded her chest. Titus had overheard Carl say he would remain with her at the hospital, Sahel concluded.

"He's not seeing straight when it comes to you," Titus spoke again.

"It's been the three of us for all these years, since we were children. He was your best man."

"Things change when you get married," Titus said.

Sahel pondered the strange and unique quality of her relationships with Titus and Carl, the whole of their friendship. Sahel had no girlfriends throughout her childhood. She felt too unsure of their motives each time they tried getting to know her, never found them interesting.

With the exception of the two years following his parents deaths—time Titus had spent with his paternal grandparents—Sahel spent her entire childhood with Titus and Carl.

As a child she played with Titus and Carl nearly every afternoon. Titus and Carl had studied at her house, the three of them attending St. Maria's Parish school, and Oakland Catholic Pre, after which they entered Cal Berkeley. Their connections went deeper than what bound many blood relatives. And yet those ties, sturdy and heartfelt, held a dark side for Sahel.

They were like siblings, their souls knotted by a million strings, some visible, others not, and all woven in a tangle that, should anyone try to unravel the intricacies, would produce a madness swallowing all.

Much like the relationship with her parents, Sahel's bonds with Titus and Carl brought with them divided loyalties. Lillian forever criticizing Essien drew Sahel's ire and anger. Sahel stood caught in the middle between Titus and Carl. Even Carl could behave like Lillian. Sahel's memory of Carl reprimanding Titus revealed that.

Sahel had made a clear choice in marrying Titus. Had the accident not occurred, would she have married him?

That she had done so, refusing to engage the subject of choosing another neurosurgeon to direct her care, sent mixed signals to not only Carl, but also Titus, her husband.

Chapter 22

T

he next morning Sahel had placed a cup of water in the microwave when footsteps entered the kitchen. "Let me do that," Essien said. "Water that's been heated in that contraption is no excuse for making tea." He ushered her to the table and set about boiling water on the gas range.

"What will I do when I don't have you to boil water?" Sahel half smiled.

"You'll cross that bridge, as they say, when encountering it," Essien said in his comforting voice. "Water boiled in that contraption of a microwave doesn't taste right."

Sahel smiled. In her present circumstances she would not think of lighting a burner on the range. For those rare occasions when neither Zelda nor Geraldine could be present and neither Titus nor Essien had arrived home, carefully shaped strips of masking tape identified the numbers on the microwave panel. Sahel needed more time alone, away from those who loved her, to learn to maneuver independently.

With fear and loathing, she contemplated the day when Essien would die. "But that's just it. You won't always be with me."

Titus had highlighted this concern when pleading with Sahel to let him marry her. "Your father loves you, but he won't always be around. I created this mess, let me clean it up."

"Is that how you see me," Sahel had said. "A mess to be straightened out?" She had been lying against Titus's chest, Carl downstairs calling the paramedics.

"You don't get it, do you?" Titus had sighed. Moments earlier he and Carl had wrestled the butcher knife from Sahel wielding it wildly. "Can you just let me love you? Please. I don't care how, but find a way. I want to marry you. I need you." Then as now Sahel could not see nor imagine what she could give Titus that he lacked and deserved, or that another woman could not better provide. Yet the darkness held a pathway of surrender to his loving.

Marrying Titus, living with him, had seemed the right and the only thing to do, even before Essien had invited them to move in with him. "Sahel knows the house, its layout," Essien had justified. "When you are away, I will be present," he had said to Titus.

Yet, in her mind, Sahel had joined Titus with her mother. The reality of day-to-day interactions with Titus had, little by little, distinguished him from the person Sahel knew Lillian to have been. Sahel had never heard the words, "I'm sorry," exit her mother's lips.

Though easily frustrated and despite having a penchant for precision and accuracy, Titus proved supportive and easygoing with the residents training under him. Never once had Sahel heard him yell. Neither had she ever heard evidence of his disparaging residents on concluding operations that had not gone as all had hoped, or produced desired results.

128

Residents, men and women, who called the house and found Titus not home, spoke to Sahel in almost loving and grateful fashion, "... for the opportunity to train under Dr. Denning."

The voices of the residents held a respect for Sahel equal to that which they held for the surgeon teaching and mentoring them, a man her love strengthened, and whose life and purpose her presence and living defined.

"Sorry to bother you, Mrs. Denning, but please let Dr. Denning know that his patient, Mr. ... is looking great."

Others would say, "I'm following Mrs. or Mr. ... for Dr. Denning throughout the night. When I'm not on the floor, the nurses will call me if anything arises." Sahel also knew that upon arriving home Titus would call the resident and speak for perhaps twenty minutes in review of the cases, in what Sahel deemed teaching mode, and a small debriefing, which he then ended with compliments or words of encouragement and always his gratitude for the resident's presence and assistance.

Sahel greeted by name any of the four residents working on Titus's service. Her heightened sensitivity to sound enabled her to recognize their voices, to which she attached their names, over time.

Once she had agreed to relay their messages to Titus, usually en route home, she then asked, "And how are you doing?"

"Pretty good. We had a long case today. I'm sure Dr. Denning will tell you about it." And then as always, no matter who the resident surgeon was, their voices enlivened. "Great as always when watching Dr. Denning in action. This is a small training program, not highly ranked. But I feel so lucky to be here and training under him. He's so wonderful and patient with us."

In their desire to follow in Titus's path and that of other cardiac surgeons, the residents presented their personal best in their efforts to care for Titus's patients.

The one female cardiac surgery resident provided Sahel the greatest insight into Titus the surgeon-teacher.

"Hello. This is Donna Milford, one of Dr. Denning's residents." The resident had called at about 5:30 one afternoon. "May I speak with him?"

"He's not here," Sahel had said. Out of breath and gasping, she had nearly missed the phone call.

"I'd like to leave a message for him about one of his patients," the young female surgeon had said.

"Oh. Hmm. Uh." Sahel had fumbled. "I'm not able to write it down," Sahel had said, and then on recovering, "I mean, it's a little bit hard to grab a pen and pap—"

"Oh, Mrs. Denning, please forgive me. I forgot it was you. So sorry."

Sahel and Titus had been married for barely two months. While the heaviness of Sahel's initial depression in response to losing her sight had lifted somewhat, the shock of her inability to perform simple tasks had not, and was in fact gaining momentum in Sahel.

"It's quite all right. I'm all right," Sahel said, easing into her strength, that of creating a situation of comfort and safety for others. "What is it you would like me to tell him? Let's see if I can remember it. This'll be my task for the day."

Carefully Donna Milford listed out the three things about the patient that she wanted Titus to know. "Now you know he's going to call you back," Sahel said, and then offered a light chuckle.

"Oh, yes, Dr. Denning is like that. He's a really good mentor. As surgeons go he's also very nice to work under." Donna then added, "The Berkeley General program was the only one that accepted me. I'm grateful to be here."

Donna's words dropped like a rock from Sahel's chest into her stomach. Donna spoke of a person Sahel had yet to meet or realize existed.

Titus arrived twenty minutes later. Proud of herself for having maintained composure during the call, Sahel relayed the message, while hoping that she had properly conveyed all the information Donna had given.

Titus dialed the resident. After greeting Donna, the tone of his voice quickly transformed from calm to concern. The patient's condition had worsened. Sahel forced her chest to expel air.

Titus said, "We did the best we could. And so did you in running the code. Of that I'm sure. It was a hard case. His heart was badly damaged." The patient, a fifty-six-year-old wife of thirty-one years, and mother of three, had died, just hours after surgery and less than thirty minutes since Donna's call to say that all appeared to be going well.

Titus asked, "Would you like me to speak with the family? It's not a bother, I can come in." Donna would handle it. "Are you sure?" Titus said and then added, "Call me back if you need to talk about what they say. Let them know I will speak with them tomorrow."

Before hanging up he said, "And Donna. This is not your fault. It happens. Keep your chin up."

Titus's words to Donna Milford sounded like those of a Titus, another person, Sahel had yet to meet. Not that Titus was unkind to Sahel. But in hearing Titus speaking with his residents, and particularly with Donna Milford, Sahel heard a calm and caring attitude, a graceful nurturing that she had never recognized. Recognition of this loss left Sahel sad.

Two months later Sahel answered the phone and recognized Donna's voice. "It's so nice to hear from you," said Sahel.

"Same to you, Mrs. Denning."

"I hope things are going well."

"They're getting back on track," Donna said. The female resident among three men and Titus then listed two pieces of information concerning a patient on whom she and Titus had operated that day.

"Please tell Dr. Denning that the patient is resting well. Everything looks good."

"I will. And I hope you have a quiet evening." Sahel was about to end the call. She didn't want to pry.

And yet— "Mrs. Denning," Donna started.

"Yes."

"I just want to say that I have really appreciated Dr. Denning's support these last few months."

"It can get difficult sometimes," Sahel said. "I know that the service has been extremely busy."

"The last time I called," Donna interrupted again. "The patient I left a message about? She died. I almost quit the program. Well, in a way I did." The voice of the young surgeon cracked into what Sahel imagined as a stifled sob. "I wrote a resignation letter," she said. "But Dr. Denning wouldn't accept it. When I didn't come to work the next morning, he called me and said as far as he knew I was still on the payroll, and my patients were waiting to see me," Donna explained.

"Later that day he said that the most important lesson we can learn as surgeons is that doctors aren't fired due to a patient's death when we have given our best and done all that is medically possible. In some cases we may pay an unfair price because someone acted stupidly or rudely. But if we treat our patients with respect and dignity, give them the best service, and pray, all will end well."

Donna added. "Since he spoke to me, I've learned to pray." Sahel's eyes filled with tears.

It pained Sahel, long after the conversation with Donna Milford, to consider how many times Titus had prayed for mercy and forgiveness in having hit her with the car. Each time Sahel entered the hospital and encountered nurses, particularly those who had attended her after the accident, she sensed their deep empathy, sometimes even their pity that such a meticulous surgeon, Titus Denning, whom they greatly respected, had made a most terrible error to which he openly and freely claimed responsibility.

That he had accidentally hit Sahel with the back of his car dealt Titus an emotional blow.

Sahel knew that some wondered about Titus's ability to move forward.

How had he recovered?

Had he recovered?

Sahel felt the ache that remained behind the persona of the cardiac surgeon respected by fellow surgeons, staff, residents, and patients. And yet she feared drawing close to, loving and most of all receiving love from someone who so physically resembled her mother.

The first time Sahel had witnessed Lillian experience pain and fear had been during Lillian's first heart attack. Fear of dying had swirled in Lillian's eyes. Not even when learning that Titus's parents had instantly died in a car crash had Lillian displayed such distress and depth of vulnerability.

Essien now touched the back of Sahel's hand.

"Here is your tea. It is hot," he said. Essien placed her hand beside the hot cup. The reverie of considerations and recollections faded. Sahel exited the memory.

"I can't remain dependent upon Titus or you," Sahel said. "I need to take some classes, for the blind."

"Is this something James has suggested you do?"

"Why do you say that?" Sahel turned towards his voice.

"You have changed since meeting him," Essien said.

Sahel recalled the strength of Titus's arms in carrying her up the stairs, the softness with which he laid her upon the bed, his lips lingering upon hers, and—she grew warm. She turned, desperately wished to have been able to see her father's face. A thoughtful man, Essien's words conveyed a depth of meaning that dug underneath the physical senses of Sahel's body teeming with memories. Essien Ohin did not expend energy of thought and word on just any idea.

Sahel said, "I know James in ways in which I have yet to understand Titus. Or Carl." The thought of Carl's friendship without her father's presence delivered a chill. She explained her vision.

"The night of the medical dinner I was sitting alone. Carl had just left. He was frustrated again that I won't have the surgery." Sahel omitted how the pull of Carl's advances had left her feeling guilty that she had abandoned him. "We had argued."

"Moments later I sensed someone nearby, someone familiar, and who knew me. I felt he was watching me, and only me. I tried brushing it aside. Told myself that I was imagining things." Sahel clasped her hands. "A vision came before me. A woman and a man. They were arguing. I saw this in my mind, images, the first I've seen since losing my sight." Sahel shook her head; an air of disbelief remained. "The man spoke the woman's name. Sunetra."

Essien softly inhaled.

"The man told the woman he loved her. Begged her to trust him. But she wanted her independence. I could tell. She was me. I was her." Sahel then told of the voice that spoke to her as she held Titus's arm, the two of them walking amid the crowd, all of them on their way to the ballroom at the corner of Porter and Fourth. You don't want to be here ... You'll be okay. It reassured me. The voice inside my head."

Her hand now to the cup of hot tea, Sahel recalled how she had responded to what the voice had said.

"Later and in the ballroom I hadn't even cleared my head of the vision, when someone lifted my hand. I thought it was Carl who had returned." Sahel grew warm in recalling her hope. "I didn't know how I was going to get through the meal and not make a fool of myself." She had felt lonely and exposed. Again she reclaimed each moment.

"I thought it was Carl who had lifted my hand, that he had returned. But it was James."

Characteristic of her father when weighing the thoughts of another, he said after some moments of silence, "We all carry two stories within us. Two voices, perhaps." Sahel listened very intently. "The lie of our reality. And a myth that is the truth of lives." Sahel lowered her head.

"As a child you grew up torn between your mother and myself." Her father continued. "Your playmates, Titus and Carl, brought stability. Now that you are married to Titus, that stability has been upset."

"Are you saying that I should not have married Titus?" Sahel asked.

"You have always loved him, despite yourself." Essien spoke matter-of-factly. "Acknowledging and acting upon this truth, you find yourself back where you were as a child with your mother and me. Torn and confused."

The wings of her father's words spawned the remainder of the vision that Sahel had yet to experience.

The sad truth of James and Sunetra arose within the eye of Sahel's mind and revealed itself.

Sunetra, her doe eyes outlined in kohl, and filled with the anger of betrayal and disappointment, stood before James. "I love you," James pleaded once more. He looked like a man reduced to boyhood. Sunetra, his mother, the Madonna, was now transformed to the rage-filled goddess Kali, blood dripping from her teeth, having torn the truth from his heart.

Sunetra's hand held a gun.

Sahel translated the vision to her father as she newly experienced it.

James looked to the gun in Sunetra's hand. "What are you doing? It's only the cleaning crew." James frowned. "I saw their cart in the hall."

"There's someone here," Sunetra whispered. "In this office. They aim to hurt me and you. Us."

"Who? What are you talking about?" Again James eyed the weapon, and knitted his brows. "Let me have that." He reached for the gun in Sunetra's hand. She pulled away and then with eyes growing big she aimed the gun at the doorway. Footsteps drew near and grew louder.

James turned towards the doorway opening to the outer office.

Ravesh's portly frame crossed the threshold. His dark face with a mustache registered shock, and then despair, on seeing Sunetra's face, and her hands holding the gun, her finger pulling the trigger. James turned to Sunetra. She fired again. The glint of death bounced from Ravesh's eyes and onto the walls, illuminating the entire room, and binding their souls.

Blood spurted through the bullet wounds in Ravesh's chest and stained his white shirt. He slumped to the office floor. James rushed to Sunetra's father. Ravesh's body shook as if caught in the web of a seizure. Silent and still, Sunetra stood looking down upon James cradling Ravesh's crimson-stained chest.

"My daughter," Ravesh uttered. He looked to Sunetra, then his eyes focused upon the ceiling. James grasped Ravesh's fingers. "My daughter." He rasped a second time. Breath, then blood sputtered from his lips, growing purple. "Tell her ... I forgive ... I forgive her."

"Dial nine-one-one," James shouted back to Sunetra, staring and still unmoved. The gun hung by her side as if hooked to her fingers. "Put that thing down and call the paramedics!" He slid his hand under Ravesh's spine, the crimson flow pouring out of his heart onto his white shirt, and brought him to his lap in an effort to help him breathe. The footprints of death left a deep trail.

Again and surprisingly, Ravesh spoke once more. This time James met the gaze of the man who was to be his father-in-law. "My daughter ... I love her. Love her too ... *purdah* ..." Ravesh made an effort to speak once more. His gaze then returned to the ceiling. His hand, fully limp, slid from James's palm.

James looked back to see Sunetra speaking on the phone to the paramedics. "Yes. Someone's been shot." She gave their address. "Please come," her voice had trembled.

The gun lay upon James's desk. His heart slowed, cementing the image of Sunetra no longer speaking on the phone, but instead gripping her head, eyes wide and swirling with fear and regret, and then staring at her father lying in James's arms.

Sahel shivered on having envisioned the full results of what had ensued from James and Sunetra's argument. Essien said, "You have received a great gift with James befriending you, and you welcoming him into your life."

Sahel absorbed her father's words.

"You are like Ohia, the man who received the gift of being able to speak to animals." Sahel's father told her the story of Ohia, and his wife Ariwehu.

"Beset with bad luck, they were very poor. Everything they touched turned to ash. About to lose their clothes to simple wear and tear, and with none to replace them, Ohia and his wife risked having to go naked and were unable to leave their house except to draw ridicule. And then one day a wealthy man allowed Ohia to draw sap from the wealthy man's trees. From the sap Ohia and his wife would make palm wine, which they would sell. Ohia cut holes into the trees and in the evening set up gourds underneath to catch the sap at night. Ohia rose the next morning only to find the gourds broken and sap gone. Hopeful and persevering, Ohia repeated his ritual another night, placed new gourds his neighbors so kindly gave him underneath new trees to catch sap. He and his wife awoke the next morning to find the new gourds broken and the sap the gourds should have collected gone again. Disappointed and angry, on the third night Ohia not only set up the gourds under

new trees, but stayed in the forest to guard the gourds. In the middle of the night an antelope came, poured the sap that had drained from the trees into Ohia's gourds into those of the antelope, and then broke Ohia's gourds. Ohia followed the antelope. Ohia was weak from hunger and desperation, but rage fueled him. He followed the antelope back to his village where the leopard was king. Ohia pled his case to the leopard king as to what the antelope had done. The leopard king agreed with Ohia. Antelope had stolen Ohia's sap. 'And that is wrong.' The leopard king ordered antelope to return to Ohia all the sap antelope had stolen. Ohia and his wife turned the sap into palm wine, and sold it. And even after splitting the proceeds with the wealthy man who owned the trees, Ohia had much to live upon. Then one day Ohia overheard some mice talking about having seen some gold behind Ohia's house. After finding the gold, the mice then buried it deeper into the ground. Ohia went behind his house to the spot where he saw fresh dirt, dug into the ground, and found the gold. Ohia was now a very wealthy man. Life became good for them. Ohia and Ariwehu even had a son. And so Ohia decided to take a second wife. But the second wife was very jealous. So jealous was she that whenever Ohia and Ariwehu spoke to each other the second wife would accuse them of grumbling and talking badly about her. Ohia and his first wife grew silent. Somberness rose up like trees between them, casting leaves of solitude, loneliness, and alienation. And then one day Ohia again overheard the mice talking and telling jokes. Ohia laughed. The second wife heard him, and as always, assumed he and Ariwehu were speaking and laughing about her. Ohia's second wife went to the elders of his village and pled her case that Ohia and Ariwehu were mistreating her terribly. The elder, who was also a deep friend to Ohia, asked that Ohia come forth. Ohia was caught, torn."

Sahel listened intently.

"He could lie to his new wife, let her think that he and Ariwehu had been speaking about her. Or he could tell the truth of what had happened, that he was actually laughing at what the mice had said. This would reveal the truth of his gift. And that meant death." Essien took in breath, sighed.

"You see, when Ohia followed the antelope back to the village over which leopard ruled, Ohia gained the gift of speaking to the animals. When the leopard king ordered the antelope to return to Ohia all the sap the antelope had stolen, the leopard also commanded Ohia to never tell anyone about the gift he had received, that of his ability to speak with and understand the language of the animals. Ohia was tired of the groaning and constant complaining of his second wife. She had ruined the good life that wealth had brought him. He also respected the elder of his village to whom the second wife and brought her case."

Sahel pulled at her fingers, what she always did when anxious and afraid.

Essien said, *"After giving all his wealth to Ariwehu and their son, Ohia then told the elder of having followed the antelope who had stolen the sap and of pleading his case to the leopard king that ruled antelope's village. Ohia then died."*

The story Essien shared touched Sahel on many levels. Never had her father shared with her any of the myths and wisdom from his native Ghana. She lowered her head and wept.

Born and raised in Accra, Essien Ohin had not returned home since leaving forty years earlier for America where after graduating from college, he earned a Ph.D. in economics and a J.D., though never having sat for the bar.

Essien loved teaching at the University of San Francisco. But Sahel longed to see the country from which she had inherited half her DNA. The idea and wish had caused Lillian to frown in extreme distaste, so much so that Sahel stopped mentioning it, though she had held onto the desire.

Essien said, "James has delivered you a light by which to see the truth of your life and who you are."

"You were a prisoner, chained to this house by Mama for over a decade," Sahel said. "The last five years she couldn't even leave her bed without the help of the nurse or sometimes you. I'll not put you through that again."

"Then promise not to take anymore medication like you did. Yes." Essien said. "You could have died as you had planned," Essien said. "Just as easily as you could have died, Titus and

Carl could have saved you to remain unconscious in, as they call it, a vegetative state, dependent on one of those machines to keep you alive. That I could not have stomached."

Sahel's father then said, and with greater force than she had heard in his voice for some time, "You are nothing like your mother. But you find yourself in a situation that has Carl and Titus at odds—much like when your mother's heart was failing."

Sahel recalled the endless hours she and her father spent in Carl's office listening to Titus and Carl present their cases on how to attend Lillian's bad heart. Titus had advocated surgery, which he would perform. He was desperate to save Lillian, his mother's best friend. Carl had reasoned against the procedure leaving Titus teetering upon his wits.

"Carl argued the risk of her having another stroke was too great," Essien said. "Regarding the loss of your sight, Titus and Carl have now changed roles. Carl pushes for surgery; Titus presents infinite and valid reasons against it."

"I'm afraid," Sahel said.

"So was you mother."

Sahel lifted her head and again absorbed her father's words along with all that lay between them.

"Carl Pierson, the boy, could do nothing but incite your mother's vehement anger. She despised him for his brown skin." Essien sighed as Sahel cringed at the truth he so calmly spoke, a truth that lived with Sahel as close as the air that filled her lungs through the constancy of her breathing.

"As a woman whose heart was failing and who feared death perhaps more than others, she leaned upon Carl's arguments as a neurosurgeon against the surgery Titus proposed. I was amazed at how much she and Carl held in common."

"They were nothing alike," Sahel said.

"Perhaps in looks," Essien said. Sahel considered her mother's complexion, fair as milk. "The color of our skin is but skin deep," Essien continued. "Underneath its surface an ocean of similarities and differences lurk unbeknownst to our eyes. And our thoughts."

Sahel trembled in the face of her father's observations,

interactions, and the motives driving them, both of which had escaped Sahel's awareness when sighted. Again she felt exposed.

With less frustration stirring in his voice, Essien said, "Take classes for the blind if you wish. But do it for yourself, not me or Titus." Then plainly and calmly, and betraying the accent of his native Twi, "You are the only person who finds Sahel Ohin Denning burdensome."

"I want to go back to seeing clients." Sahel released the words from her lips.

"James has truly affected you." Essien repeated the observation and comment he had made at the outset of their conversation.

Sahel considered what she had spoken, and then repeated her desire. "I want to go back to work." While the words felt distant, her desire to work with clients again lay close to her heart.

The voice that had burst through her consciousness on the night of the medical dinner now rose within and spoke. *You cannot remain in this house hiding from life and yourself.*

As if having emerged through the riptides of Sahel's thoughts, an image of the woman wearing the red cape formed on the shores of Sahel's mind.

Sahel recalled the time her spirit had left her body and she had found herself in the waters of the San Francisco Bay, swirling underneath the Golden Gate Bridge, bright orange like the sky set aflame by the western sun in its afternoon descent. The woman had flashed her palm, and said, *No. You cannot come here. It is not your time. You have much work waiting for you to complete. Important work.*

Now for the first time Sahel recalled the woman's second missive. *You must go back. People need you. You need you.*

The inner voice with which Sahel had become accustomed and that of the woman in red, sounded alike, as if one and the same.

Essien now said, "You are much like Ohia in the story. Do not let the wealth of your gift of loving deeply and with passion blind you to the abiding love that has always stood before you."

Sahel sat still upon the chair at the kitchen table.

"Titus loves you. He has always done so. And will continue

to. If only you can accept his love. Receive it for what it is."
With that Essien left.

Sahel grasped her cup of tea, still hot, but not so much as to burn her tongue.

Chapter 23

S

ahel's conversation with her father sat upon her thoughts.
Throughout the weekend she pondered the myth he had shared.

*... Beset with bad luck, they were very poor. Everything they
touched turned to ash. About to lose their clothes to simple wear
and tear, and with none to replace them, Ohia and his wife,
Ariwehu, risked having to go naked and were unable to leave
their house except to draw ridicule.*

And then, "You are much like Ohia in the story. Do not let
the wealth of your gift, your many gifts to giving and loving
deeply and passionately all whom you encounter, blind you to
the abiding love that has always stood before you ... Titus loves
you. He has always done so. And will continue to do so. If only
you will let him ..."

Sahel and Titus attended Sunday morning Mass to find as always Essien and Geraldine waiting for them. Afterwards the four returned home for brunch on the patio.

"Has anyone heard from Carl?" Sahel asked. Immediately she felt guilty for even thinking of him. If before meeting James she wondered and worried about Carl, now since her collapse and Carl's insistence that she remain in the hospital for tests, Sahel felt the need to guard her actions. She did not want to mislead Carl and fuel his desires.

Her refusal to undergo the surgery Carl so desperately urged her not to dismiss hardened the die cast in his abandonment of the Church when Sahel lost her sight. Carl was fighting with Sahel for more than her acknowledgment of his love. He truly needed her to regain her sight.

Having denied him both wishes had driven a wedge between them, one threatening to open into a wide gulf. Carl was angry and frustrated. Unlike Titus, who when not receiving his desires, responded in a biting fashion, direct and to the point, Carl channeled his disappointments into a slow-growing momentum, that like the ocean appearing calm and serene, could at any moment rise and overwhelm.

And yet, despite his obsession to have Sahel undergo the surgery, Carl's presence soothed her. After Titus, Carl came next in Sahel's short line of close friends, those with whom she felt no need to explain her feelings and actions, people who always had her back, and for whom she too would give her life.

Geraldine's arrival onto the patio interrupted Sahel's reverie. "Carl just called to say he's on his way," said Geraldine, the woman who loved her father. "The cantaloupe is on the table, fresh and juicy as you like it. Your father picked two up on the way home." Sahel imagined Geraldine smiling. She lamented James's preference in seeing her and not Geraldine.

Carl arrived for brunch. After speaking with Geraldine of James's condition, he and Geraldine joined Sahel, Titus, and Essien, eating on the patio.

Brunch edged towards an end with Titus receiving a call

from the hospital.

"I've got to go in and see a patient," he said to Sahel.

"Will it be long?" She wanted him close.

"No more than an hour," he said. "If I'm lucky." Gently he caressed her shoulders, kissed the top of her head, and whispered, "I love you," and left.

Later and back in the study with Carl, Sahel interrogated him on the matter of James not wanting to see Geraldine. "Have you asked James why he refuses to see Geraldine?" Sahel asked. "You see him every day."

"It's not my business," Carl said. He touched Sahel's arm. She was sitting on the sofa in the study, he beside her. "Blindness has made you a little sleuth," he chuckled.

"It's not funny. And I don't like being a go-between separating Geraldine from James. She's his godmother," Sahel said. She's stood by him through so much."

"His *godmother*." Carl repeated. "Not his mother. And even if she was his mother, James is an adult."

That's never stopped you from trying to influence someone, or as Titus calls it, coerce them, Sahel thought.

"Titus is your husband. He's too close to your situation to see straight."

"Funny. That's what he says of you." Sahel now laughed.

"I'm your doctor."

"You're also my friend, a very good one. But not my husband. Which puts you somewhat similar to Geraldine with regard to James."

"Touché."

Sahel imagined Carl smiling but without joy. Though not as obvious, Carl held a competitive nature as fierce as Titus's.

"I've scheduled your appointments for the tests. Monday, Tuesday, and Wednesday morning at 10," Carl said. "Geraldine has agreed to drive you to the hospital."

These were times when Titus was either in the middle of performing surgery or seeing patients.

"Thanks, but I could have asked Geraldine."

"You haven't, and neither has Titus," Carl said. "These tests are serious, Sahel."

"And where will you be when I'm having them?"

"Where I should be. Beside the tech administering them. I want to know the results ASAP."

"And what will you do on receiving them? Rush me to surgery against my will?"

"Hopefully not. I don't like dramatics. It plays well for television, but horribly in real life, particularly in the operating room."

Carl touched her hand. "I'm scared," she said.

Sahel's concern for others had left the terrain of her physical needs cracked and parched like the *sahel* of Africa, dry and desperate for water. In considering all that she had learned from James, and then what her father had shared, Sahel had concluded that as in the past, she was avoiding her own physical needs.

Sahel lowered her head.

"I know you are," Carl said. He rubbed her arm and then caressed her. Against her will she leaned upon his shoulder. "The woman who would be my sister. And I her brother," Carl whispered. "What will become of us?"

Again, Sahel recalled the words of her father telling the story of Ohia and Ohia's wife Ariwehu. "Ohia was caught, torn. He could lie to his new wife, let her think that he and Ariwehu had been speaking about her. Or he could tell the truth of what had happened, that he was actually laughing at what the mice had said. This would reveal the truth of his gift. And that meant death."

Sahel recalled the choices Ohia faced, deliberated them, then closed her eyes upon the omnipresent darkness and squeezed Carl's hand.

Monday morning, long after Titus had gone to the hospital and Essien to the university, Sahel sat upon the couch in the study, trying to understand the full meaning of all that her father's words had not said. So enveloped in trying to unravel the hidden and overt meanings of Essien's revelations was Sahel, that she did not hear when Zelda announced Geraldine's arrival.

146

Geraldine's voice startled her. "I've come to drive you to Dr. Leonard's," she said on entering the study.

"Oh, I'd forgot about my session," said Sahel. She turned her head.

Sahel had risen early that morning and dressed, in preparation to go to Berkeley General to undergo the tests Carl had ordered.

Inside Geraldine's sedan, on their way to the office behind Berkeley General where Dr. Leonard saw his patients, Sahel noted Geraldine's uncharacteristic quietness. She had been so yesterday when after their talk, Sahel and Carl had joined Geraldine out on the patio for lunch.

"I wonder how James is doing," Sahel mused.

The last few days had left little energy to think of James. Sahel had spent her weekend absorbed in trying to decipher her father's dispensation of the story of Ohia. Carl, with his anxious need to figure out what had caused Sahel to faint twice, would be waiting in the lab for her arrival to have the CAT scan.

And then there was Titus hovering in protection mode. He had, on returning from the hospital late Sunday night, declared his determination to obtain a second opinion concerning the neurosurgical procedure to return Sahel's sight. Following her session with Dr. Leonard, Sahel would begin the first battery of tests Carl had ordered.

"Carl says he's faring as well as can be expected," Geraldine said.

"You haven't seen him?" Sahel asked in an effort to ferret out whether Carl had told her of James's wishes. "Why haven't you gone to see James? This is all very difficult, but you can't give up on him."

"I will never abandon James. Although I can't say the same of him." A tinge of bitterness coated Geraldine's last words. Guilt slipped over Sahel.

In the wake of her silence, Geraldine added, "Sunetra's spirit is alive in him. If only I could find a way of banishing her, and all memories of her from his thoughts!" Geraldine lamented.

147

Sahel was certain that the voice rising within her was that of the woman she had encountered underneath the waters of the San Francisco Bay, the woman in red—Sunetra. Sahel felt the rumble of Sunetra's spirit residing within. Shame of disloyalty to Geraldine coated Sahel's insides.

"You're scheduled for tests later this morning. And I know Titus has his misgivings about your seeing James," Geraldine said. "But when will you be available to visit him?"

"I'd really like to see James," Sahel said. "But in the light of your concerns about Sunetra's spirit, perhaps I should—"

"You can divert his mind," Geraldine rushed to speak. "Make him forget her."

"Don't say that."

"For god's sake. You saved his life. I've seen him with you. You give him peace ... and perspective," Geraldine said. "James likes you. He believes in you. I saw what you did," she reiterated. "I was certain he was going to die. Carl and Titus had counted him dead. I saw their faces." Geraldine then whispered, "Sunetra was near. I felt it. And then you came in and made her go away." She lifted her voice, spoke firmly, as if without fear. "You're why James is still here. You give him hope."

"I only listen." And honor the inner voice. My inner voice.

"You do more than that," Geraldine said. "You give James what he needs. You make space for his words, his feelings. That's more than Sunetra ever offered."

A voice rose inside Sahel's head. *Listen to Geraldine. Do as she says.* The voice now spoke with what seemed different desires.

"I'd really like to see James," Sahel said again, now distrustful of the voice—that of the woman in red and embodying Sunetra's spirit. She spoke with hesitation. "Perhaps in the light of his thoughts about Sunetra, yearning for her—"

"He's not yearning for her. It's her, her spirit that's come back for him! She won't be happy until she's destroyed him. And he's dead."

"Maybe she wants to give him hope." Sahel was digging.

"There's no hope with her around."

"But she's dead," Sahel spoke against her own experience in

148

an effort to calm Geraldine. A hypocritical act, but ... "James has AIDS. He may not have long to live."

"Dead or alive. I don't want him with her," Geraldine said. "It wouldn't be fair. What sense would it make?" Geraldine shook her head. "James is a good person. Sunetra was only thinking of herself. She shot Ravesh, and throughout the trial said nothing. She let James be convicted of a crime that he didn't commit."

"Did she come to trial?" Sahel asked.

"No. Too ashamed," Geraldine said. Adding beyond the bitterness soaking her words, "She called every night asking of him."

"I'm sure she was hurting."

The car came to a halt. Sahel assumed they had approached an intersection. "You have to see him," Geraldine pleaded. Her words came directly at Sahel. "He needs you. You're his only hope. You can't sit idly by and do nothing. You'll be just like Sunetra."

"I have my session with Dr. Leonard. And I don't know how long it will take for me to undergo the tests Carl ordered," Sahel said.

"The lab for the CAT scan is right in the hospital," Geraldine said. She was adamant. "We'll go directly there when you're finished with Dr. Leonard, and the other tests can't take that long. They only require blood being drawn. James is just upstairs. He'd love to see you. Please," Geraldine begged again.

Surely it hurts you that he doesn't want to see you? The question turned itself over in Sahel's mind. She wondered. *Has Carl even told you James doesn't want to see you?* Sahel grew angry that he, most likely, had not.

Sahel entered her session with Dr. Leonard. Ninety minutes later and across the street at Berkeley General, she underwent the CAT scan. Throughout the testing Sahel heard the technician address Carl, reporting on each finding. Titus was in the operating room performing an eight-hour heart bypass. On completion she took the opportunity of Carl being paged to the emergency room to quickly leave. Geraldine then guided Sahel

149

up to James's hospital room on the fifth floor of Berkeley General.

Sahel felt strange and torn, duplicitous, about honoring Geraldine's request and her own eagerness to see James. Sahel cared for James and valued his presence in her life.

And yet Sahel had no doubt that Sunetra's spirit lived within her, Sahel's, body. Sahel's soul had merged with that of the one entity Geraldine feared was working against all efforts to keep James alive.

Sahel spent the first half hour with James, assuring him she was fine. She said nothing of the CAT scan she had undergone or the blood tests Carl had ordered.

"How is Carl following up on figuring out why you fainted?" James said. "He's not going to leave it alone."

Sahel grew uneasy. She hated not being able to see James's facial expressions and the movements of his body. "He can be pigheaded and stubborn," Sahel said.

"He loves you, too," James said of Carl.

"I was tired," Sahel said of having collapsed.

"It takes that much energy talking with me?"

Sahel loathed, grew more frustrated with her inability to see whether James was smiling or serious. "I haven't had this much going on in my life since the accident," she said.

"I don't want to add stress to your life," James said.

"You haven't," Sahel said. A momentary silence flooded the space between her and James. "For the first time since everything happened, I feel hope."

"Meeting me did that for you?"

Sahel nodded. "Getting to know you has changed me." She recalled the shrill sound of the heart monitor indicating James's heart had stopped. "And for the better," she added. Another silence rose and died.

James said, "You were the conduit, the portal that brought Sunetra back to me."

Sahel grew cold and anxious in knowing how much Geraldine hated Sunetra.

Sahel now said to James, "A voice told me to go to you."

"Sunetra," said James. "The first time I saw you, I sensed her

150

presence, that night in the Masonic Ballroom. Every time I'm with you she comes. Just like the other day when you visited. She's here now."

She had been on the brink of asking James why he did not to want Geraldine to visit him when James said, "I was gang raped and infected with HIV while in San Quentin."

The statement jarred Sahel, left her disoriented. And then her thoughts settled. The idea of James or anyone undergoing such a violation drew Sahel's ire and compassion fueled by the indignation she felt towards those who had perpetrated such a beastly crime. The experience of a woman being raped was nothing simple, could not be minimized.

That James, a man, had undergone a similar attack carried a set of injuries and emotional wounds equally as vicious and virulent, and not unlike that of women, delivering its own brand of shame. That he would probably die from the attack left James's burden nothing short of enormous.

James said, "Going through the attack obliterated all hope that I could reunite with Sunetra in anyway. Until then I had considered her death, the impossibility of seeing her again in this life, terminal imprisonment, a sentence that death would end. I would see her in another life, the next life, hopefully. That was my salvation."

"With the rape, I became ambivalent about seeing her in death," he continued. "I had no escape, and hoped that perhaps by the time I reached death she would have moved on to another life, and found someone else. I didn't want her to see me like this. Not in this life, or any other. Never. "

"You were viciously assaulted," Sahel said. "You didn't cause this." She wished to hold him, as a mother would a child, and care for him. An inexorable ache filled Sahel's chest. She touched her heart, massaged it. The pain deepened.

"You're the first person I've told. Geraldine, of course, knew that it happened. But she doesn't know the details."

Sahel's chest remained heavy with all that she imagined James was holding inside. The shame, the hurt, the ...

She let go of her cane, stood, and made her way to James's hospital bed. "Give me your hands," Sahel said. She extended her palms. James grasped them. His hands were shaking. "I want to know what happened," Sahel said. "Let me see what you went through."

Chapter 24

T

he phenomenon of experiencing what another had previously
undergone proved powerful. It lent her strength, and
underscored her fears. Sahel entered James's consciousness, his
sphere on life. Never had she held such depth of empathy. While
holding his hands, Sahel saw and experienced the prison rape as
if she were in James's body.

James had been on his knees scrubbing the floor of one of the
dingy prison bathrooms when three men—one black and two
whites, all twice his size—had approached him from behind.

"Say, what you doing, broker boy?" said the one with a
shaved head and sallow, pimpled face. The sleeves of his orange
jumpsuit, rolled back, revealed swastikas tattooed on his
muscled arms.

The smallest of the three led the other two, also donning orange, in surrounding James, who continued scrubbing the cement floor, plastic yellow gloves covering his hands, and ammonia burning his eyes.

The young skinhead bent over and leaned towards James. "I need some money."

With the green sponge in his right hand, and propping himself up with the left, James continued his task. "I don't have any," he finally said when they remained.

"Well, that's a shame. 'Cause I'm told you used to handle money."

The swastika-tattooed leader of the three leaned back, and with hands to his waist, let out a loud laugh. "Imagine that, a nigger sellin' stocks and bonds."

The other two chimed in with their laughter. Slowly James lifted his head and met the eyes of the black man. The man's foot came down on James's left hand. James fell from his knees and gripped his hand. But for the yellow glove, the palm and fingers of his left hand would have shattered.

Again James raised his head and this time glimpsed the face of the third man. His straight sandy hair matched the cold and piercing look of his eyes.

The black guy, next to him, shorter, and with thick eyebrows, was bald.

The tattooed guy took James's left arm. "Get his other," he ordered the bald Tookie. The sandy-haired quiet one lifted James's feet.

James kicked and tugged, almost freeing himself and nearly hitting Tookie's jaw. The swastika-covered guy punched James in the jaw.

James's body hit the floor. "Whatcha' gon' do, King?" Tookie said to the Aryan neo-Nazi. He and the quiet white guy held James to the stone floor.

"Since I can't get no money, I'm gonna' fuck his brains out. Then he'll know his place."

"Better yet, forget where it is you come from." King flashed a knife and cut open James's orange pants.

James glanced back and glimpsed King unzipping his pants.

154

An erect penis, crimson and ready to manifest the assault, appeared.

"No," James screamed, while tugging and kicking to free himself.

"He's a feisty one," said King.

"Let go of me! I haven't done anything to you!"

"You will now." King grinned.

James's spirit quaked.

King lowered himself upon his knees, and spread his legs over James, flailing ever more violently.

The two others grasped James's arms and held him down. His cheek and stomach lay flat against the cement floor. James broke away, turned over and tried kicking King in his crotch.

"Did you see that," said King. He turned to Tookie and the other white inmate, then to James, "I'm gon' have to break you boy."

King knelt upon James. His eyes grew large. He came into James. Unable to move, James's soul fell still, grew rigid.

Against the burning smell of ammonia filling his eyes and nose, James began to cry. A dull groan escaped his lips, his world sinking, life as he had known it abandoning him.

With each push of King's groin into him, James felt eternity with all its hope of renewal and resurrection slip away. He closed his eyes.

And then she appeared, drew near him, Sunetra. "I'm so sorry." She mouthed the words.

James imagined himself reaching out, but unable to grasp what he so wished to hold.

Each thrust of King's forced entries penetrating his anus pushed James's spirit, bit by bit, into his stomach, then up his esophagus, and with his every breath taken and released, from his nose and mouth. James's vision had blurred, but not from tears, rather from the loss of connection with his body, and the power that lay inside it.

He began to shake, his body vacillating between numbing chills, and hot, searing anger. He lay upon the cold, gray cement of the floor, his brown body naked, and his eyes fixed upon the corner where the walls opposite him met.

A torrential headache overtook Sahel. She tightened her grasp of James's hand. All went black. The experience ended. "You're bleeding," James said. With his finger he wiped her nose. "There. It's gone."

Sahel stepped back. Unsure of what was happening, where she was, or whether she had exited the experience she searched for. She lifted her cane. Unfolding it, she then found her purse.

"Are you all right?" James called to her. His voice sounded far away, as if he were in a tunnel.

Still in the throes of the experience, Sahel found her way to the door.

During the drive home, Sahel said nothing to Geraldine of what James had shared or allowed Sahel to see and experience. She also mentioned nothing of having bled from her nose.

Sahel had been sitting upon the couch later that afternoon, and with Geraldine gone, when Zelda announced Carl's arrival.

"I have the results of your tests," Carl said, sitting next to Sahel. "They're all negative, except for a small shadow on the CAT scan." He lifted her hand.

"What is it?" Sahel asked. She said nothing of having visited James or of her nosebleed when holding his hand in the whirlwind of disorientation that arose as her consciousness merged with James's and she experienced his sexual assault.

"I don't know. I want to repeat the CAT scan in a week." Carl held an uncomfortable curiosity about the shadow that had appeared on the CAT scan. Worry filled his voice. "Of course if we did the surgery, then—"

"No." Sahel flashed her palm.

Titus's warning of Carl played through her head. "He's being hasty. I want a second opinion."

And then there was what her father, Essien, had advised. "Titus is your husband, not Carl. And you are like Ohia, who received a great gift. Take care that you do not grab for too

156

much and lose all."

For the first time Sahel wondered about her mother's spirit, where it now dwelled. Or was she in the beyond? Sahel said to Carl, "I married Titus."

"As long as you're blind, you're tied to him," Carl said.

"You think I'll leave him on regaining my sight?"

"Titus is afraid you will," Carl said. "He's imprisoned you."

"That's not true."

"That you'll leave him? Or his fears of you doing so?"

"Both," said Sahel.

"Then prove it. Have the surgery."

"I won't put him through that again," Sahel said. "Nor you."

"You're dying now. Each day without sight robs you of your job. We lost you once," Carl said. "You died. I watched it. The heart monitor flatlined. You need your sight back."

"No! It's not fair to Titus or Daddy. I won't!"

"When are you going to start thinking about yourself, Sahel? All your life you've seen to everyone and their needs and ignored your own. Your mother, your father, now Titus."

"My father?" Sahel was incredulous. "How does he play into this?"

"He never stood up to your mother. He's a nice man, but he let you down, Sahel. Your mother was horrible to you."

"Mama gave him plenty to deal with."

"Your father's a grown man. He should have stood up to her."

"You're talking about something you have no understanding of."

"I know when a person needs tending." Carl lifted her wrist. Sahel pulled away. Memories of James's rape arose vibrant and fresh: James's cheek pressed against the cold, grey cement floor, yellow plastic gloves still upon James's hands, sweaty and perspiring, the green sponge with which he had been scrubbing lying beside the bucket of water. The sharp smell of ammonia crawled up Sahel's nose. "Titus has put you in a cage, like your mother did, made you his pet. Again your father's standing by. And doing nothing."

"I'm not his or anyone's prisoner. You sound like Mama,"

said Sahel. "I love Titus."

"You're bound to Titus in the same sick way that James was and still is attached to Sunetra." Carl's words shook Sahel completely free of her memories of James's attack.

Sahel turned to Carl's voice. "How would you know about Sunetra?" she said.

"James loved Sunetra," Carl said. "Geraldine told me all about her."

"And *she* loved him," Sahel said.

"Then why did she let him be convicted for a crime she committed? Her suicide was an admission of guilt." Carl went on. "It's just like you, and Titus. Titus hits you with the car, and you let him off."

"It was an accident. Pure and simple. I've forgiven him."

"That's what James said of Sunetra shooting her father, that Sunetra mistook Ravesh for a burglar having broken into the offices of the brokerage. He ended up in federal prison. And with AIDS. Shooting her father was Sunetra's way of getting back at him for putting James in charge of the company. It was three months before Sunetra and James were to marry."

"You think this is some kind of game I'm playing with Titus? That we're playing house in the wake of having lost my sight. In case your other patients haven't told you, blindness is no fun." Fury rose in Sahel's throat. "It's horrible, painful, shameful. At times I don't know how I'm going to survive. I wish it had never happened." Her voice slowed, the painful truth of her admission threatening to engulf her.

"My other patients have told me. And they all would give their right arm for any possibility to regain their sight," said Carl.

"I get angry at times. It's hard," Sahel continued. "I can't imagine what purpose my being like this could or would serve me or anyone. That doesn't change the fact that Titus didn't see me on the pavement. There was no way he could have. If he had, he wouldn't have hit me. I know that."

"You're spending too much time with James," Carl said.

"Geraldine doesn't think so. Despite everything I say, she's convinced I saved his life."

158

"Geraldine is not your friend," Carl said.

"Am I crazy, or did you just repeat her accusations of Sunetra?" Sahel frowned.

"She's using you," said Carl. "James has refused to see her. She wants you to find out what's going on in James's mind."

"Why would you say something like that? If anyone has championed your cause, it's been Geraldine."

"As I'm trying to do with you."

"You're absurd."

"She'll turn on you, Geraldine, when she learns the truth of what's really going on between you and James," Carl said.

"And just what is that?"

"You're bringing her to him." Carl's words seared their presence in Sahel's mind. "You're serving as a medium for Sunetra to come to James."

"Sunetra's dead." Sahel turned from Carl.

"But her spirit lives in you." Sahel whipped her head back towards Carl. "It's true," he said. "And she's using you to help him die."

"And if you know so much, then why haven't you told Geraldine?" Sahel asked.

"I do what I feel is best for my patients."

"So you think it's best that James dies?" Sahel said perplexed.

"James is not good for you. And neither is Sunetra."

"She's dead," Sahel repeated of Sunetra. "And so is your mother. The question is, in whose memory?" Sahel asked.

"It's not so much what we remember, but what we let into our bodies, our hearts and souls." Carl spoke like a theologian, or a philosopher. "You never knew Sunetra."

"But you knew Mama," Sahel said. *Perhaps too well.*

"He's an impediment," Carl said of James.

"You want him to die." Sahel was aghast.

"The more time you spend with him, the less you can focus on what's important to you. Your sight."

"I'm trying to give James the peace he needs in these last few weeks or months, whatever time he has."

"Geraldine trusts you."

"So what are you saying?" Sahel shook her head in aggravation and bewilderment. "James has taken nothing from me." Sahel considered her ability to see images, how it had returned moments before meeting James. Much of what she envisioned related to James. "I'm seeing more now than I ever have."

"I want you to step out of this. Let James go. Give him space ... to die."

"You're ridiculous!"

Carl spoke softly. "We all have the ability to delude ourselves when we're afraid of being denied what we truly want."

Again Sahel shook her head against a rising tide of anger towards what she saw as Carl's hypocrisy.

"I want your sight back," Carl said.

"It's not yours to have. You need to find someone to love," Sahel said.

"I already have."

"You're jealous of James, of what he tasted with Sunetra."

"Now that is truly sick. Sunetra destroyed his life."

"Sunetra loved James," Sahel said. "And she still does."

Moments passed. Carl then said, "I suppose in time you'll do as you want, put me at a distance, stop speaking to me, same as James has done with Geraldine."

Sahel sensed her words had stunned Carl. "Why would I do that? For your information, I feel James is being unfair to Geraldine. Neither do I like misleading her.'"

"Then stop visiting him. Get out of the triangle between him, Sunetra's spirit, and Geraldine."

"I can't."

"Geraldine has remained loyal to James when everyone else abandoned him," Carl said.

"And whose side are you on?" asked Sahel. Carl sounded as ambivalent and torn as Sahel herself felt.

"There's more to this story than meets the eye," said Carl.

Sahel turned to Carl's voice. "And of me and you?" she said.

"I love you and would do anything to have your eyes meeting and seeing into mine."

160

"I'm seeing more now than I ever have," said Sahel and then added, "Geraldine has got to come to understand that there are things between James and Sunetra to which she was not privy."

"So there are things about the accident I don't know, that you haven't told me?"

"You weren't there."

"No, I wasn't. But I know that Titus is a hothead who's easily angered. His temper is like a stick of dynamite with a short fuse."

Sahel frowned in disgust.

"Titus's patients may think he's God because he keeps their hearts beating. But at what price? It's cost you dearly," Carl said.

"And what do you know of yourself, that your patients think you're some deity? You're just as guilty as Titus of having the God syndrome."

"At least I never started believing them."

"I think I need to have a second opinion." Sahel stood. Again Carl grasped her wrist. "Is that what you want, or what Titus demanded?"

"I want it. But just as you know, he suggested it. Now let go of me." Slivers of James's prison assault flashed across Sahel's memory.

Waves of terror and rage pulsed and rippled through her body. She grew cold.

Carl released her. "There's nothing more to say here. I think you'd better leave," Sahel said.

Moments later and against the echo of the door closing, Sahel clutched her shoulders. The smell of ammonia still clung within her nose.

Chapter 25

A n excruciating pain had torn through Sahel's head on the advent of receiving the vision of James's being raped. The ache, like that of a limb being abruptly severed, returned when Sahel let go of holding James. Once more she felt dizzy to the point of almost fainting.

Sahel was committed to helping him. She hated the slow approach of death creeping over James and what life remained in him.

Exactly what she or he could accomplish through their friendship and dialogue had remained vague at best. James was hurting.

Sahel's presence assuaged his pain, provided him strength and hope of a better future. Like the images Sahel had now begun to receive, his presence had sowed seeds, offering a glimmer of light emerging within and illuminating the end of a dark tunnel.

Sahel determined to maintain a clear distance between herself and Carl.

James's entry into Sahel's life had at the very least unleashed an ability to communicate with those living on other levels of life.

Through holding James's hands, Sahel had entered James's thought space and experienced the images punctuated with the smells and sounds of his memory.

It was a powerful talent, one that, during the ensuing days, had put Sahel at ease and peace with her vulnerabilities, not simply as a person without physical sight, rather as an individual who wanted to love and to be loved.

Sahel's lack of sight had opened portals leading to a source of connection with others, a wellspring that provided a sense of purpose bathed in compassion. It also bestowed an awareness of the need for boundaries.

Essien's words about Ohia and his wife, Ariwehu, rose and died once more within the folds of Sahel's thoughts. *Ohia and his first wife grew silent. Somberness rose up like trees between them, casting leaves of solitude, loneliness, and alienation.*

Unlike during the minutes before the accident, when Titus had been closing in with his urgency to set a date for the wedding, Sahel now needed space to clarify how she would live with her blindness, find meaning, and make her life purposeful again with Titus. Holding the surgery as a viable option to regaining her sight distracted her from moving forward.

Sahel went back to see James the next day. Saying nothing to Titus or Carl of her headache, she told James of her difficult conversation with Carl the previous afternoon. "I don't want the surgery," Sahel said. "But I can't keep living like this. I'm holding Titus hostage."

"Has he told you this?" James asked.

"I hear it in his voice. He's in pain."

"Are you certain it's due to your blindness from the accident?"

"What else could it be?" Sahel said. Her mind cleared of

thoughts. Emotions flooded in, those she had experienced after having taken the pills and then temporarily abandoning her body and life. "It pained him when I died. The torture on his face cut at my heart." Sahel wondered about Sunetra's sense of betrayal that led to her anger, and the heaviness that arose in having shot and killed her father ultimately subsuming Sunetra's guilt of her abandoning James. Throughout the trial, he had sat quietly and blamelessly and accepted all responsibility for Ravesh's death.

"Guilt and shame drove me back to my body," Sahel said. "I couldn't have it on my conscience that I left him. Not in that way." Sahel then recalled, "Sunetra told me, 'No, go back. This is not your time.'"

"Where did you see her?" James's voice held eagerness. An energy of hope seized her, and, she sensed, James as well.

"We were under the ocean," Sahel said. "I didn't understand it when first recalling the whole experience. But now I know why. Sunetra jumped from the Golden Gate at the same time that the pills took effect." In James's silence Sahel described having died and then awakened underwater. "I lost consciousness when we arrived at the hospital. It was like I knew that Titus and Carl were going to do everything they could to save me. But I wanted to die. I was on the ocean's floor when I spied her in the distance. She was standing there as if she had been waiting for me. She wore a red caftan. And there was this red dot on her forehead."

"A bindi," James said.

"I drew closer, wanting to see her face. She was lovely, her words stern. She held up her palm. She told me I had to go back. I felt this force," Sahel explained, "as if she was holding me back. 'You don't want to do this,' she said. I couldn't go any farther. I wanted to stay there with her. She seemed so peaceful. I could see. I had my sight back. Oh." Sahel grasped her arms.

The pain of having to relinquish her ability to see that she had temporarily experienced with Sunetra seized her. *Now as then.* Again she considered all that she had witnessed the previous day when holding James's hands, channeling, and experiencing his rape at San Quentin.

"I did as Sunetra commanded. I had no choice," Sahel said. "I went back."

"The energy floating about her would not let me stay," she explained. "Then all at once I was back hovering near the ceiling. This time I was in the emergency room suite where Titus and Carl were working to save me." Tears scratched at Sahel's throat.

"The heart monitor had stopped beating. A flatline stretched across the screen. I saw Titus's face. He was terrified. Disbelief and abandonment filled his eyes. I was dead. I went cold with the pain I knew he was feeling, that I had caused." Sahel inhaled long and deep.

"I felt so sorry for what I had done. I understood Sunetra had sent me back, forbidden me to cross over, exit this life."

Sahel sobbed her way through the next few moments. She then said, "Part of me wanted to keep my sight, stay out of the body, remain dead. I had to make a decision. I couldn't stay in that place of limbo. I thought of the nuns at Oakland Catholic Prep, and what they said of purgatory. That it was only a stopping point before the final transition—death. A place where our soul could still be saved. Sunetra had given me the chance to save myself. I could go back. I didn't want to leave Titus hanging out there alone and my having died like that. I'm so thankful Sunetra told me, 'No.'" Sahel's voice trembled. "She chose for me, helped me avoid her mistake." Sahel lowered her face into her hands and this time, barely audible, sobbed again.

Moments later James broke the silence that had risen like a wall between them. "You say it as if you were weak for having come back."

She lifted her head to his words.

"It took strength to do what you did. Living is hard, enduring even more so."

Sahel nodded in agreement.

"What did she look like?" James asked of Sunetra. "Can you describe her face?"

Sahel wanted to give more than words provided. As on the previous day she extended her hand to James. He grasped it. She gave him her other hand. Sahel closed her eyes.

The image of Sunetra as Sahel remembered came before her.

The energy that had surrounded Sunetra, and had prevented Sahel from entering death, accumulated once more. The force of Sunetra's spirit and soul, what had made her alive and now existed beyond the death of her body, flowed from Sahel, serving as a conduit, into James. Once more at peace in mind and body, he sent his love and compassion, and forgiveness mixed with mercy and grace, through Sahel back to Sunetra.

A vessel through which two lovers, one alive, the other dead to this world, connected. Sahel also provided strength to James, the one left behind on earth, to greet his inevitable transition edging closer with every moment.

Sahel's ambivalence about what she was doing increased, crept alongside James's willingness and eagerness to surrender to death.

The heavy ache that had seeped into Sahel's head returned, intensified, and spread to her neck and shoulders.

The surge of life, Sunetra's spirit and soul, James's love and devotion, flowing between James and Sunetra with Sahel as the medium, increased. Sahel's body grew warm and then hot, as if every nerve was aflame. Her hands trembled to the point of her fingertips sizzling. Her temples pulsed as if about to explode. She would not let go of James.

Barely conscious, she wondered about James, how his body was managing the burst of energy settling and now igniting her corpus.

"I need you. I'm so lonely," he whispered.

Sahel knew him to be speaking to Sunetra. The full brunt of Sunetra's love for James, the completeness of her soul, entered Sahel. Bright and blinding light burst onto the dark canvas of Sahel's consciousness. Sparks of peace and purpose spread throughout her body nearly obliterating all awareness of her own existence.

Beneficence.

Grace.

Mercy.

The ubiquitous Omnipotence of God washed over Sahel's complete being and drenched her soul.

Relinquishing James's palms, Sahel's hands dropped to her sides.

Unable to move, she momentarily held his brown face, emaciated, somber, and like that of Titus when trying to save Sahel, ravaged with the pain of loss and separation. "I love you," said Sahel, Sunetra moving through her, and she speaking for Sunetra. With arms outstretched, Sahel leaned forward and embraced James.

Her body ached to have James lift and enter her. But he was too weak. And so she held him, Sahel's body working in the service of Sunetra. She kissed his face, felt the softness of his cheek next to hers tingling with the energy of the transmission across the abyss of death, an ocean and vicissitude of emotions rumbling beneath the bridge of their hearts and souls.

The pressure within Sahel's head increased. The weight of the responsibility she felt, and the desire to be of service, mounted to a point of excruciating pain. James and Sunetra's world had become Sahel's, she embodying theirs.

Sahel's corpus contained the spirits and souls of three lives, James's, Sunetra's, and her own. Sahel wanted to give way and allow Sunetra to take over. Perhaps as with James the previous day, she would regain her sight.

The hope that she might regain her sight proved powerful, and seductive, liberating. Sahel cherished her gift of internal sight and was trying with all her might to use it wisely. To expunge Sunetra would completely return Sahel to total blindness, unable to conjure any of the images she had recently experienced.

James felt warm in her arms. Self-awareness receded into Sunetra's desire to be with James. Ambivalence wormed its way once more into Sahel's thoughts. What would Titus say? How would Titus cope, make sense of Sahel's death should she give way to Sunetra? What might Carl think?

James's lips curved into a smile, like that of a little boy. "Don't leave me," he said. Sahel knew him to be seeing Sunetra, not her.

"Sunetra," he said.

She gazed upon James lying in her arms.

"I'm here to stay," Sahel whispered. She settled into her new role as medium, and liked her newly found gift. Again Sahel offered the vessel of her body to facilitate others in gaining what they needed to evolve.

Ringing filled Sahel's ears. The pounding in her head climbed to a crescendo. Reaching up, she pressed her left temple.

Sahel felt herself falling. And James with her.

Red showered upon her. She opened and closed her eyes in an effort to regain focus, to lose the red and see clearly.

"James," she called out, but could not hear him. The piercing sound of what seemed an oncoming train grew louder. The surrounding mist of redness thickened. All strength and will diminished within Sahel.

A loud and dense silence descended.

Last vestiges of pain dissolved.

The sea of red faded into black.

Chapter 26

S

ahel awoke gasping for breath, and flailing her arms against water she could not escape. "Stop the testing," a voice in the background ordered. Someone grasped her hands and brought them to her sides. Sahel was lying down.

"Calm down. It's me," Carl said. "Everything's fine. You're safe."

A light pierced the murky blue-gray waters surrounding her.

Feeling as if her lungs were about to explode, Sahel stormed her head through the surface of the misty waters, and fought to breathe. "Take a few deep breaths. Easy, now," the voice emerged from the light.

Her panicked breathing slowed. She opened her eyes to darkness.

"Not so fast," Carl said as she moved to sit up. He caught her shoulders.

Sahel lay back upon the bed. "My head," she said and

reached up for her temple.

Carl intercepted her hand and brought it back to her side.

"Where's James?" she asked. "I have to find him." Again she moved to sit up. "Oh, my god, what happened? I was with James, and then ..."

"You collapsed," Carl said.

"Where am I now?"

"In a hospital bed. I don't want you moving until—" Again Carl helped her to lie back.

"How did I get here?"

She heard the scraping of a chair's legs against the floor. Carl said, "The nurse in charge of James called and said you had fainted. You were bleeding from your nose. We did a CAT scan." Carl took her hand. "Blood is seeping from the clot behind your eyes."

"No. Not again. I told you, don't want the surger—" Sahel moaned and frowned.

"We need to go in and drain the fistula, relieve the pressure that's building behind you eyes. If we don't get in there and get it—"

She turned her head upon the pillow from Carl's voice.

"I need to get inside your head," Carl said. "This is more than about your sight. You have an aneurysm."

She whipped her head back towards Carl's voice and said, "Have you told Titus?"

"He was in surgery when everything happened."

Just then the door opened. "I came as soon as I heard," Titus spoke, his voice drawing near with each word.

"I called the OR. They said you were in the middle of your case,"

Carl said to Titus. "Sahel was fine once we stopped the bleeding."

"The bleeding?" Titus said. Sahel heard restrained anger and frustration in his voice.

Titus lifted Sahel's hand and brushed her forehead. "How are you feeling?"

"My head hurts, feels like it's going to explode," groaned Sahel, now touching her temple.

172

"We found a fistula, an aneurysm," said Carl. "It's behind her eyes and encompassing the optic nerve. This is why she's been fainting, what's causing these headaches. Her nose was bleeding this time."

Despite her intense headache, Sahel could feel the fear building inside Titus.

"I told you no surgery," Sahel said. She turned her head upon the pillow towards Carl's voice.

"Not so fast, Sahel," Titus said.

"But I—" She whipped her head upon the pillow back to Titus.

The energy of the moment resembled the first hours after the accident when all three had hoped the blindness might be temporary.

Memories of having channeled Sunetra's spirit and soul to James, and his love for Sunetra, returned.

"Listen to Carl," Titus now urged. "There's more at stake here than regaining your sight."

"It's a time bomb," Carl spoke in low voice of resignation. "The surgery is no longer an option. It's a must."

"If I had less than a fifty percent chance of survival before this, what must it be now?" Sahel insisted.

"Without it, you'll surely die," said Titus.

"And what are my chances of making it through the surgery?" Sahel said. She turned to Titus's voice, and then in wake of his silence, back to Carl.

"Thirty percent," Carl said.

A groan of fear and pain now slipped from Sahel's lips. Titus lifted her right hand, Carl her left. She began to weep. "You're not alone," Carl said. "We'll see you through this."

Titus kissed the back of her hand.

Her fears of dying melted into the warmth of the possibility of joining James and Sunetra in the beyond.

Why was life so frightening? Sahel chided within. She extended her hand towards Titus now sitting on the left side of the bed.

Titus grasped her palm, placed it between both of his. Sahel calmed within.

173

The dull ache of despair pierced Sahel when considering life without Titus. For a moment she envied James for his connection to Sunetra.

But who would serve as Sahel's conduit to Titus should she die? Better yet, how would Titus cross over? The unfairness of so purposeful a life as Titus Denning's cut short hit her like a riptide.

Again Sahel fought the waters of emotions threatening to pull her under. Cresting above the surface, she acknowledged that she did not wish either herself or Titus dead. It was absurd, like her attempt at taking her own life. And yet ...

"We need to do the surgery as soon as possible," Carl said.

"How long do I have?" Sahel gathered her emotions.

"What do you mean?" Titus said.

"How long before the fistula ruptures?" Sahel said.

"I don't know." Strain knitted Carl's words, aiming to widen the truth and reality of the situation and yet also revealing his limitations. "Six months, a year. It could be a week. Or a day."

"I want a second opinion," Sahel said.

"Sahel, please," Titus intervened. "Carl has no reason to lie."

"We're all too close to this." Sahel shook her head. "I need someone outside the circle to weigh in."

"And when you've heard what they have to say, what will you do then?" Titus demanded.

"I don't know. But I at least want to hear what they have to say."

"That's a good idea," Carl agreed.

"Please," Titus said. Growing desperation floated within his tone. Sahel felt hope ebbing out to sea, her old demons, ambivalence and doubt, riding the waves of the incoming tide and aiming to fill the void.

"Sahel is right." Carl reiterated Sahel's point. "We're all very close to the matter. Too close. I'd feel better if Sahel heard what someone else had to say."

"Can you refer me to someone?" Sahel asked.

"I can do better than that," Carl said. "I'm going to call some of my colleagues and ask who they think I should speak with and refer you to. I need to be out of this. I just want you alive."

Titus sighed. Sahel slid her hand from between Titus's and sandwiched his palm between hers.

"We'll get through this," Carl said in a low reverent voice. Last remnants of the bitter words that but days earlier had separated them now dissolved. Softly he patted her shoulder.

Once more Sahel felt at home in the darkness from which she had just eight months ago, had sought escape.

Chapter 27

E
xcept for Titus's intermittent sighs, the drive home was silent. In the passenger's seat, Sahel wished to see his face. Unable to do so, she fell hostage to memories of him working tirelessly to bring her body back to life. Slowly she began to cry.

The car slowed to a halt. An intersection, Sahel surmised. She imagined the traffic light blaring red. Titus's hand gently landed on her lap. He lifted her hand. Sahel squeezed tight his palm in an effort to calm its trembling. Titus's palm remained on Sahel's lap when, moments later, they moved off. On reaching home, the trembling had quelled.

During dinner, Titus told Essien of Sahel's third collapse, the results of the CAT scan, and then explained the nature and problem of Sahel's aneurysm. "Surgery is no longer a choice or option. She can't ignore this."

"Well, then she must have it," Essien said with what Sahel felt was a little too much eagerness.

"I'm sitting right here," she retorted. "I may be blind, but I can hear everything you're—"

"For heaven's sakes," Titus retorted. "This is serious, Sahel."

"You think I don't know that? It's my life we're talking about."

"You don't act like it. The past few days, all you've done is spend time with that ex-felon."

"James was wrongfully convicted. The D.A. found him innocent. The judge released him."

"Well, it wasn't soon enough to prevent him from getting HIV while he was in jail," Titus said.

"He was attacked. How can you say such a thing? Or don't you believe Geraldine?" Sahel said.

"I'm saying that I don't want him around you. You're getting ready to have surgery."

"It's not like he's going to be in the operating room assisting Carl or the surgeon."

"I thought you said you wanted a second opinion," Titus said with anger and frustration rising in his voice.

Sahel grew anxious with her father's silence. She turned towards Essien.

"He's not in this," Titus bellowed. "This is between you and me, not your father."

"You can't be serious," Sahel pleaded to Essien. "Don't tell me that you agree with him about James?"

"Titus is right."

"This is ludicrous! So immature," Sahel moved to stand.

"James is a good man, I'm sure. But it seems there is little we can do to save him. You, on the other hand, are my daughter. I don't want to lose you," Essien said.

Sahel considered the pain that had filled her father's voice outside the emergency room suite when Titus and Carl had been inside working to save her.

"She's my daughter. Those were my pills she took," Essien had said to Ana Desai, who had come outside where Essien and Geraldine stood.

"Titus and Carl are doing everything they can," Ana tried consoling.

"But they're her family," Essien had said. "They're too close.
"Shouldn't you be in there with them to keep them clear? They both love her."

"She's in good hands," Ana had said.

Sahel now reached out for her father sitting between her and Titus. Essien grasped her hand. He said, "The only thing Titus and I care about is you. And if James is the friend I think he is, he will understand."

Sahel recalled the surge of energy that had flowed from Sunetra to James through her. What had been an extreme headache grew more intense, her body warming to the point of feeling as if every nerve and ganglion connecting her brain and muscles was on fire. With each droplet of blood that fell from her nose, Sahel had felt her life regaining meaning, her living resuming purpose. Sahel's journey on earth veered upon a different course in the moment of affirming and transmitting Sunetra's presence to James.

Sahel's blindness had not proved an impediment. Rather it served as an agent of change, a transformation fueling her to search inward, recognizing what physical sight had overlooked, never noticed.

Now seated at the kitchen table with her father and Titus, she said, "I don't want to die."

"We don't want that either," Essien said. "Perhaps your mother would not have died had she undergone the surgery that Titus said she needed." Titus's silence left Sahel anxious. "Then perhaps she would have died during the surgery as I feared." Essien waxed and waned much like Sahel silently did, most recently and particularly concerning her surgery. "I don't know. But I can't take that risk now. I won't do that again," Essien said.

Then, as now, the risks were great, Sahel mused. Here I am back where I started. Afraid once more.

"I loved your mother," Essien said. He explained. "The thought of losing her dominated my every thought and action. Despite all she had done to you and me, her difficult way, the thought of not having her alive terrified me. I suppose I needed someone to argue with and criticize me, rather than be alone."

179

That's sick, Sahel thought. "Mama hated us," she said.

Her father chuckled. "I sometimes wonder if that is not what draws me to Geraldine. Like your mother, she is strong and determined."

"I have some patient charts to dictate," Titus said. His words were raw and brittle. The sound of his chair scraping against the floor resounded. Water running from the faucet followed, he rinsing his plate. He was in that place again, where his emotions held so tight a rein that they prevented any words from passing across his tongue.

Sahel's heart ached. She wished to hold and kiss him, say she was sorry for the argument and accident that followed, and now for the aneurysm requiring surgery.

Sahel wanted to reach out and grab Titus, hold him tight, and tell him of what she had experienced with James, that in the moment of linking James to Sunetra she had felt so close to Titus. Sahel realized the depth of her love for Titus when helping connect James to Sunetra.

The door to the dishwasher closed. Essien lifted her hand. Titus had left the kitchen. Sahel considered James lying in his hospital bed, unable and refusing to share with Geraldine his longing to see Sunetra, and join her. "Thank you," Sahel said. She rubbed the back of her father's palm.

Chapter 28

S

ahel awoke the next morning to an excruciating headache and
extreme dizziness. On Titus calling him, Carl re-admitted Sahel
to Berkeley General. During the late afternoon she received a
second opinion on the aneurysm.

She now lay in a hospital bed. Moments earlier Titus had
held her hand.

Presently, fifty-eight-year-old neurosurgeon, Aaron Blake,
spoke to Sahel. "I've also spoken to my partners and colleagues
more experienced than I, and whom I respect, shown them the
results of the CAT scan," said the surgeon who was twenty-
three years Carl's senior. "This last bout of dizziness and near
collapse shows there's no doubt about what Carl says. You need
the surgery, Mrs. Denning."

Sahel wished to have seen Blake's face.

The neurosurgeon continued. "No one with whom I consulted said to avoid the surgery. Nor did they believe you could remain alive without it. The stakes are high."

Blake explained. "Every moment of the procedure will be tedious, every incision and movement requiring accuracy and precision. There is little, if any, room for error." A thirty percent chance existed that Sahel could die. "And yet avoiding it means certain death."

"I'm concerned for my family," Sahel said. She trusted the elder Aaron Blake, a friend and former schoolmate of Calvin Bennett, the senior partner of cardiac surgery group with whom Titus worked.

"Carl told me that he's known you since childhood," said Dr. Blake.

"Yes." Sahel then said, "Carl, myself, and my husband, Titus, have been friends since childhood. This has all been really difficult." Sahel sighed. "I'd be lying if I didn't say I'm scared."

"I'd worry about your state of mind if you held no anxieties. The risk of complications is significant, more than any of us like. This is a major concern for all patients facing this type of surgery. Your concern tells me that you realize the possibility of not surviving the procedure."

Sahel brought her hands together. "Carl also said that I might end up brain dead."

"That is a possibility as well." Blake then said, "But notice I am not using the word certain when speaking of the risks. Possibility is a long way from certain death, which is the case if you do not have it." Blake's explanation washed through Sahel and took on meaning, reflecting an aspect she had not considered. Certain death.

"With the surgery I have the chance to put things in order. Without it I am behaving recklessly and uncaring," Sahel said. It was like when she had taken the pills, acting upon only her wishes. "To avoid the surgery would be a slow suicide."

"You have said it better than I." Blake's voice sounded relieved.

He had accomplished his task.

"Thank you," Sahel said. She unclasped her hands, and

extended her hand into the darkness towards Blake. "I'm going to have the surgery."

The door to her hospital room opened. Footsteps followed, after which Titus hugged her. Essien lifted Sahel's hand and kissed the back of her palm. "Thank god," Carl said in relief. Softly Titus squeezed Sahel's right shoulder. Reaching across her chest and grasping his hand, she turned to Carl's voice and said, "When can you do it, the surgery?"

"That depends on what date you and Dr. Blake choose." Carl lifted Sahel's left hand.

"There's another aspect to your treatment about which your husband and I firmly concur," said Blake. "I may have the knowledge. But Dr. Pierson's hands are young and steady. I would like him to assist me. This procedure is long and tedious. Then again, you are the patient," Blake said to Sahel.

He added, "I can give you a list of very good neurosurgeons, ones I would have perform this procedure if I or anyone in my family needed to undergo this type of surgery. Dr. Pierson is at the top of that list. But as I said, you are the patie—"

Sahel let go of Titus's hand and reached out for Carl. He embraced her. Tears slid onto her face. "You're going to be okay," Carl whispered. "I promise. I promise."

"Please don't let me die. Please don't," she whispered.

"No. Never," Carl spoke, barely audible, into her ear.

Ashamed of her indecision, Sahel couldn't believe her words.

Eight months ago she had wanted to die. Now she wanted to live, and prevent Titus any further pain life might throw upon him due to her ambivalence. Sahel buried her head into Carl's shoulder and whimpered.

Titus rubbed the small of her back.

Moments later with Carl and Aaron Blake gone, Sahel brought Titus's palm, no longer trembling, to her lips and kissed it.

Autumn

•.•.•.•.•

Chapter 29

T

he evening before her surgery, Sahel visited James.

"So you're going to do it," James said after a few moments of exchanging pleasantries, much of which consisted of Sahel querying James about his condition.

"Yes. I can't wait any longer," she said of the aneurysm.

"Life has pushed you to not only accept Titus's love, but to physically see him, witness him loving you," James said.

His adept response put Sahel to thinking. "You think I've been avoiding the surgery because I don't want to see Titus?"

"It's hard for you to regain your sight and remain Titus's wife, the person he loves. Just a hunch."

Sahel grew angry. "And how often do you have hunches like this?"

"The last time was the afternoon I received the jury's verdict," James said. "Minutes before going into the courtroom,

I asked Aunt Geraldine about Sunetra." Though Geraldine was his godmother, James often referred to her as his aunt. "Sunetra usually called her every other night during the trial, maybe every third. She might have called more if Geraldine had been more welcoming. I thought Geraldine had perhaps spoken with her, and could tell me how she, Sunetra, had taken the news."

"You were worried?" Sahel asked. "Did she call the night before the jury rendered its verdict?"

James sighed. "Three days had passed since her last call. I looked to Geraldine as I always did when sitting there. The judge had yet to enter the courtroom as I waited to hear the jury's decision. She shook her head before I could begin mouthing the words, asking whether Sunetra had called. Sunetra hadn't called her. I grew queasy, felt something slip past me, and then as if it returned, I grew warm. The feeling, a sensation, hovered. I turned back and realized how deeply I had sealed my own fate. I caught sight of Sunetra's mother, Meera, at the back of the courtroom.

"Meera didn't always come to court. I took her absence as a response to the guilt she felt. Like Ravesh, she too was eager for me to marry Sunetra. When Ravesh died it was as if we didn't know each other. Resignation hung on her face that morning. Meera knew that Sunetra had been calling Geraldine."

Sahel sensed an energy mounting within, as if what James spoke of had taken root, and now dwelled in Sahel. "Then is when I felt warmth dissipate. Life began to leave me. I knew I'd be convicted." Again James sighed. "When Geraldine arrived the next morning, I looked into her eyes and then was when I knew that something had happened. Geraldine told me that Sunetra had jumped from the Golden Gate."

"She was dead," Sahel said.

"Meera had avoided the trial not simply because she knew the truth," James said. "In her suicide note, Sunetra said that she had been home fighting with her mother, Meera, and ultimately within herself. She then confessed to having shot her father and having allowed me to take the blame. She asked my forgiveness for what she had done. And what she was about to do. Meera confirmed Sunetra had also confessed to her."

"Why didn't Sunetra explain that it had been an accident, that she had never intended to shoot her father, that you and she had thought the person coming in was a burglar?"

Moments passed. "It had been quick. But even I had recognized him. So did Sunetra," said James. "We'd been arguing about how her father had planned for me to manage the brokerage after Sunetra and I married. She was angry and hurt. She felt betrayed. Somewhere in the moment of seeing and recognizing him and her anger rising, Sunetra chose to pull the trigger. She never thought or considered that he'd die."

Sahel lowered her head, recalling how she and Titus had argued moments before her accident. A sound of whimpering rose inside Sahel's head. Both Sahel and Sunetra's soul residing in Sahel sobbed.

"Sunetra meant to shoot her father. It hadn't been planned. We had been arguing, Sunetra and I," said James. "Ravesh had told her that once Sunetra and I married, he was going to retire, that with me running the brokerage he knew she would be taken care of. Sunetra took it that her father didn't trust her, didn't think she had the stamina or the wits to run the brokerage."

The sounds of Sunetra's wailing filled Sahel and spread throughout her body, pulverizing her last bits of defenses.

"Ravesh had great faith in Sunetra. He knew she was smart, more than he or I. He loved her ideas, worshipped them. He also knew that this world is crazy. Not everyone can be trusted. Women aren't frail, Ravesh once said. They're incredibly strong and insightful, immensely intuitive. And that is why we must protect them. The world seeks to destroy what is right and good. Women are what's good and what's right. They are targets, not just for other men, but for women who are jealous."

Immediately Sahel thought of her mother. Lillian had not so much hated Carl as she envied Sahel for the fact that both Titus and Carl loved Sahel. "Ravesh was right," Sahel said. "All of us as women want to be loved. Sunetra had both you and her father Ravesh loving her," Sahel said.

"Like you have with Titus and Carl," said James. "But you also want your freedom."

James's words stilled her thoughts.

"Meera was kind to me," James said. "But I always felt that she deserved, and needed more attention from Ravesh. She appeared so broken in the courtroom. Some weeks later, on the morning of my sentencing, moments after the judge gave me life imprisonment, I turned back and looked at her. She didn't turn away. Meera had wanted to see Sunetra running the brokerage, her way of escaping purdah.

"*Purdah?*" Sahel said. The word filled her mind. She had never heard it.

"Purdah is an ancient institution in India that wealthy men of Rajasthan placed their wives in and sought for their daughters in marrying them off," James explained. "Their way of protecting them."

"A young wife entering *purdah* would never have to return to the world outside. Her needs, and all that she desired, would be met from within the confines of her husband's home. Never would she set foot beyond his estate. In the most ideal sense, seclusion from the world cultivated for the young wife a sense of safety from physical ills, disease, epidemics, and problems plaguing society. Liberated from a sea of worry, she could exude warmth, transforming the building that housed them into a home. A home wherein gaining knowledge of each other, wife and husband, grew familiar, and from this recognition of the other and of their own selves reflected in the eyes of the other, the two became one."

"So it was protection," Sahel said. "Not simply a confinement."

"It allowed a process of transfiguration, for the husband along with his wife. The institution of purdah was not constituted simply of walls encasing elaborate estates spanning miles and with beautiful gardens, but with vows made to each other. Servants of every description worked at the wife's disposal as she served the husband and in all manner of things, he served her. For in his wife, the husband found salvation from the travails of the world. Ravesh wanted to revolutionize it, bring it into the twenty-first century," James explained. "But purdah was what Ravesh Desai wanted for Sunetra." James sighed. "The last word he spoke was purdah."

Sahel tried imagining what it must have been like to enter her marital home knowing she would never come out until death. Titus's words returned to Sahel. *I love you. Let me take care of you.*

A faint image of Sunetra, brown face as round as the moon, formed in Sahel's mind. She experienced James's memory. Sadness dripped from her words. "My father's against our marrying."

"Give him time." James stroked Sunetra's smooth cheek.

"So he can send me to his home in Jaipur, and imprison me in purdah?"

"Don't be ridiculous. Your home is here."

"And so are prisons," said Sunetra.

They were in Ravesh's office at the brokerage. Others who worked there were outside talking and holding glasses. Sahel surmised there was a gathering of some sort.

"Can you believe some of these women lived like that for forty years or more?" Sunetra said. She was speaking of purdah.

"I can." James smiled. "When they're as pretty as you, who wouldn't want to protect them? The outside world is harsh and dangerous."

"You're just as bad as my father." Sunetra pushed into his chest ever so slightly and curled her lips into a sharp smirk.

Minutes later Ravesh said to James, "This world is harsh. It has a double standard for women and a single standard for men." His Rajasthani accent played through, sifting each word with the passion he felt for protecting his daughter. "I need Sunetra cherished and loved. Men protect what they cherish and love. I am proud of my business," Ravesh said. "I love my Sunetra. She is all that I have of Rajasthan."

"I love her too," James had said. "And I respect what you have accomplished here. They belong together."

"That is why I have made you one of my three junior partners. Keep working as you do and loving my Sunetra and all will be well." Ravesh smiled.

In her vision of James and Ravesh, Sahel spied Sunetra looking on from the distance.

"She heard you," Sahel said on exiting her vision. "Sunetra

heard you and Ravesh talking. She saw and heard Ravesh telling you that he wanted you to protect Sunetra.

"Sunetra felt betrayed," Sahel said. "By Ravesh, but especially you." Sunetra had felt betrayed by Ravesh and James much like Titus had on the night of his and Sahel's argument, after which he accidentally hit Sahel with the car.

James gave a long, hard sigh. "One word from Meera, an explanation of why Ravesh wanted Sunetra married and me running the brokerage, might have calmed her. Meera chose to say nothing, and allowed Sunetra to think her father lacked faith in her."

"Meera was also angry with Ravesh," murmured Sahel. "Sunetra was carrying the burden of not only her anger, but also that of her mother."

Again James sucked in air. He spoke softly. "The look on Meera's face that morning told me it was all over. My life and purpose on earth had ended. I would never see Sunetra again, not in this life. And that is when I began to pray for death and my entrance into the next life."

Sahel imagined him sucking in tears. He said, "I felt vindicated when Geraldine finally told me Sunetra had jumped from the Golden Gate."

Sunetra let out a great wail within Sahel's thoughts. The sound, no longer excruciating, rippled through Sahel, shaking loose bad memories of Lillian, and the tormenting words that still lingered. For the first time, a strange sense of freedom enveloped Sahel.

Emotions rumbling through her ebbed towards calm. She said to James, "With freedom comes loneliness and isolation, fear and doubt. Mama, not Titus, has been my jailor, her thoughts and perspective on life being my warden. All my life I've been running from her, and seeking escape from Titus and his love."

The image of Titus, his hands compressing her chest, torture writ large upon his face as he fought to bring her back, sprang forth in Sahel's mind. "I saw that when I died."

"You need to let go," James said. "Have the surgery and let go."

"I'm afraid," Sahel said slowly and softly.

"Do you believe in life after death?" Once more James presented the question.

"Yes. Yes. I do." She turned to his voice.

"Then die to this life," James said. "Leave the purdah of this life. And rise to the one at the heart of your dreams. Love Titus and stop running. Stop running and let Titus love you."

Air seeped from Sahel's chest as James's words, piercing her defenses, coursed through her body.

Chapter 30

F

ather Richard arrived at 5:30 a.m., two hours before Sahel was to undergo surgery, and set about to administer the Sacrament of the Sick and Dying. While Carl, Titus, Essien, and Geraldine waited outside her hospital room, the priest gave Sahel the opportunity for reconciliation.

Sahel made the sign of the cross and said, "I was not the best daughter to my parents. I angered Mama many times. In doing so I placed Daddy in the middle. Torn between Mama and me, I know he suffered."

Of her most recent perils she said, "I have lived with a divided heart. All my life I have loved two people beyond my parents, Titus and Carl. I have loved them equally." Her voice cracked. "And then I married Titus. What this says about me only others can tell." Comforted by Father Richard's silence, she went deeper.

"Titus and Carl are good men. They are like brothers to me, each of them. But I have stood between them. This has been both a burden and blessing. If I could cut myself in half, I would give to each one part of who I am. Why God has made it this way, I cannot understand. Without their love, and their loyalties, however divided, I would not have survived life at home." She sighed.

"Mama and Daddy's marriage was strange. Then again, how can I judge? In the times I didn't understand them I turned to Titus and Carl. They gave me what only brothers can give a sister. The argument with Titus. Losing my sight. Titus blaming himself. I made a choice. Maybe this was life's way of making me decide. I married Titus to set him free. I had promised to marry him. Only when losing my sight did I come to see who Titus truly is, how much he truly loves me. And I have always loved and needed him." Sahel lowered her head and squeezed Father Richard's hand holding hers, and said, "In being true to myself, I damaged Carl's faith. It's my fault that he's stopped attending Mass." She began to sob. "I'm so sorry ... for everything. Please forgive me, God, for having taken the pills." Her sobs grew harder. "It was a painful thing to do."

Sahel forced herself to continue. "I was hurting. I hurt Titus even more." Sobs of shame and despair racked her body. Again she pleaded. "Please forgive me."

"God does forgive you." Father Richard patted the back of her palm. Sahel trembled. The priest embraced her. "God forgives you, my child, more than you or I can know." Sahel calmed and lay back.

Father Richard said, "In the name of the Father, and of the Son, and of the Holy Spirit, I absolve you of your sins." He signed the cross, and then again lifted her hand. "You are within God's grace and mercy, Sahel. He has forgiven you. Now you must forgive yourself."

Fear rose in Sahel.

"Much of what you have confessed can be stated as one problem, if we can even call it that. You have loved. And you have loved deeply. *With both passion and commitment.* This is

196

what God calls us to do. To give until we feel we have run dry." The priest, who had ministered for over three decades to Sahel, Titus, Carl, and those of St. Maria's Parish, explained.

"I have watched you from the time you were a small child. The three of you in line with your classmates arriving up to sanctuary to receive Eucharist, Titus pulling one or the other of your braids, Carl admonishing him to stop."

Sahel considered how each time they had approached Father Richard, Titus had come from behind her to lead the way, Carl remaining after Sahel.

"They were so long then, your braids," said Father Richard. He chuckled. "Seeing the three of you was something I looked forward to each Sunday at Mass. It's hard not having children of your own. In many ways, you, Titus, and Carl have become like my children, those given to me by God in the absence of my own family."

Sahel's heart warmed. On so many occasions she had approached Father Richard dispensing communion, shame overtaking her heart.

"You've been through a lot, Sahel. More than most of us care to imagine. In that we priests don't have our own families, we observe a great deal. Never have I seen you behave in the ways you describe. What I have seen is you showing love and honor to your parents, always, forever seeking to make them proud and doing just that. You have also given to others of the bounty which God has provided."

The priest squeezed her palm. "God sets out a path for us. When we avoid treading it, God divines ways to bring us to it. God never places upon us more than we can carry. Nor does He send us on a journey without sufficient provisions. You are now on that path. Your decision to marry Titus was God's will. As for Carl not attending Mass, God will make plain his path. Right now you will undergo this surgery and your family and I will pray that God brings you through alive and well, and hopefully with your sight restored."

So focused on the surgery as a way of draining the aneurysm, Sahel had forgotten that a by-product of the procedure was the possibility of regaining her sight. "Do you believe God will restore my sight?"

"I don't know," Father Richard said.

James's words from the previous night returned. *You're afraid of regaining your sight. You don't like what you see when looking at yourself. The darkness is you, what your mother so hated. In some ways making peace with your blindness means accepting what your mother thought of you and disliked, but also saw as evidence of your strength and gift of spirit—your truth.*

Sahel said to Father Richard, "What kind of person likes being blind?"

"You don't like being blind. You simply cherish the sight it has given you, the ability to see into Titus's heart. And into your own."

Father Richard offered a prayer for Sahel's safety during the surgery. Upon completion he invited Titus, Carl, Essien, and Geraldine inside, and proceeded with the Sacrament of the Sick and Dying.

The holy water hit Sahel's face. Titus tightened his grip on her hand. He was sitting upon the bed next to Sahel as Father Richard dispensed the water on each of them. "This is a reminder of the baptism under which we all have gone and through which God initiates and transforms us into His own," Father Richard said. "May we now receive renewal of strength and faith in our Lord, Jesus Christ. God is with you. He will see you through this time of challenge." The priest read from the Bible. "... The book of Titus, Chapters One and then Two.

The Apostle Paul writes to Titus, a minister in the early Church, 'To Titus, mine own son after the common faith: Grace, mercy, and peace, from God the Father and the Lord Jesus Christ our Savior. For the grace of God that bringeth salvation hath appeared to all men, Teaching us that, denying ungodliness and worldly lusts, we should live soberly, righteously, and godly, in this present world; Looking for that blessed hope, and the glorious appearing of the great God and our Savior Jesus Christ; gave himself for us, that He might redeem us from all iniquity, and purify unto himself a peculiar people, zealous of good works. These things speak ... exhort, and rebuke with all authority. Let no man despise thee.'" Father Richard placed his hands upon Sahel's forehead.

With that the priest brought his hand to Sahel's, held by Titus. He repeated the last line of scripture he had read, "These things Speak ... exhort, and rebuke with all authority. Let no man, no man despise thee."

Father Richard said, "With this oil I bless you." He touched Sahel's forehead and with the oil signed the cross. "Peace be unto you, my child. God is with you, now, forever and unto eternity."

He then set about dispensing the Eucharist. In this instance and unlike during Mass at St. Maria's, Titus opened Sahel's hand to receive the wafer. Since the loss of Sahel's sight, Father Richard had placed the wafer in Titus's hand, which Titus then placed upon Sahel's tongue.

Sahel received the wafer in her palms, turned to Titus, and whispered, "Let no man despise thee," Sahel said. "No man, not even yourself." She lifted her palm to Titus. As in the past, Titus placed the wafer on her tongue.

"Let no man despise thee, not even yourself." Father Richard's voice continued low and constant as he administered Eucharist to Carl, then Geraldine, and Essien.

"Thank you." Sahel clasped Titus's hand. On returning, Father Richard touched their hands. He concluded the Eucharist by leading them in the Lord's Prayer. Titus lifted Sahel's hand, both their palms warm, moist and trembling.

"Our Father, Who art in Heaven. Hallowed be thy name. Thy Kingdom come. Thy will be done. On earth as it is in heaven. Give us this day. Our daily bread. And forgive us our trespasses. As we forgive those who have trespassed against us. Lead us not into temptation."

To this Father Richard said, "Deliver us, Oh Lord, from every evil, and grant us peace in our day. In your mercy keep us free from sin and protect us from all anxiety as we wait in joyful hope for the coming of our Savior, Jesus Christ."

Along with the others, Sahel then said, "For the kingdom, power and glory is yours, now and forever."

Sahel's surgery lasted for six hours.

During this time she traveled deep within the terrain of her heart and soul.

Chapter 31

B

etween the vast ribbon of land separating the Sahara from the plains and savannas of the south stood a grand kingdom of the sahel.

Queen Holna, its ruler, resplendent in red, a turban as her crown, surveyed the palace court of clay. Prince Rahim, her husband, was due back any moment. He and his army of 10,000 had been at war with the kingdom ruled by Bessima. Bessima was Queen Holna's mother.

It was a dream, Sahel's dream. And all within the dream sprung from the web of affections that bound her to those she loved.

The woman to the right of Queen Holna spoke. "How would

you have me instruct the royal courtiers to prepare for Prince Rahim's return?" Queen Holna turned to the young woman beside her, the monarch's words having broken the silence. "The courtiers," the woman repeated. "How would you have them receive Prince Rahim's return? Surely you have prepared a great feast. The Prince will be tired but—"

"I pray for his safe return." Queen Holna raised her palm. "Once he is here we can make the appropriate celebrations, but not too grand. Many soldiers remain in battle and unaccounted for. Not until we have won the war, and those who have survived have returned, and we have honored those injured and lost, can we truly feast. "

Disappointment shone upon the face of Holna's most senior lady in waiting. "Yes ma'am." She bowed in acceptance.

"In the meantime I will pray," said Holna. The young queen started across the clay floor, was nearly to the other side when the front doors swung open. Prince Thane, Rahim's closest friend, burst inside. Holna moved towards the tall and muscular Thane. "Where is Rahim? Is he with you?" she asked.

Covered in a sheen of dust he knelt before her and lowered his head. "A sandstorm blew in from the Sahara. Our last battle cost us many casualties," Thane spoke with one elbow upon his knee and never looking up. "I fear we have lost him."

Holna felt herself crumbling within.

Prince Thane jumped to his feet and caught Holna, breaking her fall. With Holna's lady-in-waiting he ushered Holna upstairs.

"I want you to go and find him," Holna ordered Thane once she had reached her private quarters.

"You, my Queen, must lie down. The heir to the Kingdom of Purdah lives within you." Since she had entered her eighth month of pregnancy, the news of Rahim's possible death might harm the child she carried.

"And without Rahim I am nothing. We are nothing." Holna bit back tears.

The lady-in-waiting removed Holna's shoes and then lifted her feet onto the bed. Holna lay back. "I have sent for the palace physician," said Thane. "I will wait until he arrives."

"Summon advisor Qadir," Queen Holna said to Cynda, her lady-in-waiting.

Cynda again bowed in obedience and left.

"What will you do with Qadir?" Thane asked.

"He provides good counsel, particularly in times of distress."

"But if Rahim is lost, nothing can bring him back."

"Did you see him fall in battle? Have you seen his body?" Holna demanded. She sat forward upon the bed. "Where is his camel?"

Thane knitted his brows, his face taking on a curious frown.

"What evidence do you have that he is dead?" Holna questioned further. "In fact, why are you not out trying to find him?"

"My men are tired and need replenishment. Our camels are tired. The sand has blinded and tired us. The *gods* of the *sahel* have turned against us. I assure you, as soon as the men have eaten and the sands settle, we will return."

Holna examined the band upon her left hand. "You say that Rahim has disappeared. And yet you have no corpse." The idea of Rahim's demise would not leave Queen Holna.

"I have not lied." Thane drew closer.

"What if soldiers from my mother's camp have taken him?"

Thane's eyes retreated in consideration of Holna's inquisition.

"I could dispatch a spy to enter the ranks of her soldiers. If he is not there, but yet alive, perhaps she has taken him to her palace in Koresh. With her soldiers away and fighting ours we could storm the walls and rescue him."

At that Advisor Qadir entered the doorway. "You called, my Queen?" He bowed. Holna motioned for him to enter.

"Prince Thane advises me that Prince Rahim has disappeared in the heat of battle. No one saw him fall, nor do we have a corpse or his camel."

"Then he is yet alive," said Qadir.

"That is my sincere hope," Holna conceded. "The possibility that soldiers of my mother's forces have captured him looms large."

"Prince Rahim is worth more to her alive than if dead."

Qadir's words revealed his quality of quick thought, a gift to Holna and the Kingdom of Purdah over which she ruled. "Should your mother have taken him prisoner, she might then seek to coerce, if not blackmail you, into surrendering as ransom."

"Never!" Thane shouted. Holna's gaze brightened.

Qadir turned to Prince Thane as did Queen Holna. "Our queen would never bend to Bessima's will in that way or any other," Thane said. He shot Holna a quick glance as if fearing he had over spoken.

"We must first search for Prince Rahim, determine whether he has died or been taken prisoner," Holna said.

"Yes, my Queen." Thane clicked his heels. "As soon as we have eaten, I and my men will return to the desert." He bowed once more and left.

The royal physician arrived, and examined Holna. On seeing that all was well with her and the child she carried, he left. Holna slept, though fitfully.

Later that evening Queen Holna took dinner with Qadir as her guest.

"Thank you for coming at such late notice," Holna thanked him.

They began their meal of chicken and vegetables.

"You are my queen, I your gracious servant." Qadir did not look up from his plate.

"Yes, but you have a family," said Holna. Advisor Qadir was married to Cynda, Queen Holna's lady-in-waiting. "Tell me, how are Masha and Adar?" Qadir and Cynda had two children, aged five and three respectively.

"Growing as fast as the day is long," Qadir said. A smile brightened his brown face. "They are a true blessing." His smile took on a bittersweet glow. "And to think we came so close to none of this happening." That Queen Holna had permitted them to marry greatly disturbed some at the palace court. He looked to Holna.

"You are thinking of Cynda, and her fear that I would not permit the two of you to marry," Holna said.

"You are the first to allow such a thing."

"You love each other. Serving me, the palace, and the Kingdom of Purdah cannot come before your own needs. Otherwise you would work as slaves."

"Decisions like these have angered your mother, Queen Bessima, and caused her to split the kingdom, return to Koresh, and retaliate."

"Purdah will live." Holna gave a brief smile and returned to cutting her chicken.

"Yes, but will you?" Qadir asked. Lines of worry and anguish spread upon his forehead and deepened. "With Prince Rahim missing we are in great peril."

"You truly fear him dead?"

"Forgive me, my Queen, and in no way does what I speak express my wishes. I pray a long life for you, Prince Rahim, and the child you carry. But were Prince Rahim dead, the choices standing before you would be quite simple. Storm the walls of Koresh where Queen Bessima resides and leave not a man standing."

"She is my mother."

"Yes, and we all know that she has wished many times over for your death." Qadir spoke truth.

"You fear she will use Rahim as a pawn to force me into relinquishing Purdah to her control." Holna said on meeting Qadir's gaze.

"And if that is the case, you must grant her wish."

"Surrender the kingdom?" Holna swallowed hard.

"Only your governance as Queen of the Kingdom of Purdah."

"But who will lead the people, my people? They look to me."

"We look to you and Prince Rahim, but not for orders and commands. We honor and respect you, obey your requests out of the love you show to us time and again. Acts such as your decision to allow me to marry Cynda are what make serving you so wonderful and quite easy. Your decision to honor our love, mine and Cynda's, and that of others like us, present an example that we, your loyal and grateful servants, have taken to heart. Under previous rule none were allowed to marry except by permission of the monarch. It is in response to acts such as this that men eagerly answered your call to fight Queen Bessima when she threatened our people and our lands." Advisor Qadir continued. "Their wives, our wives, encouraged us to join the ranks and fight. Prince Rahim's decision to fight with and among the men signaled that you and he do not rule over us." A pervading sense of sincerity filled Qadir's dark eyes. "You live among us.

"Your governance does not guarantee our loyalty, rather it is your love and respect. Should Prince Rahim remain alive, all we ask is that you do whatever it takes to unite with him. Allow the child you carry to be born within your and Prince Rahim's grasp. We will do the rest. Bessima may establish herself as ruler but our love for you and Prince Rahim will topple her."

Worry over Rahim's safety and well-being dissipated into a warming calm.

Prince Thane returned the following day with news that Queen Bessima's officers had indeed captured Prince Rahim. Again, as always, he knelt before Holna seated upon the throne of the reception gallery, Advisor Qadir standing beside her. "They've taken him to your mother's castle in the land of Freedom," said Thane.

The fetus within Holna jumped at the sound of Thane's announcement. She caressed her stomach. "How ironic," Qadir murmured. "A person held captive in the land of Freedom."

"I have sent men to storm the tower walls where it is suggested that Prince Rahim is being held," said Thane.

"No," Holna said. She raised her hand. "Recall them."

"But how are we to rescue him?" asked Thane. He lifted his head.

"I will do that." Holna said.

"Forgive me, my Queen," said Thane. Again, he lifted his head from his position of kneeling. "But you must not allow advisor Qadir's weak-minded ideas to sway you from a strong show of strength and good common sense."

Holna met Thane's hardened gaze. "Advisor Qadir is neither weak-minded, nor does he lack common sense. His consultation on this matter goes deeper than what you realize or can comprehend."

"But Our Gracious Majesty, how are we to surrender our leader and hope to keep the Kingdom of Purdah, the people of Purdah—"

"I am the ruler of Purdah!" Holna hoisted herself to stand. "The decisions I make reflect not simply my concerns, but those for my people, our people. My father, King Suva, established an atmosphere of love and grace, during his reign. My mother, Queen Bessima, hated him for that. So much so that despite my love for Prince Rahim, she tried to place me in marriage to you. She did not consult you. She did not consult me. Instead she moved forward with her plans with no concern for how this would affect us."

Holna stepped down from her throne and touched Thane's forehead, indicating for him to stand. "I have lived differently. I have loved. Something Queen Bessima has never done. Her method of rule has always been that scheming. But coercion and blackmail have no place in the heart of love. And love is what I have for my people, this child that I carry." Holna looked down, and touched her stomach. "And Rahim." She smiled at Thane and then stepped back upon her throne.

"I command you to take soldiers and ride as fast as you can to the Land of Freedom. Seek reception with Queen Bessima and tell her that I will surrender Purdah to her. But for that she must return Prince Rahim safe and unharmed."

"My Queen, are you certain that—" Thane's lips trembled.

"Go! Ride as fast as your horse will carry you. Obey my command."

Stunned, Thane regained composure. "Yes, my Queen." He turned and left.

With the door closed and Thane on the other side, Holna turned to Advisor Qadir and quivered in the wake, having ordered Thane to honor a command he so obviously loathed carrying out, and that she yet had come to believe was the best. "You have been a good and merciful leader, Queen Holna," said Qadir. "God will bless you."

"And will my child have a father?"

"You have already bequeathed her more than any lifetime could hold. Both you and she are blessed." Qadir smiled.

"She?" Holna gripped her stomach, teeming with life and hope, and looked down at her abdomen.

"Cynda's dreams have portended that you are carrying a girl," said Qadir. "She will look like you and will rule the Kingdom of Purdah as you have in the footsteps of your father, King Suva."

"But I am surrendering the kingdom as you have advised," Holna spoke, astonished.

Qadir drew near and in a low tone, said, "Unlike what Prince Thane has led you to believe, he has always loved you. Your mother schemed. But getting Thane to love you was not something you had to work hard to achieve. Much like Prince Rahim, he has sought to serve you in numerous ways. You are right, Queen Bessima used him to her advantage to coax you into marrying Rahim. Queen Bessima always knew where your heart lay. She also knew where Prince Thane's lay, too."

"He was her pawn," Holna said aloud in realization. "But why would she divine such a plan? I have always loved Rahim."

"Your mother knew that you would not resist King Suva's wishes for you to marry Rahim. But she did not trust that you would also love Rahim, not without outside insistence. Queen Bessima does not believe love provides strength," Qadir reminded.

"She wanted me to marry and love Rahim?" Holna grew ever more confused.

"She believes that love is the root of all destruction. In her eyes, giving your heart to someone, while pledging faith and fidelity to another, renders one weak and vulnerable, exposed."

"She wanted me to marry and love Rahim since Father chose him as my husband," said Holna. "So that she could usurp my rule here in Purdah and take over," she thought aloud.

"She exploited Thane's love for you as an alternate plan in case you married Rahim without loving him," offered Qadir.

"Loving Thane while married to Rahim," Holna began, "would ensure the fall of Purdah."

"A house divided cannot stand."

"Neither can the temple of a divided heart remain whole," Holna said. "Two men loving one woman." Again she thought aloud.

"For these reasons I greatly fear that Thane works with her now," said Holna's royal advisor. "But not towards the same purposes. He wants you. As always, Queen Bessima's purpose is to rule the Kingdom of Purdah. In so doing she will govern the person who has most threatened and frightened her—you, Queen Holna, who has loved openly and freely, the most powerful way to govern."

Torn by Qadir's words, Queen Holna clenched her hands and pulled at her fingers. Again she caressed her stomach and began to cry. "This is so unfair to Prince Thane, what my mother has done. And Prince Rahim, his life hangs in the balance betwixt and between so many desires."

Qadir's dark eyes shone firm and bright as they had been against the light of the candles, as they had during their meal last evening. "I have always loved Rahim. Though my heart wished me not to, I could do nothing other than open my soul to him."

"It was never your heart whose door remained closed to Prince Rahim, rather your mind, your thoughts, the part of you that Queen Bessima has sought to control."

Advisor Qadir's words cut through the mist of doubt and ambivalence enshrouding Holna's anxious soul and cast further warmth upon her heart ravaged by the chilling fear of having lost Rahim.

Prince Thane and his party of men rode to Bessima's castle in the land of Freedom, but not in time to prevent the soldiers ahead of him from storming the tower where they had been told Queen Bessima's officers held captive Prince Rahim.

Word of Thane's failure to arrive in time reached Queen Holna.

"You must go to Queen Bessima," Qadir advised. " Cynda and I will ride with you."

"But what of your children?"

"They need Purdah. And Purdah is you."

Holna kissed her fingers and placed them upon her stomach.

She then ordered stablemen to saddle horses for her, Advisor Qadir, and Cynda.

Despite the war between the two kingdoms, the night was peaceful. Stars lined the dark sky as none but the syncopated rhythm of twelve hooves meeting the soldier-trodden earth sounded. With each passing moment, Holna feared an ambush from the soldiers of the Kingdom of Freedom, over which her mother ruled.

On arriving at Queen Bessima's palace, Holna found Rahim standing in the middle of the reception area, the blades of two cutlasses to either side of his neck. His hands were tied behind his back. Seated upon her throne, Queen Bessima, ebony hair caressing her face as fair as milk, appeared at ease with what her plans had wrought.

"Welcome, dear daughter," she said on Holna entering the large and spacious room. Holna willed herself not to look at Prince Rahim. The thought of losing him to death at her mother's command nicked at Holna's heart. To see Rahim bleeding would send blood gushing from her heart.

"I have come to surrender," Holna said. She approached her mother and moved to kneel.

Thane rushed to help Holna onto her knees. "He still loves you," Bessima said loud and clear. She turned to Rahim. No longer able to avoid Rahim's gaze, Holna wished to strike Bessima, kill her mother for all the pain she had caused both Rahim and Thane.

And then Holna realized the depth of meaning delivered in the words of Qadir's counsel she had received during the meal two nights earlier: "You have ruled with love and grace as established by your father, King Suva. Love has made you a strong leader. Subjects rush to honor and obey you because of this. Love is the power you have over Bessima. She could never rule in this way. And for this she will fall."

Holna pulled her gaze from Rahim. He was shaking with fear, his lips trembling, body worn, and eyes red betraying the weariness of what Holna knew had been lack of sleep and food and most probably unending torture. "I love you," she said to her mother. Queen Bessima's eyes widened with what seemed fear and pain. Holna spoke again lest she lose her strength and succumb to anger and despair. "I love you," she pleaded to Bessima. "You are my mother. I will never hate you. But I despise the things you have done, how you have pitted Prince Thane against Prince Rahim, all for the price of your controlling me, perhaps even destroying me. Compassion and sorrow cover my heart for who you have been and still remain. Only from the depths of a great and aching wound, one that has corroded your heart and soul, could you have acted and continue to behave this way. May God and the Heavens have mercy on you, and all who serve you."

A great silence fell upon the palace hall against the resonance of Holna's declaration.

And then Holna felt herself smiling. Bessima never winced. The walls of the castle of Freedom that had withstood centuries of sandstorms that had blinded many a Saharan traveler and those of the *sahel* began to shake and rumble. All turned their heads with eyes glistening with fear and confusion as they surveyed the rubble encasing them. Bit by bit, slab by slab, the walls fell around them. Dust filled the great palace hall of the Kingdom of Freedom. Holna's soul quaked amid the Armageddon of the mother she had known and feared.

Seconds later and with Qadir's help, Holna searched through the rubble, and uncovered Rahim. His eyes were closed, his body limp, cheeks scratched and forehead bloody. "Oh, my dear! Please don't die." Holna lowered her lips to her husband's ... was about to kiss him ... And then ...

All went dark.

Sahel awakened to find herself standing at the entry of the sanctuary at St. Maria's Parish. Carl stood beside her. Heads

211

turned and the expectant eyes of the congregation settled upon Sahel and Carl as they started down the aisle. Joyous and grateful that she had regained her sight, Sahel turned to Carl, and through the veil covering her face, gazed into his eyes.

Again he patted her hand. About to smile, Sahel then realized that like Carl, everyone in the sanctuary was wearing black. She looked down upon her dress. Like her veil, it too was black. Slowly she looked to the front of the sanctuary where Father Richard stood, his face solemn and hands by his sides. A casket lay stretched behind him. The priest's eyes, sad and brimming with melancholy, beckoned her to come forward.

A wave of torrential sadness overtook Sahel. Pain rippled through her chest. She wanted to double over. With his hand to the small of her back, Carl forced her to remain standing.

"We'll get through this," Carl whispered. "You and I." She looked to him. "It's what Titus would have wanted," Carl said. "You and I, sticking together." Unable to speak, Sahel shook her head. "No." Again she met Carl's gaze, looked into his eyes, entered his soul. And there she saw Queen Holna with Advisor Qadir behind her, the two of them working to uncover Prince Rahim from the rubble.

"We cannot find Prince Thane," Cynda, Qadir's wife, yelled. Holna, her thoughts upon Prince Rahim, continued lifting pieces of the rubble covering Rahim.

"Let us help you, my Queen," Qadir advised. "Lest you risk losing the baby." This vision sat upon the thoughts resting in Carl's soul.

Sahel stepped back, attempted to pull her arm from being entwined with Carl's. He caught her wrist. "We must go through this. You miss Titus. So do I. But—"

"I don't love you," said Sahel.

"Don't do this, Sahel," Carl said.

The congregants grew concerned, their sadness melted into anxiety.

"I won't go through this," Sahel shouted back. She whipped around. In the doorway at the back of the church leading from the narthex into the sanctuary stood James Bolton. Sahel moved to go towards him, took two steps towards him. He flashed his

212

palm.

"You must go back." He spoke the same as had the woman in red.

"But I don't want to be here! I don't love Carl. I don't want to marry him!"

"This is not a wedding," said James. "But Titus's death. Marrying Carl." Sahel dropped to her knees.

She began to sob. "Funeral. Wedding. It's all the same."

"You are the master of this vision," said James.

Sahel lifted her head to him towering over her. She met his gaze as she had Carl's when entering the sanctuary moments earlier.

"This is your life," James said.

Feeling eyes upon her, Sahel turned back. Carl had now reached the altar. He stood with Father Richard. A Bible lay open in the priest's hands, a ring stood upon the crease of the pages, the pear-shaped diamond that Sahel's mother, Lillian, had kissed and that Titus had then slid onto Sahel's finger.

Sahel scuffled to her feet. With tears covering her face, nearly blinding her, she rushed to Father Richard, grasped the ring from within the Bible, and kissed it.

Again, all went black.

Chapter 32

S ahel reached for her forehead upon awakening. "Oh. My head."

"Not so fast," Carl grasped her hand.

"It hurts." Sahel touched her temple. Her head ached more than anything she had experienced, the pain too profound to describe, as if a sledgehammer had found its way inside and was continually pounding against her skull. "There's something stuck inside my head," Sahel said. Her sight had not returned.

"The nurse is coming with some medication for the pain." Carl massaged the back of her hand. "The surgery went well." Elation filled his voice.

"The surgery?" Slowly Sahel recalled the hour leading up to the surgery. Confessing her shortcomings to Father Richard. His giving her last rites. The thin Eucharistic wafer settling upon her tongue, Titus having placed it there. Holding his hand as she, along with her father, Carl, and Geraldine recited the Lord's Prayer. Titus's hand had grown warm and stopped trembling on Father Richard bringing the prayer to a close. *Grant us Peace and mercy, dear Lord in this moment of this, your day. Keep us free from all worries and anxiety as we wait in joyful hope of Your return, the coming of our Saviour ...*

Sahel now said to Carl, "Where's Titus?"

"He's outside with your father and Geraldine," Carl said.

Amid her dizziness and her headache, Sahel's mind slipped back to the evening prior to her surgery. "James. How is he?"

Carl let go of her hand. "I want you to raise your arms," he instructed, and evaded answering her question.

Sahel followed his instructions and lifted her arms. On his request she flexed her finger and then as he asked, she lifted her legs. He pulled back the sheets. "Bend your knees." Again she obeyed. In reply to the last of his commands, she flexed her toes. "Great," Carl said, joy streaming through his voice and reaching a new high. "Everything seems to be in working order. With the medication your headache should subside." Again he lifted her hand.

"I don't want to go back to sleep." Sahel fought to speak clearly. The movements had tired her.

"Believe me, I'd like nothing better than to talk with you. But there'll be time for that," Carl said.

Sahel felt the cold alcohol pad upon her hip. The pinprick followed, accompanied by a small amount of burning. Both of that subsided along with the ache pounding against her temples. "Thank you, Melinda," Carl spoke to the nurse.

"You're quite welcome, as always, Dr. Pierson," the nurse said.

Sahel tried imagining her smile. Carl was quite a dashing bachelor.

"James," Sahel uttered again. The sheet covered her once more as Carl pulled back her eyelid. The click of his penlight told Sahel he was checking for any signs of her eyesight having returned. "It's a bit early for this, but—"

"Oh, my head," Sahel gasped. Against the pain subsiding in her head, the dizziness increased. Again she touched her temple and felt bandage on her forehead. Gently Carl lowered her hand.

"In six months there'll be no scar."

"Scar?" Again Sahel lifted her hand. Carl again caught it. "We had to cut an opening into your forehead," he said.

A lobotomy? Sahel thought. "But I thought you said you were going to go through my nose ... Oh, Dr. Blake." Sahel recalled speaking with Aaron Blake, the neurosurgeon who'd offered the second opinion concurring with Carl's prognosis. *The procedure is no longer an option you can choose or avoid. It has to be done. Or else you'll die.*

"We tried going through your nose." The ebullience in Carl's voice dipped. "But we needed a better view to drain the aneurysm."

"Oh, yes. The aneurysm." Sahel remembered. She was going to die without the surgery. So much had vanished from her immediate memory.

Slivers of the dream then flashed before her. Images of Queen Holna, Advisor Qadir, Prince Thane, Queen Bessima, and Cynda pressed upon her thoughts. A bright vision of Prince Rahim with the two blades at his throat burst upon the stage of consciousness and obliterated the other recollections. "Titus! I need to see him!" Sahel tried sitting up. An image came of Father Richard at the front of the sanctuary, the casket containing Titus behind him.

"I'll have him come in," Carl said. "But only for a few minutes." He guided her to lie back down. "You need your rest."

"I'll rest when I see him. Is he okay?"

"Other than worrying about you, I'd say he's fine. Why wouldn't he be?"

"Where is he?" Sahel reached out her hand. Carl grasped it. She hit it back.

"What's wrong?" Carl said with a chuckle. "I've never heard you this way."

"What do you mean?" Sahel's headache had gone. Sleep would remain at bay but a few more seconds.

"This need to see Titus. Your worry about him," Carl said. "Did you have a dream during the surgery."

"Why do you ask?" Sahel said.

"Many of my patients experience dreams during their surgeries. It's quite common." Carl lifted her palm a third time.

"I was just worried," Sahel lied amid sleep fast encroaching.

Memories of her time in the Kingdom of Purdah ran clear, then solidified. "I was so afraid," Sahel murmured with a slur. "You and Titus ...you were there. But you ... you," Sahel's words slowed even more, "... you had sided with ... Queen Bessim ... Ma-ma." She drifted to sleep.

The hours Sahel remained awake grew each day, as did the time she spent with Titus. And yet her sight did not return. Titus grew troubled. Sahel sensed it each time he came to her hospital room, and on his leaving. With each departure his lips trembled in their lingering longer upon her forehead. On the fourth day after surgery, Sahel overheard him question Carl outside of her hospital room.

"I thought you said the surgery would return her sight."

"I said it was a possibility," Carl defended. "Never did I make that promise."

"You did before discovering the aneurysm or that fistula," Titus retorted.

"The focus of the surgery was draining the fistula, eliminating it. Without that she would have died."

"But what about her eyesight? Wasn't the fistula at the bottom of why she can't see?"

"I thought it was," Carl said. Tiredness roared in Carl's voice like that of a hungry lion. The words of Prince Thane in her dream returned. *You are my Queen. As such you can never surrender to Queen Bessima. She is your mother. You are the leader of Purdah. We need you.*

Outside Sahel's hospital room Titus shouted to Carl, "I need you to be honest with me, honest with Sahel. Will she get her sight back? Can she? Is it a possibility?"

"I don't know. Truly I don't." Carl's voice was flat and penitent.

"Damn you, Carl Pierson."

Sahel turned her head upon the pillow and wished for Titus's words to disappear, that he had never spoken them.

Carl entered Sahel's room and closed the door.

Silence settled. Sahel imagined Carl searching for answers, and what to say to her. She told of her dream as best she could recall.

"You were defending the Kingdom of Purdah over which I ruled, but you were also serving Mama in some way. She had tricked you. She was using you to gain control over me."

"Why would I do that?" Carl said. "Better yet, why would your mother go through me to get at you when she's always had Titus at her beck and call?"

"In reality Mama didn't always have Titus at her whim. She couldn't bend him."

"He's always felt you should marry him because your mothers were best friends," said Carl. "When you said, 'No,' he hit he you with the car."

"That's not the way it was." Sahel sat up in anger. "And you know it."

"I'm sorry." Carl lifted her palm. She pulled back. Memories of Sahel's dream returned. Her anger gradually subsided.

"He lost control, became angry when you told him, 'No,' that you weren't ready to marry."

"I was avoiding what I've always felt. My resistance of what Mama wanted turned in on me when she died. Loving Titus, letting him love me, receiving his love, it's always frightened me."

"Love is never scary when it's true and sincere."

For the first time, Sahel grew afraid of Carl, of better yet the pieces of herself that she felt she represented. She wished now to have not told him of her dream. "The simplest interpretation of a dream is that the dreamer is everything and everyone in the dream," she said.

"Then who is Thane? Or better yet, who am I to you since it

seems you have assigned me the role of this Prince Thane?"

"I never assigned you any role in my dream." Sahel felt her words echo against Carl's desperation when proffering Titus an answer moments earlier.

"He's hurting," Sahel said of Titus. She recalled the sharp edges of the crossed blades to Prince Rahim's neck in the dream. The fear filling Rahim's eyes in the dream matched that in Titus's eyes when he had fought to get Sahel's heart beating again. "Titus is my husband. I love him. I want to go home. The surgery has been a success. I'm still alive."

"We have to wait for seven days to pass." Carl spoke with severity.

"My sight hasn't returned and he's scared," Sahel said of Titus. "I'm losing him." Silence returned, this time stalwart and prickly. Sahel felt herself distanced from Carl, whom she sensed growing agitated.

Again she considered her dream, the pain that raged through her when entering the sanctuary at St. Maria's. Despite the intensity of the onlookers of the congregation, happiness had filled Sahel in being able to see. Her sight had returned. And then she had turned to Carl. Titus is dead, he had said. The somberness on Father Richard's face, that of his body robed in white, and standing in front of the casket had affirmed the truth of Carl's words.

She said to Carl, "Titus is trying to remain strong, put the pieces together. Just like me. I've got to move on. Not just for myself, but also for him. He's got to see that I can live without my sight. That all I need is him."

"He wants to see you, have you see him. I want the same," Carl said.

"You're not my husband."

"I'm your doctor. And Titus is speaking with Aaron Blake each day."

"Please tell me he's not treating Dr. Blake the way you did after the accident."

"He's equal opportunity." Carl chuckled. "You've got to give him that."

"He deserves more."

"You've given him your life."

Memories of having taken the pills swept through Sahel. The torture on Titus's face thirty minutes later as he labored to get her heart beating again swept over her. "I almost took my life from him once. I won't do it again."

"You need to rest." Carl pulled back his hand.

"I need to leave this hospital and get on with my life. A life without sight."

"You need to give time for the effects of the procedure to fall into place."

Sahel felt the bandage upon her head. "Titus will be home with me. I'm on antibiotics. You've not been averse to making house calls."

"Nor will I hesitate re-admitting you at the first sign of trouble arising." Defeat resounded between Carl's words.

"I'll tell Titus the minute I sense something isn't right," Sahel promised.

"More than that, I'm going to have a visiting nurse checking in on you each morning for the next week. I'll be by in the afternoon."

Sahel didn't like the idea of a nurse intruding on her mornings.

It took hours to get going. Never did she feel presentable. Sahel had descended into hell during the hours and days after the accident.

The ensuing year had delivered her onto a harrowing journey beset with a darkness wherein lurked strange beasts, their souls dispensing a scent of familiarity. Despite their ubiquitous nature, hot breath forever flowing between their teeth and scorching Sahel's neck, she had survived the surgery. Her soul lived. "Can you have her come around 10:00?" she said to Carl.

"Ten a.m. it is." Again he grasped her hand and then slowly let it go.

Chapter 33

S

ahel's third morning home from the hospital delivered a sense of peace. Five days earlier she had entered the wormhole of undergoing the procedure and exited alive. Twice she had met and avoided death. The first time she had crossed into the beyond by the actions of her own hand. There Sahel had met Sunetra, whose soul and spirit had pushed Sahel back to the surface of life where Titus had pulled her from the tentacles of ambivalence and purgatory, waves of death thundering in the waters beneath, and back onto the shores of the living.

Sahel's second journey towards death took her to the Kingdom of Purdah, a world wherein its inhabitants symbolized and mirrored Sahel's reality, both waking, and internal.

She crawled out of bed and made her way to the bathroom where Titus was showering. "You're going to work this morning?" she spoke into the mist and steam against her face.

"Only for a few hours." Titus had taken off the last week. "Calvin wants my consultation on a patient. He may also want me to do the surgery." It was 9:00 a.m. "I should be back by noon."

The shower door opened and a rush of steam followed, further dampening Sahel's face. "I should get ready for that visiting nurse," Sahel said. Titus enfolded her into his arms and placed his lips upon hers. "And then we can have lunch. Or perhaps walk the lake."

"That would be nice." Sahel smiled. She kissed his still-damp chest.

Titus's body grew strong and firm against hers. "I don't think I would be much good operating on someone's heart right now," he whispered. "It's good being here with you."

Sahel pulled his wet body closer into hers. "I like having you here."

Titus kissed her forehead.

"Ohhhhh." She touched her bandage.

"Sorry." Titus patted her bandage and then kissed it. Again he lowered his lips to hers, where they lingered.

Moments later, sitting on the end of the bed, Sahel wondered about the strain Titus experienced in maintaining his grip. She turned and said, "Carl told me the surgery went for six hours."

"Yeah, it did." A drawer closed. Titus was dressing. "I was really worried," he said. His voice was near. If only she could see Titus face-to-face, eye-to-eye.

She felt his finger upon her lips. "You survived," Titus said. "That's all that matters."

"Are you sure?" Memories rose in Sahel's mind, those of Titus reprimanding Carl for Sahel's sight not having returned, despite the surgery.

"I'm very sure," Titus said. He then recited the scripture from the book of Titus, the one that Father Richard had read while administering Sahel the Sacrament of the Sick and Dying hours before her surgery. "These things speak, and exhort, and rebuke with all authority. Let no man despise thee. I'll be back in an hour."

Three hours later Sahel awoke to a warm body snuggling next to her. "You came back," she said groggily.

"Like I promised," whispered Titus. He slid his hand underneath her waist and drew her into him.

"I looked a mess when the visiting nurse arrived," said Sahel.

She rested her head upon his chest. "You looked fine." Titus kissed her lips, and then shifting her onto the pillow, he kissed her chest, bare and warm.

"Oh," Sahel murmured. With immense reverence, he spread her legs and then infused her body with his passion and thankfulness over the fact that she had survived.

Satiated from having supped from and fed the other, they slept. Hours later Sahel woke to Titus kissing the back of her neck. Again he pulled her close.

Fully awake, she turned over. "I want to see James. Carl says he should be leaving the hospital soon. I'm sure he'll need some help."

"It hasn't even been a week since your surgery," Titus said. "Carl won't like that."

Sahel pulled herself up. "I feel fine."

"You're doing that now. Pretending nothing's happened. Focusing on others as a way to avoid—"

"I've got to get on with my life at some point," said Sahel. "Helping others is what I love, makes me feel alive."

"What about us?" Titus said.

Sahel felt him sit up. She said, "I have to learn to live with my blindness."

"You mean going back to work?"

"Perhaps," said Sahel.

Titus pulled away and left the bed. "Where are you going?" Sahel called out. She heard him enter the bathroom. Sahel found her way after him. "Titus, we have to talk about this," she said on reaching the doorway. "Titus?" She lowered her head. "Titu—"

225

"I don't like this," Titus said. His warm breath hit her face as he spoke. He then moved away. Sahel turned and followed him back into the bedroom.

"This what—my wanting to see James, or the fact that my sight hasn't and may never return?"

"I'm here with you," Titus said. "Why do you need to see James?"

"He's alone. I care about him."

"Yes, but what about—

"I care about you," Sahel continued.

"Where do we figure into all that you care about?" asked Titus.

"What's that got to do with me wanting to visit James? I thought you said—"

"Don't tell me what I said. I know completely what I said!" Titus yelled. "You're not the only responsible person in this relationship," Titus said. "Everything doesn't rest on your ability to accept whatever life throws at us."

"Being blind is not easy for me."

"You seem to have a hell of an easier time with it than me."

"It's my sight that's gone! Not my life!"

"And I stole it! I took your sight away!" Titus left the bathroom. Finding her way, Sahel followed him back into the bedroom. Silence deepened against Titus opening drawers and then the closet. He returned to the bathroom, slamming the door behind him. The shower went on again, this time with Sahel locked out. The sound of the water died. The door opened seconds later, bringing with it the fragrance of his cologne. Titus whisked by her.

"Where are you going?" Sahel said

"To where I'm of some use. Good use. I've certainly made a mess of things here." Sahel felt him whisk by her. Sharply he added, "And don't blame yourself. If I hear those words again, 'It's my fault ... I'm sorry' ..." he sighed aloud.

"When will you be back?" Sahel said.

"I don't know," Titus murmured.

Sahel's throat grew scratchy, tears bursting through the cracks. She silenced a whimper.

226

"You didn't make any of this happen," Titus whispered. "It's not your fault that Rahim died."

"Rahim?" Sahel lifted her head. "What do you know of Rahim?" Silence rose again, this time with coldness. "Titus? What do you know of Prince Rahim?"

"He loved you," Titus spoke with a clarity devoid of emotion.

Sahel took in the objectivity of his words.

"It was my dream," Sahel uttered, thinking aloud. Like the dizziness she had felt when waking from the surgery, confusion now set in. "I don't understand."

"You're not the only one around here who dreams, has fears and wishes." Frustration and anger resounded again in Titus's voice.

"I love you," Sahel said. "Truly I do."

"And Holna loved Rahim," Titus said. His words drew near, softened. "Why can't you let me love you—surrender the kingdom like in the dream?"

Sahel shuddered at all Titus knew of the dream. Her dream of Purdah, the grand kingdom of the *sahel*.

"But I did," Sahel finally spoke only to shake her head in realizing that she had referred to herself as Queen Holna.

Again a drawer opened across the room. Titus had moved away.

"I did what Advisor Qadir told me," Sahel pleaded. "I surrendered to Bessima."

It was all so crazy, unruly and chaotic like Sahel's memory and instinct, she and Titus discussing her dream as if it were his too.

"I know what I did," she spoke again but received no response. Unlike Prince Rahim emerging from the rubble with Queen Holna, Titus was gone.

Chapter 34

S ahel was halfway through her session with Dr. Leonard when she recalled Titus's words. "It's not your fault that Rahim died." She spoke the words to Dr. Leonard and then thought aloud, "I had been married to Prince Rahim." Sahel had told the psychiatrist of her dream, and about the players as best she remembered

She relived the pain of recognizing not simply who she had been, but had become. Each of Sahel's realities, that of the dream and her waking life, was but an alternate or parallel experience. Each mirrored the other, both revealing and uniting disparate aspects of her mind and soul. "How could he have known?" she said. Titus, it seems, had shared the dream with her.

"Have you asked him?" Dr. Leonard queried.

She had not. "He said I wasn't the only person in our marriage who had worries and concerns, fears and dreams," said Sahel. "I've never seen this side of Titus," Sahel lamented. She leaned back into the sofa, lifted her cane now folded, and stroked it. "First I'm channeling Sunetra, who's dead. Now Titus is invading my dreams."

"Why does it have to be your dream, and his presence an invasion?" Leonard asked.

"It's like he's inside my head. Like he was in the dream with me."

Sahel offered an oblique response to the psychiatrist's question. Sahel recalled, in the dream, how frightened and terrified Queen Holna had felt when seeing the two blades of the axes held to Prince Rahim's neck. "I was her, Queen Holna. She was me. I in her, she in me." Sahel then thought and said aloud, "Like Sunetra, Holna's soul had merged with mine, Holna's spirit, the essence of what made her distinct, kept her alive and fighting for Prince Rahim. Together we became one." Sahel lowered her eyelids. Red colored the dark spaces of her blindness. "In the dream it was as if I was watching both from outside of me and Queen Holna. And then there were times when we were one, with no distinction."

"So it was a lucid dream," said Dr. Leonard.

"I've felt that way sometimes with James," Sahel continued, answering the psychiatrist in what seemed a monologue. "When we're talking, Sunetra is so close. And then I've sensed her gone. But she's inside, hidden and quiet, moving through me. I feel the energy of her love and desire to reconnect with James."

"And what happens when you feel this love, her desire?"

"I want Titus. I want to be near him, to hold him, kiss him. A similar urge comes over me when I'm visiting James. It's Sunetra inside me, wanting to be with James. I hold my ground by going deeper into conversation with James. The headaches started when I realized what was happening. I resist for as long as I can. It takes all I have. Then I blank out."

The existence of these two realities within her, that of her dream in the Kingdom of Purdah and Sunetra's spirit dwelling inside her body, not only left Sahel perplexed, but had also taken its toll.

Still Sahel craved the energy of Sunetra's spirit coursing through her body. She also longed to return to the Kingdom of Purdah in her dream and this time with intentions that would hopefully reshape her waking life.

"I always knew it was a dream. And then I didn't," she said moments later of her time in Purdah.

"When did you become aware, or better yet, when did the dream shift into a full-blown reality that you no longer knew was a dream?"

"The second and last time I looked to Titus. I mean Rahim. No—"

Sahel then recalled, "I looked to Prince Thane, then Mama, Queen Bessima. And that's when I knew that she had been using him all along. Like Advisor Qadir had said. Mama used Prince Thane, no Carl, to—" Sahel absorbed her words. "And then there was the wedding, no, the funeral. I was so happy." Joy filled Sahel, now as then. "I could see. My sight had returned. I turned to Carl, thankful for urging me not to give up hope, to go through with the surgery. There had been no threat of an aneurysm. I had chosen to have the surgery of my own volition. And then ... " Sahel recalled the shift. "I looked at my dress. Carl and I were entering St. Maria's. The sanctuary was full. Everyone was looking at me. For a moment I thought we were getting married. But I didn't want to marry him. He looked so sad." Images of the ebb and flow of the final moments of the dream passed before her mind's eye.

"Father Richard was standing at the front of the church. A casket was behind him. Before Carl said anything, I knew. Titus was dead. Just like Rahim in Purdah." Sadness overwhelmed Sahel as the events, more vibrant than when first experienced in the dream, assumed their place in her store of memories. Straining, she swallowed tears.

"There was a glow about the sanctuary. Sunlight filtered through the stained-glass windows like when we were children, Titus, Carl, and I, and Titus leading the line up from Sunday School below so that those of us who had taken our first Communion would receive Eucharist from Father Richard. Moments later it all started," Sahel said. "My fainting spells, the

231

increased blood pressure. Because of them, Carl ordered a CAT scan. That's how he discovered the fistula." Again Sahel spoke her thoughts, connected the cause-and-effect of events that demanded she undergo surgery. "The dreamer is any and everything in their dream," she said. "But what if other people have experienced the same dream, shared the experiences with you?" Sahel was searching for answers in a reality where she feared none existed. "I don't feel this dream is truly mine, not with Titus having had the same one."

"It troubles you that he has shared this experience, the dream, with you?"

"But it's mine." Sahel's possessiveness grew. "It's like our minds have merged."

"As with your and Sunetra's souls, and spirits?" said Leonard.

"Shouldn't you be questioning me about my stability?" It angered Sahel that the psychiatrist seemed so open to accepting all she had shared.

"Do you feel unstable? Are you hearing voices? Thoughts of suicide, or harming others?"

"This is insane. I'm having hallucinations, for crying out loud!"

"And the definition of insanity is ... " said Leonard. "Visions of loving Titus, wanting him, concern for him and his emotions?" The psychiatrist offered possibilities.

"Something's happening to me. I'm changing. I've changed. I feel Titus pulling strings since he entered my dream."

"Perhaps he's been there all along."

The psychiatrist's voice again gripped her attention. Dr. Leonard's suggestion offered both comfort and doubt. He said, "You seem to have little problem with giving your mind and thoughts, your body, over as host to Sunetra's soul, her spirit. Someone you don't know, never met when she was alive. And yet, the thought of Titus, who has been with you nearly all your life, your mothers undergoing their pregnancies at nearly the same time, sharing your dream frightens you to the point of anger." Leonard's words presented an unsettling truth.

"I'm out of control when I'm with him."

232

"But it's also when you're most yourself," said Leonard. "Maybe the real Sahel, the true Sahel, whom you've kept hidden, is directing all of this. Maybe she's trying to come through. And when is any of us ever truly in control?" he added. "Some say it is but a fantasy, that we have a modicum of control. That it's never truly in our possession. Nothing but the illusion of it comforts our fears. Perhaps the presence of Sunetra within you, you hosting all that she could not bear to accept in her life, has pulled the sheath away from your eyes, revealed what you, like her, refused to see."

"In that case she's trying to save me from making the mistake she did," said Sahel. Perhaps manifesting as Sunetra. At that, a burst of energy tore through her, like a wave beaching upon the shore.

The quake of awareness rumbled through Sahel.

Dr. Leonard asked, "Have you seen James since your surgery?"

"I'm going to visit him when I leave here."

"I'm curious as to what James has experienced in his recent dreams," the psychiatrist said.

Despite her curiosity, she refused to question Leonard, inquire as to what he had meant or was after. Sahel grew still.

Leonard then said, "It seems that Prince Rahim died in Titus's experience of the dream?"

Sahel tried shoving past the last images of her dream, the terra-cotta walls of Bessima's castle tumbling down and then the casket in the sanctuary of St. Maria's.

"I couldn't bear losing Titus, not a second time." The pain of his having left the summer when she was eleven, and the news of his parents' deaths, swept in from the past delivering a fresh pain. She recalled her father delivering the news.

"Mama was so sad when Titus's parents died." A sense of loneliness, wide and deep like the ocean, filled Sahel and amplified the meaning behind her father's words. "She loved Titus's mother, Cecile. Titus's mother loved Mama. They talked each day, out on the front porch, drinking iced tea, while Titus and I played out back with Carl."

Sahel said, "I've never met any of Mama's family." Neither

had Sahel traveled to Ghana nor to Louisiana where Mama was from. "I was her bad secret," said Sahel. Bitterness coated her throat. "The results of Mama's dirty act of having slept with Daddy, a black man, a dark man, from Ghana, Africa. Her parents wanted her to abort me." Sahel pulled at her fingers.

"When she died, Daddy called no one. We were her only family, me, Daddy and Titus." Sahel's throat went dry, bolts falling from the doors holding closed a dam of emotions.

"Mama always said that Titus's mother, Cecile, was closer than any of her sisters. Mama had eight. Her choice to marry Daddy and have me meant that she was dead to them—her mother, her father, and all her sisters."

Again, tears encroached, drew near to all the unlocked spaces of hurt and rage, sown and pocketed by Lillian's disdain for Sahel clothed in the darkness of her skin, standing in stark contrast and so disparate from Lillian's, like that of buttermilk.

"It's hard being in the middle. Half American. Half Ghanaian. Trying to mediate the war of unspoken words and anger between Mama and Daddy."

"Then step out of the center."

"I married Titus," Sahel said.

"But you care about Carl."

"This is ludicrous." Again Sahel shook her head.

"Ludicrous or frightening that you're that tightly bonded? That he loves you despite your loathing yourself for your darkness, of both your skin and the loss of your sight?"

Sahel gripped her cane as if it were a sword with a blade as sharp as the daggers that had been at Rahim's neck in the dream.

Her frustration mounted. The idea of her mother, Lillian, having used Carl, played upon his desires for Sahel to attract and hold Titus, like Queen Bessima had done in the dream, nauseated Sahel. The slow ebb of a headache threatened to intensify. "Carl and Titus have always been competitive. It's part of their friendship."

"And as with your parents, you held in the middle, easing the tension."

Sahel knitted her brows in an effort to confront Leonard's words. "I can't abandon Carl. He's my friend, Titus's friend.

234

They're my best friends, the two of them. They're the only ones who know what it was like for me living with Mama. She was a terror." An image emerged of Queen Bessima upon the throne of the Kingdom of Freedom, Sahel as Queen Holna faced her. "Prince Thane had stood to my left, Titus to my right, Advisor Qadir and his wife, Cynda, behind me."

A few seconds passed. The session gained steam and continued. "There's a lot to be gained by discussing your experience of the dream with Titus," Leonard said. The thought of doing so, if indeed Leonard's suggestion held water, also frightened Sahel.

"You and Titus are man and wife," said Leonard.

"That doesn't mean he can own my dreams," Sahel said fuming.

"Sharing your dream is not the same as invading your darkness. Titus's presence in your dream does not erase the meaning it has for you. In fact it may even—"

"It's my dream! I don't want him there!"

"But he is."

The psychiatrist's silence drew Sahel's ire. Her anger seeped into the core of her hurt. She said, "This is not right." Sahel shook her head. "I'm behaving like a child."

"You're in touch with your anger."

"That bothers you," Sahel said.

"Are you asking or stating?"

Again Sahel shook her head. More indecision.

Slowly she wound her fingers around her cane, the tension increasing in her hand. She wanted to throw the thing at Leonard. But her hand had grown numb. "It's been nearly seven days. Titus was expecting the surgery to return my sight. Any changes that result beyond my being alive would have occurred by now."

"You're certain of that?"

"It's what Carl and Dr. Blake told me. I'm just happy to be alive, not to have that time bomb of an aneurysm ticking in my head and ready to go off at any minute."

"You speak as if you've done a duty of some sort, undergoing the surgery." Leonard's words were soft and close.

235

Sahel imagined him having leaned forward. "It was something I had to do. I couldn't put Titus and Daddy, nor Carl or Geraldine, through what I went through when I took the pills, not again."

"Tell me what you went through," Leonard said.

On hearing his question, Sahel realized she had meant to say, "... what I did ..." A psychotherapist also, she could not excuse herself from the Freudian slip by saying, "That's not what I meant."

"It's hard watching someone working hard to save you, fearing they've lost you because of something they've done, and you knowing that you played your role in everything that happened. It's especially hard when you know that person loves you more than you love yourself. You feel horrible, angry with yourself."

"You're talking about Titus," Leonard said. Sahel nodded.

"It wasn't right taking those pills." She began to cry.

"And yet it dominates your thoughts."

"I can't seem to escape it. It's as if I owe Titus my life. I owe him for bringing me back. Seeing him down there pushing on my chest, his face torn with grief and disbelief, and hurt ... " Sahel shook her head. Still the memory remained.

She said, "It wasn't until Sunetra started visiting me and I met James that I started seeing images. After I lost my sight with the accident, I couldn't see anything. Everything was dark. I couldn't even recall memories. Nothing. And with this dream I saw everything that happened. All the images have returned. My memories. I lost them after the accident. But now I have them back."

"What's one that you recall?"

Sahel relaxed farther into cushion of the sofa. "Me and Titus and Carl, our hands in the water, dirt beneath, mud." The image took shape in her mind as she spoke. "Sunlight on the water. Titus's hands next to mine. Carl's on the left of mine."

"Your hands were in the middle," said Leonard. Again Sahel nodded.

"But it's not that way anymore. Titus and I are married."

"Do you regret marrying him?"

"He needs me. And I need him."

"What about Carl?" Leonard said.

"We're too much alike. I've come to see that." Sahel let out a facetious laugh. "Imagine that. It takes being blind to see what's always been there."

"Are you afraid of Titus's love?"

Sahel fell still. "I don't deserve it."

"But you do deserve Carl?" Leonard's statement was truly a question.

"He would know what to do with me, how to handle me."

"And how is it you need to be handled?"

"Titus worries too much."

"You're his wife."

"I'll be okay."

"You took the pills."

"Titus takes things too much to heart."

"You mean like when you tried to end your life?" the psychiatrist asked. "What were you fleeing from when you took the pills?"

"It's always been with me—the darkness—even before I lost my sight."

"Your blindness is your darkness," the psychiatrist said.

"I can't see."

"Titus's love, or yourself?"

"It's pouring in on me now," Sahel said. "It's all around me, fills the darkness. I can't avoid it."

"So when you took the pills, you were trying to escape Titus's love?"

Tears showered Sahel's eyes. "In the Kingdom of Purdah, I felt myself, saw myself, loving him back. The love I have for Titus came through. I couldn't fight it. The only war was with Queen Bessima—my mother. It was so clear." Sahel's lips trembled. "That was my battle."

"There was also Prince Thane. You realized how Queen Bessima had used him."

Again Leonard's words hit hard.

"The surgery saved my life. Carl was there with Dr. Blake helping him."

"Yes, and at a great risk."

"So what are you saying?"

"I'm suggesting that you're torn, not so much between Titus and Carl, but as you yourself have acknowledged, between accepting and avoiding Titus's love. That is the war."

"If that were the case, then I would not have undergone the surgery," Sahel said.

"Which is precisely why you had it."

Now Sahel was more confused, more so than she had ever been when trying to choose between her love for Titus and loyalty to Carl.

The idea that her mother had used Carl, placed an added burden upon her. Excruciating guilt edged upon her.

"You've fallen in love with Titus, allowed him to enter your body and soul. I know this not because of your increased intimacy," said the psychiatrist. "But because of how much Titus's feelings affect you. That he has shared the dream you experienced during the surgery speaks to that."

Leonard continued. "Carl has urged you to have the surgery since the accident. But not until he found the aneurysm, and you realized that you might die, did you decide to have it. And this is where it gets interesting."

"You knew the odds of surviving the surgery—fifty percent that you could die, twenty percent that complications could occur and leave you brain dead. But still you fought. You did that because, as you say, you couldn't put Titus through losing you again, and what you experienced, separation from the one person who has not only loved you, but has shown anger when you didn't accept his love. Titus cares. And you feel that care each time he hurts."

"Carl's been angry too," Sahel retorted. "We argued before he discovered the aneurysm."

"Yes, but his anger has not troubled you the way Titus's frustrations have. You feel Titus's pain. Just as with your dream, that is also his dream; you share his emotions. When he draws close you feel love, something you did not know or experience with your mother. I'm not saying she didn't love you. But you didn't feel her love. You didn't experience or know it in the same way as with Titus. And this is where it gets particularly interesting." Leonard's voice filled with an excited sort of worry.

As with Carl when Sahel awoke from the surgery, the psychiatrist sounded tentative, but hopeful that she could handle a truth he was about to speak. "Titus is like your mother in so many ways." A second shower of awakening rained upon Sahel. "But he does not direct his anger at you."

"How about when he hit me with the car." Sahel regretted her response.

"You said he was not at fault. You've consistently defended him."

"Perhaps I don't want to do that anymore."

"You've said over and over, described how you were on the pavement searching for the engagement ring he gave you."

"My mother touched that ring. She kissed it."

"After which Titus slid it on your finger."

She recalled the gentleness with which Titus had taken her left hand and slid the ring bearing a pear-shaped diamond onto her third finger. He had been standing across from Sahel on the other side of the hospital bed on which Lillian lay. Titus had lifted and held Sahel's hand over Lillian's abdomen.

Lillian had given a weak smile and then, looking on, her eyes had grown red and glassy. The words she had spoken then returned to Sahel now. "He loves you more than I ever could." Sahel's mother had seemed resigned, apathetic, almost without hope.

Sahel said, "My mother never received last rites."

"The priest didn't make it in time?" Leonard said.

"No. She refused him, said she didn't deserve forgiveness." Sahel grew cold and numb. Tears now slipped onto her face.

Chapter 35

S

ahel ended her session with Dr. Leonard, and Geraldine walked her across the street to Berkeley General where she visited James for the first time since her surgery.

On reaching the door to his hospital room, she once more felt awkward when about to enter, knowing that James still refused to see Geraldine.

"All that matters is that he's still alive," Geraldine had said when they had exited the elevator onto the fifth floor where James's hospital room was located. "There's hope as long as he's speaking with you."

Sahel also felt a traitor. She harbored Sunetra's soul, had edged from ambivalence in doing so, to finding strength in serving as the link connecting Sunetra and James.

Inside James's hospital room she made her way to the bedside and grasped his hand. "You made it," James said. The warmth of his hand that had shrunk to what felt like skin and bones conveyed his thankfulness. James's life was slipping away, time running out.

"How are you feeling?" he said.

"The headaches are subsiding," said Sahel. She was now sitting on the chair as she had during past visits. "The dizziness has also faded."

"So they drained the aneurysm."

"It's gone," Sahel said.

A moment of silence followed and then, "What about your sight?" James asked the question that all pondered with hope and fear.

"It's been a week. I don't think it's—"

"How's Titus handling it?"

"He's angry, hurt." Sahel knotted her fist against the cane. "Blaming himself more now than ever."

"And Carl?"

"He tries to hide it, but he's disappointed too."

"And you?"

Images she had experienced for the first time since losing her sight ran across the stage of Sahel's mind. "Why did you ever come back and remain alive?" Sahel asked. She was speaking of when James's heart had stopped.

"I guess for the same reason you came back to Titus."

"But you love Sunetra," said Sahel. "It wasn't my time. Sunetra told me, 'Not now.'"

"I also needed to help you."

Sahel lowered her head, slipped closer to the edge of tears. "You sound like a man in my dream."

"Would that be Advisor Qadir?" James said.

She lifted her chin towards James's voice.

"I was there with you all the way through the surgery," James said.

"In Purdah?" Sahel said.

"The Kingdom of Purdah." James spoke with a certainty and clarity that shook Sahel.

"You saw Sunetra," she said.

"Cynda," James said.

"What does this mean? You were in my dream."

"We live in different places. And at various times. I know that now. When we've finished our work in one place, we move on," James said. Joy filled his voice. Sahel wished to see his face, hold his hope, and transcend her fears that now deepened to a throbbing ache.

"I feel like a traitor," said Sahel. "Geraldine has brought me here thinking that I would help you find a way to live."

"You've been doing the work required of you in this place and at this time." James's words flowed empty of fear against the canvas of tranquility blanketing his voice.

"You really believe in life after death?"

James chuckled. "A doubting Thomas, Catholic, no less."

Ambivalence. "We come in all denominations and religions." Sahel smiled against tears wetting her face.

"How well I know. I was one of them. That is until I found myself in the Kingdom of Purdah with you."

Surprised by another of James's revelations, her thoughts fell still.

"Sunetra's been coming to me in my dreams since she died, and I was sentenced to San Quentin. But I've been afraid all this time."

James explained. "I refused to accept that it was really her, that it wasn't my imagination, or the conjuring of my hopes and wishes. I've wanted to die," he said. "But I had no idea that there was, really is something that follows death. I thought I'd be alone, that everything would end when my life on earth came to a close. Now I know. I've seen the other side. You took me there."

The Kingdom of Purdah. Sahel felt her anxiety and fears turning into excitement and hope. "Why did you come back?" she spoke the rhetorical mantra.

"The same reason you're here right now. I'm doing the work I was put here to do."

Again James's words pricked her doubt, relieving it of steam.

"The first time I saw you, I felt Sunetra's spirit, her energy. When you told me of the voice inside your head, the pieces began sliding into place. If she could come to you, then that meant what I had seen in my dreams was real. The day of your

243

surgery, I slept for six hours straight. And dreamed."

"You were in Purdah?" Sahel's thoughts continued, this time aloud.

"We've been in Purdah all along. The Kingdom of Purdah is all around us."

Sahel considered James as Advisor Qadir entering her royal quarters and then seeing Cynda. "She was there when the dream opened. Cynda, Sunetra. And then you came."

Clarity and understanding settled upon her defenses, kneaded and softened by James's words. Sahel then said, "Titus had my dream like you."

"It's not just your dream," James said.

"I suppose this is where you're supposed to let me touch the holes left by the nails that were in your sides."

Sahel's thoughts floated back and forth between the present and moments before the surgery when under the effects of the anesthesia, sleep had overtaken her.

Father Richard reading the scripture from the Book of Titus had hung heavily in her mind. "To Titus, mine own son: ... Tell my people these things speak ... Let no man despise thee."

James said, "Maybe it's Titus's dream. And you've been pulled in. Who's to say?"

Titus was practical and directed. Sahel had never seen him as a person who gave attention to his dreams.

James's use of the word ... *been* ... pushed open a door that led to myriad possibilities concerning what had been, and was now occurring.

What if my life is his dream—Titus's dream?

Sahel felt herself growing dizzy, the world around her spinning.

She touched the bandage, a square covering the incision that Dr. Blake, in his efforts to drain the aneurysm, wove around her cranial nerve, made to gain a wider view of her brain.

The fistula had been thick, and difficult to pierce, Carl had said.

Against Carl's fear that Sahel might die or end up a

vegetable, Blake had persevered, ultimately sealing the door that, if not eliminated, led to certain death.

James spoke. "Sunetra always said that our consciousness could never handle all the possibilities that life delivers. A person could spend his entire lifetime meditating to expand his consciousness, but without experiencing human love, and physical touch, all remained a mystery. The greatest ashram, the grandest cathedral, the most holy of all temples, is the union of two hearts committed through life and unto death."

"Knowing that, why did she kill herself?"

"Reciting words is not the same as experiencing the concept they convey. Death changed her. It brought her back to life. And to me."

An image of Sunetra again clothed in red emerged upon Sahel's thoughts and robbed her words. The robe turned to purple. A crown appeared and sat upon Sunetra's head.

Sahel's temples began to throb. The pounding of her thoughts intensified. Her head grew heavy. "I need to lie down." Again she touched the bandage covering the incision on her forehead. "The Kingdom of Purdah," she uttered. Sahel felt herself growing weak. "A dream." James's words grew shallow. Sleep encroached upon Sahel and she was unable to resist its soft tentacles.

"*Purdah.*"

Chapter 36

S

ahel awoke to someone holding her hand. She was lying down.

Echoes of James's voice surfaced in her mind. Purdah. "What happened?" Sahel asked.

"I discharged you from the hospital with the understanding that you would take it easy," Carl said. Sahel felt the weight of him sitting upon the bed.

"I hadn't seen him in over a week," Sahel said of James. A deep and thick silence permeated and enwrapped her words. "I hope my fainting didn't frighten him."

"Right now I'm more concerned about you." The fear that James might have died during her time in surgery arose. "I thought I'd never speak to him again, at least not on this side." Fear had ridden her thoughts minutes before the effects of the anesthesia.

"There was no way I was going to let you die," Carl said.

"You're not God."

"No, but I can pray." He squeezed her hand. "Throughout the surgery. The statue of St. Joseph that Father Richard used that morning looked upon me and Dr. Blake."

"Six hours." That's a long time to have a saint looking upon you.

Sahel then chuckled. "You remember Sister Amethyst and Oakland Catholic Prep?"

"Do I?" Carl said with a tone that told Sahel he was smiling. "She was cute. But boy was she strict. I don't know what was harder, her rules or the fact that every time one of us boys caught ourselves looking at her, we felt guilty, dirty, as if we were lusting after God's wife."

"One of God's many wives," Sahel said. "You know there was a rumor that Father Cramer had a thing for her."

"I could see them married," Carl said.

"I suppose that's why Father Cramer was always referring the girls to Sister Amethyst when questions of life and Mother Nature came up."

"Sister Amethyst did the same with us." Carl then mocked the nun. "Now Carl Pierson, I think that's a question that Father Cramer is best suited to counsel you on."

"How much did you have to watch her with those alert and observant eyes to create that voice? You sound just like her."

"Comes with the territory. Surviving Catholic school is not easy," Carl said.

"We did more than survive." Sahel's throat grew scratchy in realizing how far she had come with Carl and Titus beside her.

Now fully awake, she recalled how she had cried when James had explained having experienced the same dream as had Sahel during her surgery. She turned her head upon the pillow. Carl touched her cheek and turned it back towards his words.

"You went through a rough surgery. The aneurysm's gone. But you've got to take it easy," Carl said.

"And what of my sight?"

"It'll return."

"And what if it doesn't?"

248

"We'll deal with that later," Carl said. "For right now I need to—"

"I have to go home." Sahel forced herself up, swung her feet to the other side of the bed, and moved to stand. Carl grasped her arms. "Let me go." Sahel pushed him away.

"We need to talk."

"And I need to get home. Titus left this morning and I haven't heard from him."

"I've spoken with him."

"You told him I fainted? More for him to worry about." Sahel shivered.

"He's fine." Carl lifted her hand. "Sahel, please sit down."

"Are you telling me I can't go home?"

"I promised Titus I wouldn't let anything happen to you." Carl's tone grew firm, almost angry.

"You also gave him the hope that I'd regain my sight," said Sahel. She straightened her back.

Then came the silence in which she sensed Carl fumbling to locate words. "What is it you're not telling me? Another surgery? What?" Sahel said.

"I told Titus that I'd tell you about James."

Sahel scoured the words of her conversation with Carl, identifying the halts and pauses in Carl's voice. "He's dead," she said.

"How did you know?"

Again she whipped back tears.

"It was for the best," Carl said.

"Don't say that!" Sahel gave into the anger welling up. And then, "He was ready to die." She sighed and absorbed her words, succumbing to a truth that in its bitter sharpness also held comfort. "It was also what he wanted."

Carl said, "Titus and your father are with Geraldine making arrangements."

"He wanted to be cremated."

"Geraldine is planning a full burial."

"Then she needs to be told," Sahel said.

"She's taken it pretty badly."

"And how does she think he had it?"

249

"Titus and I both agree that you don't need to get involved in this," Carl said. The clarity of his statement fell like the doors of a prison closing upon Sahel inside. "You've done enough. Right now you have a different set of priorities, that of resting for the next four wee—"

"Stop telling me what to do, Carl."

The hard silence that followed hewed a wide gulf, one that mere words or the breath of deep friendship could not easily smooth over.

"As your doctor, I really think—"

"You think. That's what you do, Carl. Analyze. But I feel. And right now I'm feeling the loss of someone who taught me more than anyone I've met. Jameson Harding Bolton. He was a friend. And now ..." Sahel shook her head and began to cry. Sahel wiped her face. She would not sob. "He lost everything in this life and somehow managed to love and give. He held out hope that he'd be reunited with the person he loved. And now he's there." Again Sahel wiped her face with her wrist. "I'm glad for him." Sadness and loneliness enveloped her.

"He understood so much about me, what I couldn't accept or see."

"You helped him, too," Carl said.

A groan of loss and sadness escaped Sahel's lips. In resistance to the sobs, Sahel crossed her arms and tightly hugged her chest. She doubled over. Carl's hand softly landed upon her back.

"You're always so concerned about others and never yourself," Carl pleaded in a whisper. "Your mother, Titus, now James. We all miss him. But I think he'd want you to take care of yourself."

"You didn't know him!" Sahel screamed.

"I saw everything Blake did. The aneurysm inside your head was like a small plum. Had we begun the procedure any second later, it could have burst and ... I love you," Carl whispered.

"You can't keep saying that. Not if you really do love me."

"It's true."

The door to Sahel's room opened. She sat up, her attention flew towards the door.

"Titus," Carl said. The door closed. Sahel shuddered.

"Carl told me about James," said Titus. He lifted Sahel's hand. "I'm sorry." She drew near, embraced him.

"Where is Geraldine?" Carl asked.

"Essien drove her home. They're at her house," Titus said. "The funeral is the day after tomorrow."

"How is she?" Sahel asked.

"We all need to support her." Titus sounded sad and broken. As with James, change now threaded Titus's voice. His words held a different rhythm, alluded to a new melody of heart.

"I want to go home," Sahel said.

"What does Carl say?" Titus said. Sahel felt him turn as he spoke the words.

"I ordered a quick CAT scan. The tests came back and she's fine."

"Thanks," Titus said. Sahel wished to have seen his face.

Evidence of the transformation in Titus's voice, the moments afterwards, harboring the possibilities of various outcomes, grew ever more tense.

Sahel reached out for Titus. He took her hand. Again she said, "I want to go home."

Chapter 37

T

he drive home was silent as a thick mist of fog moving in from the ocean, enveloping and obscuring all it encountered. Too afraid to ask, Sahel wondered how much had Titus heard of her conversation with Carl, what had he seen.

She recalled Carl's protestation, *I love you.*

You can't keep saying that.

My silence doesn't make it any less true, he had said.

I love you too, but not like that, Sahel had said. The door to the hospital room had opened and Titus entered.

The memory ate further into her as she rode in the car beside Titus. Sahel wished for the ability to go back in time, re-state her case to Carl, and make him realize the futility of his pursuit.

Despite her fears Sahel spoke and severed the silence

between her and Titus. "Thank you for being there for Geraldine."

"She's really broken," Titus said.

"Fortunately, James had made his peace. He was ready," Sahel said.

She considered Lillian having refused Essien's offer to call Father Richard to administer last rites. *It's too late*, Lillian had said, her voice raspy and barely audible. She had lifted her hand, trembling and withered from a heart that, in those last moments, fought to make each beat. *I can't be saved. I don't deserve it.*

Titus said, "At least he wasn't alone." The compassion in his words awed Sahel. And yet she remained mindful of how she and Titus had argued, Titus revealing that he had shared her dream.

"You hadn't wanted me to visit James," she said.

"I was wrong," said Titus. The car moved along. "It's horrible to have lost the person you love and to have no one who understands."

"You understood," Sahel said. She extended her left hand across the seat towards Titus. "It was difficult losing Mama."

"Yes, but the love was strained between you two. I imagine losing your father would be different," said Titus.

A chill covered Sahel's shoulders. She crossed her arms over her chest, each hand massaging the arm of the opposite hand in an effort to create warmth.

The car moved along. Sahel wished for them to approach an intersection where the light was red. Instead, the sedan continued, the universe having directed all the lights to flash green.

"Death frightens me," Titus said. "I fight so hard to save my patients. The men are like my father. In the eyes of every woman on whom I operate, I see the eyes of my mother looking back and asking me to save her."

Again Sahel shivered, in the realization of the enormous burden Titus had carried since life had ripped his parents from the earth and left him an orphan. The weight of his plight settled upon Sahel's heart like a stone slab. Her soul let go of memories embedded in her consciousness, images of her mother Lillian, words she had spoken, ghosts fighting to remain alive, and haunting Sahel's every breath along the path of darkness she traveled.

Sahel wished to roll back the door of Titus's soul and drink in the light of his love, then re-infuse him with all his devotion had given her. "You're a good person and excellent surgeon," she said.

"All I could think of was you when Grandpa Avery, my mother's father, returned from the hospital to my aunt's house, and told me that both my parents had died," Titus said.

He had been eleven when his father had driven Titus and his mother across the country to New Jersey to visit his mother's sister, due to deliver her first child. One afternoon a week after their arrival, and during the drive to the hospital where Cecile's sister had given birth, an eighteen-wheel big rig had crossed the yellow line and slammed into his parents' car, killing them instantly. Titus had remained at the house with Cecile's parents.

Titus said, "I didn't think of your mother or your father or Carl. Just you. All I wanted was a sunny day in your backyard. We'd make some mud cakes, let them dry in the sun, and somehow everything would be okay."

Tears scratched at the door of Sahel's throat and heart. She forced a swallow, hoping saliva would moisten her mouth, and dissolve the tears.

"The day you took the pills, and I found you, all I could think of was I'd have no one to make mud cakes with. No dirt and water. No sun. When your heart stopped beating, I felt my whole world coming apart, life slipping from under me. No reason to live." He sighed.

Sahel grew warm. The sensation of Titus's palms, hard and sweaty, pressing upon her chest returned.

Titus said, "I guess that's what you must have felt like when you lost your sight. I took that from you." The penitence in his voice cut at Sahel's heart. If only the surgery had restored her sight. "I was so hoping … And Carl said the surgery might bring your sight back."

"I don't care about my sight." Sahel touched Titus's thigh. "I just want to love you. And let you love me."

255

"I wonder if my love is good for you. Look what it's caused."

"I thought we talked about this," Sahel said, her frustration mounting. "What happened the other day when you went in to see that patient Calvin wanted your consultation on? You said you had made peace with this. You saw the patient, came back."

They had also argued about James. "We made love." Sahel continued. "Then it's like something happened. Everything changed."

Titus said, "Rahim dies in the dream." His words cast a chill.

Sahel's possessiveness about the dream returned. Again Titus's knowledge of the dream felt like a boa coiling around Sahel, its prey. "James had the dream, the one I had. He told me before he died today."

"He was Qadir," Titus said.

"Yes. And Cynda, Sunetra, his fiancée. They were married in the dream—in the Kingdom of Purdah."

"He's with her now," Titus said. His words amazed Sahel even more. "She spoke to me in the dream, told me that Rahim would die. She comforted me."

Sahel grew terrified that not only was she losing grip on reality, but now her sickness had infected Titus.

The car slowed to a halt. Soft, clear, and with deliberation, Titus's words came at her. "I wasn't Rahim," Titus said. "I was Prince Thane."

Chapter 38

A
n hour after reaching home, Sahel came downstairs prepared to join Titus at the kitchen table for the dinner that Zelda had made. As Zelda prepared to leave, while Sahel was walking her to the front door, she expressed her concern for Geraldine in the wake of James's death. "Please tell Mrs. Payton that she is in my prayers." Sahel opened the door as Zelda spoke. "I will offer a novena for her at Mass tomorrow morning."

"She'll appreciate that," said Sahel. Zelda grasped her hand.

On hearing Zelda's footsteps die while moving down the steps, she closed the door, only to meet Titus's voice drifting from the study. He was speaking on the phone with Essien. "The funeral home says that 10 a.m. will work. Has Geraldine contacted any of James's colleagues at the brokerage? I see," Titus said after some moments of silence. Despite Sahel's insistence on not to, Titus told Sahel's father she had fainted once more. "It was when she was with James," Titus said, "—as he was dying."

Sahel cringed. If but a moment could pass without someone in the house worrying about her!

"Yeah. Yeah. Sahel is fine," said Titus to Essien at the other end.

The conversation between Sahel's husband and father continued several more minutes.

Sahel had asked Geraldine to say nothing to Essien of what the nurse had found when she entered James's hospital room. Sahel had been lying on the floor as James, his eyes closed, lay still upon the hospital bed.

"No. No. She's fine. Carl ran a CAT scan," Titus said in another attempt to reassure Essien that Sahel was fine.

Sahel closed her eyes and wished for the blindness to dissipate, to open her eyes and see clearly, if not for herself, at least for those who loved her.

"... No I think a morning service on Thursday will be fine," Titus said, and then of Sahel, "She'll have tomorrow to rest."

With frustration tearing at her, Sahel maneuvered her way from the foyer back to the kitchen. Her heart ached as she found and lowered herself onto a chair at the kitchen table. James was dead and yet concern for him remained vibrant as ever. When would it stop?

She had to regain her independence. Pondering how she might set about doing that, she yet again pushed from her thoughts Titus's revelation in the car. Carl is Rahim. I was, I am Prince Thane. He dies, not me.

A wisp of air brushed Sahel's face. Titus had entered the kitchen and walked past her. She heard him open the microwave. A bowl went down on the table.

Titus said, "Your father will be spending the night over at Geraldine's." He spoke in a matter-of-fact way that awed and shocked Sahel even further than during their ride home in the car.

Surprise, sadness, and her forever-present guilt stilled Sahel's tongue during dinner and when, hours later, Titus crawled in bed beside her. After hearing him flick off the lamp, she reached

258

out and touched his back. Gently she stroked it. Unlike on other nights, Titus did not move. Carefully, cautiously, she traced his shoulders. He did not turn towards her, nor did he indicate for her to stop. Unable to conjure words, Sahel eventually turned over and with her back to Titus's drifted to sleep. Moments later she awoke to find herself enveloped in his arms, warm and strong. In thankfulness and yearning for atonement, she kissed the back of his palm. Having enveloped her, he did not move.

Deeper into the night, Titus's beeper sounded.

Barely awake and caught in the throes of memories, now visual since having met James, Sahel ached for the times when her beeper had sounded. People had needed her to lend them strength.

Titus and Carl seemed to only want her weakness, out of their need to feel strong. Only after losing her sight did Carl directly express to Sahel the depth of his affections. She had known they existed, sensed their presence. And yet something about her losing her sight, her inability to see him compounded with her brush with death delivered by Sahel's own hand, exhumed Carl's vulnerabilities.

Then again, it was only after losing her sight that Sahel had found the strength to marry Titus, to become his wife.

Perhaps that had been the trigger to Carl's protestations and vigorous declarations.

Titus ended the phone conversation and got out of bed. "I need to go to the hospital," he said.

"But I thought Calvin wanted you to take some time off."

"That patient I went in to see the other day. Paramedics brought him into the hospital." The sound of Titus's voice came from across the room. That his words were muffled indicated he was dressing.

"Calvin wants me to scrub in." Calvin Bennett, the senior partner of the cardiac group to which Titus was the last to join, was not one to issue a command, and then rescind it. "Why would he tell you to come home, take some time off and then call you in?" Sahel said. "Who's the patient?"

The door to the closet went closed.

"I'm not certain."

259

"Is it your patient?" she asked.

Now sitting up, Sahel moved to get out of bed. "You should rest," Titus said. He touched her shoulder and then said, "Carl and your father are both worried."

"I'm fine."

"Don't push your luck, my friend," Titus said with what Sahel imagined as a smile. Sunshine infused his words. Images of water, dirt, and mud cakes flitted across her mind. Titus touched her head.

She lifted her face. His lips grazed hers.

"When you get home ..." Sahel said, "—perhaps we can—" She fell silent at the touch of Titus's finger stroking her cheek. Again the guilt of what she determined as betrayal—judging Titus to be like her mother, convicting him on the basis of his skin color, resisting his love and trying not to love him back—overwhelmed Sahel.

"I need to go," Titus said. His finger left her face.

The door closed. Titus's footsteps on the other side moved down the stairs, on his way to the hospital. Sahel drew the covers upon her body, and fell asleep.

Quiet, bitter memories flickered across Sahel's thoughts, banishing the darkness.

"I want to get married now," Titus had said. It had been early evening, lights lining the driveway and the steps leading up to the front door, illuminating the dusk settling slowly and evenly.

"And I need time," Sahel had said. It had been minutes before the accident, Sahel facing Titus, the two of them at the back of Titus's car.

"Time for what?" He squeezed his palm tighter around the keys to his sedan behind which they had been standing.

"Time to plan for the wedding, get a house, move my stuff," Sahel said.

Sahel's mother had died five months earlier and she was still recovering. A psychologist and therapist adept at caring for others, Sahel said nothing of the pain of her loss of her mother to Titus or anyone.

260

"You can't just get married and have everything fall in place."

"If you love each other it will."

"We're two adults with full, professional lives," Sahel said. "I have to prepare my clients."

"I didn't know our private lives were also privy to your clients," Titus said. Adamant, he frowned, knitting his brows.

"Well, I can't imagine you planned to get married one day and perform surgery the next. Patients aren't stupid about these things. They—"

"Have you told your clients that you're engaged? Surely they see your ring. Or don't you wear it when you're with them?"

"Why would you ask such a thing?" Sahel said.

"I don't know—you're so private about your work."

"That's what clients pay me for, privacy and confidentiality."

"Oh, come off it, Sahel. This has nothing to do with your clients. It's between me and you."

Sahel's lips fell still.

Again, Titus asked, "Have you told them?"

"I'm not going to discuss my clients with you."

"Since you're so concerned about how things in your life might affect them, and as you say, getting married is a big change, I thought that you might have—"

"I'm taking care of my clients. You just take care of your patients," Sahel said. She started past Titus. He caught her arm. She pulled back.

"Our mothers were best friends, closer than sisters." Titus spoke low and calmly. The lines upon his forehead had betrayed disappointment and hurt. His voice dipped further. "They wanted us together. You promised your mother."

Sahel started away once more. Again Titus grabbed her wrist. Sahel refused to turn back. "I love you. Need you." Titus's words, too raw, and real, conveyed how she felt despite her mother's insistences and warnings. Sahel had urges of her own. She would not succumb to them. Titus reminded her too much of Lillian.

Sahel tugged back her hand, ripped her fingers from Titus's grip.

Minutes later and up in her room she looked down upon Titus then pacing across the driveway. The lack of direction in the pattern of his footsteps conveyed a pain that spread across Sahel's chest, and radiated throughout her body. She grew cold, placed hands across her chest, and grasped her forearms.

Then she felt it gone. The ring. The fingers of her hands lay empty against her forearm. Sahel inspected her left hand. It was there minutes ago—on the third finger.

Sahel tore out of the bedroom, ran down the stairs and out onto the driveway. Titus was no longer pacing. He had gotten into his car. Frantic to find the ring, Sahel had knelt upon the driveway. She had not seen the car coming. In frustration and hurt, Titus had decided to go home. Sahel's Rover had been parked in front of his black sedan. There had been no other way except in reverse.

Sahel recalled Lillian extending her hand. Her trembling fingers had reached towards the engagement ring Titus had given Sahel. "Let me see it." Her eyes, weakened by death hovering within her pupils, had glistened momentarily.

A brief surge of energy had filled Lillian's voice weakened by a heart ebbing towards its last and final beats. "So pretty," she said. Her face, pale and sallow, had taken on a hint of color.

Titus had given Lillian the pear-shaped diamond perched atop a four-pronged. Sunlight from the window by which Essien and Carl had stood filled the stone and bounced off the gold setting.

Lillian kissed the ring symbolic of life, love, and eternity, and gave it back to Titus. He slid it onto Sahel's finger. Lillian would die that afternoon.

"I love you," Lillian had uttered. "Really I do." The broken pieces within Sahel shattered by her mother's bitter words and angered actions came together.

It was as if Sahel's mother was rescinding all she had said prior to that moment of Titus sliding the engagement ring onto Sahel's finger, that when kissing it she had infused all her efforts and purpose for living into her last words to Sahel.

Five months later, and on the night of the argument, Sahel had released a sigh of relief when spying the engagement ring upon the driveway. In her mind Titus had still been pacing, not in the car and never moving in reverse.

The momentary glow of the taillights had brought the ring into focus and helped Sahel to find it. She reached out and lifted it from the grey pavement.

Exhaust fumes filled Sahel's nose. Red crowded in. She fell, slamming her head onto the cement.

"Sahel. Oh, my god. What were you doing back here?" Titus's voice came seconds later. Sahel had momentarily lost consciousness. That he had not driven over her remained a miracle. "I thought you were in the house," Titus said.

Sahel felt him lift her into his arms. "You slammed your head on the pavement. How do you feel?" he asked.

"Look at me," Titus said. He gripped her face and head. "Let me see into your eyes."

She blinked several times. Try as she might she could not see into his.

Chapter 39

S

ahel awoke with a start when she sensed the warmth of a hand upon her arm. She moved to sit upon realizing she was not dreaming.

The hand was not Titus's. "I didn't mean to startle you," said Geraldine. "Zelda said you were upstairs sleeping."

"I was tired." Sahel said. "And Carl wants me to ..." Placing her hand over her mouth, she failed to stifle a yawn.

Now fully awake, Sahel said, "Oh, my god, I'm so sorry. James."

Concern and penitence softly peppered her tone. She reached out.

Geraldine sat upon the bed and embraced her.

"I can't believe he's gone," Geraldine said and then fumbled for words.

The two cried upon each other's shoulders.

That afternoon Sahel ate soup and sandwiches with a salad prepared by Geraldine.

"That was really good," Sahel said on taking the last bite of her chicken salad sandwich. "But I feel horrible." Sahel wiped her lips with the paper napkin. "We should be cooking for you in the light of—"

Geraldine lifted Sahel's hand empty of the napkin she had placed on the table. "This was addressed to you," Geraldine said.

She handed Sahel a large envelope.

"Will you open it for me?" Sahel asked after feeling its dimensions. She handed it back to Geraldine.

"It's an iPod," Geraldine said following the sound of paper tearing.

She lifted Sahel's hand and placed the device and its accompanying headphones upon her palm.

Sahel shivered on Geraldine folding her fingers over the device. Alone in her bedroom upstairs, Sahel placed the headphones over her ears and then pressed the dial on the iPod Geraldine had given her.

James's voice streamed through the headphones into her ears.

"That you're listening to this says two things. You survived the surgery. And I have died." Again, Sahel trembled.

"Thank you for agreeing to listen to this. In a way it's my last will and testament. Nothing's left of what I earned, all spent on court costs, and then medical care. I refused to let Geraldine go broke on behalf of me. She now owns my house. Feel free to visit anytime you like ...

"I love Geraldine. She's taken her responsibilities as godmother seriously ... I refused to let her visit me because I couldn't have her see me this way. Not now. It would have been too much for her and m ..."

His voice choked up.

Moments passed. James's voice returned, and again filled the speakers of the headsets. "You were a blessing, Sahel. You saw my love for Sunetra right from the start, grasped the root of all that's gone wrong in my life. Never did you ask me about my parents, my childhood or early life. You accepted what I said without judgment."

Sahel gave a lamenting smile.

"As for Geraldine, she'll always believe that had I not fallen in love with Sunetra, all would have gone well in my life … We don't choose with whom we fall in love … Or loves us. I hope you consider that when thinking of Titus … And in deciding how to address your feelings for Carl. Because of your mother, it's been difficult for you to receive Titus's love … And to show yours for him." James's voice grew soft and dependable, worthy of truth like that of Advisor Qadir in the Kingdom of Purdah of her dream. "You have loved Titus all your life."

Sahel's thoughts flew back to the previous evening and being in bed with Titus, his back to her, he at first not responding to her touch, and then hours later, she awakening to his arms around her.

Sahel grew hopeful of deciphering the dream. Yet she wished to tell James that Titus saw himself in the dream as Prince Thane, not as Prince Rahim to whom Queen Holna was married. Sahel considered Queen Bessima in the dream and then her mother, Lillian. If only she hadn't pushed so hard, given me room to see Titus for himself, who he was and apart from her!

James's voice continued flowing from the iPod. "Surely, in the wake of your mother's death, you've recognized the differences between her and Titus." James having never met Sahel's mother had delivered another dimension of observation, a more objective set of eyes to the situation binding Titus and Carl and herself.

James spoke. "There's no way Titus is like your mother. Not the way you yearn for him. You would have married Carl if you didn't love Titus, and he didn't love you. The entire friendship would have ended. You've clung to Carl out of guilt of loving Titus, something Carl would never have permitted had the situation been reversed." James added, "Titus holds a piece of you, what your mother never let you see of yourself. And only the darkness has revealed."

Tears dropped onto Sahel's lap.

"I'm afraid of death," James said. "That Sunetra will be on the other side waiting for me is not a certainty. But life is drawing to an end here. I don't have the strength to fight death."

James had recorded this message before Sahel's surgery.

Sahel was thankful for her conversation with James the previous day—her last moments with him wherein he explained his transformation, the energy of the change propelling her to look deeper. She grasped the iPod tighter.

James's voice continued. "I'm sure there are times when Titus wished he hadn't fallen in love with you. It would have made it so much easier for you."

Sahel's chest ached at having gone so long ignorant to the depth of Titus's commitment, and his love. Guilt arose as she recalled Carl's confession about his love the previous day.

"Promise me one thing, Sahel," James said. "Call these numbers."

James recited them. "Geraldine will give them to you. They will connect you with an agency that offers classes for the blind. They even provide tutors who will come to your home, work with you one-on-one. Do this, and everything with you, Titus, and Carl will fall into place."

Once more Sahel embraced the iPod that had delivered James's gift, unto and beyond death. Carl's confession of love drifted into the backwaters of her thoughts.

Chapter 40

G

eraldine was prepared to remain with Sahel until Titus arrived
home. Essien would be in a meeting at the university over in the
city that extended to long past five. "I don't mind staying here
alone until Daddy or Titus comes home," Sahel said. On
speaking the words, she wished she had not. Luckily, Geraldine
clarified her position. "Perhaps I can put it another way. Please.
Let me stay. I don't want to be alone."

"Of course." Again, Sahel reached out for Geraldine. "I'm
sorry. I've come to see myself as nothing but a burden. And
after listening to James on the iPod."

"Is that what was on the iPod?" Geraldine asked, then, "I'm
sorry. I shouldn't pry."

"Not at all," said Sahel.

"Which reminds me," Geraldine started. "This paper was also
in the envelope."

She opened Sahel's palm, and placed the piece of paper upon
it. "It's a list of numbers."

"He told me," Sahel said. A bittersweet smile took shape

upon her lips. She and Geraldine had entered another embrace. Sahel was again about to cry when the doorbell rang. "Are you all right?" asked Geraldine. Sahel nodded.

On returning from having answered the door, Geraldine announced that Carl had arrived. "Forgive me, Geraldine. But how are you doing?" Carl said. He had entered the study with her. "I'm sorry about James," he said. Imagining him standing by the doorway, Sahel wished to see his face.

"It's hard," Geraldine confessed in acquiescence. She sighed hard and deeply. "But he's in a better place, where he wanted to be." A wave of guilt shattered Sahel's heartfelt concern for Geraldine's loss. She had channeled Sunetra's spirit, had harbored Sunetra's soul within her.

Geraldine left for the kitchen, saying that she wanted to make some tea. Carl sat beside Sahel seated upon the leather sofa. "She's gone to cry," Sahel said, still held hostage by her guilt.

"At least she has the strength to let herself do that," Carl said. He heaved another sigh as if of defeat.

"Long day?" Sahel asked. She reached for his hand.

"It's not that," Carl said.

"I miss James," she said.

Carl touched her cheeks, newly moist, and wiped them of tears.

"Perhaps you miss James too," Sahel said.

She sensed an uneasy stillness rumbling about and within Carl. Sahel offered what she felt certain would lift his spirits. "I followed your orders and slept late until Geraldine arrived. We ate lunch and did nothing you would find taxing." She smiled and patted his hand. Her tears receded. "I was a model patient."

"That's good," Carl reciprocated. He sucked in air. Sahel grew anxious in his silence.

"You're worried about something," said Sahel. "What is it?" She felt Carl turn towards her. He grasped her other hand and lifted both palms.

"I need to talk with you about Titus," Carl said.

"Let's not go there again." Sahel pulled back her hands. "I love Titus and nothing's going to change that. I realize I may have misled you, but—"

"Have you spoken to him today?" Carl said.

"No. He left early this morning to assist Calvin in surgery. He should have been home by now. I suppose the case ran over. But—"

"That's what I need to speak with you about."

"What's wrong? Has something happened?" Sahel asked. Carl released another sigh. "Carl?" she said.

"The patient died," Carl said. "During the operation."

"How far were they into the procedure?"

"Over halfway. It was tedious."

"Titus will be feeling badly." Sahel recalled the drive home yesterday, Titus describing how he viewed his patients. "I wish Calvin hadn't called him." Sahel moved to stand. Carl grasped her arm. Sahel turned her head back towards Carl's voice. "Have you spoken with him or Calvin?"

"I was hoping you had."

Sahel's worry increased. "Where is Titus?"

"We don't know."

"What do you mean you don't know?" Sahel was now angry.

"The patient who died was the Mayor Jackson."

A cold tremor slid through Sahel.

"Titus took it badly. He and the team tried for half an hour to save him. Titus called at the time of death. Calvin offered to speak with the mayor's family. Titus said he'd do it. No one's seen him since he spoke with the mayor's wife and sons."

"Surely it wasn't his fault."

"It was an emergency procedure. Long-standing heart disease." The weariness of defeat again permeated Carl's voice. "With high-profile figures you never know what will ensue. The hospital's legal team is already preparing for a case."

"And what of Calvin and the partners?"

"They have full confidence in all that Titus did. The attorneys for their malpractice insurance agree. Titus was not at fault. He did nothing wrong."

"That's why Calvin called Titus last night and asked him to come in." Sahel leaned back into the sofa cushion. "The emergency patient was the mayor," Sahel said.

"Calvin had called me too, asked if I thought Titus was up to it."

Carl conceded. "I said Titus would be the best judge of that."

"How could you? After what you said to me before I left the hospital?" Sahel said. She reprimanded Carl. "If there was ever a time he didn't need to see the inside of an operating room, it was last night. I'm certain he heard what you said. Every word of it."

"He left a resignation letter on Calvin's desk," Carl said.

Sahel bit her lip, and drew blood. Titus's words returned from the previous afternoon during their drive home. *Every woman I attend is my mother, every man my father.*

"There were two other letters, one for me and one for you," Carl said. He placed it in her hand.

"What did yours say?"

"He asked me to take care of you," said Carl.

Chest pounding and temples pulsing, Sahel handed back to Carl the envelope containing her letter from Titus. "And mine?" Against the paper crackling of Carl tearing open the envelope, Sahel prayed for Titus. Carl sighed. "What is it?" Sahel asked.

"He says that he's sorry for how he destroyed your life and that ... " Carl stopped.

"What does he say?" Sahel demanded.

"That you're better off without him," Carl said.

"He's wrong!"

"He's included divorce papers," Carl said. "He's signed them."

"No. This is so wrong." Sahel shook her head, and then wrapping her arms around her stomach, she doubled over and, for once, didn't fight back the tears.

Chapter 41

S

ahel would not accept that James was dead. Nor would she accede to divorcing Titus.

They were at James's gravesite.

Father Richard read from the Bible. "As she had come naked from his mother's womb …"

The priest continued speaking words intended to comfort and Sahel recalled her vows.

"… For better, for worse …."

"… so will he return as he came."

"… For richer, for poorer …."

"… He will take nothing from the fruit of his labor that he can carry in his hand."

"… In sickness, and in health … I thee wed."

Father Richard read more scripture. "Here is what I have seen to be good and fitting: to eat … drink, and enjoy oneself in all one's labor … for this is his reward … as for every man to whom God has given riches and wealth, He has also empowered him to eat from them and to receive his reward and rejoice in his labor; this is the gift of God."

Work.

"I love you," Sahel prayed in her grief of losing James. And yet there was more—she labored to understand—so much more to what Sahel had known of James's living.

Geraldine had refused to open James's casket and make public his withered body. Sahel and Essien had concurred.

Sahel tried conjuring an image of the small gathering according to Geraldine's description. "Just a few of his friends. Those who remembered him."

"James would have been touched. I am touched," Essien had said of the gathering.

All gathered back at Essien's home following the interment. "It seems so silly," Geraldine had commented while riding in the limousine up Highway 80, "—going past James's house," to the gravesite in Rolling Hills Cemetery, and then past it once more on their way back to Sahel and Essien's home in Oakland.

Sahel gave thanks for having been with James during those last minutes of his life. "Yes, it is," she had concurred.

He was with Sunetra now. At least that is what Sahel prayed and believed.

I believe. Help my unbelief.

Back at the house and seeing to their guests, Sahel maneuvered about, finding her way past and between congregants who attended the repast. Against quips and fragments of guests' conversations, she prayed ... *Titus will come back.*

One person said to another. Had you seen James since his release?

... *I need him. He needs me* ... Sahel whispered within against another voice speaking. "I couldn't believe it when Sunetra jumped from the bridge."

... *Bring him back, oh God. Please.*

Still another person said of Sunetra, "She truly loved James. If only she could have shown that in the end."

One person whispered, "Success taints everything."

"You mean the need for it," a last one lamented.

Sahel sighed. *Please, God, forgive me. Titus, I'm so sorry ...*

The guests' statements, though blunt and politically incorrect, sounded, on careful consideration, honest and genuine. They had seen and witnessed, even experienced, what Sahel could not, what she would never view or share with James. Likewise, those speaking would not know the James Bolton she had come to love and respect.

If only she could have seen. ... success taints everything.

"Sahel." Essien's hand landed on her shoulder. "This is Cole Newhart. He was a friend," Essien said. "He worked with James at the brokerage."

"Pleased to meet you." Sahel extended her hand into the darkness, Newhart grasping it. "I'm glad you came."

"I would have felt horrible had I not," said Newhart. "Thanks for contacting all of us."

"I'll be right back." Essien patted Sahel's shoulder and left.

"Your father's a nice man," Cole said.

"So was James."

"How long had you known him? Your father says that you and James were very close."

"Only about a month."

Newhart's silence betrayed his confusion.

"So you worked with him at the brokerage," Sahel said.

"Yes. We lost track of each other when he left." Newhart sounded anxious, almost guilty.

"You mean after the trial and his conviction?"

"Yes. It was difficult, you know ... "

"I would imagine San Quentin's a very difficult place to enter, even if to visit someone you liked," Sahel proffered.

"I went one time," Newhart explained. "James refused to see me. I held no grudges. Probably would have done the same, had it been me."

"I'm sorry for having misjudged you," Sahel said.

"No, it's quite all right. Some part of me felt I should have returned." Newhart sighed. "I never knew he had AIDS."

"He contracted it in prison. He was attacked."

Newhart's silence fell heavily and then, "If you don't mind my asking, how did you and James meet?"

"At a medical dinner," Sahel said. "My husband was receiving an award, Surgeon of the Year. Geraldine coaxed James to accompany her. He sat next to me during the meal." Sahel smiled as she reminisced. "He was the most interesting person that I'd spoken with in a long time. People assume your lack of sight leaves you brain dead. James was just the opposite. He was eager to talk. A warhorse for the weary."

"Apt description. That was James," Newhart said. Sahel imagined him smiling. Newhart then said, "Have you always been without sight?"

"No. There was an accident. About a year ago."

"That would have been about the time that Ravesh was killed," Newhart said.

"Shot by Sunetra," said Sahel. Months later, after James was wrongly convicted, he received his sentence. At the same hour and moment of that afternoon, Sunetra threw herself from the Golden Gate and Sahel attempted to end her life. Sahel considered how in the waters of the San Francisco Bay underneath the Golden Gate Bridge, she had encountered Sunetra's soul.

Again Newhart sighed. "I suppose there are certain events that interweave our otherwise disparate lives."

"How do you mean?" Sahel asked.

"You lose your sight, which I'm sure was difficult. James, whom you don't know, loses practically everything that gave meaning to his life, his freedom, his work, Ravesh and Sunetra. A year later he's released and meets you. I'm sure there must have been a purpose in all of it," Cole Newhart said. "If only we could see it."

Again Sahel smiled, this time in a bittersweet manner.

"None of us ever thought for one moment that James had killed Ravesh," Cole said. "I knew that something must have been wrong. The D.A., the evidence, what little there was of it. Sunetra went into seclusion. And then with her jumping from the bridge."

"What became of the brokerage?" Sahel asked.

"I bought it ... with another partner."

"You purchased it from Ravesh's wife, Sunetra's mother?"

"After everything that had happened, she'd had just about enough of living in America," Newhart explained. "I'm told she returned to India, a place in Rajasthan. Last I heard, she had entered an ashram, what they call *purdah*."

Sahel chuckled in spite of herself. "It's not a place, *purdah*, that is, at least not physical. It's a way of life." She then explained, "Purdah is an ancient tradition wherein wealthy men of India kept their wives at home, did not permit them to travel outside or beyond the husband's estate. It was a kind of protection."

"Very ancient I'm sure," said Cole. "No woman of today would want to live like that. Then again, I'm certain Sunetra's mother doesn't want to see anyone."

"You'd be surprised," Sahel said. "She needs to heal. One thing purdah has in common with an ashram is that both hold an experience wherein the inhabitant, or person living in it, withdraws from the world, by choice, or by force. With Sunetra's mother being a widow, I imagine that she has chosen to enter an ashram."

"As a matter of fact," Cole said, "I was told that she had remarried. A friend of Ravesh, who's now a widower. The man's wife had died about the same time as Ravesh."

"Then perhaps Ravesh's widow has entered *purdah*." Sahel mused on the synchronicity of occurrences and then her experience of being torn from the world, the protection that Titus, brash at times, had provided too. "This last year has been not unlike being forced into *purdah*. I resented it. And then James came along. He helped me gain footing, find a way when everything else in me had stopped."

"He was a really good person," Cole spoke, his words brushing past Sahel's, but in rhythm with their meaning. "I wish I could have seen him one last time."

"Perhaps you will. Perhaps all of us will. In another life."

"That would be nice. That would be very nice," Cole said. He expressed his condolences once more and then left.

Carl came to Sahel out on the patio in back. "James seemed to have a fair number of friends. Too bad they couldn't have seen him during those last weeks and told him how much he mattered to them."

"Is that how you feel about Titus?" Sahel said.

"Have you heard from him?" Carl said, subverting the question.

"No," Sahel answered. "Have you?" Carl went silent. "Have you any idea where he's gone?" Sahel asked.

"I've called all the guys he trained with. Of course I said nothing of what had happened with the mayor. Just that he'd had some family problems and his wife hadn't heard from him in a couple of days."

"Did you tell them that we'd had a fight, weren't getting along?" Sahel quipped.

"No, Sahel. I was only trying to help find him—do what's best for you."

"What's best for me is what's best for Titus," said Sahel. "I'm not going to sign those papers. I won't abandon Titus."

"He certainly doesn't mind leaving you," Carl said. "What if he doesn't come back?"

"He's hurting," said Sahel.

"He left once before," Carl said. "And this time he's bound you to him, left you hanging. These divorce papers are nothing but a sham, his way of leaving the dirty work for you."

Sahel recalled how, unbeknownst to her and Carl, even Lillian and Essien, Titus had transferred from the surgical training program at UCSF in San Francisco to the one at Columbia in New York.

"He's trying to set me free."

"Perhaps Titus wants his freedom. Like when he married Alice," Carl said.

"Have you called her?" Sahel's voice was firm.

"You'd take him back even if he went there?" Carl asked, still pushing the offensive.

"I love him. We did him wrong."

"Titus is a grown man. All his platitudes about loving you and he leaving you with divorce papers that he's signed. I can't

278

believe you're letting him off the hook so easily."

"You sound like Mama."

"Whatever you may have thought of your mother, she was consistent. She never left your father high and dry."

"Perhaps she was too afraid. Mama was sick. And I'm not speaking only of her heart," said Sahel. "And when did you start championing her cause?" She recalled Prince Thane and Queen Bessima in her dream. "Mama spared no love on you."

"Why do you always fight what's available?" Carl said. Again he avoided her question.

Sahel turned from Carl. He touched her shoulders. Sahel pulled away. Essien called out her name. "Oh, there you are. I don't mean to interrupt you and Carl. Cole Newhart and some of the others are readying to leave. I thought you might want to thank them once more for coming. If you like, I can tell them you are—"

"No. I'd like to thank them," Sahel said. Carl touched her arm as if to lead her back into the house and to Cole Newhart and the others departing. Sahel brushed aside Carl's hand, pulled away, and said, "Carl was just leaving." Extending her cane, she found her way inside to Newhart and the others.

Chapter 42

C

ole Newhart and others with whom James had worked at Ravesh Desai's stock brokerage extended final appreciations to Sahel and Essien for having invited them to attend the funeral.

Engaging with Cole had revealed to Sahel how closed off she had become since losing her sight. Her reclusiveness and withdrawal lay rooted in the distance at which, prior to her blindness, she had always kept others.

Sahel felt certain Titus had overheard Carl's confession of love.

The death of Oakland's mayor while Titus had been performing surgery had provided but the fuel, the tipping point, and exposing sides of both Titus and Carl, aspects of Carl Sahel had avoided. How long had Titus possessed the divorce papers? When had he requested them drawn up? She considered the letter Titus had written to Carl, asking him to care for her. Sahel was determined to have someone but Carl read Titus's letter.

Carl desperately wanted Sahel's love. But his need, though great, brought no balance to the scales of Sahel's heart when weighing the ache of the orphan residing within Titus, the man-child forever doomed to attempting to resurrect his parents or prevent their deaths by saving each patient whom he attended.

In all his actions of fixing malfunctioning hearts, Titus desperately sought the family he had lost, parents and people to and with whom he could safely belong, and who would accept him not only in his strength, but also whenever his weakness and fears took over.

Sahel sighed in weariness. The loss of her sight had distilled from within her dearest childhood friends, now men, their boy souls yet developed, full of love, and yearning to evolve.

The following night at dinner, Sahel said to Essien, "It's time for me to start learning to live with my blindness, and achieving some independence. It's the only way Titus can feel safe if he comes back."

"You doubt that he will?" asked her father.

As she had told Carl earlier, Sahel now repeated, "If Titus wants a divorce, he'll have to come back and tell me in person." She lifted the documents. "I won't sign them unless I hear his voice saying he doesn't love me anymore."

Titus's desire to operate on Sahel's mother had been an attempt to connect with his mother, Cecile. A burning wave of sadness gripped Sahel's chest. She edged onto the precipice beneath which roared a sea of unshed tears.

"Use this time in waiting to move forward as you have planned," said Essien. "Grant yourself freedom from not simply Titus wracked by his guilt, but from Carl continually blaming him."

Sahel's blindness had given Carl an edge with which to make Titus his whipping boy. "He's lost his connection with God," Sahel said of Carl and thinking of his refusal to attend Mass. "It all started when I married Titus."

The last time Sahel had known Carl to enter St. Maria's had been to serve as best man when Sahel wed Titus.

"The three of you need time apart," said Essien. He patted Sahel's shoulder. "In time you'll come back to each other, having become closer friends and better persons."

"You really believe that?"

"I know it. And so do you."

An excruciating heaviness that defied thought and words settled upon Sahel's shoulders when she contemplated the guilt Titus felt in having hit Sahel with his car. Though an accident for which Sahel had quickly forgiven him, the tentacles of its aftermath now threatened to strangle her in Titus's choice to leave and bequeath her to Carl's care. "I am not a thing to be given by one man to another!"

"Then remain committed to what you have decided to undertake," Essien said. "Now tell me of your plans." He sounded energized and eager. "What have you proposed for yourself?"

"I'm going to take classes."

"Where? What kind?"

Sahel reached in her pocket, lifted out the iPod containing the message James had recorded, and then the envelope. She handed the envelope to her father. "James wrote down the names and numbers of various agencies that work with the blind," Sahel explained.

"They offer classes, one-on-one tutorials. James left me a message on the iPod." She held it up. "He said he'd made some calls, asked about various ways I could get some training." Against the sound of her father unfolding the paper, she said, "He listed tutors who deliver lessons in the home."

"I see," Essien spoke. Sahel imagined him perusing and reading the paper.

"I want to hire one."

"I think that would be a good idea. But are you up to this?" Worry again resounded in Essien's voice. "A lot has happened in the last few days."

"I've got to get on with my life," Sahel said against the tension mounting within.

"You fear Titus will not return?"

"Perhaps if I do this, he will have something to come back for."

Sahel felt a wall rise between her and her father. She said,

"Titus feels guilty for the accident. No amount of my telling him he's not at fault will get him to see—" she stopped short. Her lips trembled. Essien grasped her palm. He brushed her face. Sahel wanted to latch on to her father's hand, hold it forever, never let go. "I need Titus. I need him terribly. I've always needed and wanted him." She had never spoken those words. "I was too afraid of letting him in, receiving his love, because I saw him like Mama."

"Titus is nothing like your mother," Essien said.

"I see that now. Or rather in the absence of sight, I've come to see clearly."

"The darkness can be comforting."

Sahel turned to Essien.

"Your loss of sight has tried me in so many ways," her father started. "I would never have wished this upon you or anyone. And yet ... the Sahel I have come to know, the person life had revealed my daughter to be, is so much more than I could have imagined."

"But how can you say this?" Sahel asked. "I've been so horrible to Titus and you. That stunt of taking the pills ..." Essien lifted her hand.

"We are all weak and struggling. This last year with all its hurt and messiness has allowed me to give you what I never did when you were a child. It has been my time to let you know how much I love you, what you mean to me not simply as a daughter, but as a person for whom I hold great and much respect."

"This is so much like the dream," Sahel mused. "What dream is this?"

Sahel told of the Kingdom of Purdah, Queen Holna, the princes Rahim and Thane. "There were also Advisor Qadir and his wife, Cynda," she said. "I knew them all, felt so much familiarity with them. It wasn't until I told James of the dream that it all gelled and I recognized who they really were. It was like coming home. James had the same dream as me and at the same time, when I was in surgery." Sahel then told of Titus speaking of the dream.

"He had it, too—my dream. But Titus saw things differently."

"Then it was his dream, too," said Essien, echoing Dr. Leonard.

"I was certain that Prince Rahim was Titus. I saw him, Titus, there in the Kingdom of Purdah. We were married. And just like in waking life, Carl was there. He was Prince Thane."

"Did he feel for you there as he does here?"

Ashamed and in awe of her father's directness, Sahel confessed, "Even more. In the dream I saw Carl as he really is. He would stop at nothing to have me. Like Mama, he has this determination, this passion. It's frightening. Carl is quiet and soft, certain and clear.

But behind all that there's a fierce determination to have what he wants. He's like this silent bulldozer mowing down whatever is in its way, but making no sound. You don't realize he's coming. Carl is so much like Mama, what I've always feared lurked behind Titus's feelings. I see that now."

"Was your mother in the dream?" Essien asked. He sounded troubled and yet hopeful.

"She was Queen Bessima. Like here she was my mother. Our kingdoms were at war. She didn't like the way I governed. I didn't burden the people with rules that limited their lives. I wanted them to be happy. I did something that no other ruler had done. I allowed and encouraged two members of the royal court to marry, Advisor Qadir and Cynda, my first lady-in-waiting. Despite this I kept them in my royal service."

Essien sighed and then asked for clarification. "You and Titus and James all had this dream?"

"Yes, but Titus's version differs from what James and I saw and heard."

"Have you spoken to Carl of the dream?"

"No." Sahel shook her head.

"Has he mentioned anything about having the dream, any dream?"

"No. But I get the feeling—Maybe it's wishful thinking," Sahel retreated into her thoughts.

"What is it, my dear?"

"It's something Carl said. No. Rather it was the way he was when telling me that the mayor had died during surgery." Sahel took in breath, tried grasping what she had sensed. "It was like Titus had died."

Sahel recalled Carl's' words like she had remembered James and Sunetra in her dream. *Titus did the best he could. But some things can't be helped. They just are.*

"I was angry," Sahel said. "Carl said that Calvin had called him, asked if he thought Titus was up for the surgery. I guess with me having just undergone surgery, Calvin was worried." Sahel grew anxious, frustrated. "But it's not like Calvin to go back on his word. He told—No, he practically ordered Titus to go home and stay with me during my recovery. And why call Carl, asking about Titus?"

"Did Carl know that Calvin had ordered Titus to stay home with you?"

"I don't know," said Sahel. Essien's question had opened a new angle from which to view the recent events.

"He is like your mother," Essien said. "As I have concluded for some time, you must be careful."

"How long have you, too, sensed he is like Mama?" Sahel asked.

"Since he was a little boy. That is why I have admired him so." Sahel's father spoke in an acquiescent tone. "Your mother felt the same."

"About Carl?" Sahel frowned. "No. Mama hated him."

"Carl frightened your mother," said Essien. "She saw herself in him."

Sahel's heart sank. "But Titus—"

"Titus only looked liked her. And that is where the similarities ended," Essien said. Images from childhood flooded her memories. Slowly, Sahel began to understand.

Sahel said, "In the dream Advisor Qadir warned me not to trust Carl."

"That would be James," said Essien.

Sahel then remembered, "Before Titus left he said he was Prince Thane in the dream. That Carl was Prince Rahim." Sahel sighed in realization. "That's why Titus has given me the

286

divorce papers. He had them drawn up after the surgery and when it was obvious my sight would not return. Titus has everything wrong. He's misinterpreted it. He thinks he's setting me free. But in the dream I loved Prince Rahim. There were no questions, no doubt. Yes, you wanted me to marry Rahim. I also loved him," said Sahel.

"And where was I?"

"You had died."

Essien returned to the dream. "And you were not torn?"

"No."

"But you and your mother, the kingdoms over which you ruled were at war?"

"Queen Bessima, Mama in the dream, wanted to rule over both the kingdoms of Freedom and of Purdah. Queen Bessima wanted power. Though I was a girl, you had passed the rule of the Kingdom of Purdah to me and not her, until I was married. And so she sought to control whom I married. Queen Bessima would rule through my husband."

"And it seems she wanted this Prince Thane to be your husband, not Rahim, whom I had chosen for you to marry."

"That's the way it seems." Sahel's thoughts fell into a quandary.

Again her father lifted her hand. He said, "I am not dead, neither in life, nor in you."

The weight of loneliness and isolation Sahel had endured as a child caught between her parents began to lighten, a lightness of hope and expectation replacing it. And yet slivers of doubt and worry remained. "I love him, Daddy. I love Titus and I want him back," Sahel said.

"And he shall return."

Sahel then told of how in the dream Queen Holna, Advisor Qadir, Cynda, and Prince Thane go to the Kingdom of Freedom where Queen Bessima is holding Prince Rahim hostage. "I knelt before Mama and told her I would not hate her and that, while I hated what she was doing, I would not turn against her. I was willing to relinquish the Kingdom of Purdah to Mama's rule if only she would free Prince Rahim and let him live. But as I spoke, the palace hall began to rumble. The walls began falling around us in huge slabs. Rahim was buried in the rubble. I found him and was about to kiss him. Then the dream shifted to St. Maria's. Father Richard was standing at the front of the sanctuary. I was entering the church with Carl to my side. He was holding my hand. At first I thought we were getting ready to be married, but then I saw the casket behind Father Richard. Everyone in the congregation was wearing black. Prince Rahim, Titus, was dead."

"No," said Essien. "Rahim isn't dead, and neither is your marriage to Titus." Sahel took in breath. "Trust me," said Essien. "We are all in transition—you, Titus, Carl, me, and even your mother. If I have ever believed purgatory, or what the Buddhists describe as the bardo, I do now. Most of all you must remember that I, your father—" Essien grasped her shoulders. "I am not dead. I am with you, now and all the way."

Moments later Essien said, "Your mother had earned but a high school diploma." Both Sahel and her father had earned doctorates. "She said that my education attracted her to me. Your mother held strong feelings about your becoming a psychologist, not because of the nature of your work in probing the mind, but because you were doing as I had. You were entering a world where I could offer guidance and counsel, and of which your mother knew nothing."

"But she said I needed an education because, as she said, I'm dark and no one would love me for who I am," Sahel explained. "She said the only thing anyone would see of me is my dark skin."

"That is all she saw. And yet two men both in life and your dream have and are still vying for your affection. Both Titus and Carl—one man who has a fair complexion like your mother, and another dark like me and you—have worked all their lives to make you happy."

Sahel inhaled deeply and long, and then on angling her head, asked, "Could Mama have been jealous?"

"Much like Ohia's second wife," Essien said of the Ghanaian myth he had shared with Sahel. "You directed anger for your mother's shortcomings at Titus."

Sahel began to cry.

Later Essien said, "I'll make the calls for you in the morning."

Sahel breathed deeply and for the first in a long time felt tensions slipping away. "Thank you," she said.

"Did you think I would stand against it?" Essien asked.

"I could use this time to search for Titus, make calls instead of taking the classes."

"Why not do both?"

Sahel gave a bittersweet smile. "Then again, perhaps Titus would be better off without me."

"Is that what you believe?"

"Look how long it's taken me to say what I truly feel. I never even tried before, instead focused on being independent, and separate, acting as if I didn't need him."

"And so that is what you were doing when you were on the pavement of the driveway searching for his engagement ring?"

"Mama touched that ring. It meant a lot to me that finally I was doing something that made her happy," Sahel said. Her lips trembled when she whispered, "She said she loved me."

"Perhaps that is the truth you still cannot accept. That your mother wanted something for you that you also wanted."

"You're suggesting that the only reason I grew close with Carl was to get back at Mama?"

"Your mother exploited Carl's love for you and your need to stand separate from her. This was her way of trying to ensure you would marry Titus."

"But she kept pointing the way. Putting Titus in my face, reminding how wonderful he was."

"And you kept resisting her. But you never married Carl."

Sahel sighed in admission of the truth of her father's words.

"Remember your dream," Essien urged. "Let it do the work. You married Titus, not out of resistance to you mother. And not because it is what she wanted. You married him because you love him."

"Only in blindness could I see this," Sahel said.

"These classes are but one more step in this process of having married Titus," Essien said. "Taking them you give yourself the person you thought you did not deserve. And also to love the person who feels she has done nothing to deserve your love. And that person is you, my daughter."

Tears slid onto Sahel's face. "I've hurt him so much," she said of her actions toward Titus. "And just like Mama, I've used Carl. I've got to let Titus know he's not Prince Thane, that he's Rahim."

"We all have our roles on this stage of life. And we must play them. To the best of our abilities and to the worst. Our roles, not anyone else's."

"But I've confused Titus." Sahel shook her head. The frustration of Titus pressing to set a date for their wedding enveloped her. "Why won't you marry me?" Titus had said. "I love you. Always have. Our mothers were friends." The torture on his face was palpable. "I can't understand it. You promised your mother that—"

"This is not about my mother!" Sahel had shouted.

"Everything in your life is about your mother, Sahel. All you've ever done and do is connected to trying to protect yourself from her. You think I don't know how she treated you, all the things she said?" His hurt seemed to deepen as did Sahel's.

"You don't know anything," she said.

"She beat you. Just like my father beat me." The truth of Titus's words sent ripples through Sahel. Her heart stole an extra beat and then slowed.

"Your mother was sick. She thought you were ugly because you are dark and not light, like her or me," Titus said.

"Shut up!"

"I don't care about that." He grasped both Sahel's arms. "None of that matters. It's never mattered to me. My mother loved you." He drew her close. Sahel avoided looking into his face.

"She told me to love you, that you were a beautiful person. Always. And you are." Sahel had fought to free herself. Titus's words continued filling her memory. "When I see you, I see her, my mother. She could have passed for white. But in my heart, you are everything she was all about. I don't want to live without you. I can't! I won't!"

Sahel had pulled away. Titus reached for her, grasped her hand.

She continued forward and the ring slipped from her fingers, Sahel unaware.

The memory dispersed. Sahel lifted her father's hand, and said, "Titus saw through me. He saw everything. My fears, my anger, all my pain, everything. Titus hit me with the car, saw himself as having become like Mama. But it was truly an accident. I've got to tell him that, though I hate this blindness," she knotted her hand into a fist. "I hate not being able to see his face, yours, Geraldine's, and Carl's—but the darkness has brought me closer to him, let me see who he really is and how much I love him."

"And you'll do that. He'll come to see," said Essien. "Right now he needs time to heal. We can run. But we can never escape or hide from who we are or those who love us. Their voices travel wherever we go. They never leave us."

Essien embraced Sahel. She laid her head upon his shoulder. Then, bending over, she placed it upon his lap. And there she remained, her father gently patting her hair.

Chapter 43

T

he next morning and with Essien's assistance, Sahel began contacting the agencies whose numbers James had listed on the paper. Within an hour of speaking with the first agency, Sahel had scheduled her first private lesson with an instructor for the blind. The woman who was to be Sahel's instructor arrived at 3:00 p.m. the following afternoon.

"Nervous?" Romina asked Sahel after the two had greeted.

"As I ever could be," Sahel said, and plastered a smile. Essien had left the study.

"That means you're ready to learn, and you've set some goals for yourself."

"You're good," Sahel said. The heaviness lifted from her chest and she resumed breathing.

"When I read that you're a psychotherapist, I knew I had to be on my game," Romina said.

"I haven't been on mine since the accident—for the last year," Sahel lamented.

"How'd you lose your sight?"

Sahel explained the accident, said nothing of Titus having disappeared. "I need to learn everything I can and regain my independence, for my marriage, my husband, and most of all for me."

"Then let's get started," Romina said. "I brought you some items for beginning to do just that—labels for your clothes, and two kinds of watches and clocks for you to try out."

Again Sahel smiled against her fears. She reclaimed her old tenacity; or rather it ensnared her.

Romina took Sahel's hands and placed the tags on her palm. "They're engraved with Braille," Romina said as Sahel felt the tiny formations of dots upon the surface of the tags. "Consider this your first lesson in learning Braille."

Halfway into the ninety-minute session and after she had introduced the watches and clocks, Romina said, "I'm also going to teach you cane technique."

"So I'm not using my cane properly?" Sahel lifted her cane and unfolded it. Memories of Carl secretly giving it to her and Titus's anger that ensued, rose but soon drifted away.

"What you're doing is fine," Romina said. "It's just that mobility outside the house and even inside where there are stairs requires refinement of what you're doing."

"I always wondered whether I wasn't using it properly."

"Not to worry," Romina said. "From what I've seen, you're far ahead of the game. You'll find this easy." She patted Sahel's hand.

Sahel recalled when she had first returned home after the accident, Titus forever holding her hand. I'm here with you, he had said. I'm not leaving. He had led her up the stairs to her room. Sahel did not have a cane.

Once in her room, she had said, "I don't know how to make this work, life with you—and me not being able to see." Sahel valued her independence. Gaining her independence as she grew into adulthood had kept her going despite the difficulties of living with her mother.

"You're not alone," Titus had said. "I did this to you. I'm here to make it work." The accident had been as much hers as his. She grew angry at his persistence, his unwillingness to abandon her. Sahel had not understood, nor had she trusted his commitment. Now knowing how he viewed his patients, shame for her actions welled inside.

"Every woman I treat is my mother, every man, my father," Titus had said.

Sahel shook herself free of the memory.

Like Titus and Sahel, Essien loved Geraldine and she, him. The loss of James left a gaping hole in Geraldine's life, one that Sahel determined Essien wanted and could fill. Sahel would not bind her father to taking care of her in his last years. Eventually Essien would die. He needed his time of joy.

Sahel identified what she needed to accomplish that she might live independently. She wanted to set free her father, liberate him to care for Geraldine, and receive the love Lillian had never given him.

And yet some part of her feared Titus might not return. Against mounting anxiety, Sahel pushed aside her worries. She extended her hand to Romina, and said, "I'm ready."

After that first session with Romina, Sahel began labeling everything, thus speeding up her understanding and ability to read Braille. At Sahel's request, Romina had devised a list of tasks she wanted Zelda to oversee Sahel in learning to do, alone.

It was a late afternoon in October when Romina said, "You've progressed faster than any student I've had."

"Thanks. I needed to hear that."

"Your advancement has nothing to do with age. And believe me, you wouldn't be the oldest or the youngest. Zelda says you're helping in the kitchen with drying dishes," Romina said. "Putting them away, setting the table and making your bed. She feels quite comfortable leaving you here alone." While she had not attempted to cook anything, Sahel had begun helping Zelda with housework, demanding that Zelda not go easy on her. "So does your father," said Romina. "I've watched you eat. There's an ease you didn't have when I first came."

Sahel smiled with pride. "You've also cut the time needed to dress to a little under an hour."

"The clocks and clothing labels are helping," Sahel said. Before the tutorials, she took over two hours. "Laying out my clothes at night helps and also lets me practice Braille."

"It shows. Which brings me to one more point," Romina said. "Have you considered how you'll continue after studying with me?" Sahel lifted her chin.

"Don't get nervous," Romina chuckled. She patted the back of Sahel's hand resting on her knee. "I'm not leaving you. But I owe it to you to be frank about what I can offer. Many people only desire to achieve so much. And while there's much more you can learn, I'm wondering if the daily tutorials are the best way for you to gain these skills."

"What do you mean?"

"A three-month training program. It's quite intensive. You'll have your own apartment alone with nine other participants living in their apartments, ten total," Romina explained. "Most are like you, adults who have lived the majority of their lives with sight and are now making the transition to living without it."

"This sounds really exciting," Sahel said. "But I have to admit the idea of living alone doing everything for myself is scary."

"I'd wonder if you weren't afraid," Romina said. "Fear means you understand the commitment involved in achieving your goals."

"I feel as if I'm a child again."

"In many ways you are. That you can acknowledge your anxieties—reconnecting with those fears and worries as you did when you were a child—says you have the desire. As with a child, you're willing to do what it takes to achieve your goals, surrender. Which is exactly what you've been doing with me. Wanting something puts us square with our vulnerabilities. For someone as accomplished as you, this isn't easy. Some people can't go back that far. The work you've been doing with Zelda here around the house is paying off," Romina said. "It's provided dividends that I think make you a perfect candidate to enter the program at the Independent Living Center and be able to do more than most who start with you."

Romina touched Sahel's hand. "You may not believe it, but the year you retreated from the world and remained stuck here in the house, hiding out, as you say, was perhaps the best thing. You're lucky that you had a family surrounding you, and that didn't rush you back into life too soon. I've seen one too many who've lost their sight try to move on as if nothing has happened. It sounds nice and strong. But it's a mixture for disaster. The loss of one's sight carries a heavy bereavement. Your life is never the same again. You have to grieve. That's what you've been doing this last year."

Romina's rendering of Sahel's last year presented hope. "Thanks for sharing that." The heavy burden of shame lifted.

"We all need to mourn the losses life presents us. And the time required for mourning is different for each person."

"I was afraid that I'd be depressed forever if I gave into it. I didn't want to let down my family and friends, to disappoint them." Sahel then told Romina of her attempted suicide. "Since then I've been seeing a psychiatrist."

"It's totally understandable. That you're able to talk about it, share it with me, says you're moving forward. Your family and friends, those who love you and whom you love, also need time to readjust. As life changes us, it also alters those closest to us. They need to mourn as well. They haven't lost you, but the Sahel they knew is no more."

Romina's words provided several aha moments for Sahel. "It's a heavy burden your husband carries, particularly in the light of how much he loves you," Romina said. "It's obvious by how hard you've been working that you love him very much."

Romina's lack of judgment surprised Sahel. "One of our friends blames Titus for my loss of sight," Sahel said. In recent weeks she had avoided Carl's phone calls, having instructed Zelda to tell him she was either asleep or out with Essien or Geraldine. Nor had she returned his messages. For this Sahel held regrets. Despite his actions that had angered Sahel, Carl had purchased and presented her the cane two months into having lost her sight.

Romina asked, "Has this friend seen how hard you've been working these last few weeks?"

On completing her lesson that afternoon, Sahel accompanied Romina to the front door. "You're using your cane well," Romina said.

"Thanks." Sahel smiled and opened the front door. "It seems you have a visitor," Romina said.

"I was about to ring the doorbell," Carl said. He introduced himself to Romina. "Dr. Carl Pierson. Sahel's neurosurgeon."

"Pleased to meet you," Romina said. "I'm Sahel's tutor."

"You're from the Lyon's Agency?" Carl said. "Sahel's father, Essien, has spoken highly of you."

"Sahel's a great student," Romina said.

"I bet. Unfortunately, she missed her appointment today."

Anxious, Sahel turned to Romina and forced herself to speak. "It was a great lesson."

"I thoroughly agree. Give yourself an extra pat on the back," Romina said. She hugged Sahel. "I'll see you Monday. Have a great weekend," Romina said.

"You do the same," Sahel said as she waved against Romina's voice drifting into the distance.

With her cane in one hand, Sahel tightened her grip on the doorknob.

"May I come in?" Carl said.

Sahel stepped back, opened the door wider, and on closing it she turned and started for the study. "I'm sorry for missing my appointment. Truly I forgot."

"It's easy to see how you got caught up—Romina's a great teacher. She has a good student." Carl's voice was soft and penitent. "Your father says she's been good for you."

"So you've been talking with him?" Sahel felt for the sofa and on finding it lowered herself on the cushion. She folded her cane. "You look great," Carl said. Restrained joy now replaced the sorrow that had floated in his tone.

"Have you heard from Titus or anyone who knows where he might be?" Sahel asked. She had not spoken to Carl in recent weeks.

Sahel had instead spoken each morning and afternoon with Calvin Bennett, who provided progress reports on his and the other partners' efforts to locate Titus. Calvin Bennett was the senior partner of the cardiac group to which Titus belonged. Essien had also joined efforts with Calvin and had begun making calls.

"I was about to ask you the same thing," Carl said.

"Daddy and Calvin and are making calls," Sahel said. "None of the people he trained with have heard from him. Every night before going to sleep, I call Titus's cell phone, thinking that I'll catch him, hoping he'll pick up. I've left nothing but messages." She sighed. "This is so unlike him. To not even return messages. I'm worried."

"You haven't returned mine. Each time I call, Zelda gives me one excuse after another."

Sahel's face grew warm, her ears reaching a slow burn in the face of Carl's honesty.

Carl then said, "As for Titus, he left once before. And we know what came of that."

Sahel knew Carl to be speaking of when Titus transferred from the cardiac surgery residency to one at Columbia. "Have you called her?" Carl said. He was speaking of Alice Whitmore, Titus's first wife whom he met while at training at Columbia in New York.

A slow tide of anxiety crept upon Sahel. "I'm not going to sign the papers," she said. Her back grew warm and her hands began to tremble. "And why would you even bring her up?"

"He married her while you were here waiting for him," Carl said, remaining firm in his cause. "How do you know he's not there now?"

"And how are you so certain he is?" Sahel whipped her face towards Carl's voice.

"He signed the papers. Titus is setting you free."

"I don't want to be free," Sahel said. "You don't get it, or you refuse to."

"I will never stop loving you."

"And I'm not having Calvin or Daddy call her. Besides, I don't have her number."

"I'll make the call if you'd like."

"I don't need you to do my dirty work for me," Sahel

snapped.

She hadn't considered that Titus would return to Alice. Now that Carl had raised it, the possibility seemed real.

"I didn't make him leave, not this time nor the first," Carl said.

"And what about when his parents died?" Sahel said.

"Surely you're not blaming me for that?"

Like Titus who had admitted having terribly missed Sahel when living with his paternal grandparents during the two years after his parents died, Sahel had also grieved Titus's absence. "No. But have you ever considered what it must have been like losing both parents and then having to stay two years with the grandparents he hardly knew? If Titus hadn't started acting out, his mother's parents would have never gotten him and moved back to Oakland. He hasn't gotten over that yet. The experience of losing his parents still haunts him. He also lost us," Sahel said. "He lost us again when, during residency, he discovered I'd slept with you."

"Well, I don't know who told him," Carl said. "I certainly didn't."

"Perhaps not directly," Sahel said. The defensiveness of his tone seeded doubt regarding the truthfulness of his statement. In Carl's silence she added, "I've been so wrapped up in trying to escape my mother that I haven't seen what's before me. Titus has always loved and needed me."

"I won't let you blame yourself for Titus having left us again," Carl interjected.

"He didn't leave us," Sahel said softly. "He's hurting and doesn't know what to do. The little boy inside of him needs us now more than ever. He blames himself for my blindness the same way he felt helpless when his parents were killed in the car accident."

"As well he should."

"You're cold and horrible and can't get beyond the competition. It's not me you wanted, but to be liked by Mama, the black woman on our street who could have passed for white. Marrying me, having me, is your way of getting her approval and getting back at her."

300

"I love you," Carl pleaded.

"No. You love competing against Titus. Mama saw that," said Sahel. "You want what she gave Titus and denied you. Mama used you, just like she used me. But I'm no longer playing her game. I love Titus. Not because she wanted me to. I love him because ... I love him. Always have. Always will." Sahel then said, "I love you too, Carl, but—"

"Then why didn't you come to me when everything was falling down around me, the walls of Queen Bessima's castle. *In the land of Freedom?* Instead, you went to Rahim."

Startled at what she was hearing, Sahel said, "Titus thinks he's Prince Thane and that you're Prince Rahim." Silence from moments earlier returned and thickened. "You were there ... in the Kingdom of Purdah ... with me, Advisor Qadir, Cynda, and Mama?" said Sahel.

"I was in Purdah, serving you as I have in all my life here."

"I slept with you as a way of getting back at Mama, not because I loved you," Sahel said. "I was wrong, but it's the truth."

"I loved you then," Carl said. His voice cracked. "Just as I love you now."

"I'm sorry, Carl. I behaved as badly as Mama." Sahel sorely regretted her actions over a decade earlier. She felt horrible and enormously guilty for her lack of sight, and insight. "I didn't love you that way," she said to Carl. "I thought I did. But—"

"I've always loved you, as both Prince Thane in Purdah and as Carl in this life."

Sahel shivered in hearing Carl pronounce himself as Prince Thane. She wished to hold him, and right the wrong she had committed for using Carl, as Queen Bessima had exploited Prince Thane in the dream, and Sahel's mother, Lillian, had done in waking life.

And yet she could no longer deny her truth. "If that be the case, that you love me, then find Titus. I need him. He needs me. He's my husband. And I'm his wife. Until he comes back and tells me he doesn't love me, this marriage remains. I'm not signing the divorce papers. *The Kingdom of Purdah* needs him. I need him. You need him," Sahel said. "We, all of us, are the

Kingdom of Purdah. This war, the internal battle I'm fighting, is holding Titus hostage." It was all becoming clear, the link between Sahel's waking life and her experiences in the Kingdom of Purdah. "Titus is captive to the demons I fight—Mama and the image she gave me of myself."

The house stood wondrously quiet as Sahel lay in bed that night.

At Sahel's insistence, her father had spent the night at Geraldine's.

"She still needs you. Go be with her."

Alone with her hopes, wishes, and fears, she pondered her need and the task to find Titus and convince him that he was truly Prince Rahim, not Prince Thane, and that Prince Rahim had survived the rubble.

She reached upon the night table, and fumbling across the surface, found her new cell phone. Opening it, and identifying the numbers indicated in Braille, she dialed Titus's cell phone.

"This is Dr. Titus Denning. I can't take your call right now. Please leave a message and I'll get back to you as soon as I can. If this is an emergency, please call Cardiac Surgeons of Berkeley at 510-868-34 ..."

"Titus, this is Sahel. I'm worried about you." Tears pierced her throat like the nail of a lost kitten clawing at the door of a house it hoped was its home. "I love you and I want you to be okay. You're not Prince Thane. You're Rahim. And I need you. We all miss and need you. And we want you to come home." Having spoken those words, she would not belabor the point. Sahel closed her cell phone, slid it under her pillow as she had every night since Titus had left, and drifted to sleep.

Chapter 44

R

omina came the following Monday afternoon. As always when the session ended, Sahel went out with Zelda for a stroll around the block. Her stroll with Zelda was as Sahel put it, "... a chance to practice proper technique using my cane, keeping it in rhythm and alignment with my back foot."

"That way when you encounter a curb or drop-off, where you have two to three seconds to react," Romina had explained, "—before the next step."

"Kind of like driving a car," Sahel had said.

During Sahel's Tuesday session the following day, Romina asked, "Have you considered what you'll do on completing the program at the Independent Living Center?"

"No, but something tells me you may have."

"I thought you might like to return to seeing clients."

"Oh?" Sahel grew interested.

"Like a former student of mine." Romina said. "A psychotherapist. She's set to complete her stint at the Independent Living Center in March."

"I hadn't thought that far," Sahel said. "That it would come so soon."

"Oh, it's approaching fast," Romina said with joy and

eagerness.

"You're a quick learner. I don't want you to lose steam. Planning ahead provides goals that keep you moving forward."

Planning also provided little time for fear and doubt to slip through the doorway of Titus's absence and lack of knowledge concerning his whereabouts. Each night before bed, Sahel contemplated the divorce papers. And each night when questions arose, forcing her to consider her stance, James's voice came forth. *Do you believe? We can be reborn?*

Sahel believed in life after death. How that occurred for each person she was not certain. Facing the gale-force winds of greatest doubt, Sahel found anchor in all her senses that said James had joined and was now with Sunetra on the other side of life. That she heard his voice during these times of greatest need evidenced that he yet lived, but in an alternate reality, not unlike the Kingdom of Purdah in which Sahel had dwelled during the six hours of her surgery.

Sahel's present battle centered on holding faith that her marriage could receive new life, that God, or the powers that be, could resurrect from the ashes of blindness her relationship with Titus.

Don't give up. He's there for you, James's voice coaxed Sahel when shadows of despair edged closer, threatening to overtake her hope. But he's not here. Titus is gone.

To this James spoke through what lay beyond the dimensions of life on earth, and said, *Sunetra also left. And she came back.*

Sahel knew this to be true. Her body had harbored Sunetra's soul, serving as the medium of Sunetra's consciousness. James said, *Without you I would have never believed and opened myself to receive Sunetra coming to me in my dreams.*

And I would have never been able to seek James's forgiveness, said Sunetra, adding, *You brought us together. You saved us.*

She grew warm realizing their souls were now together. Their voices fueled her hope and neutralized much of her despair. Yet angst remained. *Who will serve as medium reuniting me with Titus?*

A week later, Romina arrived and as usual Sahel asked, "What's on tap for today?"

"I'm not teaching a lesson today. Or rather it's not coming from me," Romina said.

Sahel had come to count on Romina's visits, her encouraging comments. *You're doing well with choosing your clothes ... Reading Braille comes easily.*

"Today I have a surprise," Romina said. The energy in her voice stirred Sahel's anxiety-filled anticipation. "I want you to meet Joan Witherspoon, my former client, the one I was telling you about."

Sahel tried stilling her trembling hand as she reached out to shake Joan's.

"Pleased to meet you," Joan said. Romina lifted Sahel's palm and Joan grasped it between both her hands.

"If you don't mind," Romina said, "I'm going to run over and do an intake with a new client who lives around the corner. I'll be back in about an hour." Seconds later the door closed.

Joan opened the conversation as she and Sahel found their places on the sofa in the study. "So this must be new for you?"

"You mean not having a session?" Sahel said.

"Talking with another blind person."

Sahel caught herself smiling. "Yeah. And in that you're a therapist—"

"Romina tells me you're a psychologist," Joan said.

"And you a psychiatrist."

"Same difference. Like you I'm accustomed to helping, not so comfortable with receiving assistance, my way of staying in control. Then I started losing my sight."

"How?"

"Retinitis pigmentosa," Joan said. "Theoretically, at forty-five years old, I'm too old but diseases don't follow textbooks."

"I had an accident," Sahel said. "A car accident. My head was injured. I'm thirty-three."

"Any scars?" Joan asked.

"No."

"So you're as good as new except for the blindness." Sahel

chuckled in that she had held the same thoughts. "We're still vain, you know," Joan said.

Sahel felt Joan lean back into the sofa. Sahel did the same.

Joan said, "After everything settled and my sight was completely gone, I discovered it was not being able to see myself that really got my goat. I never judged how others dressed. I suppose that had to do with my feeling that everyone was better dressed, prettier than me. I liked watching their behavior, their actions."

Sahel wished she could see Joan, whom she imagined to be beautiful, that she would tell Joan as much, extinguish Joan's fear and worries, and make everything right.

"It's hard when you're the person needing the compliments, and the support," Joan said. "You don't even know how to ask for it."

"It's certainly my tale," said Sahel.

Joan asked, "Are you married?"

"Wow, you cut right to the chase."

"It's a little easier when I can't see how what I say registers on a person's face—illuminates or dulls the eyes. Instead, you have to listen not simply to what is said, but also what fills or empties a client's words, and the spaces connecting and separating them. Freudian analysis by default," Joan said.

Sahel thought of Titus, where he might be and how he was feeling. She hadn't heard from him in nearly three months. "He's offered me a divorce," said Sahel.

"Has it anything to do with your blindness?"

"Everything has to do with my blindness," Sahel said.

"Not everything. All of us have fears, rifts in relationships. The blindness illuminates them and brings to life long-festering wounds and fears, like the death of loved ones and friends brings home our sense of mortality."

Do you believe? James's words returned. *In reincarnation, life after death?* Sahel's mind went farther back. Lillian's words invaded the forefront of Sahel's thoughts. *You're not like other girls. You have to be careful. Life is hard on people like you. Gives you no margin for error.* Sahel grew sad in acknowledging and accepting the vacuum of joy that had encased her mother's life. Despite the abundance of physical beauty accorded her by certain standards—skin the color of buttermilk and black hair streaming to her slender waist—misery had permeated nearly every minutia of her existence.

Lillian Ohin had died consumed by a broken heart sustained within a body of great beauty, but wherein her aching soul had also dwelled. Now thirty-three and physically stunning in her own right—eyes shaped like exquisite diamonds, angelic lashes, and lustrous hair in which Titus lived to lose his hands and himself—Sahel stood lithe, and five years from the age at which Lillian had suffered her first heart attack.

She said to Joan, "My mother wasn't a happy person."

"Neither was mine. The first thing I thought when the doctor told me I was losing my sight was, will I be able to remember how she looks?"

Sahel nodded her head in agreement.

The conversation continued, psychologist and psychiatrist moving into deeper, but no less important, terrain.

"Romina says you're returning to your practice, that you'll be working with clients," Sahel said.

"I've been open about my loss of sight. Many of my patients have chronic illnesses. They understand. They've also had time to prepare. Just as the universe sends clients to us, it guides us to them, each of us serving the other."

"But we're still responsible for them," said Sahel.

"Our clients are not as weak as we think, nor are we as strong as we'd like to imagine."

"So, how is it for you?" Sahel repeated her inquiry.

"I'm scared to death."

"I immediately transferred my clients when realizing my sight wasn't coming back without surgery, closed my practice indefinitely. I then tried relinquishing my license."

"Now that wasn't a good idea."

"A friend of mine found out, told one of my colleagues, a psychiatrist." Sahel chuckled. Her chest grew warm in remembrance of how Carl had interceded. "The psychiatrist had consulted me on a number of his cases as had I with him, concerning some of my clients. He went before the board, told them what had happened, and that I wasn't thinking clearly." Sahel's warmth increased. Again she smiled. "The board said they would only accept my license after I had undergone a year of therapy."

"Did you?" Joan asked.

"I'm still seeing Dr. Leonard. I only went to him after I attempted suicide." Joan's silence deepened. Sahel grew anxious. "Four months after losing my sight. Three months into my marriage."

"So you married after losing your sight? Or was your choice to marry a result of your blindness?"

"Both," said Sahel. One more of the various knots binding her chest loosened. She inhaled, tension throughout her body dissipating.

"Your loss of sight pulled open the door to your heart?"

"More like kicked it open," Sahel said. She chuckled. "It's been over a year since losing my sight. I'd like to go back to work, start seeing clients again, but what can I offer them?" Sahel said. "Am I even ready?" She sighed. "The only way I can salvage my marriage, create any hope of survival, is to regain my independence. Otherwise Titus will—"

"Your husband blames himself for the accident, your loss of sight?" Joan interrupted. "And let me guess. The way he wants to care for you not only suffocates you, it also intensifies his guilt."

"I couldn't have said it better," Sahel said. Joan's directness and her interpretation of Sahel's situation offered a wider perspective on Titus's struggles.

"Trust in the process," Joan said.

Romina had high hopes for Sahel. Sahel also held them for herself. She didn't want to let Romina down. She also needed to move forward, remove the burden of guilt that she felt certain was eating away at Titus.

Joan explained, "Part of the reason I entered the program at the Independent Living Center is because I refused to let down, disappoint, my clients. Many of them have been living with disabilities and chronic illnesses all their lives. The gradual loss of my sight was my opportunity to show them what I was made of, that what I had encouraged and asked of them actually worked. I had to show them that I believed in what I said. The other reason, even more important," Joan said, "is my husband. Our marriage hasn't been the best. Neither of us has been perfect. The retinitis pigmentosa gave us something to fight, other than each other. My mother didn't know how to stand behind someone through thick and thin. She admired loyalty when seeing it in others. And yet she was repulsed by the idea of needing to be supported by someone. She saw dependence as a weakness. She thought the best people stood alone, and on their own. We shouldn't need anyone." This time Joan emitted a sigh. "Arthur stayed with me when others would have gone, and long after. Had my mother been alive, I would have wished her to leave. He stayed when I abandoned myself. My mother couldn't have tolerated seeing me blind. Part of me hated myself for losing it. The retinitis pigmentosa put me in the very place I had fought all my life to avoid. I fell apart."

Sahel's throat grew hot. Her eyes began to burn. Joan had expressed so much of what Sahel had yet to glean in words. She wanted to touch Joan's hand.

Moments later Joan asked, "Can I come again? You're the only other blind therapist I know." Searching its way to Sahel's palm, Joan's hand brushed Sahel's arm. Sahel grasped Joan's hand.

"You're the only other blind person that I know." Again Sahel chuckled and said, "I'm already looking forward to our next meeting."

On hearing the doorbell, Sahel escorted Joan to the door where they both greeted Romina.

The three exchanged good-byes, Romina filling them in on her new client. Only after a long embrace with Sahel did Joan depart.

On Romina's arrival the following afternoon, Sahel thanked Romina for introducing her and Joan. "I like her honesty," Sahel said.

"It's easy when the one you're talking with doesn't have

anything to hide."

"Or that you don't feel the need to lie and withhold who you are," added Sahel.

When on Thursday of the following week Joan returned with Romina, Sahel said with a chuckle, "I see that Romina has convinced you to take me on as a client."

"I don't see clients on Thursdays," Joan explained. "I thought that perhaps we'd take a stroll around the block, get you ready for your time at the Independent Living Center."

"Ahhh," Sahel said. "Romina's ulterior motive."

"And mine," said Joan. "I need a therapist with whom I can consult now that I've returned to work."

"How's it going now that you're back seeing your clients?" Sahel asked.

"Interesting," Joan said.

Again, Romina excused herself to go see her new client who lived on the next block over. Outside, the two of them, each with her cane, maneuvered down the sidewalk. Joan said of her clients, "It seems they're happy to know I survived the loss of my sight. That I didn't retreat from the world permanently. But I get the feeling they don't want to hand me too much. That if they do, I'll crumble and they'll lose me again, or forever." Joan sighed. "It's as if they can't decide whether I'm a ghost or the real thing."

"And you're neither," Sahel said. She thought of her visit to James after her surgery, of how different he sounded.

"I had a friend. He was dying." Sahel introduced James, his plight with Sunetra, Sahel's aneurysm, and the surgery she underwent wherein Aaron Blake had drained the fistula of blood behind her eye. "A week after I'd been home I went back to the hospital and visited him. He sounded so different than the week earlier. It was as if he had been remolded, and transfigured." Sahel then said, "My surgery lasted for six hours. I had a dream during that time. I was the queen of this kingdom, where subjects had been unable to express and show their love. Only monarchs and those close to royalty were allowed to marry."

Sahel explained. "Someone with whom I had grown close had that same dream. He died the afternoon we discussed my dream."

Sahel continued walking alongside Joan, their canes in rhythm with their steps.

"Life is strange," Joan finally said. "What happens to us affects all of those around us. If we can embrace the transformations that overtake and remake us, we lend strength to those who care for us, helping them do the same."

"It's hard." Sahel considered Titus, from whom she had still not heard, and then went to her point of truth. "I miss my husband." The words eked their way from Sahel's trembling lips. She described taking the pills, her ensuing out-of-body experience, and meeting James then seven months later. Her chest grew warm in the memory of Titus, his palms crossed, one upon the other and pressing upon her chest, *"One-one thousand, two-one thousand, three-one thousand,"* in an effort to get her heart beating, the frustration upon his face, and then throwing down the paddles.

With the sun against her face, she turned in the direction from which Joan's words had traveled. "I now realize that I died. Titus and his love brought me back." She thought of James. "The friend I spoke of earlier, who experienced my dream, helped me see that. Because of him, I started these lessons."

Sahel then spoke of Sunetra. "She forbade me to die. Later I served as a conduit for her to connect and communicate with James. I had no idea who she was when I first saw her. Through me he came to see that even though Sunetra had died by her own hand, on the same day that I tried leaving this world, some part of her lived. Some part of her still loved him, had always loved him. An hour or so after we first met he asked, 'Do you believe ... in life after death?'" James's voice rang within her head.

"He questioned, forced me to think and decide, whether I believed that something lives on after this body dies." Sahel touched her chest. "Because I felt Sunetra's spirit within me, and I had connected with her soul, James trusted what he saw in his dreams, that it was truly Sunetra coming to him, that she was preparing a place for him, letting him know he wasn't alone, giving back to him what she had taken in this life, seeking repentance." Sahel lowered her head. Tears dropped from her eyes.

"James trusted me. He presented me with what I thought had died with the loss of my sight." Again Sahel fought to digest a bitter truth she found hard to swallow. James was gone. "He showed and gave me a reason to live. He died moments after we discussed the dream," Sahel said during their stroll back to the house. "I didn't see when he died." Sahel felt foolish when trying to describe what happened. "I went unconscious. The nurse saw me fall over from my chair. She called the infectious disease doctor taking care of James, and my neurosurgeon. I woke up in a hospital room. After running some tests, they concluded that I was overly tired from just having had the surgery."

"Do you believe that?" Joan asked.

Taken with Joan's interest in what Sahel deemed a convoluted story, it also intrigued Sahel that Joan had zeroed in on the aspect of her having fainted. "Every time I visited James in the hospital, I grew faint towards the end of our conversations, lost consciousness. One time my nose bled." She did not tell of having held James's hands and witnessing his experience of having been raped.

"You seemed to have had a very special and powerful relationship with James," said Joan.

The two women, psychotherapists trained in the area of internal exploration, plodded along, their canes in front of them. Sahel sensed the heaviness of Joan pondering. "What are you thinking?"

"How can you tell?" Joan asked with a chuckle.

"The heaviness of your thoughts settled on mine," said Sahel. "My head felt heavy. And then I saw a waterfall, followed by a boulder, a large round rock, rolling down a hill. Two people were in front of the rock, trying to get out of its way."

"And the waterfall?"

"I saw two people beneath it. They were swimming in what looked like an oasis, no, a tropical paradise." The images came faster and clearer as Sahel described them.

"That was me and Arthur in the river, Quatejo in the Andes, on our honeymoon," said Joan. "And that boulder we were trying to outrun, that was in an Egyptian desert."

"Egypt?" Sahel questioned with surprise. "I always thought the land there was flat."

"You'd be surprised what you find in places that appear one way, but are really altogether different. All sorts of things that you never expected." Joan spoke as if unshaken by Sahel's comments.

The two continued along. "I like talking to you," Joan said. "After losing my sight I withdrew from friends. I've reconnected with some of them. Others, well ... "

"It's hard," Sahel concurred. "They don't know what to do or say. And with the way I've behaved. My friends ... "

"The real and true friends will still be there. As for others—"

"There's plenty of time for them to return," Sahel said, unable to avoid thoughts of both Titus and Carl.

Farther along Joan said, "I think this is it. We should be back in front of your house."

"How do you know?" Sahel asked. This was Sahel's second outing during which she had strolled around the block with Joan Witherspoon. Now as in the first time, Joan had been aware of their having reached the driveway in front of Sahel's home.

"I count the paces," Joan said.

"But we were talking."

"During my time at the Independent Learning Center, I learned to keep track as I do other things. I guess you could call it multitasking for the blind."

Sahel chuckled. "Like conversing with me and keeping track of where we are, however you do it."

"Don't worry. You'll learn to do the same during your three months at the Independent Learning Center. And much more," said Joan.

"If I get into the program." The two had started off again, and had reached the front door.

"You'll get in."

Sahel reached for the doorknob and was about to stick the key into the lock when Joan touched her hand and said, "There's

313

someone I want you to meet."

"He's a neurosurgeon, no doubt, but I have a neurosurgeon."

"This one is different."

"Thanks, but I've had the best doctors," Sahel said. Old fears and anxieties began to rise. "I've accepted my blindness, that my sight won't come back."

"Hear me out," Joan said. She pulled at Sahel's hand. "I'd love for you to regain your sight, but that's not what I'm talking about."

Sahel resisted the effort of her defenses to close ranks, forced her mind to be open and receptive.

"You hold a power, a special ability," Joan said. "You see into people's minds, and absorb images of their thoughts." Sahel fell still as Joan explained. "When you told me of your connection with James, how you had helped him receive the spirit and soul of his fiancée, I didn't know what to think. But just now I felt you absorbing my thoughts and receiving the transmission of images that accompanied them."

"Did you send them to me?" Sahel asked.

"Not intentionally. But some part of me wanted you to have them."

"Why?"

"Because I need to believe in them." Joan's voice dipped as if her thoughts had retreated to a time in the past. "Suffice it to say that going back to work and greeting my clients now that I've lost my sight doesn't frighten me nearly as much as returning home to my husband."

Joan's confession of fighting to keep faith in herself and her marriage resembled James's doubt of Sunetra's spirit having actually visited his dreams. Sahel had met a kindred spirit, a person who, like James, understood so much about Sahel without needing deep explanation.

"I entered the program at the Independent Living Center fully intending to divorce my husband. But hearing you describe a physical place where I had once traveled with Arthur brought it all back, and reminded me of the love we once had. It was a gift that only you could give."

Joan said, "We come to this work as psychotherapists, first as wounded people, secondly as professionals. Whatever happens to us in our private lives happens to us as people, not as professionals who, with our degrees and training, have it all figured out. Your description of the boulder and the waterfall gave me hope," Joan continued.

"You sound like James," said Sahel. She recalled James saying, *For the first time in a long while, I felt hope.* As with James, Sahel had also given Joan hope.

Joan said, "There's a neurosurgeon I want you to see. Dr. Hansel. He's done a lot of research with blindness and what happens in the brain after blindness. His research documents the various areas of the brain that we can begin to access when we lose our physical sight."

"Like psychological illnesses that manifest in a loss of sight?"

"You're actually ahead of me," said Joan. "But not quite. Dr. Hansel doesn't approach it from the point of what would it take for you to regain your sight. He's not a psychiatrist. Instead, he focuses on what you may have gained in the way of heightened intuition and sensitivities in the wake of losing your sight. Or—" Joan then said, "—what your blindness has now allowed you to see."

Later inside the house and drinking tea at the kitchen table, Joan explained, "A few of Dr. Hansel's patients have actually regained their sight. The majority of those he works with conclude that the most important aspect of working with Dr. Hansel is what they come to realize and understand about themselves, regardless of whether they regain their sight or not."

Joan's last sentence caught Sahel's interest. She said, "I spent this last year caught between Titus, who wanted to never again have to consider the possibility of losing me, and Carl, my neurosurgeon, who desperately wanted to return my sight. I was stuck. The aneurysm forced me to have the surgery. When my sight didn't return, Titus lost all hope. Now that I've begun to move forward, I can't go back to that." Sahel released a heavy breath. "I don't know where Titus is or what he's doing. Not even a credit card statement has come through. He needs money. Where he's getting it from, I have no idea. He's hurting." She added, "Titus lost a patient during surgery. The mayor of Oakland."

Joan softly gasped. "I had no idea your husband was the surgeon who was performing the case."

"Titus and the senior partner of the group were trying to insert a valve in the mayor's heart. Losing the patient was the tip of the iceberg that pushed him over." Sahel resonated with the frustration underneath Joan's silence. "I should have seen the signs, been more attentive," said Sahel. "Titus is truly my best friend. And I let him down."

Again Joan lifted her hand. "I want you to meet Dr. Hansel. You can help him and his work. And I know he can assist you."

Chapter 45

F riday of the following week, Romina drove Sahel for the interview at the Independent Living Center in Pinole. Joan met them when they arrived, sat with Sahel as she explained to the various teachers of the Center why she would like to enter the program and what she hoped to gain. On walking back to Romina's car, Sahel thanked Joan for her support.

"It's the least I could do in the light of what you've given me, and Arthur." Joan then said, "I've cancelled all plans for seeking a divorce. I never really wanted one. It was my pride. And my hurt at being dependent. You helped me see that Arthur has always needed me. The greatest gift I could give him was leaning upon him, letting him take care of me the way I've done him."

"It's so hard for us," Sahel said. "Letting others help us." She lowered her head. Thoughts of Titus weighed heavily upon her thoughts.

"Dr. Hansel thoroughly understands our predicament. He's heard all the stories and more."

"You spoke with him?" Sahel grew energized.

"He's eager to see you. What's your schedule?" The two

agreed that Monday before Thanksgiving would work well. Romina would drive them.

On the morning she was to see Dr. Hansel, Sahel received a call from the Center informing her that she had been accepted.

"It's really going to happen. I'm starting the program at the Independent Living Center," Sahel said to Romina who arrived half an hour later with Joan. Classes began at the outset of the New Year. "I couldn't have done it without you." She reached out. Romina and Joan embraced her.

Later in Romina's car, crossing the Bay Bridge to Dr. Hansel in the city, Romina said to Sahel, "I can't think of a better student for the program. You'll make good use of everything the center offers."

"It's a hard adjustment in the first week," Joan added. "But you'll love it. All they teach is worth everything and more than you ever imagined."

Though afraid of the difficulties she might encounter in living alone, Sahel relished the idea of actually entering a new phase of her life after losing her sight. She assuaged her anxieties with the knowledge that Joan had not only survived the same ordeal, and having completed the program two weeks early, was now preparing to return to practicing psychotherapy.

Thursday of that week, Joan would return to Independent Learning Center in Pinole, and eat Thanksgiving dinner with those who had accompanied her through the three-month training. The next morning her comrades would gather their belongings and return to their lives, armored with greater strength, courage, and knowledge of how they would maneuver in the world lacking sight. Most importantly, Joan would be living back at home with her husband.

"It's scary being back with Arthur," Joan said as she and Sahel sat in the patient waiting area of Dr. Hansel's office. "I entered the program eager to learn what I needed to live on my own and adamant about our divorcing. But while doing that, I fell back in love with Arthur. It's as though time away from him let me see just what drew me to him in the first place."

"Distance can do that," said Sahel. She now spoke with Joan in an easygoing way she never experienced with another female.

An image of Titus formed in Sahel's mind, his face, lean and fair with dark eyes and thick brows, overhanging them, his gaze sharp and clear. But unlike before, he was smiling. Sahel said, "Time gives us space to step back and see what was always there."

"I explained to Arthur what I experienced with you," Joan clarified how Sahel had helped her. "He wants to meet you."

Sahel turned in the direction of Joan's voice.

Please bring Titus home. She prayed within. Allow me another chance to show him my love. As Joan had done with Arthur. *Let him love me.*

"I'm pretty stubborn and determined," Joan said. "Any person who caused me to rethink my plan is impressive in Arthur's eyes. Perhaps even stronger than I." She chuckled.

Later having reached Dr. Hansel's office and sitting in the waiting room, Joan continued. "Meeting you helped me realize I didn't want to live alone, and that I was lucky to have Arthur. Just as Titus is lucky to have you.

"You and Arthur have staying power, something I lack."

Sahel felt horrible hearing those words. For so long she had shunned Titus and avoided his pleas for her to marry him. "I'm not what you think," Sahel said, recalling how she had warned James during noon brunch on the day after Geraldine introduced him at the medical society dinner. Sahel said to Joan, "Losing my sight revealed the clarity of Titus's love."

Joan grasped Sahel's hand. "He'll be back. Anyone who can communicate with the dead can also message the living."

Sahel smiled. And at that the nurse touched her hand and called her name. "Mrs. Denning, Dr. Hansel will see you."

The familiar click of Dr. Hansel's penlight against the darkness indicated he had concluded his examination. "The aneurysm is definitely gone," he said. "As to why your sight has not returned is ... well ... I can imagine that might puzzle you. But—"

Sahel interrupted. "Joan said that you've been able to help patients bring meaning to their lack of sight."

319

"That's a nice way of putting it," said the neurosurgeon. "What I like to do is essentially study the physicality of my patient's blindness."

Sahel found that interesting, a relief to Carl's incessant desire to help her regain sight. "Most neurosurgeons feel that they've failed when the surgery they perform doesn't return a patient's sight. While I still perform surgeries, many of which are successful, I've also developed a special interest in the experiences of my patients whose sight has not returned, particularly those for whom there is no physical explanation for their blindness."

"You don't consider this a psychological phenomenon, their sight having not returned," Sahel said. She was speaking of herself, too. "I'm not averse to the idea. I happen to find it also interesting to explore what has been gained in a physical state of blindness, and stands to be lost should a person regain their sight." Sahel's thoughts began to twirl and dance.

"No one's walked into my office, having lost their sight, and said, 'I'm blind, I've had a spiritual awakening,'" Hansel explained. "But many have said, 'The loss of my sight made me stop and think, reconsider.' Better yet, I heard them say, 'When I lost my sight, I began to see or experience ...' They would then go on to share various dreams they experienced. 'Explosions of imagination,' one man termed it. Another gentleman even began writing music," said the neurosurgeon. "He heard it in his mind. Had never taken a musical lesson of any kind in his life. Nor did he sing. He was an accountant. Last year I read of a man in Boston who, in losing his sight, also experienced a cure for his schizophrenia. It just went away. He's now stopped all medications and is teaching."

Hansel then added, "One of my patients has even begun to communicate with people across the world, individuals she has never met. These people are in China. They speak. And she hears their voices while sitting in the living room of her apartment in Oakland. After a fellow researcher documented and confirmed this, I began to wonder what these people were talking about. I wanted to see if anything was taking place in this lady's brain, in fact the brains of all my patients, as a result

320

of their new abilities. I began measuring and examining their brain waves, and if possible, comparing their EEG's before their blindness to the ones I've done since their loss of sight."

Sahel asked, "Have you ever studied the brain activity of someone who communicates with the dead?"

"No, but I surely would like to." Eagerness filled Hansel's voice.

"Joan briefly explained your relationship with your friend James. And the spirit of his deceased fiancée whom you had not met and didn't know when she had been alive."

Slowly Sahel told of first meeting James, how he had asked, *Do you believe ... in reincarnation?* "I tried taking my own life ... It hurt my husband terribly ... and my father."

Sahel then told him of learning from Carl that James had AIDS and was dying.

She explained, "The night after James was admitted to the hospital, he nearly died. His heart stopped beating. My husband had been running the code. And then I heard a voice."

She told of receiving instructions from Sunetra, James's fiancée.

"I asked to be taken to him. I whispered in his ear as he lay on the hospital bed. Seconds later I heard the heart monitor start beating again. I'm told they'd worked on him for five or six minutes before pronouncing him dead.

"After that I would visit him in the hospital. We'd talk," Sahel said. "One day he told me that when he first saw me, he sensed Sunetra's presence. Something had come alive in him. It was during this conversation that," Sahel now realized, "I experienced my first headache. I fainted. Every time I visited James, there'd come a point during our conversation where I'd begin to feel dizzy. Then came the headaches. They were excruciating to the point of losing consciousness. I'd collapse."

"With the onset of the dizziness, what would you and James be discussing?" Hansel asked.

"We talked about so much. It's hard to remember." Sahel touched her lips. It felt both relieving and strange to be discussing her experiences with someone interested in neither the psychological aspects of the headaches nor in analyzing what she had undergone regarding the effects of disease and injury.

She said, "We always came around to the subject of Sunetra." She told Dr. Hansel of the shooting that killed Ravesh Desai, and added, "James was wrongfully convicted. Sunetra pulled the trigger. But James couldn't bear the thought of her going to jail."

"He loved her deeply," said Dr. Hansel. "Very much so.

"And what of you and your husband?" the neurosurgeon asked.

"My husband feels very guilty about my blindness. The night of the accident we'd been arguing about setting a wedding date. I'd been hesitant. Titus was adamant about firming up the date for our wedding. He'd been backing out of the driveway, and I was down on my knees behind the car when he accidentally hit me. He had no idea I was there. I fell on the pavement of our driveway and hit my head."

"Why were you there?"

"I was looking for my engagement ring. I'd tugged my hand from his during the argument. Not until I was in the house did I discover it was gone. I'd run back out to the driveway to search for it," Sahel said. "There was no way Titus could have heard or seen me. He had no way out except to back up. My four-by-four had been parked in front of his car." Sahel shook her head and then repeated to Hansel, "No way to leave except backing out."

Tears threatened to burst from behind Sahel's eyes onto her face. "We married six weeks later. I don't know that I would have agreed to his proposal had I not lost my sight."

"Hmm." Hansel said as if making his own assessment. "I want to run some tests. My technologist can do them here in the office. In the meantime, I'd also like to have a look at your CAT scans, particularly the ones that showed your aneurysm. Would you be willing to sign a release?"

"Sure. My surgeon was Dr. Aaron Blake. His practices here in the city." Sahel would not involve Carl.

"Yes, I know Aaron. This should go quickly." Hansel sounded excited. "Now, for choosing a day for the tests. What works for you?"

"When's your next appointment?" Sahel said. She was anxious to figure out the purpose of all she had undergone. She would not accept that Titus had suffered for naught.

"How about the day after tomorrow?"

Sahel gripped her cane, knowing that for once she would undergo tests not for diagnostic purposes, but rather to uncover and discover. "I'll be here," she said.

Chapter 46

S

ahel returned to Dr. Hansel's office two days later, the day before Thanksgiving. After performing yet another CAT scan and MRI, the technologist prepared Sahel for an electroencephalogram. "The EEG will measure brain activity," the technologist stated. From the sound of her voice, Sahel estimated she couldn't have been more than twenty-eight. "Actually, I'm thirty," Lorna said. "I've been working for Dr. Hansel for three years now."

Her voice held the excitement of discovery as she carefully placed the electrodes on Sahel's head. "He's really good."

"What do you like about him?" Sahel asked.

"It may sound trite. But he cares." Lorna chuckled. "The other neurologists and neurosurgeons I worked for were only concerned with making their patients better." The technologist placed an electrode on the crown of Sahel's head. "It's understandable," Lorna continued. "Neurologic problems are usually very difficult. But sometimes when patients know they can't get better ..." Lorna slipped into silence. She placed the last electrode on the back of Sahel's head. "To understand illness, sometimes we need to explore it, particularly when a patient's life is not at stake. We have to try to understand what's really going on. Who knows? Maybe you'll discover something you never imagined or considered."

Lorna's perspective on William Hansel's research intrigued Sahel, much like Hansel and his work itself. That he listened to the experiences of patients who had lost their sight, those who had begun to experience phenomena they had not when sighted, had propelled Sahel to rethink her time with James. No longer did she approach the experience asking, What was wrong? Rather, she asked what did it mean, what had she missed, and what might she glean for the road ahead after she completed the program at the Independent Learning Center in preparation for her return to practicing psychotherapy?

Sahel was encouraged to fall asleep during the EEG that would take about two hours. Dr. Hansel came inside the room where she lay. "How are you doing?" he softly asked.

"So far, so good."

"Lorna says you're a trooper. The tests don't seem to faze you," Hansel said with a light laugh.

"I've had my share."

"And it shows." Hansel lifted Sahel's hand. "As I said earlier, I want you to relax for this last test. We'll begin collecting data when you're asleep."

"That should be easy. I slept only about an hour last night. It's also probably the reason the CAT scan and MRI didn't bother me too much."

"Good," said Hansel. He placed her hand by her side and on the bed where she lay.

Sahel let herself relax. She was truly tired and nervous. Concern for Titus never ventured far from her thoughts. Images rose in her mind as she drifted off, those of Titus, Carl, and herself as children.

The sun shone brightly above them. As on so many occasions, they were in Sahel's backyard. The sturdy California

326

live oak in her backyard cast wide arms of shade. Steps beyond its branches lay aluminum pans filled with mud made from the dark earth Carl had dug from his mother's flower garden. A red plastic bucket Titus had filled with water stood beside the pans.

They had been Sahel's helpers, Titus and Carl, delivering the main ingredients of her mixture and the one entrée that comprised their meals. Mud cakes made of earth and water that had been their Eucharist, their bread and wine, their body and blood, the three were pouring and mixing on their altar.

One day, Carl, to the left of Sahel, had lowered his hands into the water, clear with its surface reflecting the sun at its zenith. Kneeling on her right, Titus had done the same, his hands descending to the bottom of the red bucket. Sahel's hands, already settled at the bottom of the bucket, had rested between her friends' hands. There in the sunlight, three pairs of hands, thirty fingers, extended beneath the water's surface, forming a circle.

Slowly Carl had extended his pinky finger and touched Sahel's.

"Leave her alone," Titus had growled.

"She's my friend too," Carl had retorted. The three had been four years old.

"Sahel's Mommy doesn't like you," Titus retorted.

Knelt between her two best friends, Sahel remained mesmerized by the water reflecting the noonday sunlight. Three pairs of hands, thirty fingers, pierced the glistening surface of the water and formed a circle at the bottom of the bucket.

Carl edged his finger upon Sahel's smallest finger once more.

"Get away," Titus yelled. He moved his hand through the water, and hit Carl's hand. The bucket of water toppled over, shattering the crystalline moment of silence and Sahel's transfixion.

She stood up and ran inside the house.

On entering the kitchen, an eerie silence descended upon Sahel. She walked to the living room. Through the window she spied her mother, Lillian, on the front porch with Titus's mother, Cecile.

As usual the two women sat in rocking chairs on the veranda and conversed. A small, round wooden table built by Titus's father and bearing two glasses with a pitcher of iced tea, stood between them.

Lillian spoke. "'African and dark,' my parents said. 'He's not of our kind.' They hated Essien."

Lightly, so as not to make a sound, Sahel entered the living room and lowered herself beneath the sill of the window that opened onto the verandah.

"Sahel is dark just like him," Lillian went on. "They would have never accepted her."

Sahel absorbed her mother's words and then inspected her arms.

"But she's your daughter," Cecile had said. "Surely you don't ... you cannot refuse to love—"

"I don't know how to love her," Lillian said. "She's nothing like me. Too dark for my people."

"And you, too, it seems. That's evil," Cecile scolded. "How can you not love her? Sahel's your daughter. A part of you." Cecile had been adamant. "Treat her wrongly and you'll suffer, not only in this life, but for eternity."

"You don't mean that." Lillian had been indignant.

"I didn't make the rules of life. We get back what we give out," said Cecile.

Again, Sahel looked at her arms and rubbed them as if to remove the darkness from her skin.

"Sahel is your daughter," Titus's mother repeated. "And if you can't love her, will not love her, then God will punish you." Cecile stood up. "I love her. And so does Titus. He will always love her. I've taught him to love her. He'll never stop. One day he'll take her from you. And you won't have your daughter to mistreat anymore." Cecile whipped around, and headed for the screen door.

"Cecile!" Lillian called out as her friend entered the living room.

Cecile was headed to the kitchen in back when Sahel stood up.

Their eyes met.

"Haven't I warned you about listening in on grown folks' conversations?" Lillian said on entering behind Cecile and

328

seeing Sahel. "You insolent little—" She rushed towards Sahel, raised her hand, nearly white, and drew back.

Both Carl and Titus entered the living room. Sahel turned and met Carl's gaze.

"No!" Cecile rushed forward and grasped Lillian's arm. Like Lillian, Cecile's skin, too, was fair as milk. "Don't ever let me see you hit her, or else!"

Aghast, Lillian stepped back and lowered her hand. Sahel then turned to Titus, and for a third time examined her arms. Titus looked to his mother.

Cecile said to Lillian, "You're no better than your parents and the slave masters that abused our ancestors!"

Fear and terror filled Lillian's eyes. They would return with even greater horror nine years later when the first pangs of a heart attack gripped Lillian's chest. As she had when four, Sahel at thirteen, torn and perplexed with incredible rage at her mother's judgment, stood juxtaposed to her need for love and acceptance.

I don't know how to love Sahel. Lillian's words sowed the seeds of ambivalence and ambiguity that gave rise to Sahel's inability to choose between her love for Titus and loyalty to Carl, who like her, had received the misguided choice of cards dealt by Sahel's mother.

Sahel awoke to Dr. Hansel holding her hand. "Sahel, do you hear me?" Hansel asked.

"Her brain activity is back to normal," Lorna said against his question to Sahel.

Again Hansel patted her hand. "Nod if you can hear me, Sahel."

She did.

Minutes later Sahel sat up. Hansel and Lorna assisted Sahel from the bed. "Lorna will give you some water," Dr. Hansel said.

"Thank you," Sahel replied while gripping Lorna's hand.

"How do you feel?" the neurosurgeon asked.

"Dizzy."

"Understandable." The same excitement that had entered his voice when Sahel agreed to return two days later for the testing now highlighted Hansel's tone. "I'd like to speak to you about your EEG. Lorna will show you to my office. And please bring your water with you."

Sahel entered Hansel's office. "Please sit here." He escorted her to a chair.

"I've reviewed your EEG," Hansel began.

"What did it say?" she asked.

"It's not so much what the results say. That can be left up to many interpretations. None as important as the ones you will help me define."

Sahel angled her head up.

"Tell me," Hansel began. "What did you experience when asleep?"

"I had a dream, or rather, I relived a memory," Sahel said and then recounted her memory in vivid detail as she had experienced it. "It was as if I was back there once more, as a child. But this time I saw it with the eyes of all I know now, all my experiences since then."

"Interesting," Hansel mused aloud.

"It was very painful."

"I can imagine."

Sahel had given Hansel the full dream. "The relationship with your mother is strained," he said.

"Was strained," Sahel said. "She died nearly two years ago, just about this time."

"Interesting."

"What do you see?" Sahel asked. "What does the EEG show?"

"You see me reading it as we speak," Hansel said.

"I had a flash. You're holding the strip with your left hand. The right end of the strip is a little ripped. That frustrates you."

"You have an incredible ability, Sahel. Of both sight and insight," William Hansel said. "You also attract others to you. You are not alone."

"What do you mean?" Sahel leaned towards his voice.

"I believe that you speak with those who have passed on.

330

Your EEG recorded the energy of their presence."

"My brain waves?"

"The amount of activity, number of brain waves recorded in your EEG, indicates you should have been experiencing a seizure. Had that occurred, you would not be sitting here coherently discussing this matter with me as you are doing."

"Is that why I fainted when I visited James?"

"I believe as you have theorized, that you served as a conduit for the soul of James's fiancée to communicate with him. She spoke to him through you. You filtered her presence into this reality. More importantly, they were present, or rather the energies of their spirits, James's and Sunetra's souls, were present in the room with you as you underwent the EEG. Given what you told me on Monday, I believe the energy of their spirits, their souls, accounts for the increased brain wave activity recorded on your EEG."

Sahel leaned back in her chair.

As Hansel's explanation settled upon her thoughts, an image formed. Sahel saw Titus, as an adult.

He was standing on the shoreline of a beach. The sun in the distance and over the water cast a glow upon his face, but none so bright as to dissolve the melancholy that weighed down his brows.

With his hands pocketed and the hem of his trousers rolled above his ankles, water washed in from the ocean and onto the sand covering Titus's feet, bare of shoes or sandals.

Sahel wished to reach out, touch his shoulders, and kiss his brow.

Instead she softly murmured, "I love you."

Moments later Sahel said, "The surgery to repair my aneurysm was difficult on my husband."

"How so?" asked Dr. Hansel.

"Titus was afraid of the surgery."

"It was very risky," Hansel commented.

"He never admitted it, at least not to me," Sahel said. "But Titus was counting on the procedure to restore my sight."

Tears slid down Sahel's face. "I wanted my sight back if only to lift Titus's guilt. It was never his fault." Sahel again spoke of the accident. "He had no idea I was down there on the pavement and looking for the ring." Sahel sighed and wiped her face. "I can't believe this all happened for nothing. I won't accept that." She told Hansel of Titus losing a patient. "I was too much for him. Titus never mourned the loss of his parents when he was eleven. The mayor's death took him right back to where he was over two decades ago. If only I could see him and—"

"When was the accident?" Dr. Hansel asked.

"About eighteen months ago."

"When did you begin experiencing the headaches and dizziness?"

"In October. After I met James and began serving as a medium or conduit through which Sunetra could connect with him."

"Are you sure you had no symptoms before meeting James?"

"Yes. I'm certain," Sahel said. "Why do you ask?"

"I've reviewed the CAT scans Aaron Blake sent over. I also spoke to him. The surgery you underwent was quite difficult. Aaron had intended to approach the aneurysm by entering through your nose."

"I know," Sahel said.

"Due to the difficulty, mainly its size, he was forced to enter through your forehead."

"A mini lobotomy," Sahel said.

"It's a miracle you're still alive, that you survived the surgery. The size of your aneurysm was almost that of a small plum," Hansel explained. "Aaron said he had never seen anything like it."

"Did you tell him you would be conveying this to me?"

"Yes. He felt that in the light of your recovery, the news would not distress you."

"I haven't regained my sight." The words slipped through Sahel's lips with a bitterness that she disdained. She missed Titus more with each passing day. Her soul ached for his touch, to feel him sleeping beside her. If only she had regained her sight, perhaps he would not have left. The mayor's death would not have hurt him so.

"As with all aneurysms, particularly of this size, sudden

death quite often occurs if left untreated. That you had no symptoms until meeting James makes me wonder," Hansel said as if thinking aloud.

Receiving no indication as to where Hansel's thoughts were guiding him, Sahel said, "It's because of James that I began taking classes, classes that led me to the Independent Living Center."

"Yes, but had you not lost your sight, you would have had no need for them."

Sahel shook her head. "I don't understand."

"The presence of James in your life brought on the headaches, if you will. Your relationship with him heightened the activity of your brain to a point of affecting the aneurysm. It forced you to have symptoms that brought attention to the aneurysm that had otherwise lay dormant."

"You think I'd had the aneurysm for some time."

"It takes time for an aneurysm of that size to form."

"I always thought the aneurysm had formed as a result of the accident," Sahel said.

"Is that what Aaron told you?" Now Hansel was probing.

"No," said Sahel. "And nor did my neurosurgeon in the East Bay." And yet Carl had not said that the aneurysm had not resulted from Sahel's head slamming onto the pavement when the car driven by Titus had hit her.

"Let's say you had this aneurysm two years ago, which is quite reasonable. And let's imagine that there had been no accident. Life had continued as it had been, you never losing your sight."

Sahel recalled Aaron Blake's words explaining the seriousness of the aneurysm inside her brain—"This aneurysm is like a time bomb. It could explode at any moment. You no longer have the choice of avoiding the surgery despite its risks."

At that Sahel realized what her blindness rendered by the accident with Titus at the wheel had uncovered.

Chapter 47

T

hanksgiving Day. Sahel attended Mass at St. Maria's with Essien and Geraldine.

Throughout the homily Sahel sent loving thoughts to Titus. The last credit card statements she received came from hotels in Florida.

Before going down to the car where she joined Essien driving them to Mass, Sahel had left a message on his cell phone.

Following homily and in the line moving towards Father Richard to receive Eucharist, Sahel grew fearful and ashamed. She missed receiving Eucharist with Titus present. Sobs threatened to engulf her on drawing near Father Richard.

A hand landed on Sahel's shoulder when she reached Father Richard. "Let me help you." It was Carl. He took her hand.

"The body of Christ, Sahel," said Father Richard. Sahel cupped her palms and received the wafer. "Carl, the body of Christ."

Carl led Sahel to the Eucharist minister dispensing the wine. "The blood of Christ." Sahel drank from the chalice. Moments later Carl guided Sahel into the pew and helped her kneel. Comforted by Carl's presence, she still prayed for Titus's safe return.

Back at the house Sahel helped Geraldine set the table for Thanksgiving dinner. While folding the napkins, Sahel said, "Carl left Mass before I could speak to him." Sahel folded two more napkins and then said, "It was his first time there in a while."

"Since you and Titus married," Geraldine said more specifically. A stack of plates landed on the table beside Sahel's elbow. Geraldine touched her arm. "As for not being able to speak to him, you have me to thank for that."

Sahel lifted her attention to Geraldine's voice.

"I told him you didn't need to have any more confusion in your life. Not right now."

"And what if Titus doesn't come back?"

"He'll come back," Geraldine said. "And if he doesn't, we'll find him. You, me, and your father." Sahel couldn't help but wonder whether Titus had returned to Alice, his first wife.

Geraldine said, "Titus loves you. *Very much*. Carl knows that."

"But he doesn't know how much I love Titus. I can't help but wonder if I haven't led him on. Maybe I'm not the best person for Titus."

"Titus is sensitive like you. The loss of his parents hurt him terribly."

Sahel sat in awe of Geraldine's words and her transformation in the way she viewed Titus. "He doesn't believe he deserves you," Geraldine continued. "Same as you don't believe you deserve him."

"Oh, but he does. Titus saved my life." Sahel told of her examination by Dr. Hansel.

"But I thought you have given up undergoing any more surgery."

"That's not why I went." She explained of Hansel's research. The tests he ran showed that the accident didn't cause the aneurysm behind my eye. It had been there much longer. Hansel suspects perhaps a year or more."

Thick silence settled. And then Geraldine spoke. "Without the accident," Geraldine spoke some moments later, " ... Carl might never have examined your brain. The headaches would have come, but ... "

"I probably would have ignored them, written them off as what comes with ... "

"And then it might have been too late." Again Geraldine grew silent.

Later she said, "You and Titus are so much in love with each other it's frightening." Her voice was low and soft.

"How do you know this?" Sahel asked.

"You're not the only one who dreams. Nor was James."

The ceremony took place at St. Maria's sanctuary on Christmas Eve, Sahel attending as matron of honor to Geraldine Paynter exchanging vows with Essien, and the two becoming wife and husband.

As Essien pledged his love and honor to Geraldine, Sahel recalled the words Titus had spoken to her. "I, Titus McCrary Denning, take thee Sahel Ohin as my wife in the eyes of God and man. As your husband I promise to love you for better or worse, for richer or poorer, in sickness and in health, unto death, in this life and the next."

Sahel had pledged to do the same. Now doubtful of having fulfilled her vows during the nine months of their marriage, she grew fearful of living without Titus. Sahel began to cry.

While Essien and Geraldine thanked the small gathering of guests who had witnessed the ceremony, Sahel sat at the front of the sanctuary praying. "Bring him back, oh God. Give me just one more chance to show Titus how much I love him. Grant me that.

Please." She lowered her head and drew the bouquet of flowers she held as matron of honor into her chest.

A hand landed upon her right shoulder. "It's hard to pray alone." At the sound of Father Richard's voice Sahel recalled the moment he had placed the palm of Titus's hand over her back and pronounced them Mr. and Mrs. Titus Denning.

Sahel felt the priest sit next to her. She extended her hand. Father Richard took it. Tears turned into sobs.

"Heavenly Father, we are your children." The priest softly prayed. "Surround us with your love and care. Those present with us and those whose whereabouts we have no knowledge but whose return we eagerly await."

With palms trembling Sahel lowered her head and released sobs pent up for years, sobs that turned into wails.

Winter

•.•..•.•

Chapter 48

T

hree days into January, Essien and Geraldine drove Sahel to the Independent Living Center in Pinole. Romina greeted them on their arrival. "You've really got the hang of using your cane." Romina brought Sahel's left hand to her arm. "This is really important since you'll be going to and from classes at the main building on your own." Romina then said in a low tone, "But before we get started, there's a bit of a problem."

Sahel grew anxious. "It's okay if my father hears," Sahel said.

"It seems that one of your doctors has not faxed us the agreement as required, Dr. Pierson."

"That would be Carl," Sahel said.

"Your neurosurgeon," said Romina. "I believe I met him."

Anger mingled with surprise and desperation filled Sahel's chest.

Romina explained. "We called, several times, and at different hours. His receptionist always says he's in surgery. I called this morning. Same thing."

"Would you like me to handle this?" Essien asked.

"No." Sahel shook her head. "Call Calvin." Sahel spoke with Calvin Bennett nearly every other day. On learning of her decision to enter the program at the Independent Living Center, Calvin reminded Sahel that if she needed anything she could call him. "Don't hesitate to call. Ramona and I pray for Titus and you every morning and every night."

Minutes past noon, the strident footsteps of the senior partner over the cardiac group of which Titus was a partner preceded his voice. "I'm here to see Mrs. Denning."

Calvin Bennett came to Sahel and lifted her hand. "I'm so glad you called," he said in that soft but commanding bellow that so distinguished him, and trumpeted his presence. "Wish you had told me sooner. Ramona's been asking if there was anything we could do to help other than making calls to locate Titus. I told her you'd let us know."

"Thanks so much," Sahel said. "I hate pulling you from the office. You could have faxed everything."

"No. I want to be here. What you're doing is great. All of us are rooting for you and Titus." By "us" Calvin meant himself and the other two partners of Berkeley Cardiac Associates.

Calvin performed the briefest of physical examinations and signed the documents required for Sahel's entrance as a participant at the Independent Living Center. After giving Romina the documents, he said to Sahel, "I'd like to speak with you."

While Romina delivered the documents to the administrative officials, Calvin escorted Sahel into one of the onsite examination rooms.

The door closed. Calvin guided Sahel to a chair and helped her sit.

"Now for the matter at hand," Calvin said against the sound of a chair moving. "I don't know what Carl's been telling you, but we actually know where Titus is."

Sahel's heart raced forward and then slowed at the fact that Carl had not told her.

"Titus is in New York."

Now her heart sank as she considered Titus's first wife, Alice, and Carl's warning and words of foreboding. "Have you called anyone in New York? He lived there for seven years. Alice is also there."

"Is he back working at Columbia Presbyterian?" Sahel asked Calvin.

"No. Believe it or not, cardiac surgery positions don't open up that often. Besides, I don't think Titus has working on his mind, not at the moment." Calvin's words took on a fatherly tone.

Sahel recalled Calvin's praise of Titus. The father of three daughters, Calvin had said, "If I had to choose a son ... it would be Titus."

The cardiac surgeon said, "Zena put out the word that we were looking for him." Zena, the eldest of Calvin's three daughters, was a pediatric surgeon working at Sloan Kettering in Manhattan. "One of Zena's colleagues spotted him. He was with a woman. A psychiatrist, Zena said."

"What did she look like?" Sahel asked. She thought of Missy Grosvenor, a fit and athletic blonde who, during their freshman year at Oakland Catholic Prep, had worshipped the ground on which Titus had walked. Sahel then considered Titus's first wife, Alice Whitmore of old New York stock who summered on Long Island.

"Zena didn't say," Calvin said. "I think Titus needs a rest."

"Do you think he's coming back?" Sahel said with a sigh.

"I'm certain of it." Calvin grasped Sahel's shoulder.

Sahel's hand trembled. Calvin tightened his soft grip. "I've seen this kind of thing happen with other colleagues," Calvin said. "You lose that particular patient and your whole world goes awry. It's as if all the things that have gone wrong in your life, all the pain stored up from childhood experiences, rise up and board ship with this one loss."

"But I thought Titus didn't do anything wrong."

"Technically he didn't. Emotionally he was all over the

place. Milton Jackson was our mayor, a good one. But he should never have been operated on. His heart was in a shambles. No surgeon could have repaired it. Titus had the courage to see it, but lacked the strength to convey it to the patient."

"But you called Titus, asked him to come in to see Mayor Jackson," Sahel said.

"Not for the purposes of doing the surgery. Titus was to offer a second opinion, tell Milton that neither we, nor anyone, could fix his heart," Calvin said.

"But Titus couldn't say, 'no.'" Sahel thought aloud. Titus's words levitated from her within her memory. *Every patient I meet is either my mother or my father.*

"Milton Jackson was scared and Titus wanted to save him," Calvin said. He sighed. "This is a dangerous work we do. Patients ask us to play god. Some parts of us want to. But we're men and women with clay feet. And sometimes that clay crumbles, particularly when our feet are tired."

Sorrow and dread settled upon Sahel. She reached across her chest and gripped Calvin's hand still upon her shoulder. Sahel felt herself as much to blame, if not more, for Titus's leaving. "The last two years have not been easy for him," she said.

"Forgive me, but all of this could have been made somewhat easier if Carl Pierson hadn't been taking care of you," Calvin lamented. "I like Carl and respect his work. But he's got his own set of problems that neither you nor Titus have had the time to deal with." Sahel wanted to ask of those problems, but Calvin's words, echoing with such clarity of description, stilled her tongue.

Calvin continued. "Titus is a surgeon, the best of the best. As far as getting him back home, I don't give up so easily. I'll be working on my end. You focus on the program here." He patted Sahel's knee. "Ramona and I are thrilled with your decision to come here." Again he reminded, "You're always in our prayers. You and Titus."

A flush of embarrassment crossed Sahel's face. She had never imagined Calvin Bennett the praying type. "Thank you."

"You're not alone in this. Neither you nor Titus," said Calvin. "And with a little help from me and the partners, he'll

344

see this. Be a better surgeon for it." He then added, "All of us surgeons have had our losses, those patients we wished to save, more than the patient perhaps wanted to live. In retrospect patients are often going through the motions of undergoing the surgery for the sake of their family, if not for us, their physicians. All of this, mind you, is unconscious to them. It's our job as their caretakers to make them understand. Time and maturity teach us to know when to stop and how to help the patient realize nothing more can be done. This kind of knowledge has come later to Titus than it did to the rest of us. It happens to all eventually, and when it's supposed to. Titus needed a string of successes before his time came."

"But those successes make it even harder to accept that he couldn't save the person," said Sahel.

"It's not our job to save everyone. It's physically impossible," Calvin said. "The hardest part about being a doctor, particularly a surgeon, is realizing we can't save everyone. The ultimate we can strive for is to cast no harm, and ease the pain of suffering. Oftentimes the pain we assuage is not that of illness, but rather the suffering that comes with the approach of death."

Sahel considered the difficulty of Carl to accept that the surgery that she had undergone had not returned her sight, despite saving her life.

"I need to give Titus space," she said. "If you reach him, are able to speak with him, tell him that I love him, but with no expectations. Say nothing about the program here or that I'm in it. I just want him to take care of himself. And come home when he's ready."

"I'll do that. And believe me—" Again Calvin patted her knee. "Titus will be back. He loves you. And it goes without saying, you love him."

Sahel grasped her cane and thanked Calvin for coming, "— and so quickly," she added.

"Glad to do it. Glad to do it." He took her hand. "I'm also happy to see that you're moving forward beyond this ... well you know ..."

"My blindness," Sahel said, and felt the freer for doing it.

Calvin grasped her hand. "When you complete your work here and return home, Ramona and I want to have you to dinner." He patted the back of her palm. "Promise?"

"I do."

Calvin then pulled Sahel close and laid a light fatherly kiss upon her cheek. "These things take time. Ramona and I always knew you'd come around. They take time. Take time."

Calvin escorted Sahel from the empty office out into the lobby, where he reminded Romina that as Sahel's physician he was to be called if anything arose medically, "—or otherwise. Here's my number."

Sahel accompanied him to the front door. Before leaving Calvin again whispered encouragement. "Complete this program and everything is going to be fine. Trust me. You're focused on Titus, but this will be good for you too."

Chapter 49

S

ahel began her training at the Independent Living Center two hours after Calvin signed her medical release and wished her well. The first order of business was getting settled into her apartment, one of ten owned by the Center and located within the complex across the street from the building that housed the classrooms. The one-bedroom apartments came with a furnished kitchen that contained cooking utensils, pots, pans, plates, flatware, and cups, as well as a dishwasher, washer, and dryer. While Essien explored the grounds of the complex, Geraldine helped Sahel place her clothes in the bedroom closet. On hanging the last pair of slacks, Sahel thanked Geraldine. "You've been so much help."

"It's my pleasure. Never mind that you're now also my stepdaughter."

Sahel felt closer to Geraldine, in more ways than she had to her biological mother, Lillian. Unlike Geraldine, she had not encouraged James to fight to live, to remain in this world. For that Sahel felt heartily sorry.

Sahel said, "I don't know what I would have done without you all these months. I owe you so much."

"Not as much as I owe you. If only James could have drawn strength from you and resisted the pull of Sunetra," said Geraldine. Hurt and pain filled her voice, filtered her words and drained into her tone.

Sahel made her way across the room and sat upon the bed. Disloyalty towards Lillian cornered Sahel from one end as remnants of guilt blistered her from another. Sahel had lent James energy, assisted him in making peace with the finality of death. She said, "It's because of James that I'm here and about to begin this program."

"He loved you."

"And I him," Sahel said. She felt Geraldine sit upon the bed.

Geraldine said, "I pray every night that James has made it to heaven. And that his soul is free of Sunetra. I pray for you."

"We all need your prayers," said Sahel.

"I pray for Titus too." Geraldine's words, what seemed a change of heart, rattled Sahel.

Sahel said, "I hope that I'm finished with the program by the time he finds the strength to come home."

"Do you really think he'll come back? It's obvious that you love him. But I just don't know if Titus has what it takes to keep you happy."

Anger welled in her chest, fuel by Geraldine's voice. And the reversal of her opinion on Titus. "Well, this is a change. Just weeks ago you said that we were so much alike, almost identical twins."

"I never said that."

"You implied it. You also said that Titus would be back. He loved me too much and I him."

"The latter I don't doubt." Geraldine relented. "But as for Titus—"

"What's caused you to change sides? You started out not liking Titus and favoring Carl. Then you show sympathy when the mayor dies and Titus leaves. Now you've taken up your old position. If I didn't know better I'd suspect—"

"Forgive me," Geraldine interrupted, " ... but Titus abandoned you once before. When he and Carl were residents training in surgery over at UCSF."

"Titus transferred from the training program at UCSF to Columbia."

"He left you. You, who've waited for him all your life. And now he's gone again." Geraldine's words cut like a scalpel. "You're back here with Carl and he's gone back to that white woman, the psychiatrist, he was married to."

"Is that what Carl told you?" Sahel asked.

"He didn't have to. But I do agree with his suspicions."

"And when did you learn of his suspicions?"

"He hosted your father and me for dinner the other night. Took us over to Cafe Rouge down on 4th Street in Berkeley. Carl said it was a belated wedding gift for newlyweds who have everything. I know better. He wanted to check up on you."

"It would have helped to send over my physical. If it hadn't been for Calvin coming over today ..." Sahel said, then on turning towards Geraldine's voice, added, "But wait a minute. As I remember, you're the one who told him to give me some space and not add to my confusion."

"Carl, like Titus, needed to give you space to grieve over James's death."

"I also miss my husband," Sahel said.

"That may be. But once Titus sees what you've been able to do without him standing in your way and holding you back, and despite the car accident—"

"I love Titus."

"But do you think he's capable of loving you the way you need to be loved, hovering and giving you space to flourish?"

Geraldine's ambivalence, her need to perhaps please, frustrated Sahel. And yet Sahel had done the same.

Amid the darkness of her loss of sight, she saw the frustration on Titus's face when she had offered excuses empty of reason to delay setting their wedding date. A warm steam of compassion rose within Sahel's chest. Softly but with wide deliberation she said, "I'll take living in *purdah* with Titus any day to the freedom of moving through this life alone."

"You're not alone. Carl loves you," Geraldine said.

"Like me at one time, Sunetra also wanted freedom. She wanted to escape her father the same as I wanted to get away from Mama."

"What are you talking about?"

"Sunetra wanted to manage her father's brokerage," Sahel said. "She became angry when she learned that Ravesh had made plans for James to manage the brokerage after she and James married."

"Is that what James said?" Geraldine said. "You never met Sunetra."

"She never meant to pull the trigger." Sahel lowered her head in somber understanding of why Sunetra had pulled the trigger. "Like me, Sunetra was unconscious of how deep her anger and hurt ran against both her father and James."

Geraldine sighed long and deep.

"Despite her silence and never coming forward to admit the truth, she loved James."

"That's a lie. You can't know that! She ensnared James!" Geraldine said.

"No. It's the truth. And I know it because ..." Sahel struggled to form the words. "—because she ... she ..."

"You never met her!" Geraldine repeated.

"I didn't need to. I knew her spirit. Sunetra lived inside me. I let her come in. So she could speak to James."

"Don't say that!"

Sahel felt Geraldine's weight lift from the bed and then heard steps moving away. "I harbored her soul," Sahel said. "She lived inside me. We, Sunetra and I, attempted suicide at the same moment, on the same day, when James was sentenced."

"No," Geraldine sobbed.

"Our souls met in that moment of hating life and the pain we were feeling so much so that we tried to end it all. But when I failed—" Sahel's words slowed. "Sunetra crossed over." Her words now barely a whisper, "Sunetra died. I didn't."

"You're lying! I don't believe you." Geraldine's words then

came directly at Sahel. But the ache in her voice evidenced she believed Sahel.

"I trusted you!" Sahel's stepmother screamed. "I accepted James's refusal to let me visit him at the hospital. You were supposed to keep her away. I trusted you to protect him from Sunetra. Instead you brought her right on in!"

"It's what he wanted. Sunetra loved James. The same as he loved her," Sahel said. "And like I love Titus.

"Titus has always loved me. I see that now. It's because of James and Sunetra that I do. In Sunetra showing me her mistake, I saw mine. She gave me a second chance. Just like Titus most likely saved my life when accidentally hitting me with the car."

"That may be, but unlike Carl, Titus will never be able to—"

"Carl loves me. He always has," Sahel said. "But I mean to set things straight with my husband. I will remain Titus's wife until he comes back and tells me he wants a divorce."

Chapter 50

S

o intent had she been on telling her truth that Sahel had not heard footsteps sounding and dying in the distance, Geraldine leaving the bedroom and heading towards the front door to the apartment. Only against the sound of the front door slamming shut did Sahel realize her stepmother had left the apartment.

Moments later Essien returned from inspecting the grounds of the Independent Living Center. "The compound looks good and safe," he concluded in a tone of concern but acceptance, as only a father could. Surmising that Geraldine had gone to the car, Sahel said nothing of the argument that had ensued between her and Geraldine. Sahel's father then said, "I love and I shall miss you."

"I'm already missing you, too." She reached out. Essien embraced her.

"And yet somehow I feel your mind is already slipping away

towards your work here," he whispered on pulling her tighter than she had ever experienced. "That is a good thing."

Sahel smiled and then asked, "Pray for me."

"Always," Essien again whispered and then, barely audible, spoke directly into her ear. "You have always been a good daughter. If only I could have been as good a father."

With her head against his chest Sahel sensed a sadness in his heartbeat that she felt slowing. "Oh, but you have."

"Pray for me as well," Essien again whispered.

"Always," Sahel said. She left his embrace. "Now it's time for you to go. And see to your wife." Against the tears creeping into her heart, Sahel smiled once more.

"I will see myself out," said Essien. "Remember to lock the door. And always check twice." He lifted and patted Sahel's hand as she walked him to the door. And on his leaving, did as he had asked.

The orientation meal with fellow participants in the Center's main gathering across the street left Sahel drained that evening.

She went to sleep without taking a shower.

On sliding under the bed covers, she pulled the edges of the quilt to her neck. The quilt was from James's bed. It had come with the house he had bequeathed her. James had spoken of the quilt in his iPod missive left for Sahel.

"This was a lifesaver when my sight left completely," Joan had said of her own iPod when Sahel had told her of owning one too. "It kept me from feeling alone," Joan had added. "I listened to so many books on audio before learning Braille. Still do. In some ways I think it's hampered me from learning Braille."

Sahel was determined to learn Braille despite owning an iPod and having thousands of audio recordings of books. But on this night Sahel felt alone. Not even memories of James's voice, words he had spoken of his quilt that now warmed and comforted Sahel, could dispel the loneliness and abandonment she felt.

Titus was gone. Carl had lied. The three now lived distanced from each other in a way she had never expected. Sahel wondered how, or if ever, the mysteries of life might, or could mend the rift separating them. That had been their story, that of the Three Musketeers, what fellow high school students had called them.

Anger rose within and filled Sahel's chest as her thoughts fell upon Carl saying that he had not heard from Titus. *I have no idea where he is.*

How could he? She now thought aloud. That Calvin's daughter, Zena, had seen Titus with Alice, his previous and first wife, seared Sahel to the core. Carl with his ominous warnings sounded so much like Lillian. *There's studying. And then there's studying.* Yes, Sahel had slept with Carl during their junior year in college.

She had wanted Carl to realize he could get into medical school. His grades were good. But he needed to do better on the MCAT. And that meant taking it again. Something Carl feared and of which he felt ashamed. Titus had done exceptionally well on taking it the first time. If only she could explain her actions to Titus.

Sahel's worries shifted to doubts of having helped James make peace with death, affirming him in his decision to abandon life on Earth, seek to enter the beyond where he felt certain Sunetra was waiting. What if she had not? Sahel now ruminated. Was it I that wanted to die? Did I project this onto James? Let it cloud my judgment and not encourage him to fight to live?

At least Geraldine was not alone. She had married Sahel's father, never resisted Essien's proposal, something that Sahel had not had the strength to do with Titus.

The rancid smell of betrayal would remain with Sahel for quite some time. She still felt guilty for not having encouraged James to do all he could to live.

Softly she brushed her hand across the quilt that had at one time warmed James's body. She pressed the iPod to play. James's voice flowed.

This quilt kept me warm many nights since being released from prison. My mother's mother made it to remind me of where I had come from, my ancestors. It contains patterns and squares designed and made by my grandmother's own grandmother.

Sahel was happy that James's lasts steps towards death had, for him, yielded freedom. *Our country places a high value upon freedom. But what is freedom?*

Our forefathers were brought here in chains and shackles. Today, many of us find ourselves imprisoned by family relationships that squeeze the life out of our hopes and dreams. The prisons separating us from ourselves multiply and change faster than we can understand the nature of these relationships .... And then there is the purdah *of our love, that which we hold for others, not of our choosing, but of our hearts—hearts that beat to their own drums and rhythms.*

... What are we to do when the pulsation of our arteries leads us down roads we had not intended to travel? What can we do when what lies before us, draws us forth, and captures our passion, also requires our demise?

... We cross to the other side, trusting that upon our arrival we will experience, the resurrection of hope, redemption, our rebirth.

Reincarnation, Sahel thought as she flicked off the iPod, and tucked it under her pillow. She marveled at the poet that had lived in James, unseen and invisible, enlivening so much to which Sahel had become conscious in the wake of her blindness.

Again she considered Titus and his protectiveness under which she had felt smothered, imprisonment in the *purdah* of his love.

Life with Titus as his wife had felt like incarceration. "I've turned my life upside down for you," he had declared when Sahel demanded to see James. "You seemed more concerned for him than you have ever been for me ... Is there nothing I can do to win your love, let me love you?" Titus had pleaded.

Now, as when he spoke those words, Sahel imagined the agony she had, as a spirit and out of her body, witnessed upon his face. Pain had bled onto his cheeks as if hope, like blood, was draining through the wound rent by a knife. Sahel missed him terribly. She pressed her fist upon her chest.

One-one thousand. Two-one thousand. Three-one thousand. She recalled Titus counting the seconds as he fought to save her. Sahel's ache increased when under the spell of the memory.

Throughout his life Titus had fought with death and all the casualties it had wreaked upon him, first when it had stolen his parents in the car accident. Then when he had battled against the time bomb of Lillian's bad heart. Nearly eight months after Lillian's death, Sahel's blindness had nearly rendered her a corpse, the ghost of which wandering between life and death had stood between them, and evaporating only when Titus made love to her.

The passion of Titus's chest, warm and pounding upon Sahel's, filled her with life and hope each time he entered and withdrew from her. She wished for him as James's words, his essence, swirled in her thoughts, added warmth to the quilt made by his mother, and covered and protected Sahel from her sea of doubts. Should Titus ever return, they would sleep under its protection unto death.

Sahel inhaled the history of the decades-old quilt. Softly she slid her hand from under the pillow, held tight to the quilt, and on breathing in once more, inhaled what now symbolized the scent of James's presence, his life, his soul.

James.

He had been a lamp unto Sahel's feet illuminating the darkened path on which she trod.

"You need to find him," James had said of Titus. "He's your resurrection. In him dwells all you'll need in life, salvation and reincarnation, what none of us can give ourselves alone, what Sunetra gave me and what I'm going to find. Thank you for being my family in these last days, a loved one who did not seek to hold me, but one who set me free." Those had been James's closing words.

"I love you." She whispered her statement, as much a 'Thank you,' to James as it was a call to Titus. Because of James, Sahel had made peace with the darkness and come into the light, the glow of opening the door of her heart, letting Titus enter, and receiving his love.

Come home, she now prayed for Titus's return while hoping her father was praying for her. *Come home and let me love you.*

Completing her training at the Center would allow Sahel to do that in the fullness she desired.

Chapter 51

S

ahel wanted to transcribe the message James had recorded on the iPod he had bequeathed her, into Braille. To accomplish this she would listen to James's recording and type what he said, on the computer provided by the Center. From that she would print out the document in Braille format.

James's letter printed in Braille would serve as her primer, for reading each morning and night, and expanding to what she had learned from the tags that labeled her clothes.

Eric, the supervisor and instructor of the technology lab at the Independent Living Center, considered Sahel's plan viable and smart. "You have to hold on to your passion," he encouraged. "That's what my parents taught me."

Blind from birth, Eric was a sort of pioneer in his ability to use and modify computers for the blind. "My mother believed there was nothing I couldn't do if I really put my mind to it."

On her fourth day at the Center, he explained, "Many of my friends, blind like me, were intent on rock climbing and reaching the peak of Mt. Everest. I just wanted to travel through using my computer."

"I'm certainly glad you chose this route," Sahel said. She loved Eric's energy. There was something about him and two others in the program, young like Eric and having never possessed sight, who boosted Sahel's confidence.

"You can't miss what you never had," Eric had said on welcoming her the first morning after her arrival.

By the end of the week she was not only surfing the Internet, but also typing letters. Sahel was also considering how she might acquaint Titus, on his return, with her capabilities. "You have to hold onto your passion. Hug it tightly," Eric steadily urged. "Never let it go." His words, and those of Eric's mother, anchored Sahel, as did James's. "Find Titus. He needs you."

She felt James's presence living through her as she found her way to the Center each morning and worked with Eric in the tech lab.

At the end of the first week, Sahel received a call from Essien. "So what have you learned?" her father asked. It was Friday evening, around seven. Sahel had just arrived back at her apartment from having worked late in the tech lab. As she was the last one to leave, Eric escorted her across the street to her apartment in the complex. "It's dark and you're still new here."

"I was worried," Essien confessed. "Geraldine and I have been calling for the last hour."

"I was working late in the tech lab," Sahel said and then asked, "How is Geraldine?"

"She's fine. Still grieving James," Essien lamented. "Each day she improves.

"But how are you?" His voice lifted. "Quite busy, it sounds."

"I am." Sahel said.

"Having fun, I hope?"

"I haven't felt this energized and hopeful in a long time," she said.

Essien chuckled. "This reminds me of when you were in

360

college—" Essien's voice grew wistful. "—and then graduate school. I'd get worried when you hadn't called your mother or me in a few days. Then on speaking with you, the excitement in your voice told me everything was fine. We miss you." Essien's tone turned somber.

Sahel grew warm with joy. "Believe me, I'm feeling the best I have in a long while." She had asked Essien not to visit until February. "I also have a lot to learn and everyone here is incredibly helpful."

Sahel mused upon her father having weathered life's ups and downs, and how his love remained constant and unceasing, given without mandate or obligation. She did not want to lose that. A part of Sahel feared Essien might delay or cut short his and Geraldine's travels should he learn of the heated discussion with Geraldine.

Sahel asked, "How's the semester going?"

"Same old things," Essien said with a sigh. "Students who want to learn all I have to offer, and then others who simply come to class because it is required of them to graduate, a stepping stone to bigger and better things."

"Nothing is bigger and better than you in my life," Sahel said.

"I would hope that Titus is."

Sahel pushed aside Carl's pronouncement hours before James had died, *I've waited all my life. Let me take care of you.*

Essien asked, "Have you by any chance heard from Carl?"

"You mean, has he called to say what he is doing to find Titus, or, better yet, why he refused the Center's call requesting medical records and showing me physically fit to enter the program?" Sahel translated the indictment sprouting wings underneath her father's question. "Geraldine said he had taken the two of you out for dinner as congratulations for your marriage. She told me the day you two brought me to the Center. She was helping me unpack."

"Yes, he did." Her father's voice wafted through the phone.

"Thank God for Calvin," Sahel said. She recalled his advice. *Titus needs some time. And you need to focus on getting through this program. Titus is not alone. And he loves you.* Sahel said to

her father, "It's been a long week. I'm a little hungry and—"
She wanted to lie down.

"Like all of us, Carl regrets some things he has done," Essien said. "Life always provides gifts. One option extinguished provides room for another opportunity. And if we are blessed, the option received proves more conciliatory, and cooperative to who we are."

Essien sounded as if he were picking up from where James's letter left off, James having met and adopted the poet who had always lived in Sahel's father, but fully presented itself in the absence of Sahel's mother.

She adjusted the phone to her ear.

Her father said, "I never understood why you tried to commit suicide after losing your sight. You've always been such a fighter, quiet but thorough." Essien sighed. "Your behavior was so much like what your mother would have done."

Sahel's mother had endured the physical devastation wrought by a bad heart.

"It was hard for her in the end," Essien said. He had to switch subjects. The path hewn by his words remained clear. "I'm not the person I have presented as myself. Your mother was never whom you thought. Nor I. Those last days ... were extremely painful," Essien started. "For both her, and me."

Sahel recalled Lillian's coughing spell, how it had consumed her the half hour following Titus's proposal and Lillian kissing the pear-shaped diamond ring Titus had then slid upon her finger.

In a raspy and what sounded like a sore voice, Lillian had whispered, "I love you, always have, always will." Sahel recalled how her mother had refused to allow Father Richard to administer last rites.

Essien now said, "Your mother was scared." Sahel tightened her grip on the cell phone growing warm and sweaty against her ear. "I wanted to alleviate her fears. Help her release them."

Sahel considered all the things her father could have done to assuage her mother's pain.

"She begged me not to call the paramedics, to let nature take its course. I gave her muscle relaxants. When those didn't work,

I administered the morphine." A long and metered silence ensued. "Your mother was never as strong as you." Essien resumed. "That's why I didn't understand when you took the pills. Why you would want to be with her, where I had sent her, freed her to go."

Despite attempts to clear her thoughts, an image rose in Sahel's mind. The hospital bed upon which Lillian had lain for nearly seven years had taken up every inch of space in the front room where, during Sahel's childhood, Lillian and Essien had entertained guests. Sahel, Titus, and Carl had also studied in that room during afternoons on arriving from school, or the library.

The window that faced her mother when she was lying in the bed had opened onto the veranda on which Lillian sat and confessed, to Titus's mother, Cecile Denning, her sins of conceiving Sahel by a man with skin too dark for her family's comfort, and Lillian's inability to love Sahel. "I was pregnant and unmarried. The father was black and dark, from Africa." Sahel again recalled the words with an even greater pain than when asleep during the EEG conducted at Dr. Hansel's.

Unable to see her arm, Sahel stroked it as she had when eleven years old, and crouched on the other side of the verandah underneath the sill of the window in the front room as Lillian revealed the darkness that lurked in her family. Sahel considered her mother, imprisoned from life and confined to the bed that faced that window. Purdah. Unlike then, Sahel could not examine her arm, observe its darkness that stood in contrast to her mother's milky white skin.

"My mother would have never accepted her," Lillian had said. "That's why I never went back with her or Essien," Lillian had said, explaining why she had never returned to see her parents in Louisiana. "I married Essien and kept looking forward. Until you came, I had no one in my life who felt like family," Lillian had said to Cecile.

"You have Essien. And Sahel. She's so beautiful."

"She's dark and so is he," Lillian said.

"But they're your family. And they love you," Cecile chided. Her face had been as soft and milky white as Lillian's. It had also borne love.

"Family means nothing when your own mother doesn't love you." Lillian had then fallen silent.

The bed on which Lillian would dwell some fifteen years later came to stand inches from the window beneath which Sahel crouched and heard Lillian confess her dilemma.

Sahel now wished to see her skin, dark like her father's, and then look into Titus's face and tell him, "I love you, always have, and always will—despite myself, and my mother who hated me, my mother who was as fair as you. You are not Mama."

Her father's whimpers came through the phone, pierced Sahel's memory and tugged her back. Sahel's hands trembled. She said, "You did what was best. I forgive you. Now forgive yourself."

Moments later Essien's voice rose. "Only if you can forgive yourself for resembling me more than your mother."

Cool awareness of her father's nascent understanding of her plight gripped Sahel. She shivered.

I must. I will. I do. The words floated from within the depths and slid into Sahel's chest like an infant exiting its mother's womb.

You are the most beautiful person I have ever met. Perhaps in another life we shall meet again.

James. A rush of joy filled with pain tore through Sahel. The ache she held for James gave way to the honesty of wanting, desiring Titus, his warm body near her, his passion entering and flowing throughout and enlivening her.

Sahel shook herself free of the memories, relinquished them, and then to her father said, "Good-night."

Sahel prepared a light meal, something else she had learned to do, and showered. She then slid into bed, and as on each night, pulled the quilt to her neck in an effort to shield herself from the fear of having lost Titus forever.

Questions and statements James had spoken to Sahel lulled her to sleep.

How are you doing today? ...

Sunetra came to me in my dreams ...

Love is all that matters ...

364

You gave her back to me, helped me to believe ... and trust ...
I want you to have my quilt ...
It now made sense.
Sunetra's spirit.
James's presence.
Their time together.
Sahel's entrance into the Independent Living Center.
To Titus she whispered, *You're not Mama. Never were. Never will be. You saved my life ... I love you.*

Chapter 52

A
major part of the Center's training required the participants to assume responsibility in paying their utility bills. This obliged them to go in person to the nearby post office and notify postal attendants of their new address.

Monday, the very start of the new week, required Sahel to travel to the post office seven blocks from the apartment complex where she lived with the other nine participants. The trip strengthened skills in mobility and orientation, along with providing experience of handling the practical business of life.

For Sahel the trip would also involve making the move to return to work.

Joan had suggested, "One of the first things you want to do in re-establishing your practice is to open a post office box. I find it's much easier than having mail come to my office. If something's missing, or the postman places someone else's mail in with mine I can handle it right at the post office. Call me paranoid, but I like having my mail held at the post office."

Sahel agreed. She had held a post office box before losing her sight. But, "Paying the rent to keep it open was one of the many things that slipped through the cracks after the accident. It's been over a year and I haven't paid the bill," she told Joan before setting out with Abby on their trek to the post office. "It's probably closed."

Sahel's post office had been located in Berkeley near the building where she had practiced.

"You should still tell them about your previous P.O. Box," Joan had said. "Life's funny. You never know. It may still be open."

I doubt that, had been Sahel's conclusion.

Abby, twenty years old, and having begun the program three days before Sahel, walked between Sahel and Joan, who had come along to lend assistance in walking to the post office, and, helping, if needed, with the process of opening their post office boxes.

Along the way, Sahel alternated between conversing with Abby and Joan, and silently chiding herself for having let so many things go in the months that followed her accident.

Abby said, "Coming here, and starting this program, is one of the hardest things I've done." Her words resonated with Sahel despite Sahel being thirteen years older. Now accustomed to keeping her cane in front of her back foot, Sahel listened with acuity.

"I love my parents," Abby said. "They've been really supportive. Too much so."

The sound of the three canes, Sahel's, Abby's, and Joan's, tapping their way in unison amplified what Abby would deliver next.

"Everything they've done for me has been to absolve themselves of bringing a child without sight into the world. I wish I could make them forgive themselves, get them to see I hold no grudges. They've been the best parents anyone could want."

While catering to a more mature population, adults who had

368

lost their sight, the Independent Living Center held two spots each semester for young adults, most of them blind from birth and having never lived away from their parents. Sahel drew energy from younger participants like Abby, who lived in the apartment neighboring Sahel's on the left, and Eric.

A somber tone attached itself to Abby's voice. "No matter what I say, they can't get beyond, can't accept that the only thing I lack is sight. They can't understand that it's hard to miss what you've never had. I don't need them the way they need me," Abby said.

Sahel's thoughts slipped to Titus and then onto Carl with his need to restore Sahel's sight.

Of the predicament with her parents Abby said, "It really hurt when I found they'd declined my acceptance to Yale. I worked so hard to get that. Felt that I could do no less since my mother had put her entire life into homeschooling me. She wanted me to have the best education. And she gave me that. Working to get into Yale was my way of saying, 'Thanks.'"

The diverse textures and circuitry of their lives, Abby, blind from birth, and Sahel, who had lost her sight at thirty-three years old, bore an uncanny resemblance.

"Calling Yale was the third hardest thing I've had to do," Abby said. "It hurt having to decline my acceptance, and saying it was because I was seventeen, then asking my parents for the truth and hearing them say they were afraid. All the time they said, 'Yes, you can, Abby,' and supported me in doing everything others said I couldn't do because I lacked sight. It was all a lie." Abby's voice wavered.

Joan said, "Sometimes it's only when you start asking the hard questions that your family, those you love and have depended on, begin taking you seriously."

At the post office Sahel stood in line behind Abby. During the wait, she toiled over the finer points of Abby's story.

My parents were so supportive. They loved me. But their affection was suffocating. Again Carl, not Titus, occupied the forefront of Sahel's thoughts. She considered Carl's refusal to sign the physical required for her to begin the program at the Center for Independent Living.

The attendant called Sahel forward. "I'm here to establish my new address," Sahel said. Wearily she slid underneath the window a piece of paper on which she had printed Essien's address. "I've been living at this address."

Sahel felt a sense of accomplishment in her newfound and growing abilities to use her computer, the Internet, and unlimited technologies associated with the two and available to those without sight. "I had a P.O. Box until two years ago. It was in Berkeley," she explained. "I stopped paying the bill. I imagine it's no longer open. Not that it really matters."

"I'll be right back," the attendant said. With cane in one hand Sahel tapped the fingers of the other on the counter.

Oncoming footsteps from behind the window signaled the attendant's return. "You're in luck. Your box is still open."

"Who paid the fees?" Sahel said.

"Not quite sure," said the attendant. Sahel heard what sounded like him flipping through a stack of cards. He added, "The fees for next year are all paid, too."

"Who did it? When?" Sahel gripped the counter. Her cane slid from her hand.

"I'm not certain."

"Do you have any records of how they were paid?" Perhaps Titus had done so. If lucky she could trace—

"No ma'am," said the attendant. "But their address is 2999 Regent Street, Suite 709 … Berkeley, … 9570 …" His young voice reminded Sahel of Abby's, bright and full of hope.

Chapter 53

A

nxious to learn who had kept open her post office box, and wishing with every second that passed that it would be Titus, Sahel had implored the postal attendant to research the matter. "Give me just a moment," said the postal worker.

Sahel had tapped her fingers in succession on the counter, all the while growing anxious and weary, much like she had when sitting to the table in the Masonic Ballroom at Porter and 4th, and fearful of how she would manage eating.

Moments before Geraldine would introduce James, someone lifted her hand. "How are you doing?" Carl had asked. His voice, soft and low, had alleviated some of her stress. He had lifted her hand and placed it between his palms. "I see Titus is in his element. Calvin and the old heads surrounding him." Carl had continued. "He's their golden boy."

"This is his night," Sahel had said.

"I'm worried about you," Carl said.

"I'll be fine." Sahel had lowered her head.

"Then why are your hands shaking?" Carl asked.

"This is my first time out. I want everything to be perfect for Titus. And here I am, unable to even see the food I'm supposed to—"

"I would never have brought you here," Carl whispered.

"But I want to be here. With him."

"And if I were Titus, everything would be perfect. With you here with me."

Again Sahel had lowered her head.

"Say the word and I'll take you home," Carl whispered.

"No. I can't. I won't." Sahel shook her head, tried pulling her hand from Carl's palms. "Stay for the dinner. Titus purchased a seat for you here at our table," she said.

Carl drew even closer, tightened his hold on her hand, and spoke barely audibly. "Just say the word and I'll take you away. To our own *sahel*. Where I'll make everything right. No more in between." Again, Sahel had shaken her head. "No," she whispered."

Carl let go of her hand. Sahel had lifted her head towards his voice. "I only came to check on you," Carl had said and then left. Seconds later the vision of James and Sunetra arguing had lit up the stage of Sahel's thoughts.

I've been such a fool. Sahel dropped her cane.

"Here you go, ma'am." A man's voice sounded as she bent over to search for her cane.

"Thank you," she said on reaching out and the man placing it in her hand. "Thank you," she repeated shakily but also relieved that blindness prevented her from seeing the reflection of her face in the man's eyes.

The attendant spoke and claimed her attention. "The person who paid the fees for your post office box is the person at the address where your mail has been delivered, a Dr. Car—"

"You don't need to read it to me," she said. Fumbling, she found the window separating her from the attendant and stretched her fingers into the dip underneath the window. He placed the card in her hand.

"And what would you like to do with your old post office box?" the attendant asked.

"Leave it open," Sahel had said. "And I'll also need to open one here." She then said, "For the next two months, forward all the mail from the Berkeley P.O. Box to this one here in Pinole." The words momentarily hung in Sahel's thoughts. "I'll be picking up all my mail at this box."

Sahel had not needed the attendant to read the name on the card. The offices of Bennett Cardiac Associates were located at 2999 Regent Street, same as Carl's. Suite 709, the office of Dr. Carl Pierson, stood across the corridor from Bennett Cardiac Associates at 710.

Carl had kept open Sahel's post office box and diverted mail sent to her P.O. Box to his office.

Having her mail forwarded to her new post office box in Pinole would signal to Carl that she had uncovered his actions. And yet Sahel wanted no distractions. She needed to remain focused and continue moving through the Center's program. On completion of the program, she would confront Carl.

In the days that followed, Sahel considered what Carl's actions symbolized and meant, and the consequences, both good and bad, that his behavior had portended. She reasoned that it had been through intercepting her mail that Carl had learned of her attempt to relinquish her license to practice psychotherapy.

A month after mailing her license to the Board of Behavioral Sciences, Sahel received notice that the board would not allow her to give up her license lacking two requirements. Sahel would undergo a year of psychotherapy. Her psychiatrist would have to demonstrate that Sahel was a danger to herself and her clients.

Reynard Williams, a psychiatrist, had delivered Sahel the board's decision. Unbeknownst to Sahel—prior to telling her of the board's request—Williams had also driven to Sacramento and spoken with board officials explaining her accident and loss of sight, while adding that she had been an excellent psychotherapist with whom he had both conferred and consulted regarding both their clients and to whom he had referred many patients for psychotherapy.

A colleague, Sahel had introduced Reynard to the mental health community when he had moved to Oakland seven years before. In addition to being colleagues who respected each other's work, the two had become friends.

Sahel now surmised that when picking up her mail, Carl spotted the envelope from the Board of Behavioral Heath in Sacramento containing the board's response to Sahel's decision to relinquish her license. On reading it he contacted and told Reynard Williams of her actions, an act on Carl's part that had in essence rescued Sahel from herself, and preserved her ability to practice her livelihood, to which she now was working to return.

Weeks later Essien had read to Sahel the letter from the California Board of Behavioral Health.

It has come to our attention that your decision to hand over your license is an ill-informed response to the trauma of losing your sight. Dr. Reynard Williams, a licensed psychiatrist, has described you as one of the most ethical and competent colleagues with whom he has had the opportunity to work and consult. He states that you are a much-needed asset to the Oakland and Berkeley Mental Health Community. He asks that we disregard your action of sending in your license. As such we, at his behest and guided by our own ethics, advise you to reconsider your actions.

"It was all due to Carl," Reynard had said on Sahel calling to thank him. "He's the one who contacted me."

Again Sahel had never asked Carl how he had learned of her actions. In truth she had been only too grateful that Williams had stepped in and averted her plans.

Sahel also had yet to complete a year of work with Dr. Leonard, who, in the very first meeting, stated that, despite her attempted suicide, he would not be party to helping her relinquish her license. "I won't take money from a colleague who has so much to offer clients. What I will do is help you find a way to get your life back on track."

Sahel loved working with clients, helping them fight the inner demons that stunted their lives, and hindered their will to succeed and thrive at living out their most meaningful passions.

Bound by her own beast of worry, and self-doubt, Sahel

clung to learning all she could while matriculating through programs at the Independent Living Center. She pushed aside thoughts of Carl when they arose, concentrating on the fact that had he not illegally accessed her mail, she would not have retained her license to practice psychotherapy, without which she would possess no hope of returning to practice her profession and re-entering the stream of life with purpose.

During the next eight weeks Sahel spent innumerable hours working to orient and refine her skills in using her computer, one adapted for those without sight, and that the Center provided each participant. She was determined to not simply become acquainted with the new technology available through the computer and the Internet, but to master it. From early morning to later afternoon and into the night, Sahel worked with Eric in the tech lab when she was not attending life skills classes.

On returning to her apartment for dinner, she prepared a light meal. Then after eating and cleaning up her dishes, she sat down to her computer in the apartment and resumed working, often calling and then on getting the hang of e-mail, text messaging Eric with questions. Life grew busy for Sahel. The goals she had set for herself brought order to the ramblings of her mind that could, if left unchecked, drag her into a pit of melancholy and hopelessness that loomed from not only the complexity of Carl having diverted her mail, but Titus's absence.

From the beginning of February, Sahel willed herself to forget what Carl had done. Through her daily prayers she sought and found comfort that God would care for Titus and protect their marriage from both Titus's feelings of guilt and Sahel's fears of inadequacies.

Refusing Essien's desire to have her join him and Geraldine for Valentine's dinner, Sahel instead assisted Abby and Eric in preparing dinner at Eric's. Later that evening, on returning to her apartment, Sahel encountered Essien and Geraldine waiting at her door. "I can't believe it's been nearly four weeks," Geraldine said as Sahel welcomed them inside. Sahel felt awkward when Geraldine, in giving her a tight hug, also whispered, "Your father really misses you."

Sahel recalled last month's heated exchange between her and Geraldine.

"*You encouraged him to give up. Stop fighting,*" Geraldine had said hurt in her voice. "*I trusted you.*"

"*He was ready to leave this life,*" Sahel had said in defense of her actions. "*I helped him to find his way to where he believed and I hope Sunetra was waiting for him.*"

Now as then, Sahel again felt sorry for her actions concerning James. Geraldine had hoped that introducing Sahel to James would provide him an ally, one who would encourage James to fight to live, not die. And yet for Sahel, only one choice had lain before her.

She could enter the future free from having acted out of her own needs, and those of others, or guided by the compass of James's wishes for her, desires rooted in the same terrain giving seed to the prayers for his soul to reconnect with Sunetra's.

She said to Geraldine, "I did for James what I'm also trying to do for Titus. Provide space and support to do what he needs to live. And hopefully find his way back to me, same as James was fighting to connect with Sunetra's soul. And the way Daddy wants to be with you, the woman he loves."

The apartment door closed. Essien lifted her hand and pulled her close. No words passed between them, only sighs of thankfulness.

Following dinner, Sahel served dessert, a cherry pie she had prepared.

"This is the best pie I've eaten, better than my mother's apple pie," Geraldine said, as Sahel made ready to clear the dishes. Her tone sounded absent of malice or hurt.

Yet wounded hearts did not mend so quickly. Sahel considered her father's confession of having euthanized her mother, his wife. "You don't have to say that on my account," Sahel said while she made her way to the sink.

"Let me have those," Geraldine joined her. "Please," she

376

added as Sahel stood still. "Your father needs to speak with you," Geraldine said.

Sahel relinquished the dishes and went back to the sofa. Minutes later when the water ceased flowing from the kitchen faucet, Geraldine announced, "I'm going for a walk." The sound of her heels died towards the door that opened and then closed.

Sahel leaned back onto the sofa.

"Thank you for letting Geraldine do the dishes," Essien said.

Sahel grew anxious. "Have you heard anything from Titus?"

"I was going to ask you the same."

"Calvin says Zena's colleagues and friends report he's fine."

"Where is he living?"

"I'm not sure." Sahel lowered her head.

"Or is it that you do not want to know?" Essien pursued.

"Calvin says Titus is living alone," Sahel said. "Not with Alice."

Sahel asked her father, "You've been worried?"

"Only about you," Essien said. His voice lifted.

"Then why the need for Geraldine to leave?"

"I had asked her to stay," Essien said. "She thought it best that I tell you myself."

Carl, Sahel thought. Had Essien and Geraldine learned of Carl's tampering with Sahel's mail?

"I want to take Geraldine to Ghana," Essien said.

Sahel cleared her head of thoughts concerning Carl and absorbed her father's words.

"Will you permit me, us, to do that?" Essien said.

Sahel recalled the words of his confession. *She was in such pain, your mother. I only wanted to help her,* Essien had said of euthanizing Sahel's mother. *She begged and pleaded for so long. I grew tired. I was weak.*

"You need to go, and with Geraldine," Sahel said. In truth she was ecstatic that her father had not heard from Titus, and that it appeared neither Geraldine nor her father held any awareness of Carl having tampered with her mail. Sahel said, "It's been too long since you've seen home."

"We'd like you to come with us."

"I won't complete the program until the end of March. After

that I plan to try and rebuild my practice."

"Are you certain you'll be up to it?" Essien sounded encouraged, but cautious.

"Yes. And I'd like to do it while you two are on what will be your belated honeymoon."

"But you are my child," Essien started. "How can I leave you like this?"

"You'll be back," Sahel said. She stood and reached out for her father. Hope now filled the spaces linking them, areas left empty all Sahel's life, and as she concluded, much of her father's also.

On Geraldine's return Sahel asked, "Have you set a date?"

"We were thinking about April," Geraldine said.

"That would be a perfect time. I'll be resettled in the house," Sahel said. Titus had wanted an April wedding. The reality of circumstances had deemed it take place on a cool morning in mid-July.

"Are you sure you'll be all right all alone in the house?" Essien asked. Trepidation and regret now filled his voice.

"Taking a blind woman with you is not much of a honeymoon," Sahel said.

"That's not how we saw it," Geraldine said. Geraldine's apparent change of heart set against the sadness filling Essien's voice perplexed Sahel even more.

She said, "Believe me, the time you and Geraldine are away will give me just what I need. Not that I won't miss you, but you can't stay away any less than a month. No, make that six weeks."

"So let me guess. Would two months provide you sufficient time to settle back in at home and get your practice going?" Essien said.

Sahel imagined, wished to see, the smile she sensed creeping onto her father's face. "That's more like it, what I call a grand honeymoon." She smiled too.

Chapter 54

T hat Carl had diverted her mail to his office tore at her. He had prevented Sahel from all but throwing away her career, and yet the manner in which he had achieved the ends ate away at Sahel's trust in him. Faced with Titus's propensity for brash directness, she had never considered the possibility that Carl could and would act underhandedly in equally opposing fashion.

Sahel had always considered Carl a friend, one who saw her as an equal, not someone to whom his affections might drive him to behave so deceptively, thus revealing his vulnerabilities. Carl's love for her, his need to see her looking back at him, had blinded him to honoring the boundaries of her marriage with Titus, and also blinded him to Sahel as an individual.

The attacks Carl had launched upon Titus, accusing Titus of preventing Sahel from undergoing the surgery to return her sight, now glowed in hypocrisy. And he had allowed Sahel to mistakenly believe the aneurysm had formed inside her brain as a result of the accident.

Carl had projected his fears of losing Sahel onto Titus, Sahel's husband, who had stated his fears from the start. Sahel lay ensconced in the *purdah* of Carl's own mind that which he had deemed Titus guilty of trying to impose upon Sahel.

Thoughts of anger and betrayal crept in. She would complete the program at the end of the month.

Sahel had said nothing to her father and Geraldine of her discovery concerning Carl during their visit on Valentine's night. Essien's announcement of their plans to travel to Essien's childhood home in Accra had diverted their conversation away from the possibility of broaching any subjects involving Carl.

Essien's confession concerning Sahel's mother guided Sahel in maintaining balance in her evaluation of Carl's actions and the wounds that had driven his behavior.

It was hard for your mother in the end. She suffered so much. I am not the person you imagine me to be.

It was a hard truth she had learned about her father. *Your mother was never whom you thought. I was weak and scared. So was she.*

And yet she understood.

While Sahel had spent January adapting herself to living alone in her apartment and moving around the campus, she focused her energies in February on learning as much as possible from Eric in the technology lab. Sahel entered March determined to use the remaining four weeks of her time at the Independent Living Center in preparation to move back home. With Essien and Geraldine traveling, Sahel would take initial steps at reopening her psychotherapy practice.

In the second week in March, Sahel called Reynard Williams, and asked for assistance in re-establishing her practice. "Whatever you need, I'm here to help." So eager about her decision, Williams offered to meet her at the Independent Living Center.

"I really appreciate your driving all this way out from Berkeley," Sahel said once she had welcomed Reynard into her apartment. On closing the door, she made her way to the sofa.

Williams lived in Oakland. His office was in Berkeley.

"Ramona told me you had entered a program," Reynard said. Sahel felt the weight of Reynard joining her on the couch. "This was great timing for me. I don't see clients on Friday afternoons. I'm glad you called. After everything that happened with my contacting the board—"

"I'm grateful for what you did." Sahel had not seen it that way when she had received the letter from the California Board of Behavioral Sciences rejecting her attempt to relinquish her license to practice psychotherapy. "Without your intervening, driving all the way to Sacramento, I'd be unable to return to doing what I lov—"

"I was too glad to help," said Williams. "But it wasn't just me. If Carl hadn't contacted me—"

"I know. But still I'm thankful," she said. Now, and as she had done in the three weeks since learning of Carl's actions, Sahel pushed aside her fears of confronting Carl. She remained focused on the task at hand.

Reynard said of Carl, "I saw him the other day in the hospital. Funny he didn't say anything about your having entered the program out here in Pinole."

"Carl wasn't especially keen on my decision to move out here for three months," Sahel said. "I really appreciate your helping me to re-establish my practice."

She then brought Reynard up to date on the happenings in the recent year of her life—her attempted suicide, meeting and getting to know James, and her surgery. "Everything seemed to be heading for a better place," Sahel said, "Titus slowly accepting that my sight had not returned despite the surgery ... And then the mayor died during surgery."

"We were all sorry to hear about that, both for the mayor and his family and for Titus," said Reynard. "It's difficult with every patient we lose."

Sahel slipped into concern and worry for Titus. Nearly four months had passed and she had not heard from him.

In her silence Reynard asked, "Do you know where he is?"

"New York. He's working in Manhattan."

"In medicine?"

"I'm not sure," said Sahel. "Calvin's daughter, Zena, said some of her associates had seen him around Sloan-Kettering where she works. I have no idea where he's getting money to live. He's made no withdrawals from our bank accounts."

"Sometimes we need time alone to figure things out, particularly when so much is going on in our heads. The last year has been difficult for Titus." Reynard's words provided perspective and enlivened Sahel.

She said, "He's been so focused on me that he forgot himself."

Again she considered Titus's confession. *Every female patient I encounter is my mother. The men are my dad.* "It's hard being an orphan," Sahel said. "Even when you're an adult."

"How old was Titus when his parents died?"

"We were all eleven—me, Titus, and Carl. They died in a car accident. Back in New Jersey on the turnpike. It was horrible."

"That's difficult."

"Mmmm," Sahel mused in a lamenting tone.

"The remnants of their deaths will always be with him," said Reynard. "Your losing your sight was for him like losing them all over again." Sahel had shared with Reynard the truth of the accident, the argument that had led up to Titus backing out of the driveway and accidentally hitting her.

"He won't accept that it was an accident. I never blamed him."

"He can't," Reynard corrected. "At best it will be difficult. Never forget he's a surgeon allowing himself little, if any, room for error."

Sahel lowered her head, fighting back tears. "Without the accident and my loss of sight, Carl would never have discovered the aneurysm. I would have died. I know it sounds corny and twisted, but my loss of sight brought attention to the time bomb inside my head." Sahel described her meeting with Dr. Hansel and what he had concluded.

"It's not strange. Everything happens for a reason," Reynard said. We are truly lucky and blessed to uncover that reason in this lifetime."

"I wish I could find Titus and tell him the truth. Then again, he won't believe me until I can show him that I'm okay. I've got to go back to work doing what I love," Sahel said. "Then when he returns, Titus will see that I'm okay."

"Are you okay?" Reynard asked. His question surprised Sahel, catching her off guard. "When I heard you had taken the pills, I wanted to rush over and see you."

Reynard's words took her back. "I don't think that would have been a good idea," Sahel chuckled. "I was a mess. What I did hurt Titus so much."

"We were all worried." Reynard said with a heavy sadness.

"What I did was foolish."

"It was human."

Sahel's thoughts turned serious. "Do you think I'm ready to see clients?"

"I think that your ability to ask that question shows you've given it serious consideration," said Reynard. "What does Dr. Leonard say?"

"Like me, he thinks it's a good thing, as long as I'm still seeing him. And I have no intentions of stopping."

"Well, in that case, what can I do to help you get back to work?" said Reynard. "Never forget that it'll be good to have someone to discuss cases with."

"Same here," Sahel said as she smiled with relief. "But I must admit I am nervous."

"That sounds normal."

"What if I trip or stumble and fall?"

"That's easy. There's an office in my building that's available for rent. And if that happens, have your client come and knock on my door."

Sahel laughed aloud. "So I'll have to schedule my clients during the times when you'll be there. I'm sure Aaron will love that."

Aaron, a woman with a male name, was Reynard's wife.

"Seriously," Reynard started with a serious tone. "All of who you are, and everything that you are about makes this possible. Clients need you." He patted the back of her hand. "Those that you know. And the ones you have yet to meet."

Sahel turned towards his voice.

"Call it psychic, but the day after you called me, I began receiving messages from some of your old clients," said Reynard. "They wanted to know if I'd heard from you, and whether you'd be returning to practice."

"What did you tell them?"

"That I'd look into how you were doing," Reynard said. "I find this quite affirming of your decision to return to work."

"Did you tell them I'd lost my sight?"

"I thought that perhaps you might want to give them a call and explain. I have their numbers," Reynard said. He then added, "And I hope I haven't acted too rashly." Sahel clasped her hands, interwove her fingers to avoid pulling them. "I have three potential new clients for you. I don't have space to take them on in my practice. They're eager to meet you."

"Do they know that I'm—?"

"Yes. On telling them they seemed even more determined to meet with you. One woman is putting off deciding what therapist she wants to work with until you return."

"Oh, my goodness," Sahel said. "I don't know how to interpret that."

"Take it to imply that your blindness only hinders you in working with clients to the extent that you are uncomfortable with your loss of sight and the inability to physically see the clients with whom you have never worked."

Chapter 55

D uring the next two weeks Sahel made calls and left messages with prior clients—those who had begun working with Reynard, and others with who had refused any referrals towards whom Reynard had tried to steer them. She also connected with clients Reynard had referred to her, persons Sahel had yet to meet.

Sahel managed the transition through phone conversations and e-mails exchanged with Reynard, She would meet with clients on Friday afternoons in a vacant office down the hall from Reynard.

"I meet with interns and finish paperwork on Wednesday and Friday afternoons. So if you need me I'll be close," Reynard explained.

Sahel appreciated his assistance and patience.

Friday, two weeks later, Reynard returned to Pinole and drove Sahel back to where he practiced in Berkeley.

Sahel had been to the building many times before losing her sight. It now felt like foreign terrain. "You can leave your computer here, if you want," said Reynard as he led her to what would be her office.

"Thanks, but this goes with me everywhere." Sahel pulled the computer into her breast. She had shown Reynard her ability to type client notes, surf the Internet, and send e-mails. "All touch- and voice-activated," she explained as he led her throughout the building. Reynard escorted her to all the doors. "The computer also speaks to me, lets me know what I'm doing or if I've made a mistake," Sahel said.

"This is amazing." Reynard remained animated, as he had when fourteen days earlier she had told him of her desire to re-enter practice. In two weeks Sahel would complete her work at the Center. On Friday of the week that followed, she would meet with her first client since losing her sight.

He directed her down the hall leading her back to his office. Using her cane, Sahel poked and prodded her way back down the hall from the kitchen and to Reynard's office. "I expect to get lost a couple of times, bump into things."

"You'll do fine," Reynard said. He lifted her hand, and placed the keys to the building and the office on her palm.

"I appreciate everything you've done, and are still doing," she reiterated.

Reynard made them tea. Later, as Sahel sipped hers, he asked, "Have you heard from Titus since we last spoke?"

Sahel's hand trembled as she extended it in search of a flat space on which to set the hot container. "Nothing still." She shook her head.

Reynard took the cup from her hand as she searched for a clear space on which to set it. "I don't mean to pry when asking about Titus."

"It's good to know others are thinking of him."

"We're all thinking of him. You too."

Sahel recalled how Carl had said nothing to Reynard of her having entered the program at the Independent Living Center.

She wondered about Carl's pursuit of finding Titus, whether he had continued making calls to colleagues and friends.

"Does Carl know anything?" Reynard asked. "Has he heard from him? Calvin Bennett said he was working with Carl and Titus's partners to locate him."

Again she shook her head. "No." Reynard had been doing a little checking on Carl, she surmised.

Reynard often spoke with Calvin's wife, Ramona Bennett. A psychotherapist too, Ramona had interned under Reynard. He said, "I gathered from you that Carl wasn't helpful in getting everything set for you to start at the Independent Living Center."

"Sounds like Calvin told you what happened," Sahel said. "Carl didn't sign my health form and then refused to take their calls. I called Calvin, and he immediately came to the Center."

"I can only imagine what this is like, the three of you being friends from childhood," Reynard said.

Sahel laughed amid memories of her, Carl, and Titus pouring forth. "The Three Musketeers, they called us at school," she mused with a smile. A short silence descended and made its way between her and Reynard. Sahel then recalled what Carl had pronounced hours before James died. "I'm here like I've always been, waiting ... for you." Sahel then said of Carl, "We haven't spoken since some time before I started the program."

"You know," Reynard eventually spoke, "a lot of people would swear that you, Titus, and Carl were sister and brothers."

Sahel smiled. "The people in high school who didn't like us called us the Three Stooges."

"We're not in high school anymore," Reynard said. "None of us." He then added, "I'm going to say something. Hopefully you're ready to hear this since you've decided to start working again."

A gentleman at all times, Reynard Williams was known not to mince words with his clients. Sahel respected him for that. "I always wondered about Carl and you. I appreciated his sense of duty that he came to me seeking help to stop you from giving up your license. But I always felt there was more."

"Carl loves me," Sahel lamented.

"It's hard living in the shadow of another man loving the woman you love, too," Reynard said.

"I realize Titus's pain," Sahel confessed. "I feel horrible about it. It's my fault that I've let it go this—"

"I'm not talking about Titus." Reynard's words resounded in Sahel's heart and rattled her soul.

Chapter 56

S

eated beside Eric, she marveled at his abilities and all that she had learned from him, so little compared to what remained for her to tackle, but so much more than she had known at the time of entering the program. "I can't believe you're only twenty," she said to Eric. "You should be teaching at Cal or Stanford."

"I was accepted to both, you know," said Eric.

"Why didn't you go?" Sahel pressed the button engaging the process to shut down her computer. Her session with Eric was drawing to a close.

"I still may," Eric said.

She followed the voice prompts on her computer guiding her to log out. She pressed the keys.

"Cannot compute this function," the computer said. "Do you want to explore documents?"

Eric reached over, lifted Sahel's left hand and moved it,

allowing her to feel the keys encoded in Braille, "Your fingers were misaligned," he said, then placed her fingers on the correct one for shutting down her computer.

Sahel typed in the correct letters for prompting her computer to shut down.

The voice of the computer asked, "Do you want to shut down your computer? Sahel typed y. e. s. "Computer shutting down," the voice stated.

Sahel placed her hands in her lap.

Eric sighed. Sahel heard him lean back in his chair. "I often imagined myself at Stanford," he said. "I really didn't care that much for Cal."

"You know I'm a Cal alum, undergrad and graduate school. Bears all the way." Sahel chuckled.

"What was it like there?" Eric asked. Learning she had graduated Cal appeared to have muscled through doubts and reservations he had held about the university.

"It's a busy campus," said Sahel.

"And?"

An image formed as Sahel recalled several of the buildings that she had often rushed past going to and from classes. She thought of the library, Dwinelle, and then Tolman Hall, the psychology building where she had spent hours upon days in the stacks of its library, researching information for her undergraduate papers, and then her doctoral thesis—*Self-Psychology and Self-Esteem*: an unlikely title for a writer who had received little in the way of acceptance from her mother. Sahel had fought to gain confidence by caring for and helping others to ascertain what she lacked, and so yearned for.

"Mine was an interesting time at Cal," Sahel said. She remembered Titus and Carl dueling each other in their practice sessions of fencing. Both had been members of Cal's fencing team. Their greatest competition ensued not when playing other teams, but when dueling with each other during practice sessions. The two had been each other's best and worst enemies. Sahel now said to Eric, "I had a lot of growing up to do."

"Did you do it?"

"I thought I had." Sahel's decision to enter graduate school in

390

psychology had sent Sahel's mother into a rage-filled spin. "Psychotherapist. Working with crazies," Lillian had spat. "I suppose your father put that idea in your head. You'll end up like him, with little respect and even less money to show for the trouble of gaining the degree. People only seek help when they have pains in the body. Aches of the mind are for those too stupid to realize they're weak, and no one can help them."

Lillian had wanted Sahel to attend medical school. Lacking the desire and the necessary grades in the appropriate subjects made that impossible.

With the help of her father, Sahel secured a one-bedroom apartment on Durant during July, a month prior to starting graduate school. She did not visit home nor see her mother for the entire fall semester of her first year in graduate school. While Titus had been busy choosing which medical school he would attend from all of his acceptances, Carl had consoled Sahel, assuring her that she had made the right decision in choosing to pursue a doctorate in psychology. *You're great at helping people when they're feeling down and hopeless.*

Maybe it's because that's also my constant state of mind. Sahel had kept the response to herself.

"Without you I would never have gotten into medical school," Carl had said.

Carl had scored poorly on his medical school entrance exams while Titus had done extremely well. Sahel and her father had not only demanded Carl take the test again, but also affirmed their insistence by Sahel finding him a tutor that Essien paid for.

"I'll always be grateful." Carl had smiled and then kissed her cheek. Moist warmth had traveled through Sahel not unlike the energy of freedom that now surged through her body when opening the computer. On the afternoon he received his second set of scores, greatly improved from the first, Carl had found Sahel. Then, after showing her his new scores, offered, 'Thanks,' in the best way he could. After a celebratory meal at Bongo Burger on Bancroft, he and Sahel made their way back to Carl's apartment. And there they made love.

Sahel banished the memory of that from her mind. Quickly she found the slip disk and device for scanning documents, and

391

removed them both from the USB ports of her computer. Eric had given her the scanning device during their first session in the tech lab.

She reached forward and closed her laptop.

The laptop now securely closed, she reached inside the pocket of her sweater and fingered the card she had received from the post office. Slowly she recalled scanning the card from the post office box. A cold anguish of despair spread through. The voice of the computer had read, Dr. Carl Pierson, Neurosurgeon.

Sahel ended her session with Eric and arrived home as usual past eight. Eric had informed her that upon completing the program, he was always available as with all participants who had graduated, to speak with her. Yet Sahel's streak of independence fueled her determination to learn as much as she could in his presence. Sahel was moving forward. She would complete the program in fewer than seven days. Like Joan Witherspoon, Sahel would return to the Center to assist others like herself.

Spring

Chapter 57

T

hat Essien and Geraldine's flight to Accra departed SFO at 5:00 p.m. allowed four hours for Essien to fret away his time assessing what he had packed that could remain home, and what he was leaving at home that he might need or wish for during their travels.

It also provided Sahel space to contemplate the e-mail she had sent Carl.

... I suppose you're surprised to hear from me and like this, that I'm typing on the computer. I know you like getting e-mails from your patients. And since I'm one of your patients ... Sahel tried imagining Carl's face, the beam or dullness in his eyes while reading on the computer screen the words she had typed.

... I learned a lot at the Center, most of which centered on using my computer and the Internet. It's really freed me up. So much so that I've returned to work. I also have to thank you for that.

I appreciate your alerting Reynard of my having mailed in

my license to the board. I will forever be in your and Reynard's debt ...

Sahel wrote nothing about having re-established her practice, and that she now worked in an office down the hall from Reynard.

Geraldine opened and closed her suitcase one last time. Sahel abandoned her thoughts. "I've told him we won't be gone forever," Geraldine lamented.

"He's excited, and worried," Sahel said. She was sitting on the bed beside Geraldine's second suitcase, also locked and ready to be taken downstairs.

"So am I."

"The two of you'll be fine. Trust me. If you can tolerate America, then—"

"It's not Ghana or America that troubles us." Geraldine's tone was crisp and clear. "It's you, here, alone in this house. What if something happens?"

Geraldine's tone also bore a comical and ironic twist. "I lived alone in the apartment for three months."

"That was different. This is a house. In the apartment you were on the compound, and part of the program at the Center."

"If I didn't know any better, I'd swear you were overcome with motherhood, perhaps going through a bit of attachment anxiety." Sahel chuckled. She struggled to find an opening, a way to ask Geraldine about her change of heart. Geraldine's ache and mourning of what she felt was Sahel's betrayal had hung thick and heavy between them.

"This is not funny," Geraldine said.

Sahel stood. "And that's why I've agreed to call Reynard at least once a day."

"No, twice, once in the morning and again before you go to bed," Geraldine corrected. "I mean it. We've instructed Reynard to e-mail or call us if he doesn't hear from you. And you know what that means."

Essien had sworn that he would fly back to California the minute he felt or learned Sahel was experiencing problems or difficulties.

"I know. And believe me there'll be no need for that." The

onus lay upon Sahel to keep her father and stepmother in Ghana the entire three months she had encouraged them to stay and travel there.

"I really need some time to myself." Sahel made her way down the stairs with Geraldine. So much had happened.

"Your father and I feel as if we're abandoning you."

Sahel's closing words in the e-mail she sent to Carl reclaimed her attention. She typed, *I'd like to see you.*

Her thoughts jutted back to the conversation with Geraldine.

"Your fears of leaving me alone is a great way to avoid feelings of guilt and resentment," said Sahel.

"About what?"

"Your anger at me, for starters." Sahel moved her foot from the last step of the staircase and onto the ground floor. "And secondly, your fears about marrying my father and letting him love you."

"I'm happy to be married to your father," Geraldine said.

"So is he. As am I."

A piercing silence descended.

"Two very good men have loved me. I don't feel I deserve that."

"You deserve every bit and more," said Sahel.

She reached into the darkness and found Geraldine's hand. "Unlike my parents' marriage, yours with Paynter's was happy." Sahel squeezed Geraldine's trembling palm. "He would want you happy."

"You're right," Geraldine said, "about everything. I'm sorry for having accused you of siding with Sunetra. Saying that you two were alike."

"Apology accepted." Sahel smiled. "All's forgotten."

"Not so quick," Geraldine said. Her tone wavered. "You're not going to let me off the hook so easily."

"But you've done your penance."

"And so have you," rebutted Geraldine. She touched Sahel's arm. "In her craziness, your mother was working to make sure you had someone, a husband to love you."

Sahel grew anxious as Geraldine spoke with ease.

"Your mother may have loved Titus as her favorite between

him and Carl. But she also knew that Carl loved you."

Sahel's chest began to pound, its pulsations echoing through her.

"Both Titus and Carl love you. You have your mother to thank or blame for that as much as yourself."

Myriad words presented themselves, but none approached describing the intricacies of what Geraldine had described concerning Lillian.

"She hated me so much," Sahel said.

"But we can only hate that for which we hold love, more love than we have for ourselves."

A patch of prickly bumps rose upon Sahel's back.

Geraldine's words unfolded a truth Sahel could never have delivered herself.

"I was hard on Titus," Geraldine said. "I shouldn't have been. I also misjudged you and Carl."

Sahel's heart slowed.

"Besides loving you, Carl's also brown like you. I thought the two of you should be together." Sahel's stepmother continued. "I didn't like Titus because he's fair. Like Sunetra's mother, Meera. I always thought Meera looked down on James, because he was brown. I even surmised she looked down on Ravesh like your mother looked down on you, and your father. That your mother loved Titus so much made everything worse."

"Mama was hurting," Sahel spoke softly. "Titus was her link to Cecile."

"As are you," Geraldine said. "It's hard being a dark-skinned woman in America. People look down on you, judge you by your darkness. Can't see beyond your skin color. It's as if your dark skin blinds them to all that lives within you. And then your parents, mothers particularly, offer what they call words of wisdom.

You're dark, and you may as well get used to it," Geraldine recited what the older women had said to her as a child. "*No one's going to like or see you the way they view white girls or light-skinned black girls*."

"'*High yellow*,' my mother called the women like yours and Titus's mothers."

398

"Titus's mother was kind. She liked me. Loved me. She told Titus to protect me."

"And Titus has done just that. Same as Paynter did throughout our marriage. He cared for, and loved me as if I were the fairest woman in the world," Geraldine said.

"And that's what you were for him," said Sahel. "The most beautiful woman in the world. The same as you are now for Daddy. I can only imagine the gleam that lights up in his eyes when he's with you. I hear it in his voice. The spark that came alive when you agreed to marry him."

"He didn't ask to marry me, your father," Geraldine said. "I asked him. His response nearly broke my heart," Geraldine's voice cracked once more. "'Thank god for your boldness in asking, Geraldine.' Your father appeared as if he were about to cry. When I asked him why, he seemed so relieved. He said, 'I was afraid you might not have me. Now I know you want me.'"

Sahel extended her arms. Geraldine took her hands and embraced Sahel.

"It's time for you and Daddy to allow yourself some fun. You're not abandoning your first spouses, just taking the love you have for them and moving on."

"Thank you," Geraldine whispered. "Thank you so much."

Sahel felt her shoulder grow damp. Geraldine's tears.

A knock rose from the door. "The cab's here," Geraldine called out to Essien. "Bring the bags downstairs. We're going to be late, unless we leave now."

Sahel and Geraldine approached the doorway while Essien assisted the driver loading his and Geraldine's bags into the cab. "I didn't ignore what you said," Geraldine said.

Sahel smiled.

"It is hard for me to enjoy, to have fun. It's always been that way," Geraldine said. "That's something I think all black women share. In truth, all women around the world."

Geraldine squeezed Sahel's hand tightly. She then said, "Do one thing for me."

Sahel leaned in.

"Tell Carl what you learned from Dr. Hansel. Explain to him that however crazy it sounds, Titus hitting you with the car forced you to undergo tests that revealed the aneurysm. And that without it, you would have died."

Sahel nodded.

"You love them both," Geraldine said. "But only one saved your life. And now he's hurting."

"But Titus needs to know the truth, too."

"He will if you do what I say. *Trust me*. I'm your step-mama. And on this, I know best. *Tell Carl*."

Geraldine's missive left Sahel dizzy. Despite their disagreements, the love between them had grown powerful. Sahel had experienced with Geraldine a kind of acceptance that, even in their differences, had been impossible with Lillian. "Thank you," Sahel said.

"For what?"

"For being you," said Sahel. She patted Geraldine's hand.

"All of the suitcases are in the cab," Essien announced, his voice drawing near. Grasping Sahel's shoulders, he drew her close and kissed her forehead.

On leaving her father's arms, warm and strong, Sahel relinquished his hand. She then caught the last words of his instructions concerning the house and the alarm system. "I am told the police will be here in five-minutes flat if you press this." He opened her hand and placed the remote to the newly installed alarm system upon her palm.

Sahel folded her fingers upon the device.

"We don't have to do this," Essien said one last time.

"I'm fine." Sahel placed her free hand to her father's arm and considered Geraldine's words. "*Like you with Titus and Carl ... I love both Essien and Alfred*."

"Geraldine and I don't need a honeymoon," Essien reiterated.

Sahel pulled her father close and whispered, "But I need you to have one." Sahel and Titus had not taken a honeymoon.

"What will you do about Titus?" Essien said. He had spoken softly. "It has been nearly seven months and we've heard nothing."

"He needs time," Sahel said. "Perhaps I'll send him an e-mail, now that I have my computer."

"Sahel, I don't like this. I tolerated your focus on getting through the program at the center. And you completed that. Now with Reynard's help you've returned to work. It is now time for you to—"

"Essien, we need to get going," Geraldine called out once more. "It's one o'clock. Check-in at the airport opens at two."

"Your new bride awaits," said Sahel. She pushed her father towards her stepmother's voice.

Reluctant and resistant to leave, Essien embraced Sahel once more. "Take care of yourself." His cheeks were wet. "And don't be too proud to call Carl."

Sahel's heart sank. "I love Titus."

"You love them both. That has been the problem all along. I see that now. If your mother were to return this moment, I would be at a loss, much as Geraldine would be should her Alfred reappear." Essien took Sahel's hand. "I appreciate your forgiveness. Now give yourself what you exhorted me and all your clients to allow ourselves."

Forgiveness. The word shot through Sahel's mind.

Again Essien kissed Sahel. She let go of her father's hand. Geraldine gave her a last hug and kiss.

And then, "One last thing," Geraldine added. "I noticed your mail hasn't started coming back here. Tell the postman to have it forwarded from the apartment."

Sahel's thoughts flitted back to the postal attendant. "Your P.O. Box is still open. Here's the address to where the mail for your P.O. Box has been diverted. Most likely the same person who paid the bill has been getting the mail. Would you like us to look into this?" The post office attendant had asked when Sahel had frowned and expressed surprise and confusion. He then added, "Mail tampering is a federal offense."

Now as she had on so many occasions in the recent past, Sahel pushed aside thoughts of Carl. "Yes, I need to do that," she said to Geraldine.

Chapter 58

S

ahel was halfway through her session with her first client before she realized she was having fun, enjoying working again.

"I was scared of coming to this first session," the client, Mary, said. Twenty-three, and newly married, she had never sought out therapy or counseling. "I had no idea what to expect. Whether you'd like me. If I'd like you."

She added, "Everyone in Ben's family has done therapy." Ben was Mary's husband of three months. "His sisters seem to take it as their religion."

"You did say Ben's father was a psychiatrist," Sahel asked.

The space between Sahel and Mary seemed to widen. The silence filling it bore down like a hot oppressive wind that lacked any space for coolness. Sahel felt as if she were traveling across one of the many savannas of the Sudan bordering on the *sahel*.

"What are you thinking right now?" Sahel said. She had

asked this with previous clients, her former way of intuiting if and where the client's thoughts had rambled. Sahel now posed the question because she could not see Mary's face.

"I miss my father," Mary said. "I miss him terribly." Mary's father had not attended her wedding. At the outset of the session, Mary had spoken of her father's absence, saying, "I don't know why I'm here other than my husband suggested I might want to try therapy. He said he'd pay for it."

"What would you have wanted your father to do had he been present?"

"Dance with me at the reception. I didn't need him to escort me in, or give me away. I knew what I was doing. Had made up my mind that Ben was the one for me. I love him." Mary hesitated. "I just wanted my father to be there, dance with me and tell me that everything was going be all right. That it was okay to love, to open my heart and take someone in."

"You worry about your capacity to love?"

"So many people around me don't seem to be able to do it, or want to," Mary said. "Our society is about doing it all on your own, alone and by yourself. Everyone says you're weak if you want someone in your life, and forever."

"Well, I don't know if all people feel that way."

"My friends certainly do. I had a dickens of a time getting bridesmaids; I mean the ones who aren't just doing it because there's nothing else on their agenda, who want an excuse to buy a new dress. People who're really happy for you, and who have found that lifelong mate they want to work things out with, build a relationship."

"Are you and Ben experiencing any problems?" Sahel was searching. The words—
someone to work it out with—had left her uncomfortable and awkward.

"Well, look at my father. He left my mother. Marriage takes work. And I haven't had anyone that I'm close with to show me the how of working things out," Mary said. "Things won't be perfect, not like they seemed to be in Ben's family when I first met him."

"Your parents aren't you and Ben," Sahel said. "How perfect

did things for your parents appear in the beginning?"

"I liked the way they talked about everything; didn't hide stuff. Then I learned how Ben's father had died."

Sahel ran her palm across the lap of her pants.

"He was with another woman, his mistress of thirty years."

Sahel knew Ben's father was deceased. Mary had not stated the circumstances until now. "How does the way Ben's father died affect the absence of your father at your wedding?"

"They were both absent from our wedding, our fathers."

Sahel wished to see Mary's face. As she had on so many occasions with clients whose faces she had beheld, Sahel began to dig and explore, but not into what their eyes conveyed. She listened intently to Mary's voice, her words, the spaces between them, and what lay hidden in all Mary did not speak. "You haven't said anything about your mother."

Mary sighed with what sounded like relief. "The wedding has been a strain on her."

"You speak as if some disturbance has continued from the wedding."

"It's been hard letting me go. Ben and I live just down the street from Mom. For her it's as though I'm miles away."

Sahel felt confused, lost. She wanted to understand. But Mary needed her space.

Mary then said, "I'm married and my mother's not. She likes Ben and thinks he'll make a good husband. She told me so."

"How so?"

"'He loves you,' she said. 'I can see it in his eyes. He loves you very much. It's in his voice, in everything his does.' She said that the day before the wedding," Mary explained. "Then is when I knew our relationship, mine with her, would never be the same. We would never feel close as we did in the past, at least not her to me. I was now different. She was telling me that. Because I had someone who really loved me. And believe me, my mother is a cynic and a pessimist. If she says something is the real thing, then it's real a thousand times over. Talking about a doubting Thomas, she's it."

Sahel's mind began to flit. *Doubting Thomas. Cynic. Pessimist.* Mary's words rang a sad bell in Sahel. Her mother,

Lillian, had held her own idiosyncratic views on life. And yet, despite all, Lillian had never doubted Titus. "And what about you?" Sahel said to Mary.

"I trust her. I don't like her opinions on most things. But I know that she's honest and real," Mary said of her mother. "What you see is what you get."

"Not like Ben's family. Or his father," Sahel said.

"It really hurt Ben the way his father died. I met him a month after his father's funeral. Ben was a mess. Didn't trust anyone, felt betrayed. We had both just finished college and were trying to make our way out in the world. Ben was still standing in awe of his father and all he'd accomplished. Ben's father had completed medical school at twenty-two, four years earlier than most. Ben said he was brilliant."

"He was also human."

"Aren't we all?" Mary's voice was tight.

"You said that Ben's sisters saw psychotherapy as their religion. Perhaps they're simply using it as a way to understand life. I can't believe that Ben's father was having this affair for— what did you say—thirty years, and no one suspected anything." In Mary's silence Sahel asked, "What's your real concern about Ben and his family?"

"Could my mother have made a mistake about Ben being in love with me? Why do Ben and his sisters feel the need to always have a therapist in this life? It seems he sent me here so that I wouldn't bug him about what he's truly feeling. 'Go talk to your therapist, Mary,' he says. 'And I'll talk to mine.'"

"Is that what he said?"

"That's what it felt like," Mary said. "I got really nervous when Dr. Williams said he couldn't take me on. He came highly recommended. A friend of mine who's dating and wants to get married gave me his name. He's seeing him."

"Your friend is a man?"

"We graduated Cal together. Now he's in law school. He and his fiancée have a lot going on. He likes talking to Dr. Williams. Says Dr. Williams lets him know he's not strange."

"Do you feel strange, now?" Sahel ventured.

"I did when I first walked in."

Sahel worried of her blindness, whether that would or had presented a problem for Mary.

"When Dr. Williams told me you had lost your sight, I didn't know what to say," Mary said. "But I was intrigued."

"How so?" Sahel again forced herself to pursue the comment.

"That maybe because I thought I'd see some part of myself I wasn't ready to meet that would overwhelm me, tell me I was hopeless." Mary sighed.

"Then halfway through the session, I realized you're the right one for me. That the powers that be of the universe had put me with the right person."

"What let you know that?" Sahel said after softly breathing a sigh of relief.

"I don't know how to say this. I hope I'm not offending you. But the fact that you're blind and willing to work with clients says a lot about you."

Anxious joy flooded Sahel. "How so?" she asked.

"I don't think I could do it. Be without sight and listen to other people's problems. Neither could Ben's father. Work with clients you can't see, but who can see you."

"It takes trust. And patience with others," said Sahel. "Most of all with yourself."

Mary's fixation on Ben's deceased father, Mary's dead father-in-law whom she never met, intrigued Sahel. If she understood that, she might discover a key to assisting Mary in determining why she followed Ben's advice to enter psychotherapy. "You seem taken with Ben's father, whom you never met."

"Like my father, he was absent—"

"Not just from your and Ben's wedding, but your lives as well."

"You're good, Dr. Ohin," Mary said.

As before losing her sight, Sahel was using her maiden name.

"Thank you," said Sahel.

Before she could suggest another session, Mary asked when she could come back the following week. "This has been really helpful. I realize I have a lot to talk about. Stuff that, in truth, I really don't want to share with Ben, at least not now."

407

Sahel and Mary agreed to meet the following week, the same day and time. Mary left, closing the door behind her.

Sahel leaned back in her chair excited and thankful that she'd been allowed to resume work. Her heart warmed with thoughts of Reynard and then Mary. Each of them had made decisions that helped her. And from Mary's statements she was glad about her choice.

Only time would tell. Reality set in. While Sahel had experienced moments of fun, she now realized that her blindness was something out in the open for her clients to see and present in their need to discuss. She would speak to Reynard about how to handle it.

She would also discuss her feelings, some disjointed and some intact, with Dr. Leonard. Sahel was seeing him in an hour. Until then she'd bask in the newness of her accomplishment, of having completed the Independent Living Program and subsequently having returned to her work as a psychotherapist.

Sahel had never imagined doing such, and so soon. And then James Bolton entered her life. She thought of him daily. His presence had supported her in matriculating through the program at the Independent Living Center, most particularly in learning as much as she could from Eric.

Now that she had returned to work, a final task lay at hand—that of confronting Carl about having diverted her mail to his office.

She also needed to contact Carl. Sahel stood and made her way to the desk. She opened her computer, logged onto her e-mail, and began typing.

Chapter 59

S

ahel settled into her session with Dr. Leonard. As with Mary she found herself relaxed, "... and grateful to be alive." She had added that she rarely used that phrase regarding herself.

"I don't think I've ever heard you use it," said Dr. Leonard.

"I was nervous during the session with Mary. I wanted her to like me," Sahel confessed, "to think me capable, despite being unable to see her."

"And?"

"She felt my blindness allowed me to see aspects of her invisible to physical sight. I'm sure a lot of her statements are mere idealization. Months from now, if she's still coming, she'll probably—"

"And what about your gratitude for being alive?" Leonard asked.

"Where did it go?"

Sahel lowered her head and smiled. "I'm not comfortable receiving compliments," Sahel said. "In my old life I didn't need them. Better yet, I hid my need to hear them."

"We all want to know that we're doing a good job. Praise never hurts anyone when it's truly deserved," said the psychiatrist. "These last eighteen months have been challenging," he added.

"I miss Titus, wish he could be here to see what I'm doing."

"Are you more able to let him love you and take in his love, now that you've completed the program at the Independent Living Center?"

"Something's changed. I feel differently. I want him," Sahel said. "I need him. And I don't feel ashamed of that. I don't resent him loving me." Sahel then added, "I'm afraid he won't come back, that I've realized all of this too late."

"It's important to let Titus have his feelings when he returns."

"You think he left because he was unable to be himself around me?"

"Titus was orphaned when he was eleven years old. A truck driver smashed his 18-wheeler into their car. Titus's father wasn't at fault, but he was at the wheel of the sedan. A sedan with four doors like the one Titus, also with no malicious intentions, was driving when he backed into you."

Sahel cringed, crossed her arms and gripped her shoulders, at the similarities in the events of Titus's life. "I could never blame him," she said. "Refuse to be angry with him. But he doesn't trust me and thinks I'm pretending, hiding my anger."

"Stop blaming yourself for what happened that night," Leonard said. The psychiatrist's words called forth what Essien had said. "Accept Titus's love. Receive it for what it is. The gift of a boy who has lost everything."

The psychiatrist said, "You've learned to live without your sight. The darkness has enabled you to see past the color of Titus's skin and recognize him for who he is, a husband who loves you very much."

Sahel considered the intricacies of thoughts Leonard described, and the feelings, quite real and authentic, to which Sahel and Titus's tightly held belief, often erroneous and mistaken, gave rise to.

The psychiatrist said, "Titus and your mother are distinct and

410

separate, both quite different from each other."

"I won't sign the divorce papers. I can't."

"Titus feels he doesn't deserve your love, should instead receive your wrath, same as you don't feel worthy of his love because your skin is darker than his."

"You, like many in our profession, desire to fix things. We want to make everyone and everything okay," said Dr. Leonard.

Sahel toiled with recollections of Carl blaming Titus for the accident. "The mayor's death pushed him over the edge."

"An edge that he approached when surgery failed to return your sight."

A sharp pain pinched at Sahel's chest. She covered her mouth to stifle a moan. "It was too much. He fell apart."

"Sometimes breaking apart is the first stage of putting things back together."

"James taught me that." Sahel grew warm with gratitude. "I owe him so much."

"And yourself." Leonard then said. "So much of what you have done with Titus has been instinctual. The pain you experienced as a child growing up under your mother has guided you about how to love Titus. Knowing how to be present without getting in the way and becoming an obstacle, rather a silent help—it's been your gift, both as a psychotherapist to clients, and as a wife and lover to Titus."

"But I've brought him so much pain." Sahel leaned back into the sofa. As always, she found difficulty in acknowledging her strengths and embracing her goodness.

Leonard shifted direction and asked, "Has Carl responded to your e-mail asking him about keeping your post office box open?"

"You mean whether he has explained why he had my mail sent to his office?" Sahel asked. In Leonard's silence she said, "No."

"When do you plan to?"

"I've been waiting for him to respond to my e-mail," Sahel said. "He's probably ashamed. And I'm still angry."

"About what?"

"He tampered with my mail!"

"He also kept you from giving away your ability to practice your profession."

Sahel pulled her fingers as if to dislodge them from her hand.

"This is my fault. If I had set a date for the wedding, that would not only have calmed Titus, but have also sent a clear message to Carl, letting him know there was no hope for us. That I didn't love him."

"When are you going to let others deal with the consequences of their actions? What's done is done, Sahel."

"And what am I supposed to do when my actions have influenced theirs?"

Leonard gave a long sigh. After a moment of silence he said, "James gave you a wonderful gift." Sahel directed her attention towards the psychiatrist's voice. "If only you could use your interactions with him as a template for relating to others, and to yourself."

"James wasn't my husband. I didn't need him like I need Titus."

"You in fact needed him more," Leonard retorted.

Sahel whipped her head towards the psychiatrist's voice.

"James let you see what happens when you hold too tightly to what you love. He also taught you how to let go, and what happens when we do."

"But Sunetra was dead," Sahel said.

"You allowed her to enter your body."

Sahel began to wonder how she had done that. It seemed so far away, that month last autumn when she first heard Sunetra's voice, not knowing what or whose voice had spoken from within. "I felt I had no control over my life. I was lost. There was nothing I could do."

"And what can you do now?" Leonard asked. "What can any of us do beyond creating an illusion of control?"

"Is that what my work has been?"

"On some level. Helping those who, like yourself, have heretofore provided you a task to divert your attentions away from your own wounds."

"But I thought our work was supposed to bring our emotional hurts into focus. Without that, we lose our way in helping others. In fact we're not really assisting them."

"The work you did with James helped him accomplish his goal of dying. It also brought into clarity your emotional wound rooted in the relationship with your mother, which forms the very core and essence of your strength."

"It's also where I'm most vulnerable," said Sahel.

"Yes it is. But you're refusing to sign the divorce documents." Dr. Leonard brought the discussion back to its roots. "You're remaining faithful to your heart and instincts, remaining present to Titus but allowing space within it for him to heal and find his way home to you."

"You think he'll come back?" Sahel was afraid.

The question is and has always been, "Will you be there on his return?"

Sahel considered her return to seeing clients. The long days she had spent working years earlier now felt a blur, an escape from the intense loneliness she hated, isolation that arose from a clear avoidance, outright refusal to acknowledge her love for Titus.

Immediately Sahel thought of Carl, the numerous hours he spent in surgery, working on Saturdays and Sundays, even his refusal of Romina's call requesting Sahel's recent physical.

She said to Dr. Leonard, "Work has been our escape, mine and Carl's. It's where we feel strong, and purposeful, needed and in control. Take it away from us or remove us from it, we disintegrate."

"I like to think that what you call disintegration is rather your becoming whole," said Leonard. "Like when you were with James. And perhaps your client this morning."

Again the psychiatrist reminded, "Each time life knocks us down and we fall apart we have the opportunity to put the pieces of ourselves back together, not as who we're told to be or feel we should become, but as they truly fit, and who we really are." Dr. Leonard then added, "I'm saying this regarding both you and Carl."

Chapter 60

C

arl escorted Sahel to his Rover and helped her inside. The passenger door closed as did the driver's door seconds later.

"So where to?" Carl said. "Lake Merritt? I haven't been there since we last strolled around it." He cranked the Rover.

"I'd like to go to Rolling Hills and visit James's gravesite," said Sahel. "I haven't been there since the funeral."

"Then Rolling Hills it is," Carl spoke without hesitation.

Some minutes into the ride, Carl asked, "So how are things going with you and Reynard? I hear you're sharing an office."

"Not exactly. I'm renting an office in the building where he works. Reynard's office is down the hall from mine."

"How many clients are you seeing?"

"I have five. Two on Wednesday afternoons, and three on Friday afternoons."

"I suppose that nixes all possibilities of resuming our

Wednesday afternoon walks around the lake," Carl said. In Sahel's silence he asked, "So how is it working with clients again?"

"Better than I expected." Sahel smiled.

Carl gave a nervous chuckle. "I suppose that lets me off the hook for not signing the medical release required for you to enter the program at the Independent Living Center."

Calvin Bennett's words concerning Carl's refusal to sign the release rose within Sahel. "Carl's an excellent neurosurgeon. But like us all he's human. You might want to push him a little bit more on the issue of his hesitancy to contact and speak with Titus."

"I meant you no harm," Carl said of his actions. "I just didn't feel it was time for you to be on our own. Obviously I was wrong."

"We all make mistakes. Thankfully, Calvin was available," Sahel said. Her anger towards Carl having dissipated, Sahel remained clear on what she would say to Carl. And when. "Have you heard from Titus?"

"I thought he might have contacted you."

"No. Or at least I don't think he has," said Sahel.

The Rover slowed to a stop at what Sahel surmised was a light or stop sign. After a few seconds it took off once more and on speeding up, Sahel concluded they had entered onto the freeway. "Wouldn't you know?" Carl said.

Sahel brushed her hand over her cane folded and lying upon her lap. "What's the sky like?" she asked, ignoring Carl's question.

"It's crisp and blue. The sun is shining," Carl said as if caught off guard. "I'm sure you felt the warmth." It was mid-May, nearly three weeks since Essien and Geraldine had left. Sounding calmer, Carl said, "It's a beautiful day to be alive."

Sahel relaxed into the front passenger's seat. She smiled and said, "I thought I would be a horrible therapist, in that I can't see my clients' faces, and their movements. I worried that in being overly dependent on the inflections and emotion in their voices, or lack of it, I wouldn't be able to get the gist of what they are saying." She sighed in relief of what she had experienced. "I couldn't imagine how with my lack of sight I could help them, or that anyone would want me to help them."

"Reynard tells me you have a waiting list," Carl said. He sounded both eager and wary.

"Going through the program at the Independent Living Center got me going again. Without Reynard sending me those referrals, I fear I may have fallen back into a slump. He's really been kind. I feel blessed."

"You're a good therapist. You helped me," Carl said.

Sahel recalled the time in their junior year at Cal. Carl's spring semester grades had dropped. He had been distressed. She had kissed him. The scent of Carl's freshly showered chest beating against hers arose from the past. "You were never my client. Nor could you be," she said.

"Still, you cared." The warmth of Carl's words settled upon Sahel's chest as had Carl's lips, warm and devouring hers. Though she had loved Titus, they had not been married. She had slept with Carl, accepted his thanks for helping him because Lillian had hated Carl. This was Sahel's rebellion, her 'yes,' to her mother's 'no.'

Her chest relaxed. Last remnants of her anxieties faded. Carl asked, "Have you heard from your father and Geraldine? I'm sure he's glad to be back home. How long has it been?"

"Nearly forty years. He was a little afraid in returning. Fearful of what he might find and what was present among what no longer existed."

"Life changes so fast, particularly when you're away and out of touch," Carl said.

"He calls every day," Sahel said of her father.

"If you're ever lonely or need someone—"

"I'm not."

"I was just saying," Carl started again. "That since you're not driving—"

"I appreciate that you're available, like when you contacted Reynard about me wanting to relinquish my license to practice psychotherapy. You really saved me."

"I would hope that if the situation was reversed, you'd do the same for me," Carl spoke tersely.

"I'm not afraid to be with myself," Sahel said. "Despite being unable to see what's around me. I've come home."

Minutes later she said, "I learned a lot at the Center."

"It shows. The therapist you met there, the one who lost her sight, gave you the boost you need. This way, if the surgery doesn't work—" Carl stopped short.

Sahel's heart broke, and for the first time, not for herself. She ached instead for Carl. He needed Sahel's sight more than she, same as Prince Thane needed Queen Holna alive, and ruling the Kingdom of Purdah more than Queen Holna.

The Rover slowed and shifted right, moving onto what Sahel concluded was an exit from the freeway. It entered what felt like a turn and came to a full stop. "The cemetery is just up ahead," Carl said.

Seconds later they came to a stop. "Rolling Hills Memorial Grounds," Carl said. The driver's door opened and closed. Sahel's door opened. Carl helped her out. "It's over this way," he said.

Sahel unfolded her cane. With her cane outstretched before her, and in rhythm with her stride, as she had learned, Sahel walked with Carl towards James's gravesite.

Carl's trembling hand had calmed upon reaching the headstone. He helped her to kneel. Sahel slid her hand along the granite face and then fingered the words etched upon it:

Jameson Bellamy Bolton, 1967-20...
Beloved Son, Fiancée, and Friend.
May He Find Rest, and Love

Sahel's thoughts traveled back to the medical society dinner at the Masonic Ballroom. It had taken place some eight months ago during the previous September, Indian summer. *Reincarnation is my life, my hope.* James had made the statement no more than two hours after Geraldine had first

418

introduced Sahel to him. *Do you believe? I need to know*, he had asked following his pronouncement.

You must believe something, he had said with the passing of some seconds. *You're taking too long to answer.*

I don't know what I believe, Sahel had said.

We all believe in something, James had countered. *The challenge is accepting what we believe, not punishing ourselves for hoping, or letting ourselves love. Not imprisoning ourselves into loving too little.*

Again Sahel fingered the etchings upon the headstone marking where James's remains were interred. She also ached for having loved Titus, what she now feared was much too little, and greatly past the time when he most needed her.

Chapter 61

S

ahel moved to stand and Carl helped her up from kneeling at James's gravestone. Back upon her feet she said, "I've made peace with my blindness."

A dark and fearful energy filled the silence emerging from Carl and creating an abyss between them.

"Titus won't accept that," Carl said.

"I just want him to come home. I need him to come home."

"That may never happen."

"Is that what you believe? Or hope?" Sahel said. "I haven't filed the divorce papers and never will. Titus will have to tell me in person that he no longer wants me as his wife, and file the papers himself."

"And if he does?" Carl said.

"I won't be marrying anyone else. Titus is the only person I've ever loved. I see that now." Sahel felt Carl's pain in being found out. "You should also add when speaking to him that I don't know how many of his letters I've missed. For the last year my mail has been diverted elsewhere."

An even more dreadful silence ensued.

"I'd have never backed you into a corner," Carl said.

"You mean you wouldn't have hit me with your car."

"I have always loved you," Carl pleaded with a whisper. "The argument would not have happened."

"Is that because you loved me? Or rather like Narcissus, you needed to be seen?"

Carl let out an aching sob that rattled Sahel's soul. Her heart pounded. "I love you," he said. "Can't you see that?"

"If you ever held for me the kind of love you're speaking of, it died when you instructed the post office to forward the mail from the P.O. Box, and all that went to Daddy's house, including Titus's letters, to your office at Regent Street."

"Be angry with me if you need. But that's no reason for you to give up hope on regaining your sight," Carl whispered.

"I underwent the surgery. What happens now and in the future is out of my hands. *And yours.* All I know is that Titus saved my life. I'm indebted to him for that."

"A life you nearly succeeded at ending as his wife!"

"I was living a lie," Sahel said. "I saw myself as a burden, my blindness as a curse."

"What the hell else can it be?"

"You, of all people should know. The aneurysm may have caused my blindness. But it didn't result from Titus hitting me with the car." Sahel continued. "The aneurysm had formed much earlier. Without the accident you might never have discovered it."

"Don't say that!"

"It's true and you know it," Sahel said. "But just like you let Titus think he was Prince Thane, not Rahim, you also left him to believe he had caused my blindness."

"Titus hit you with the car. One day you were seeing. The next you'd lost your sight."

Sahel told Carl of her visit with Dr. Hansel. "He used the same words as you when describing the aneurysm, ' ... *the size of a plum* ....' Only Dr. Hansel was clear. The aneurysm began forming long before the accident, perhaps as far back as three years ago. Titus hitting me with the car only served to bring its presence to light."

"When the aneurysm formed is not the point," Carl said. "For god's sake, don't sit around and waste your life being—"

"Blind?"

Carl's pleadings, amplified by his desperation, resounded upon the hundreds of headstones surrounding them, reminders of those who had once lived among them, and created a bridge linking Sahel to her friend from childhood.

Carl sniffled in between sobs.

Sahel said, "Had the accident never occurred, and I not lost my sight, the aneurysm would have exploded and I would have died never knowing what happened. Titus's love set me on a course that save my life. Along the way I also found myself. Now with Titus gone, he might never know this. And that he's not Prince Thane."

"It was just a dream!" Carl shouted.

Sahel spoke of the dream. "The caving in of Queen Bessima's castle, the destruction of the Kingdom of Freedom wasn't the end of my life. It signaled the beginning of my life with Prince Rahim," said Sahel. "But Titus believed he was Prince Thane who was a danger to me. That's why he gave me the divorce papers and left. He was releasing me to you, the person he believed would protect me. But you knew better."

"I was always true to you. I served you honorably and honestly," Carl spoke as Prince Thane.

"But you're not Prince Rahim. And neither am I to live my life with you." Sahel said, "My mother, Queen Bessima, used you, as Prince Thane. She exploited your affections for Queen Holna, the same as Mama made you a tool for achieving her ends in my life. She manipulated your love for me to ensure Titus remained interested in, and married me.

Mama saw Titus's competitive spirit. She saw yours as well. Keeping you in the picture was her way of keeping Titus on guard. Mama didn't like you, yet she never demanded you to go away. Instead she attacked me for being your friend. In this way she gave me a path to rebellion. And, if her plan for me to marry Titus failed, I would have you, a doctor, like Titus, to step in and take his place. I would not be alone."

Sahel said, "Mama used you the same way she married Daddy when she realized she wasn't going to get the kind of Creole man she wanted—one educated and successful, both of which she was not."

Carl wailed as if fighting to retain the last bits of life and hope. The words Sahel spoke, her reminder of the dream they had all shared, their time in the Kingdom of Purdah, exhumed a sad truth, that being revealed dispelled a past wherein each had absorbed the other, Sahel, Titus, and Carl.

When I was a child, I spake as a child, I understood as a child, I thought as a child: but when I became a man, I put away childish things (1 Corinthians 13:11).

"The dream's not over," Carl said. "I keep having it. Each night when I lie down and close my eyes I see you, whom I have served and to whom I gave all I had. But every night you go to him. Blood is spurting from his neck. But you go to him. Every night! I see you running. To Prince Rahim. Titus. He's dying. But you still go to him."

"But he's not dying," said Sahel.

Again Carl sobbed loudly. "He is until you go to him."

Sahel relived the dream, she as Queen Holna, Titus as Prince Rahim.

"No! No!" She screamed while running to Rahim, the walls of Queen Bessima's castle tumbling in around them. A large slab of wall hit Rahim's head. He fell, but not before one of Bessima's guardsmen nicked Rahim's neck with the blade of a saber.

"Rahim! Rahim!" Holna knelt and lifted his head onto her lap.

"Please don't die. Not now. Not now. We're almost home."

"Then die with me," Rahim whispered. "Kiss me. And die with me."

Holna leaned over, placed her lips on Rahim's. Instantly she

424

found herself lying down ... upon a gurney. Bright lights shone around her. Hands worked upon her chest, pushing, thrusting, willing her heart to beat. "One-one thousand. Two-one thousand. Three-one thousand."

Settled once more in her body, Holna opened her eyes and coughed.

All went black.

Sahel said to Carl, "He forgot who he was, Titus. Where he had come from. Where we had come from."

"So did I!"

"No. You remembered only too clearly. You knew that you were Prince Thane. Mama knew. But Titus had forgotten. That's why Mama was pushing me to him. Just as in the dream. Like in the Kingdom of Purdah. She never counted on me losing my sight and seeing what I couldn't unless blind to myself, who I truly am and who I really love."

"I won't accept this," Carl said.

Sahel recalled Dr. Hansel's words. "I read an article about a man with schizophrenia who in losing his sight regained his sanity. The schizophrenia left. He returned to teaching piano. No more medicines. No need for therapy. He has a full round of students. And a waiting list of those who want to work with him."

She then considered Essien's missive on her decision to hire a person to find Titus. *A detective can only help you locate what is lost or what has left you. What you most long for stands right before you, abandoned by your own need for independence and fueled by your fear of love.*

Now as when a child and playing in her parents' backyard, the warmth of the bright sun filtered by the leaves and branches of trees bathed Sahel's face and body. Kneeling to a bucket she lowered her hands into the water, clear and pristine like the northern California sky canvassing Oakland.

Carl, to her left dipped his fingers beneath the water's surface. On reaching the bottom he stretched his finger to touch hers. Titus, his left shoulder touching her right, did the same.

425

With Sahel's hands in the middle, Carl's and Titus's to either side, their fingers formed a circle.

A bucket of dark earth that Carl had brought from his mother's flower garden stood but steps away. Titus had supplied the water collected from the spigot attached to Sahel's house.

Earth, water, sun, and sky.

It had been their Eucharist, their bread and wine, their corpora and blood, each of their souls providing altars of transformation for the other.

Flesh of flesh.

Soul of all souls.

Carl dropped to Sahel's knees. His sobs turned into moans. He was clinging to her legs like a little boy, the young Carl who, like Titus, knew his role in helping her mix and pour the mud cakes.

Sahel reached into the darkness and touched Carl's head at her thighs. He batted back her hands. She rubbed his head. He tightened his grasp upon her legs. A flow of trembling sobs escaped him, and entered Sahel.

Hours later ...

Sahel had locked the front door and, with the remote, engaged the alarm system, when the doorbell rang.

"Did you forget something?" Sahel called out, having started back towards the door thinking of Reynard who had just left.

Moments earlier he had delivered Sahel her copies of the new set of keys to the offices where she, Reynard, and several other psychiatrists and psychotherapists saw clients.

Reynard had been waiting for Sahel when she arrived home with Carl from visiting James's grave at Rolling Hills.

"I had new deadbolts installed," Reynard had said. "We can never be too safe." Sahel's practice having quickly grown she had begun working into the early evenings.

"I really appreciate everything," Sahel had said.

"Think nothing of it. Besides, Titus would never forgive me

should I let something happen to you at work, or anywhere else for that matter."

Against the warmth spreading across Sahel's heart, sadness had filled her chest.

"Don't give up," Reynard had patted her hand after placing the keys upon her palm and then folding her fingers around them.

"Keep working. And don't give up."

Those words along with the ones Dr. Leonard had spoken in her recent session had pushed Sahel's thoughts to the back of her mind when the second round of doorbell chimes resounded and she started back towards the front door.

"Reynard, is that you?" Sahel asked on bringing her hand to the deadbolt.

"No." The voice on the other side sounded as if from a woman.

"My name is Alice Whitmore. I'm looking for Sahel Denning, Titus Denning's wife."

Chapter 62

S

ahel opened the door and invited Alice inside. "Would you like some tea?"

"No thanks. I don't want to trouble you," Alice said. "It's no bother," Sahel pressed.

"I'd rather not."

She showed Alice into the study.

Once seated Alice commented, "You look well. Titus told me about the accident."

"Thank you. I've gone back to work."

"I'll have to tell him," Alice said.

"I was told he's been working in New York?" Sahel said. She leaned forward.

"For a while. I don't know where he is right now."

Alice explained, "Titus spent some time out at my parents' place in the Hamptons. He needed a place to clear his head. My parents always liked him." Alice added, "When you didn't answer any of his letters he—"

"What letters?"

"He wrote at least five. I mailed two of them. To this address. That's how I knew where to find you."

Carl. My post office box. *You need to switch your mail back to the house.*

Essien would have given Sahel the letters had they arrived there.

Instead much of her mail had gone to the post office box in Berkeley.

"Perhaps his friend Carl might know about them," Alice said.

"Titus spoke to him at least once a week when he first arrived." Sahel grew warm, her anger rising, as Alice spoke. "Carl told Titus to mail the letters to your post office box, and informed him that you had begun a program at a center for the blind."

But what about the weeks before I entered the program? Four to six weeks had passed from the time Titus left until Sahel moved into her apartment at the Center in Pinole where she had purchased a post office box and learned of Carl having directed her mail to his office on Regent Street in Berkeley.

Now with what Alice had said, Sahel realized Carl must have diverted her mail to his office while she was still living at home, most likely even before Titus had left. Anger bordering on rage towards herself, and then toward Carl, spread throughout Sahel. Sahel clasped her hands, interwove her fingers and rested them upon her lap.

Alice said, "Titus said he didn't want to cause you any more pain, and that if anything happened, Carl would be there for you."

"Why would something happen?" Sahel grew dizzy with disappointment and loathing.

"I don't know what kind of relationship you, Titus, and Carl have. The three of you seem close. I don't have anyone in my

430

life from as far back as you three have been friends." Alice's words now came pointed and clear. "At some point we all have to decide what it is we want, who we love, and how we're going to share that love.

"I married Titus because I loved him," Alice said. "My parents thought he was a beautiful person. But Titus didn't love me. He never spoke of you. I never knew what or who was standing between me and him. At times during our marriage, he would have this far-off look. When I asked him about it, he said he was just thinking of home, Oakland, and how he missed it. I told him we could move here. Always he said, 'No.' One day when I was preparing to take some of his trousers to the cleaners, his wallet fell out. He was still asleep. I lifted the wallet and two pictures fell out. One was of you and Titus. I had never seen him smile like that, not even on our wedding day. The other was of you. The Oakland he was thinking about, what filled his eyes and took him away when saying he was thinking of home ... it was you."

Sahel recalled Titus's description of learning about the death of his parents. "All I could think about was getting back home to Oakland. And seeing you. That's what kept me going. Knowing you were here. You're the only thing that's left."

Alice now said, "I ended our marriage by asking Titus about the woman whose picture was in his wallet."

"What did he say?"

"That you were the person he had and would always love. He only married me because he grew tired of competing against Carl for your attention, and frustrated with your refusing him, not letting him in, not allowing him to take care of you."

Sahel's heart sank.

"Carl loves you very much," Alice said. "But you might want to ask yourself why, with all these opportunities, you haven't married him."

Sahel had been drowning in the unblemished waters of Titus's love.

"Titus said he left you divorce papers," Alice said. Sahel swallowed hard. "I don't know if you've signed them. If you're trying to decide. Or what. But don't keep blaming him for

431

something that wasn't his fault. It's killing him."

Sahel knew that Alice was speaking of the accident. But Sahel was thinking of her mother, and how Titus's resemblance in skin color to Lillian had distracted and blinded Sahel to his love.

Alice said, "It's hard to see someone suffering and you don't come close to having what's needed to heal them." The pain in her words pierced Sahel's heart. Like Geraldine, Alice had relinquished Titus to Sahel's grace and mercy. If only Titus would find his way home and give Sahel another chance at redemption.

"Only the key to the heart can liberate the mind from its own tyranny," Alice said. "I remind my clients of this every chance I get."

Anger followed by hurt slipped into Sahel's chest. That hurt fomented into a dream the night following Alice's visit. In it Sahel revisited the time following her surgery and James's death.

As in waking life the procedure Aaron Blake had performed, assisted by Carl, had failed to return Sahel's sight. Sadness gripped everyone. Sahel, Titus, and Carl were hurt.
James had died. Then Titus left. Their sorrows streamed into rivers of anger that flooded the countryside of their lives.

"This war, this internal battle I'm fighting, it's holding Titus captive to my inner demons." Sahel pleaded to Carl. "The ones Mama spawned when she looked at me and I saw the hatred in her eyes for my dark skin."

Sahel and Carl were seated upon the sofa in the living room, where the three had studied as children, gathered as teenagers, and to where they now retreated as adults when the world and its trials threatened to swallow, and separate them.

"I want Titus back. We need him," Sahel said of Titus's absence. "All of us. We are the Kingdom of Purdah."

"No! You are the Kingdom of Purdah," Carl said.

Sahel felt Carl's hands, precise at wielding a scalpel, grasp her shoulders. He drew her close.

"Let me go," Sahel said. She leaned back, trying to escape his hold.

"Titus is gone. He ran away just like he did the last time."

"I love hi—"

Carl's lips touched Sahel's, silencing hers.

With cheeks scorching, her body grew hot. Anger singed each nerve, burrowed its way into every sinew, and exploded through her pores. "I don't love you!" she screamed.

Then ... a burst of light ... the shadow of a face ...

"My head." Sahel grasped her temples to soothe pain, sharp and searing.

"What's wrong?"

"Leave me alone!" She batted Carl away. The pain moved to her forehead and increased against the sharp light penetrating her eyes.

With hands to her face, she stood and started away.

"Sahel, wait," Carl called after her.

Her palms had still been to her eyes when hands caught and steadied her, and enfolded her into their arms.

"Let me go!" she twisted away and turned around. Sahel pulled her hands from her eyes, and saw Carl. He knitted his brows, looked past her.

The reflection in his eyes, the shock upon his face, revealed the person standing behind Sahel. She whipped around and lifted her gaze.

Titus.

"Oh, god, no!" Sahel flew up in bed having awakened from the dream, and grasped her head.

"Bring him home." She prayed of Titus. "But not that way," as it had been in the dream.

Sahel wished terribly to see his face. "But only Titus's face. *He saved my life*. Let that be the first thing I see."

Against hot tears and trembling hands, Sahel pleaded, in this late season of her time in purdah, "I don't want my sight back unless I can see him, first."

Titus.

Indian Summer

•.•..•..•.•..•.•..•

Chapter 63

Sahel exited the cab and handed the driver three twenty-dollar bills. "Thank you, Mrs. Denning," said Ahmad, the cab driver. Now a year from the day James had entered her life, Sahel still used her married name. She had also encouraged Essien and Geraldine to extend their stay in Ghana for an additional six months.

A hand took hold of her arm and helped her out. "You're quite welcome, and thank you," Sahel spoke to Ahmad.

"I only drove you here," Ahmad said. "This gentleman assisted you from the car."

Carl spoke. "It was enough to let you come down here alone."

"Thanks," Sahel said to Carl, "... but Ahmad and I have

become good friends. I'm one of his best customers." Sahel refused the change Ahmad offered.

"You are also a very nice person," said Ahmad.

"So are you," Sahel said with a smile.

"Thanks, Ahmad," Carl said to Ahmad. "Don't worry, we'll be driving Mrs. Denning home tonight."

"Very well," said Ahmad. He said to Sahel, "I shall be here to pick you up tomorrow morning at ten."

"See you then," said Sahel.

Carl led Sahel onto the sidewalk of 4th Street in Berkeley. They started towards Cafe Rouge a few steps beyond. With Carl having wrapped his right arm around her left, Sahel had folded her cane.

The two of them walked as they had in the dream when entering St. Maria's sanctuary.

"So how's it going?" Carl asked. It was Saturday evening, and the warmth of Indian summer caressed Sahel's face.

"I had a new client this afternoon."

"Working on Saturdays. You're getting busy. And you arrived on time," Carl said. He warned before entering Café Rouge, "It's a bit noisy," and placed his arm around her. "We're eating upstairs."

Sahel moved forward, guided by Carl, the din of conversations around her no longer casting a mist of disorientation.

On reaching the space upstairs, Carl led Sahel to their table. "It's in the corner over here." He guided her to a chair. "It's quiet up here."

"Thanks," Sahel said. "But what I want is to meet her." She was excited.

At the table Carl made the introductions. "Nora Adams, this is Sahel Ohin Denning. Sahel, this is Nora, my fiancée."

"So we finally meet." Sahel extended her left hand into the darkness. A hand grasped her palm. "I can't tell you how happy I am to finally meet you," Nora said. She released Sahel's hand.

Before Sahel could bring it to her side, another hand, soft and strong, fastened its grip around her palm.

She frowned and turned left.

"It's good to see you." The voice was deep and firm, betraying a pulsating constancy of love.

"*Titus*," Sahel said. She reached for her chair. It went under her. She lowered herself onto the seat and placed her cane in her lap. "When did you get back?"

"Three months ago," he said. "I've been working over in the city."

How could people not know? *Not tell me.*

Carl spoke from across the table. "I just found out."

"I told only a few people," Titus explained, "asked them not to say anything,"

Sahel had heard rumors. She had refused to believe them. *Too much to hope for.*

The dream that had come the night following Alice Whitmore's visit wormed its way into Sahel's thoughts. *Only Titus,* Sahel had prayed. *I want his face to be the first I see.*

Titus said, "You look well." He was sitting beside her.

Sahel grasped her cane, sought to quell the flood of emotions spilling over levees of defenses now crumbling. She said to Nora, "I'm sorry this happened on our first meeting. I hope Carl explained. We have a strange relationship, Carl, Titus, and me."

"He's told me everything." Nora's voice broke through with crystalline clarity. "Even how Titus saved your life."

"It was her idea for the meeting," Carl said of Nora.

Sahel tilted her head.

Titus said, "I met Nora in a yoga class over in the city. We started having coffee after class. Got to know each other."

"I do bikram yoga every morning at 5:30 a.m.," said Nora. Like Carl, and now Titus too, Nora lived in San Francisco. She said of Titus, "When I saw first him in the opening class I felt I knew him. He reminded me of someone I couldn't quite place."

"My hair was longer," said Titus.

"You let your hair grow?" Sahel reached out.

Titus took her hand and brought it to his head. "I cut it yesterday."

"How long had it gotten?" Sahel asked.

"Quite," said Nora.

Sahel ran her fingers through the two inches of Titus's mane, still thick. And surrendered her thoughts to the prayer to which she had clung: *Only Titus, let me see him, his face.* She now dwelt in the castle of the *Kingdom of Purdah* where seasons held no end, no beginning.

Titus continued explaining. "One morning after yoga class when Nora and I were having coffee, she said she was dating a neurosurgeon, Carl Pierson, and that they were engaged to be married in the spring. The rest is history."

History, Sahel thought. She fingered her cane folded and lying upon her lap, said to Titus, "Did Nora explain how you saved my life a *second time*?"

A bolt of energy surged through Sahel.

Light, as in the dream, pierced her eyes.

She blinked. Darkness peeled away. The shadowy haze that followed drizzled clear. Sahel smiled upon the reflection of her face sparkling against the black canvas of Titus's pupils. She caressed his cheek, smooth, and with an olive undertone.

Titus's lips curved up.

She met her husband's gaze, saw him as he was. *As he had always been.*

To Carl across the table, and whose hands had assisted in draining the aneurysm waiting to explode in her head, she whispered, *"Thank you."*

Sahel gave Titus her cane.

He knitted his eyebrows, thick and black, like his freshly cropped mane.

"I don't need it," she said.

His eyes widened in disbelief. "But—"

"Take me home," Sahel said. She grasped his palm. "I'll explain."

Titus gazed into her eyes. And knew.

Sahel's soul enlivened. Vibrancy entered her body.

She grew warm.

Bibliography

Kathleen Arnott. African *Myths and Legends*, Oxford University Press: Oxford, New York, Toronto, Delhi, Bombay, Calcutta, Madras, Karachi, Petaling, Jaya, Singapore, Hong Kong, Tokyo, Nairobi, Dar es Salaam, Cape Town, Melbourne, Auckland, Berlin, Ibadan. 1962. pp 2-12

———

"'You are like Ohia, the man who received the gift of being able to speak to animals.' Sahel's father told her the story of Ohia, and his wife Ariwehu.

'Beset with bad luck, they were very poor. Everything they touched turned to ash. About to lose their clothes ... '"

The myth recited by Essien in <u>Chapter 22</u>, pp. 136-138, taken from:
The Man who Learned the Language of Animals
Ghana (Akan,) the 2nd story in African *Myths and Legends*, Retold by Kathleen Arnott

Acknowledgements

Sincere thanks to Joy, a friend and sister in spirit, and soul. You loved *Seasons in Purdah* on first reading it. Your adroit perception into Carl's persona clarified all contained in Titus's heart, thus setting straight the plot. As with the narrative of Sahel's journey, you have been and are for me that friend who makes your presence quick, and forever ready to help when life throws curve balls, and we need someone to hold us steady. May the Universe and all the Goddesses and Gods make real the dreams you have committed your thoughts, and actions to manifest.

Many thanks to Lori Zue, Karlyn Thayer, Shonelle Bacon, Jennifer Magnani, and Naomi Long—five editors whose suggested changes and comments lifted this story from the dungeons of my convoluted imagination, and deeply internalized critic. Eleven years in the making, *Seasons in Purdah* challenged my commitment to writing, dared me to become a novelist. The four of you pulled me ashore after a decade of writing and toiling alone. Your insights and keen sense of detail mid-wifed *Seasons in Purdah* to its present from. While much remains for me to learn, your kind and diligent assistance taught me even more about the art and skill of crafting fiction. You also boosted my confidence. *What more could any writer ask for?*

And what would a story be without an enticing book cover? Overlooked, most probably.
Immense thanks to Iryna Spica for your intensely imaginative eye, exceptional patience, and the unique ability to develop images symbolic of the story and message between the covers displaying those images.

Once again, to my husband of three decades: *These words would never have made it to print, on either paper or electronic screen, without your support in ways seen and unseen.*

445

For my daughters, *Perhaps the words and sentences I spend days and hours shaping and refining at the computer will host my spirit when the soul who is my essence no longer dwells in this body.*

To all my readers—those who have downloaded both free and purchased copies of all or any of my books, *Thanks for your support.*
I'd love to hear from you.
www.anjuellefloyd.com

Peace and blessings to you and yours.

www.ingramcontent.com/pod-product-compliance
Lightning Source LLC
Chambersburg PA
CBHW031413240626
47154CB00001B/15